THE FORE

SAMANTHA YORK

THE FORESHORE

CROMER

PUBLISHED BY SALT PUBLISHING 2025

2 4 6 8 10 9 7 5 3 1

Copyright © Samantha York 2025

Samantha York has asserted her right under the Copyright, Designs and
Patents Act 1988 to be identified as the author of this work.

*This book is sold subject to the condition that it shall not, by way of trade or otherwise,
be lent, resold, hired out, or otherwise circulated without the publisher's prior consent
in any form of binding or cover other than that in which it is published and without a
similar condition including this condition being imposed on the subsequent publisher.*

This book is a work of fiction. Any references to historical events, real people
or real places are used fictitiously. Other names, characters, places and events
are products of the author's imagination, and any resemblance to actual
events or places or persons, living or dead, is entirely coincidental.

First published in Great Britain in 2025 by
Salt Publishing Ltd
12 Norwich Road, Cromer, Norfolk NR27 0AX, United Kingdom

GPSR representative
Matt Parsons matt.parsons@upi2mbooks.hr
UPI-2M PLUS d.o.o., Medulićeva 20, 10000 Zagreb, Croatia

www.saltpublishing.com

Salt Publishing Limited Reg. No. 5293401

A CIP catalogue record for this book is available from the British Library

ISBN 978 1 78463 360 6 (Paperback edition)
ISBN 978 1 78463 361 5 (Electronic edition)

Typeset in Neacademia by Salt Publishing

Printed and bound in Great Britain by Clays Ltd, Elcograf S.p.A.

<dedication>

PROLOGUE

THE SEA

NEWS of death came in with the tide. Gently, the sea pulled itself across the pebbles of the bay and caressed the feet of the women gathered to wait on the shoreline. Around them lay treasures which the storm had wrenched from the sea's clutches: the bleached, splintered bones of a boat's hull; the fans, whorls, and jagged spikes of seashells; gelatinous mounds of amber and amethyst jellyfish which quivered in the sun. Amongst the wreckage, a seal's carcass stared hopelessly at the sky through milky eyes. Later, the islanders would take what they could salvage from its flesh, before the circling gulls and flies could commence their feast.

Huddled beneath shawls, the women gazed into the distance at the wooden boat bobbing closer with each swell of the tide. Barely noticing the waves gradually lapping against their feet, they craned their necks, and some ventured out even further into the water, oblivious to the cold.

Not a word passed between them.

The vessel sat within the treacherous strip of ocean which separated the island from a cluster of towering sea stacks. Jutting out from the depths like blackened, fossilised shark teeth, the stacks rose hundreds of feet into the air and were home to thousands of nesting gannets. This banquet of eggs and pungent meat was a prize for which husbands and fathers would ascend the dizzying heights of the stacks, sleeping for nights amidst the salt spray and piercing bird cries. But this time the women knew, their intuition alerting them like the sudden rumble of a subsiding cliff edge, that the men would be returning with something other than just plump seabird chicks.

As the boat drifted closer to shore, a dozen heads and brawny bodies appeared. Arms strained against heavy wooden oars.

What seemed like hours passed by before the body lying prostrate across the centre of the boat finally became visible, but a tangle of nets obscured the figure's head from the desperate gaze of the wives and mothers who waited anxiously on the beach.

At this sight, there was a sudden frenzy of movement on the shoreline. Where previously the women had stood as still as the distant sea stacks, several now dropped to their knees, rocking backwards and forwards on the sand, wringing their hands and trembling. Others waded further into the swell, determined to be the first to reach the boat and help tow it back to the shore. Men leapt over the side, torso deep in the surf, grappling with ropes and trying vainly to shoo away the hoard of women eager to push their careworn bodies through the surrounding breakers.

After a struggle, the boat was pulled into the shallow water of the bay. Women swarmed around it. Some ran into the arms of their awaiting husbands and clung to them, moaning and sobbing, their bodies shaking. Others desperately scanned the throng of men, trying to fathom whose face could be missing from those of the living.

From the midst of this sombre scene, two of the men broke free from the crowd and made their way across mounds of kelp and sea foam to a solitary woman who hung back from the commotion. The smallest of the two men could barely walk; occasionally he stumbled, his legs seeming to strain under the effort of keeping his aging body upright. His eyes were wide and stared fixedly ahead of him through sea swept knots of hair, while his companion kept a strong arm around his shoulders, guiding him to his waiting wife.

Back at the shoreline, several of the men began lifting the body from the boat. Hushed voices spread among the women.

"It's Flora MacKinnon's youngest lad . . ."

Murmurs spread and heads turned to view the woman waiting

at the far side of the beach. The taller of the two men, Donald Gillies, kept an arm around John MacKinnon as he spoke to Flora, a woman whose age and heartaches had eroded her once striking face. What words passed between them could not be heard by the women gathered around the boat, but they did not need to be. They understood those words as sharply as if they were being spoken to them, for those were the words that made them wake, sweating, from their beds at night; the words which they had repeated in their minds countless times when their men were absent, as clear, and as terrible, as a cormorant's mocking cries.

Half out of curiosity, half out of sympathy, women turned to observe the scene and braced themselves. They braced themselves for the terrible scream, the crumpled fall to the ground, the distressed cries that would inevitably follow. But the screams did not come.

Two young women, Ann and Mary MacKinnon, pushed to the front of the crowd to view the solemn figure of their mother-in-law. Mary, the youngest and slightest of the two, strained forwards with her child balanced on her hip, ready to offer soothing words and coax her husband's mother away from the awful sight which lay behind them. Ann, however, held herself back, her strong arms wrapping themselves protectively around her thrice pregnant stomach, her handsome face ashen with dread.

Flora MacKinnon stood as still as ever. Her eyes flickered past Donald and John to the body the men had now lain out on the beach. Flora stirred, and soon she was striding resolutely towards the shore. The women, observing Flora's silent march towards the corpse of her son, stepped aside and created a path between mother and child.

Upon the boy's cadaver, purple bruises had formed against bone white skin and his clothes were stiff with salt; two cloudy eyes stared blankly up at the blazing sun and his lips were parted slightly, as if awaiting a lover's kiss. At the back of the young boy's head, a mess of congealed blood and matted hair was flecked with fragments of skull.

"It's a reckoning!"

A lone, trembling voice filled the air, and the islander's turned to Ann MacKinnon, hushing her in sharp reprimand for breaking a silence which did not belong to her. Ann hung back, still nursing the soft curve of her belly.

Flora, seemingly unaware of the other woman's outburst, knelt by her son's corpse. Once again, her fellow islanders waited for the howling and lamenting to commence, but Flora uttered not a sound. All that could be heard was the gentle lapping of the ocean, the shrill mewing of the seagulls and the occasional bleating of lambs as they roamed the pastures beyond the beach. Some of the islanders glanced away, almost ashamed to bear witness to the spectacle of the bereaved mother who had yet to shed a single tear. Instead, Flora MacKinnon bent down and pressed her forehead against her son's cold brow, holding him there in her arms, unmoving, as the gulls cried, and the sea swept across the shore.

In due course, the remaining men gathered to carry the corpse back to the MacKinnons' croft. The women followed; pity mingled with guilt as they escorted Flora and her weeping husband from the beach, before the tide could reclaim what was left of the land.

As they departed, the sea crept closer.

CHAPTER ONE

THOMAS

THE Reverend Thomas Murray staggered out of the blackhouse. Clinging to the side of the crude dwelling, he clutched his stomach and gagged. After a prolonged period of retching into the grass, Murray fell back against the wall, gasping and heaving. Turning to the water barrel behind his lodging, he splashed cooling spring rainwater across his face and down his throat, eager to rid himself of the rancid tang of gannet meat which had lodged itself there, causing him to retch up what little remained of the lining of his gut.

It had been a full week now since he had arrived on this remote island, and it seemed his only tangible memories since then revolved around the process of passing various bodily fluids. The journey to the isle had taken him through weeks of discomfort. It had started with a bone rattling coach journey which brought him from Inverness and ended in several perilous attempts at sea crossings. Murray was surprised when he finally made it off the boat onto the tiny beach at Eilean Eòin, where he had promptly fallen to his hands and knees and vomited onto the wet sand. The men who had brought him to his post had gazed on him with a mixture of contempt and pity, before departing back to the comforts of the more hospitable inner isles. Even now, Murray's stomach lurched at the memory of the boat deck tumbling beneath him. After the relentless torment brought about by his multiple sea voyages, he had then spent the best part of a week confined to bed, sick with a fever that even the largest storm the island had seen in over a decade could not shake him from.

Murray stumbled back into the sparse little blackhouse which had become his new lodging. The doorway led into the byre, where two sheep and one mangy cow had bedded down overnight. The air stank of damp straw and stale urine. Walking past a wooden partition, Murray unsteadily entered back into the dense fug of the living space. The room was dimly lit by a solitary lantern hanging from one of the wooden beams above and a central hearth fuelled by peat, over which a soot blackened kettle was suspended on a long chain. In the corner of the room there was a large wooden box bed: a supposed luxury on the treeless isle. The Reverend had spent many claustrophobic nights confined inside its dark wooden panels, tossing and sweating into a coarse, scratchy mattress, no doubt infested with lice. On a rickety wooden table, one of the few furnishings to adorn the dwelling apart from a quern stone and a few broken pieces of crockery, was the offending plate of gannet and boiled potatoes.

The seabird swam in a thick layer of fishy grease. It was the first meal the minister had eaten in a week, and upon first taste the fatty meat was reminiscent of overcooked goose and pickled herring. Reluctantly, Murray once more took his seat.

Across the table sat a stout woman wrapped in layers of dense wool, with an ancient weather-beaten face.

"You don't like *guga?*" she asked bluntly.

The minister groaned and pinched the bridge of his nose between thumb and forefinger. His attendant for the past week, at best, could be described as a difficult woman. Her late husband had owned the croft he currently resided in and despite now dwelling with her eldest daughter's extended family, she had taken it upon herself to oversee matters once the new Reverend moved in. So far, the widow had made a conceited effort to show that she was unhappy with Murray's presence in her former home.

"I fear the fever has yet to reside." He tried his utmost to force a smile in response to her taunting question, reminding himself that he was here to judge the moral character of these people, not their primitive cuisine. "It is certainly an interesting dish." He took another tentative bite and felt his stomach lurch in protest.

The widow harrumphed and with a clatter started clearing the table.

"I suspect I just need another day of fasting," Murray said, attempting to appease her: he would after all, find it more difficult to complete his mission if he did not ingratiate himself with these backwards folk. "My thanks to you, Aileen."

"Ailith."

"Yes, of course. Thank you, Ailith."

Murray closed his eyes and did his best to imagine he was home in Inverness with Caroline and her home baked plum pudding, rather than sitting in a hovel which stank of bile and sheep shit, with an old woman whose most obvious qualities were a sharp tongue and a dull wit. Perhaps it was mere ignorance that kept the islanders in their precarious existence, he considered, but ignorance was no excuse for corruption and sin. Even in the midst of his fever-tossed arrival, Murray could not help but sense something creeping and sinister lay at the heart of this island; it was his duty to locate it, dig it out and place it, root and stem, into the cleansing fire of God's grace. He felt his lips curve upwards slightly in anticipation. This assignment, placed upon him by Church and State, would be the making of him. He would make sure of it.

Fumbling at his coat pockets, he pulled out a crinkled parchment, creased from the number of times he had clenched it within his fist. He placed it on the table and smoothed it out. He need not worry about the old widow, for the islanders had no grasp whatsoever, and seemingly no interest, in deciphering either the English tongue or the written word. And so, he read the letter again, hoping that with each examination he would find himself closer to the recognition he had so long deserved.

To the Reverend Thomas Murray,
I write to you by way of the Presbytery of Inverness-shire, on

behalf of my Master, Chief MacLeod of Clan MacLeod, to offer to you the role of Missionary Curate on the island of Eilean Eòin. This would take the form of a year long posting, but it is vital that you understand the significance of what could seem such an unpromising parish.

Before you dismiss this offer, you should be aware that the current occupants of the island have yet to find someone of appropriate faith to guide them towards a Christian life, for they are, unsurprisingly, negligent of any religion besides their own paganistic superstitions. Many curates have failed to accomplish necessary progress in converting the population; we recently employed a Reverend by the name of Buchan, to attend to this post, but unfortunately sickness has forced him from this role, hence the Presbytery directing me to you.

Truth be told, Sir, we suspect these islanders to be guilty of a variety of vices and barbarities, themselves having had no guiding authority such as Law or Church to steer them away from evil. As such, this role will comprise of far more than sermons and preachings. His Lordship requires you to root out any malfeasance you may encounter and report these findings directly to the tacksman, who visits the island on a bi-yearly basis, or upon the completion of your post. The inhabitants of the Outer Isles have long been a thorn in the MacLeods' side, as it is as unprofitable for his Lordship to keep them as it is for them to exist on such scant rations as they do. It is also feared that should another uprising occur, the islanders will be easily led. Therefore, it is hoped that in uncovering any crimes or transgressions committed by these people, we will be better able to repurpose the islands and earn due subservience from their current populace, who have yet to earn their place in an enlightened world.

This will be no simple feat, and I understand if this offer lacks incentive. His Lordship will provide you with a yearly wage which will complement your current post, rather than

replace it. However, there will be few comforts on the isle, and it is this which has proved the failing of our previous missionaries. Nevertheless, I hope you will agree, Sir, that this role is an essential one, and one which could prove revelationary to a man of God such as yourself.
We eagerly await your response.
Richard Tavis, Secretary to Chief Norman MacLeod
Dunvegan
Year of Our Lord 1727

As Murry scanned the now familiar epistle, he deliberated over the Presbytery's choice in recommending him. Just as he had at home, he tried to read the relevant lines in a way which supported his preferred interpretation: that he had been offered this post due to his fine reputation as a minister skilled in purging his flock of sin. It was not because he was low ranking; negligible; expendable . . . Once again, he looked down to find the parchment was once more compacted into a tight ball in his fist.

Shaking off his fears, he hastily banished the letter to his pocket and watched as Ailith scraped what remained of the boiled potatoes onto the plate in front of him.

"Eat it. You'll waste away, young lad, the way you're heading," she admonished, shuffling towards the door.

Murray flinched at the term, "young lad". As a man now considerably past his thirtieth year, edging perilously closer to his fortieth, he could hardly be considered youthful. The islanders he had met so far had been treated harshly by the elements, and he could not help but wonder if his less ruddy complexion and the lack of lines on his face made him appear less aged to them. Once again, his thoughts strayed to Inverness and Caroline.

"Ailith?"

The widow grunted her response, barely turning from the door.

"I don't suppose there have been any other boats which have stopped by recently?" he asked. "I'm expecting a letter."

The old woman looked incredulous. "No ships will be coming near for weeks. Especially after that storm. Perhaps if you weren't so busy heaving your guts up and tossing about in that bed you would have noticed that."

Murray felt a stab of irritation at the widow's lack of empathy, but conceded he was foolhardy for even thinking a letter could have arrived so soon, given his new circumstances. Nevertheless, it had been almost a month since he had spoken to his wife, and although he had sent several letters from various stages in his journey, he had yet to receive any word from her.

"You're welcome," Ailith muttered, picking up her shawl and wrapping it around herself. "I'll be away now, Father. The MacKinnons are burying their youngest lad this afternoon and I reckon I'll find as fine a company there as I will anywhere else today."

Murray's face grew hot.

"Firstly, I'm not a Papist, and therefore not anyone's father," he snapped. "Reverend will suffice. Secondly, why was I not informed of a burial? Correct me if I am wrong, but I had been led to believe that the Chief of Clan MacLeod, that's your laird, Madam, had appointed me here to administer to the rites and sacraments of this community? I do not imagine for one moment that this family will want their son buried without a proper, Christian service?"

Ailith stared blankly at the minister but offered no response to his sudden outburst. Murray sighed and composed himself. Whilst any foolish Papist notions of last rites were to be scorned, it was vitally important that he made himself visible to the community on such an occasion.

"See to it that the boy is not moved from the house or interred until I am present."

Ailith did not seem to deem his instruction worthy of a response.

"I will be at the chapel as soon as I can." He looked at her pointedly. "Please, convey that exact message to the others. If you wish, you may go."

The old crone turned and made for the door, shutting it heavily behind her in a manner which made his head throb. Once more he turned his attention to the miserable meal in front of him. After taking one mouthful it became apparent that the potatoes had soaked up the remaining fatty liquids on the plate and were now oozing with the taste of gannet.

Pushing his plate to one side, Murray crossed the room and opened the byre door, allowing his face to be greeted by the fresh, sea breeze. It was a relief to stand outside the putrid smog of the blackhouse, which with its one tiny window covered in sealskin offered virtually no light or fresh air into the room. Fixing his eyes towards the horizon, Murray's gaze passed over the tiny, incomplete missionary's chapel which had been abandoned by his predecessor. Instead, he looked to the sea.

Miles of perilous ocean stretched out before him, with nothing between him and the vast continent of the New World which lay far beyond his gaze. Closing his eyes and allowing himself to be embraced by the wind, he imagined that Caroline would eventually feel the same breeze on her face, flushing her cheeks and blowing wisps of coppery hair from beneath her linen cap. His fist clenched around his silver wedding band, and for some time he was lost to the harsh surroundings of the island.

"This is what God wanted you to do, Thomas."

The final words his wife had spoken to him echoed through his mind; carried like gauzy threads of gossamer on the breeze. Murray remembered her standing by their own cottage door, softly singing as she collected blooms of meadowsweet and bell heather. Resting his head against the mossy stone of the blackhouse wall, Murray imagined his wife as she was on the day their son was born, slowly kneeling to pick another floral sprig, one hand resting contentedly across her loosened bodice. Then, suddenly, his wife's soft singing had become a wordless gasp for air. Flowers had fallen to the ground and scattered.

As if manifested by these memories, the wind rattled fiercely against the door and carried with it the ear-piercing sound of a woman's cries. The distant lament pulled Murray from his thoughts. Looking towards the crofts further down the hill, he observed a large party of islanders making their way towards the small village cemetery at the edge of the chapel. To the rear of the group, the women were keening: clawing and scratching at their hair and faces in a primitive display of mourning. A group of men carried between them a figure bound in sailcloth.

Barely containing his fury, Murray began marching down the grassy hill towards the funeral congregation. Still unsteady on his feet, he skidded on the wet turf and came close to making the remainder of the journey down the steep slope on his backside. Correcting himself, he carried on, thankful that the islanders were too focused on their blasphemous mockery of a ceremony to have noticed his predicament. Striding purposefully forward, he arrived at the chapel as the congregation were still sluggishly making their way across the bay. After clambering over the wall of the island's crude churchyard, he positioned himself next to a freshly dug grave. Hurriedly brushing the muck from his breeches and fighting back a wave of nausea, he tried to affect an air of composure as the funeral procession inched closer.

All around him the bitter sea squall pounded against motionless stone cairns, whipping its icy tendrils through the marram grass, and buoyed along by the breeze came the haunting, melodic wailing of women.

CHAPTER TWO

FLORA

It was not the first child she had lost, but it was the first that she had buried. Looking upon the lifeless form of her youngest child being lowered into his grave, cradled tenderly in the arms of his father and two surviving brothers, Flora wished that she could summon a genuine tear. Instead, she trembled in the bitter cold, disguising her shivers as sobs as her neighbours mourned on her behalf. Inside she was crippled with a dull pain, but since the day her son's storm damaged, mutilated body had been brought back to her, she had not been able to cry. She had lain awake for the past five nights, her boy's corpse lying just beyond the partition separating her living space from the byre and waited desperately for the grief to hit her. Yet now she stood, watching as other mothers wailed and tore at their flesh for her child, while she remained silent.

With an aching awareness, Flora listened to the soft thud of Donnchadh's body hit the earth and felt a sudden twinge of longing as her boy's form was obscured from view. It had been barely seventeen years since she had first held him against her breast.

As she scanned the crowd she observed Mary, the wife of her second son, Fergus, nursing her infant granddaughter beneath her shawl. Flora stared longingly at the child. She thought of her lost daughter, and how there had been no opportunity to grieve then, no grave to weep over, no memorial cairn to sit and remember her by. No mourners had gathered to lay her little girl to rest, but that was the last time Flora had allowed herself to shed tears so freely, and even as her son's body was vanishing beneath her feet, it was still the memory of her daughter's soul which plagued Flora's thoughts.

Despite the relentless battering of the elements, Donnchadh's grave was soon filled, and Flora allowed herself to shuffle forward to the front of the congregation. The earth lay clumped in freshly dug sods which stood out from the springy turf surrounding the grave. Just yards away stood the burial cairn of Flora's parents and siblings, now so old that thick moss and lichen had crawled between the pebbles, binding them together.

John placed an arm around his wife's shoulder and pulled four round stones from beneath his belted plaid, giving one each to Flora, Fergus and his eldest son, Michael. Flora felt the stone sit snugly in her palm, warming to her touch, before she planted it firmly in the ground at the head of the grave. In procession, each member of the family deposited their stone on the growing cairn, while the remainder of the congregation scrabbled around in the turf for their own. Michael's wife, Ann, hesitated before she placed her own tribute on the cairn, hastily moving back when the deed was done to distance herself from the gravesite. Flora looked to Ann but could not catch her eye. She noticed that some of her other kinsfolk seemed unsettled as they crowded the cemetery; some hovered by the edges as if afraid of getting too close. Flora understood the unease all too well: a death such as this forecast ill luck was on its way, swept in on a high tide. Flora did not fear this, for to her Donnchadh's death was already a penance bestowed upon her by the sea, but if anyone else suspected this, they wisely chose to keep their fears unspoken.

"This is idolatry."

Summoned by a stranger's voice, Flora rose stiffly and looked across her son's grave. She beheld the owner of those words hovering at the edge of the crowd: a tall, slender man whose thin lips were set firmly on a beardless face which betrayed no warmth of feeling. Flora observed that he could not have been a great deal older than her eldest, and that the windswept hair escaping from the confines of a thin ribbon binding it at the nape of his neck was the same burnished brown as her own sons'.

Flora quickly surmised from the unfamiliar words and outlandish dialect that the strange man must be Reverend Buchan's successor. The elderly cleric had left the island with the first buds of spring, taking nothing with him but a terrible fever and leaving nothing but an incomplete structure which he claimed was a place to house God. Unlike her neighbours, Flora had paid little heed to the man's lectures and preaching.

Perhaps it could be attributed to his relative youth and sickly pallor, but Flora felt a sudden wave of sympathy for the new Reverend, who stood out sharply from the islanders in his closely fitted black clothes and odd, three-cornered hat.

"This is idolatry," the stranger repeated, his face flushing red.

Most of the mourners ignored him, but Flora could see that John and her sons were eying the clergyman anxiously. Desperate to break the dreadful silence, she took a bold step forward.

"I am very grateful to you for coming, sir." Flora looked up to meet his eyes.

The young man narrowed his eyes and opened his mouth, but unprepared, took several moments to respond.

"I am sorry for your loss, madam." He paused and straightened himself. "But I'm afraid I cannot allow this kind of superstitious, pagan ritual to continue while I am tasked with caring for the spiritual wellbeing of this island's inhabitants."

"I don't quite understand your words, Father . . ." Flora could recognise that the man was offering some form of condolence, but there was a coldness to his voice, as well as a trace of unease which she found both unsettling and pitiable.

In this moment, Flora felt a sturdy arm wrap around her waist and a firm hand rest once more against her shoulder as her husband came to stand beside her.

"As you can see, Father, my wife has just buried a child," John growled. "We'd be thankful if you could leave her to mourn. She's in no fit state to make introductions today."

As John spoke these words, Flora set her jaw and gently bit the inside of her lip.

"I meant no offence to your wife, sir. I was just explaining that..." The Reverend caught himself mid-sentence, before resuming in a quieter tone. "I only meant to say that it is important that you and your wife honour your son in a way which is respectful to God."

"Who said anything about disrespect?" John's voice set as hard as granite.

The Reverend's head twitched to one side. "I did not mean..."

"Are you alright, Ma?"

Another voice joined the fray. Michael and Fergus positioned themselves on either side of Flora and fixed their gaze upon the Reverend. Flora took Fergus' hand in hers and gazed up at Michael, who now towered above both her and his father.

"I'm fine, boys." Flora patted Fergus' hand. "Get yourselves back home. Those bairns of yours will want feeding."

Michael shifted, but after taking one last icy glance at the Reverend, departed with his own growing family.

"Are you sure you'll be alright, Ma?" Fergus hovered at her side. Flora gave a shaky smile and nodded, gesturing for him to join his wife and babe. With a final squeeze of his mother's hand, Fergus left to follow Michael. Flora turned back to the Reverend, who licked his lips slightly before once again speaking.

"The fact is, madam, that your son is in God's hands now, and hopefully, he'll be welcomed warmly into the house of the Lord. But no amount of scratching at the dirt will help him into Christ's embrace." The Reverend's voice rose as he drew his body upright to reveal an imposing height which dwarfed Flora's brethren. "Those stones are empty gestures; they merely serve to venerate death. We cannot permit false idols."

Silence hung ominously at the end of the Reverend's words.

Flora felt the air thicken as the remaining mourners all turned to observe them.

"My wife can mourn our son how she sees fit." The lines on John's face deepened.

"Aye. And we don't need guidance from the likes of you!"

Donald Gillies, the Mackinnons' closest neighbour, stormed his way across the tiny graveyard, positioning himself close to Flora. "The last one of you lot was a good enough man but did little in the end to actually help us. We don't want any more of your kind here. Why can't that fancy laird or bishop of yours send strong, working bodies that can pull their weight around here?"

The Reverend tried to stammer a reply, but was cut off by Donald's wife, Margaret.

"Aye! Or why doesn't he send us more sheep or grain? It's feeding, not praying that we need."

There was a grumble of assent from the congregation, and several other voices shouted across their own grievances.

"As you can see, priest," spat Donald, "you're not wanted here."

A rising tide of fury could be heard gathering over the graveyard. Flora could see in his eyes that the Reverend was growing increasingly anxious, but his doggedness to his cause refused to be cowed.

"I have been sent to this island for your benefit, not my own." The stranger trembled as he spoke. "Yet thus far, I have received no welcome, not one hint of gratitude from any of you."

"Here's your gratitude, priest!"

A stone bounced off the Reverend's chest, leaving a clod of mud on his fine woollen coat. Despite the cleric's ghostly pallor, his cheeks once more reddened with rage as he opened his mouth to speak. But another stone soon followed, whistling over the Reverend's shoulder, narrowly missing the side of his face, and knocking the hat from his head. Despite the strong arms of her husband and Donald holding her back, Flora could contain herself no longer.

"Stop it! For shame!" Flora shouted. "My son is lying in his grave, and you all behave like a pack of squabbling gulls."

The crowd froze.

"I don't care why this man is here. If you don't want his service, then pay him no heed and mind your own." Flora steadied herself, feeling her body starting to buckle under the weight of fresh words. "Now leave before I say something we'll all regret later!"

Lowering their heads, many of the group looked shame facedly down at the grass. Slowly, they began to trudge home, ready to return tomorrow to the monotony of their daily lives upon the island. Donald and Margaret Gillies sidled up to Flora.

"I'm sorry, Flora," murmured Donald, and like many of his kinsmen he cast one last disdainful look in the direction of the Reverend.

"Do not fret over me, Donald," Flora sighed, turning quickly to Margaret in a desperate attempt to divert her neighbours away from further conflict. "If you're worried, come to the house later. There are some bannocks I've made from the last of the grain supplies."

Margaret looked to her husband for permission. After a pause, Donald nodded and steered his wife away. Several others cast apologetic glances at Flora as they once more abandoned the barren little churchyard.

"Come home now, *mo chridhe*," John whispered, turning and pressing his brow against her shrouded head. Flora looked longingly at the freshly dug earth. Walking to the head of the grave, she pressed her hand against the uppermost stone. It was done. Closing her eyes and allowing the wind to touch her face, she reluctantly let go and followed her husband.

Turning, Flora's eyes searched for the Reverend amongst the cairns, but looking around, she saw that he was already storming up the grassy slope beyond the village towards his lodgings, fury evident in each step.

Flora stared into the hearth and inhaled its comforting, peaty scent. Reaching down she petted John's sheepdog, Morag, who lay placidly by the warmth of the fire, tail slowly thumping the earth floor. John and Margaret's voices continued to echo hazily from behind her, their words blurring together as they savoured their meagre meal. Flora's fingers picked through a warm crust of bannock and rolled soft, doughy balls out on the palm of her hand. This was the last bread that would probably pass her lips for months and she knew she should be savouring every bit of it, but despite her attempts she could summon no enthusiasm for the taste.

The wind suddenly picked up and clattered against the door. Morag whined and skulked from her place by the hearth to huddle in the corner of the cow's byre.

"Dearie me, this looks to be as bad as the last one!" Margaret exclaimed. "I really should be going, Flora, before this picks up anymore."

Margaret rested a hand on Flora's arm and rubbed it reassuringly. Flora glanced up and placed her hand lightly over Margaret's, offering a slight nod, allowing Margaret to kiss her on the head before she turned back to John. Her neighbour had always strived to be near her in times of grief; it sometimes felt as if Margaret did this less to comfort Flora and more in the hope that she too could learn from such fortitude in the face of disaster. Flora knew her friend was entirely misunderstood about her, but still she appreciated her presence. Margaret had been by her side ever since she was a small child tottering around the graves of her brothers and sisters.

"Are you sure you'll be all right on your own tonight, John?" Margaret collected her shawl and lowered her voice to a whisper. "You know I could stay and keep her company for a bit. Just so she could have another woman to talk to."

"Thank you for the offer, Margaret, but I'd rather we were alone," John replied, his face haggard and voice cracked. Rising from her place by the fire, Margaret leaned across to John and wrapped her arms around him.

"It will all be fine," she said. "The worst part is over with."

Although she knew her friend meant well, in the ensuing pause Flora closed her eyes and swallowed back her frustration. There were no words that could possibly be spoken which would make everything fine.

"Flora," her husband called sharply. "Margaret is leaving."

Flora exhaled.

"Goodbye, Margaret. Take care on the way back home."

"Don't you worry about me," Margaret replied. "Just you rest and let that lovely man of yours take care of you." Flora noticed the flash of envy on Margaret's face as she braced herself to return home. Donald Gillies was a good enough man, Flora thought, but John had always been the kinder husband of the two.

More platitudes were exchanged before John escorted Margaret outside, watching as she vanished into the evening's fading light. Flora listened as her husband closed the door and returned to the hearth, sitting down heavily on the stool beside her. The croft was now silent save for the wind still whistling through the eaves. An almost palpable emptiness hung between the couple. Flora continued to stare intently into the dying embers of the hearth, listening to the soft crackle and hiss of the fire as it slowly subsided.

"So, are we to sit quietly like this for the remainder of the night?"

Flora looked up at the sound of her husband's voice and saw in the dimming light that his eyes were glistening. John's craggy face was set firmly, but beneath his beard Flora could see his jaw quivered from fighting back tears. Most men would be ashamed to show such weakness.

Flora shook her head despairingly. "I don't know what you want me to say, John."

"I'm your husband." John's voice cracked. "You should be able to talk to me."

Flora flinched, but once more returned to gazing into the smoky air.

"I'm worried about you, Flora. The last few nights you've turned away from me in bed; it's as if you don't want to touch me. You won't even cry around me."

"Would you rather I cried every night?" she said abruptly. "Would you rather I screamed and howled the place down?"

"No, I just want you to say something. Anything! Instead, you barely even look at me. Do you have any idea how worthless that makes me feel?"

"I don't know how to feel, John!" Flora cried. "I'm an unnatural mother. Say it! It's the truth, isn't it?"

"You know fine well that's not what I'm saying. You're the best mother our boys could have asked for. But you've barely spoken a word to me since Donnchadh . . ."

The name hung tremulously between them. Flora wanted to reach out to her husband, to hold him and comfort him and put into words the confused haze of emotions she was experiencing. But she could not. Instead, she bowed her head, looked down upon the crumbled remains of the bannock in her lap and picked the crumbs from her woollen skirt.

John sighed heavily. "Flora, you can't blame yourself for what happened. This is nothing like the last time."

At these words, Flora's head jerked up and she stared at her husband, her face falling.

"If anything, it's my fault," John continued. "I was there and even I couldn't protect our boy. We should not have stayed so close to the cliff edge; I was the more experienced one and I should have known better. The wind was just too strong, and we couldn't hold on to him . . ." John's body began to shake. He hurriedly rubbed his sleeve against his eyes and took several deep breaths.

After what seemed like minutes, Flora reached out and touched her husband's hand.

"No, John, I won't let you blame yourself. The storm took our boy; not you, not Donald, not any of the men who were there that day. Nobody could have stopped what came for him."

He turned to her, his eyes glassy in the dimming light.

Flora tightened her grip on his hand. "You're a good man."

John smiled shakily and planted a kiss on his wife's cheek. "I'm sorry, *mo chridhe*."

"Me too."

The couple touched their foreheads together and sat that way for some time, until the last of the embers hissed and was almost extinguished.

"We should wrap those up," John said suddenly, nodding to the remaining bannocks which nestled snuggly in a basket lined with cloth. "Can't have them going stale."

"There are too many to last long anyway. Seems wasteful." Flora leaned against John's shoulder and brushed the remaining crumbs onto the floor. Her mind drifted once more, and she was struck by an idea.

"I'll give them to the new Reverend as a welcome gift. It's the least we can offer after that shameful display earlier."

"Forget about that, *mo chridhe*. He had no right upsetting you."

"You know that wasn't his intention, John. These mainlanders have a different way about them. Besides, it was me who made a spectacle of him in the first place." Flora contemplated the bannocks. "I don't imagine he's been offered much to eat these past few days. He looked as pale as milk whey."

John shrugged his shoulders. "If it pleases you, I don't see the harm," he grumbled, getting up to prod at the hearth. "Just be careful around him. I've seen men like him before."

Flora ignored the warning. She needed to get away from their house, even if just for a moment, for they had not left it since the storm, other than to bury their son. She needed a stranger's words too, someone who knew nothing of her and who could speak to her without the dreadful knowing of what had taken place. She rose wearily to her feet, her joints cracking and her hips protesting as she straightened. The pain was familiar but grew in strength each day. She gracefully accepted it: it was merely more penance. Crossing to the chair nearest the door, she reached down to pick up her shawl.

"You can't possibly be thinking of doing it now." John looked aghast. "It's getting dark out there and that wind is picking up something fierce."

"It's a ten-minute walk, John," Flora retorted. "The worst won't pick up for a while yet. Anyway, I think the poor man will need some succour and a kind word tonight. He's probably feeling awful about what happened earlier on."

"His wounded pride is not our responsibility. And besides that, I'm not having you trudge up that hill in this weather."

"The longer we argue about this the more likely I am to be caught out in the worst of it," Flora muttered, swinging her shawl around her shoulders and up over her head. She stooped to pick up four of the bannocks which she carefully wrapped in cloth before heading to the door. As Flora passed through to the byre, Morag raised her head from between her paws, her eyes wide and her tail twitching nervously.

"Flora, please," John implored, "you're not thinking clearly."

"Isn't that how grieving mothers are supposed to behave?" Flora looked pointedly at her husband over her shoulder as she opened the door and strode out into the elements.

Clutching the bannocks to her chest with one arm and using the other to keep her shawl from blowing off her head, Flora watched as the waves swelled against the shoreline. Grey clouds gathered over the horizon and the tall blades of seagrass whipped back and forth. At least the wind was blowing easterly and would help to push her aching body up the steep slope towards the Reverend's lodgings.

Squinting against the wind and the dying light of the evening, Flora looked back towards the graveyard and tried to discern her son's burial cairn. She could see that the wind was beginning to loosen some of the haphazardly stacked stones around the cemetery wall and the missionary's chapel. She tried to look closer but was soon startled from her thoughts by a sudden rush of air buffeting against her skirts. Glancing back once more at the tideline, Flora saw it had risen to swallow the beach. Her ears were assaulted by the shrill scream of the wind. Flora froze. A memory resurfaced from deep within her.

Clasping at her skirts and hugging her gift in the crook of her elbow, she began to slowly climb the hill, shaking off her feeling of unease. The tide and the wind followed her as she steadily made her way up the slope, both elements consuming the island inch by inch as the sea again stirred to sweep up its secrets.

CHAPTER THREE

THOMAS

THE lantern flame sputtered into life, casting a warming glow over the bare walls of the Reverend's lodgings. As daylight subsided and the winds picked up, Murray noticed to his dismay that there was a steady trickle of water seeping through a corner of roof turf nearest the byre.

With a deep sigh, he set down the lantern and shrugged off his coat. Rubbing the material between his thumb and forefinger, he tried to remove the dusty imprint left by the muck covered stone that had bounced off it earlier that day. Murray still simmered with barely suppressed rage towards his assaulters following the incident. Clutching the material in his fist, he flung the garment to one side and glowered at the rush strewn floor.

His head throbbed as the failures of the day returned to punish him. He could feel them pressing against his skull. Every mistake and disaster in his life had brought him to this empty and friendless place. It was a penalty he would have to accept; only through consuming himself in his mission for the next year could he return to the mainland with any trace of his dignity intact. The islanders would have to bend to his will eventually, for although they did not know it, it was he who held their fate in his hands.

Reassuring himself with this, Murray walked over to the wooden chest by the side of the bed: the only furnishing in the entire dwelling that had any connection with home. Murray ran a finger over the embossed lines which formed a lion's mane on the carved lid; the paint was faded and cracked after years of being transported from one armed campaign to another across the Low Countries, France, and the length of the British Isles. Dried shards of red and yellow flaked away under his fingertips: his father's only legacy to an unfit son.

When he remembered back to his boyhood, Murray thought of his father's tirades against the corruption of Papism, and the horrifying stories of The Killing Time; stories which had kept him awake as a child. He remembered the vividly told tales of hordes of men confined to dank, open air prisons to freeze before execution, and of adolescent girls tied to palisades and left to drown for refusing to swear an oath to a Papist king as head of the church. Murray was a mere babe when his father had first fought the rebels loyal to James II at Dunkeld and Cromdale. His mother had birthed him on the road to Killiecankie. From then on, she followed her husband from barrack to barrack with her infant son strapped to her back. Murray's most fragmented and distant memory was filled with flashes of grey and red marching in line over a haze of green to the sound of drums and pipes. Knowing that he did not have the stomach for a military career, as had incessantly been pointed out to him, Murray had convinced himself that the Clergy was the only way of honouring his father's ideals.

Opening his father's chest, Murray began to rummage through books and spare parchments to extract a small collection of letters. In amongst the bundle was a very brief correspondence from his sister, a letter of appointment from Clan Chief Norman MacLeod, and several communications from the Presbytery of Invernessshire. On the broken wax seals of these letters was the emblem of a burning bush and the words, *Nec Tamen Consumebatur*: Yet it was not consumed.

Digging deeper and finally finding what he was searching for, Murray sat on the edge of the box bed and with slow, tender movements unfolded the letter. He carefully studied her handwriting, following its elegant loops and curls.

My Loving Husband,

This letter will no doubt have reached you by the time of your departure from Fort William, and I am hopeful that it shall suffice for you in prelude to your voyage to Eilean Eòin. I know how badly you take to travel, so I hope that the sea remains calm for you and you are not brought to any greater discomfort than our parting necessitates. My next correspondence shall not be with you until you reach your destination and are too far from me to turn back from your course.

I have recently arrived back from a visit to your mother, who it grieves me to say makes no improvement. One must take comfort in the knowledge that she no longer seems to feel the pain of her losses. As I sat with her yesterday, she was smiling and speaking your father's name as if he too were in the room with her. Her eyes were blind to me but full of an innocent joy. Elizabeth and Frances keep their mother company most days and wish to be remembered to their brother. Elizabeth's belly grows by the day and if the child is a boy, she has said that she may name him after his good and Godly uncle.

For now, life carries on as usual for me. I have the garden to occupy me, and I am enjoying the warmer weather. Do not concern yourself over how I ail on my own. Understand Dear Husband, that our separation is a necessary evil which will reap its rewards in the House of the Lord and bring great pride and joy unto me, your wife. Remember the words I spoke to you on our parting and do not allow Earthly feeling to push you from your path.

Know that I pray for you and will continue to do so every day.

Your Dear Wife,
Caroline Murray

He traced the name several more times before folding the letter back up.

Murray remembered the conversation he and his wife had had when he was offered the missionary post. He knew Caroline's delicate state of health would not cope well with the harsh realities of island life and was eager to reject the Presbytery's offer. There were other, more experienced and committed ministers who would have more readily taken his place, but the crestfallen look on his young wife's face when he had admitted this to her shamed him into a change of heart. Sitting across from each other in their tiny parlour, Murray remembered how his wife had clasped his hands and told him he could not turn down an offer to directly administer to the Lord's wishes; bringing the reformed faith to those in the most unreachable places was a divine mission which would be the making of him. Everything inside him revolted against the notion, but his wife's fervent reassertions of faith, both in God and in him, pushed him into accepting.

Gazing up at the plain, wooden cross he had affixed to the wall opposite his bed, Murray clasped his hands to his brow, praying he too could demonstrate the level of commitment to Christ that his wife showed.

Looking up at the water leaking from the thatch above his head, he thought bitterly of the little recognition this calling had brought him. Closing his eyes, he listened to the steady fall of rainwater. His chapped lips parted slightly as in his mind's eye he returned to a cottage on the outskirts of Inverness, where his wife was tending to a rush light. The chill of the blackhouse dissipated as a growing warmth spread across his body.

A sudden, violent surge of wind hammered against the door to the byre and jolted Murray from his imaginings. It was only when the door was struck again, that he recognised the deliberate pattern of a person knocking. He was slightly perturbed that Ailith would come to tend to the house on such an inhospitable evening and surprised she would deign to ever return after the events of earlier in the day. Rising from the bed and picking up the lantern, Murray stepped through to the byre, treading carefully past clumps of hay to reach the door.

The door swung open to reveal a bent, huddled figure on the threshold; a shadow slowly emerging from the gloom. Holding the lantern aloft, Murray was startled to recognise the mother of the deceased boy. Her withered hands clutched a sodden bundle of cloth and bread.

"I'm so sorry to disturb you, Reverend." Above the howl of the wind, the woman's voice was gentle and reserved. "I just wanted to apologise for the misunderstanding earlier and bring you something by way of an apology. I hope you don't judge us too harshly; it's been a difficult few months and . . . Oh, I'm sorry, I can see I've startled you when you were readying for bed . . . I just . . . Oh, it was silly of me really. What must you think of me? An old woman roaming about so late and in such foul weather."

Murray surveyed the woman carefully. He estimated she was considerably past her fiftieth year, but age seemed hard to distinguish on the islands. Beneath her shawl her face had the same weather-beaten hue familiar with most of the islanders, but the lines on her face did not convey the same severity: there was a softness to them. Softness begot weakness. Perhaps this weakness would prove useful.

"Anyway, I brought you some leftover bannocks as a way of trying to make amends," she continued. "They're from the last of our grain supplies, but they're still very fresh."

The woman pressed the bundle into his hands. Her grimy, rough-skinned palms briefly brushed against his fingers. He flinched.

"I won't keep you any longer in this chill air, Reverend. John, that's my husband, will be frantic with worry if I don't return quickly. I hope you enjoy the bannocks." She turned to leave.

"Wait!"

The old woman halted, turning back around with careful movements. Opening the door wider, he took the moment of hesitation to regain some semblance of composure.

"Mrs MacKinnon, am I correct?"

The woman gave a slight nod.

"Please. Come in for a moment out of the cold. I would not want your husband to think I'd given you no hospitality in return for your kindness."

Murray saw the woman's fleeting hesitation; the quick look back over her shoulder to the crofts at the bottom of the hill, the clawed hand worrying at the stiff wool of her shawl.

"Yes," she said slowly, "I think I would quite like that, thank you." The doubt seemed to evaporate and was swiftly replaced by a warm smile. "Old bones need some relief. Only it will have to be quick, I'm afraid."

Opening the door wide, he invited her over the threshold, leading her through the byre and into the living space. Lowering herself stiffly, she sat on one of the small, three legged stools by the hearth. He scrutinised her movements as the she took a sweeping glance around the dishevelled room, her gaze eventually landing on the leaking rafters.

"That will need fixing before long," she said thoughtfully. "I could ask my boy, Fergus, to stop by and re-patch the turf if you would like, Reverend."

"I dare say that would be helpful, Mrs MacKinnon." He considered the way she nodded to herself in acknowledgment of his words. There was a sad desperation about her; a franticness which seemed forever on the cusp of divulging more than was appropriate.

"My Fergus is a good lad. He'll do whatever his mother tells him." She smiled, casting her eyes downwards. Murray could not tell whether this was from discretion or fear of judgement. He wracked his brains, striving to maintain cordiality and escape the growing silence.

"How many children do you have, Mrs Mackinnon?"

He realised his error almost as soon as the words had escaped his mouth. Hurriedly, he tried to redeem himself in the woman's esteem. "I mean, they must be of some comfort to you in this difficult time. I am terribly sorry for your loss."

The old woman waved her hand. "Don't worry, you have not

offended me, Reverend. I have two grown up boys, both with their own families now. Two of my children, including my youngest boy Donnchadh, I've lost to the sea."

Murray's occupation often revolved around the consolation of others, and he had always considered himself a calming influence in the lives of his previous parishioners. Nevertheless, there was something unreadable yet tragically vulnerable about this seemingly kindly woman that made him apprehensive: it was as if she could read his every thought and feeling more than he could ever come to understand hers.

"I suppose I'm lucky in some ways," the woman babbled on. "I haven't as many children as some women my age, but none of mine were born too soon and none succumbed to sickness, not even during the sickness which claimed so many around the time my Donnchadh was born. The sea also took my daughter, but she was much younger, barely more than a babe when she was lost." She seemed to stare into empty air. "She's still there now. The sea, I mean. But they say drowning is quick, don't they, Reverend? Not lingering like sickness or hunger. It would just be like slipping into a deep sleep."

The woman turned to him, pleading and wide eyed.

"I'm sorry," he said awkwardly. "I've been too familiar . . ."

"No. No, I need to talk about such things." Her face was again impassive. "Everyone at home expects me to do nothing but sit and feel sorry for myself all day." She gave a slight, nervous laugh. "Sometimes I feel . . . But I can talk to you. You're an honourable man. A man of faith."

Murray felt tense. His urge to interrogate this woman was muddied by a sense of mutual pity and a growing realisation of the bleakness of both their situations.

"Do you have children, Reverend?" the woman asked suddenly.

He winced. The conversation was becoming too personal. Trying to stifle his feelings and regain control, he replied, "I have a wife on the mainland."

"You must miss her terribly."

"Yes."

He could hear the faint remnants of the fire crackling in the hearth; the dying embers highlighted every line on the woman's face. To his dismay he found that he no longer felt in control of the interaction; this aging woman made him feel increasingly uncomfortable, and her mere presence seemed to mock and undermine his purpose. Murray watched as she stirred from her place by the fireside, and he rose awkwardly. It was as if he were standing to respectfully acknowledge a lady exiting the dining room, or to escort an elderly matron to her seat in church. He admonished himself for the absurdity of his action.

Flora MacKinnon slowly eased herself to her feet. "I can see you are tired, Reverend, and really I must get home."

Thankful for an end to this absurd charade, Murray escorted her outside, kicking aside the musty straw of the byre and leading her to the door. The rough, homespun wool of her shawls brushed gently against his arm, and he drew back quickly, as if scorched by a stray tinder. "Thank you again for the bread, Mrs MacKinnon. Are you sure you would not prefer me to escort you home?"

Once again, the woman feebly waved her hand at him and smiled. "I've trod the same path many a year."

Relieved, Murray stood and watched as she weaved her way steadily downhill, the wind catching at her many layers of clothing. He felt a sinister shiver stroke his spine. Not knowing what to make of this, Murray watched through the dim light of his lantern and the fading twilight until he could see she was safely at the bottom of the slope, where she vanished from his view, phantom-like into the setting sun. If there truly was evil afoot on this isle, he had little doubt that Flora MacKinnon would be the first to lead him to it.

CHAPTER FOUR

FLORA

THE following morning the women and children gathered on the beach to pick the meagre meat from the bones of the storm. Driftwood jutted from the sands like a broken ribcage, and the remains of birds, fish and crustaceans littered the shoreline as the women stooped to collect what was not already rotting into their baskets. Young girls stood in the shallows, bashing and scraping the limpets off rocks with heavy stones. Some of the younger children attempted to help, until their momentary fascination in tearing small creatures from their refuge soon abated, and they instead amused themselves by running back and forth through the surf, swinging long glistening strands of kelp in circles, while trailing them along the sand for the crofters' dogs to chase.

Flora sat transfixed, watching the children playing and taunting the waves. A gutting knife lay in her lap, coated in blood and gleaming with scales. Although the islanders preferred the briny tang of gannet meat, when nature's whims presented such sustenance, it would be foolish not to take full advantage of the bounty on offer. Still, Flora could not help but be distracted from her duties, staring longingly at the children as they played.

"Grandam?"

Flora turned to see Michael's eldest child, Janet, standing by her side with a small fish proudly held aloft for her grandmother's appraisal. Flora curled her lips into a smile and nodded. "That's wonderful, *m'eudail*. Shall I ask your mammy to save this one especially for your supper?"

Her granddaughter flushed crimson and toyed sheepishly with a loose thread dangling from her sleeve. The girl had always been nervous around her. Flora blamed the child's mother, who seemed stubbornly reluctant to share in the pleasures and pains of childrearing.

"I got this one for you, Grandam." Janet's voice was barely more than a whisper.

"Oh!" Flora affected surprise and bent forward conspiratorially. "I shall have to keep this one hidden then, so nobody else pinches such a fine catch for themselves." Flora made a show of tucking the fish under her shawl, knowing full well that the whiteness of its gills and the slightly putrid smell already emanating from it would mean it would have to be discarded.

Janet gave a shy nod, chewing on a thumbnail before turning to watch her younger brother, Malcolm, further down the beach. Their mother, Ann, observed with one hand on her hip, the growing mound of her belly pressing against the basket she carried.

"Janet!" Ann called out to her daughter and made her way forward. "Stop hassling your grandam. You're a big girl now and should be helping."

"She does not bother me." Flora smiled and bent forward to run her fingers over the child's hair. Ann, seeming not to notice, took Janet by the shoulders and started distractedly fussing at her clothes, which had become unpinned and were in disarray. Flora watched carefully, yearning for connection. "How do you fare, Ann?"

Ann's head jerked around; her expression was distant. "Well enough," she murmured, avoiding eye contact and continuing to toy with her daughter's plaid. "The babe is quickening fast."

"You know I am here to help if you need anything. I'll be there when the time comes."

Ann finished refastening Janet's earasaid and straightened. Flora watched as the girl, restless from all the attention, wriggled free of her mother and scampered across the sand. Ann sighed and wiped her hands on her apron.

"I want my grandmother there to attend to me."

Flora felt wounded by the blunt delivery of those words. It made sense, of course. Ailith McQueen was the oldest woman on the island, and no woman still living had not had her in attendance when their children were delivered. But Ailith was a bitter old woman at the best of times, and some of the sense of entitlement she possessed over her position as island matriarch seemed to have seeped through the generations. Flora tried not to let her annoyance show.

"I see," she said slowly. She could see that the young woman was itching to be away. Ann did not return Flora's attention, but instead craned her neck to watch anxiously as her children crouched low to the tideline and dug their hands in the wet sand.

"Ann?" Flora tried to catch her daughter-in-law's eye. "Is there something troubling you? Besides the baby?"

"How can you say that?" Ann turned on her heel and faced Flora. "You know more than any of us that something isn't right. It feels wrong. Everything feels wrong. It feels like something is coming for us . . . Coming to swallow us up."

"You shouldn't talk about such things. It's just the storm and . . ."

"It's more than just the weather," Ann snapped. "It's like a quickening in the air, in the way the sea moves: it's like that last month before the babe comes. Your Donnchadh was just the first, I know it. My grandam says this isn't the first time we faced a reckoning. I was a child; I can barely remember the last time, but you . . ."

"Be careful with your words." Flora tried to keep her voice steady. "This is not a reckoning. It's normal this far on in a pregnancy for you to . . ."

"Then why do you not weep for Donnchadh? Why do you not mourn for your son?"

Flora flinched.

"I grieve how I see fit," she said quietly. "You must not lose control of yourself, Ann. It won't be good for the baby if you worry yourself so."

"No . . . I mean . . . I just don't want the baby tainted by death is all." Ann's eyes shifted towards the sea.

"And it won't be." Flora levelled her voice as she regained control. "We'll all be there for you when the time comes, just as we were before for Janet and Malcolm."

"Perhaps," Ann responded distractedly and paused, saving herself for her parting words. "Besides, if anything is coming, surely it will not be coming for me. I have a clear conscience."

Flora's skin prickled and suddenly the cold was more potent than ever. She tried to gather her thoughts into summoning a reply but before she could even open her mouth, Ann was hurrying back to her children.

"Nothing is coming for us, Ann!" Flora yelled, but the sea drowned out her voice and her words passed unheard. A whistle of wind brushed past her face. Flora halted for a moment, her thoughts of the present suspended as she felt herself closing her eyes to the silence it summoned.

A sudden wave crashed against the rocks at the mouth of the bay and Flora's eyes flew back open. She felt exposed sitting out on the beach with the other women and thought that the further she could get from the settlement, the better. Rallied by this urge, she turned away from the sea and looked back down at the bloody mess of fish in her lap. She had not been paying due care to her work and now her hands were smeared with briny gore. Wiping the gutting knife on her skirts and hurriedly brushing away the scales, she picked up her basket and headed back towards the settlement.

While crossing the machair, she could see the circle of men were still sat by the village wall, deep in their morning discussion. She was eager not to be seen. Pulling her shawl up to cover her head, Flora skirted the wall, passing by her house and instead taking the coastal track which passed the cemetery and wound its way around the side of the bay; a path which led to rocky inlets and hidden coves. Hopefully, the time elapsed between John returning from the meeting and her returning with a full basket would be enough for his incessant worrying to have subsided. Crossing by the edges of the tumble-down dyke which bordered the cemetery, Flora took a fleeting look across at her son's grave. Some of the stones had loosened in the night, but the cairn remained.

The further she looked, the more signs of the storm's destructive path exposed themselves. Most prominent was the condition of the chapel. The wooden beams which for a time had supported the roof had rotted through with rainwater, collapsing in on themselves and leaving a gaping hole through which the sodden turf had fallen. Now the building stooped miserably under its own weight.

In amongst the rubble, the Reverend stood pathetically observing the carnage. Putting a tentative hand to steady himself against the doorway, he seemed to peer inside the remnants of the chapel, as if trying to locate a safe path of entry or find anything salvageable. A short time passed before he retreated, submissive and seemingly defeated.

Flora hesitated. Her eagerness to acquaint herself with this stranger had become mixed with embarrassment at the ease in which she had unburdened her thoughts to him the previous night. She raised her hand upwards in greeting, but before she could even announce herself with a friendly salutation, she slowly lowered it again, her fear getting the better of her. More than her apprehension over humiliating herself socially, she felt unsettled by her recollection of their previous conversation. The Reverend was distant in a way which made her uncomfortable. She could sympathise with him, even relate to his current isolation from those around him, but she could not shake off the disquieting thought that he wanted something from her. Something more than she was prepared to give.

Compelling herself onwards, she held her shawl to her face and, with a sense of purpose, prepared herself to hurry past the cemetery wall. John, Ann, the Reverend; all of them could wait while she sought solace in her most hallowed place: the cove.

Her son's bones may have been rotting in the earth, but the bones of her lost daughter perhaps still littered the shoreline, picked clean by an array of tiny creatures. Flora always hoped that one day, as she examined rockpools in search of shellfish, she would find a piece of her daughter waiting for her beneath the surface.

※

Beyond the sanctuary of the bay, the land crept forth in jagged fingers to meet the sea. Following the narrow path from the island's settlement, eventually the coastline petered out into the small pebbly cove which could be accessed by a gradual descent from the cliffs above.

Past the rocks at the back of the inlet, away from the frothing water's edge, was a tiny, almost imperceivable gap in the cliff, which, if small enough or brave enough, a person could crawl through into a network of caves. In summertime and during low tide when Flora was young, the children had sometimes dared each other to enter the cavern. It was a long-held belief that it contained a selkie's tomb. Fireside stories reported that centuries ago, a young crofter had found an injured selkie stranded on the rocks and entranced by the beauty of her human form, had hauled her ashore to take as a wife. The crofter burned her velvety soft pelt and the selkie had pined away, barely lasting a week on land before dying and being buried in a shallow grave, safe inside the cave where her spirit could not wreak vengeance on those who had wronged her. Lately, few on the island would venture there, some convinced that they could still hear the selkie's anguished cries.

Around the rocks at the cave's entrance were a series of shallow pools encrusted with jewelled anemones and draped with green, hair-like strands of gutweed. It was here that Flora gathered her skirts and waded barefoot in her search for cockles and whelks. Collecting them in the deep woollen pockets of her skirt, she staggered forwards, wincing as she hauled herself upwards with one hand grasping at a barnacled rock.

The sea hissed. Cold, salt air caressed her face and whipped up her hair.

Flora looked up at the horizon and frowned, barely noticing the shrieking gulls swooping down to protect their nests, or paying heed to the gutted fish slowly spoiling at the bottom of her basket. After weeks of stormy weather, the sea was remarkably calm, and as she scanned the shoreline, the steady flow of the tide ebbed its way further up the rocks towards her ankles.

Making her way precariously over the kelp strewn foreshore, she headed back towards the path. The tide had piled the seaweed in deep mounds beneath her feet, so thick that she could not feel the hard rock beneath. Flora kept her head down, carefully watching each step she took. Sun-blackened bladderwrack crunched beneath her feet amidst the slippery sheen of the kelp, which lay in dark, seemingly endless strands, rotting and secreting an aroma of brackish decay. Flora swatted at the flies buzzing around her face.

She stumbled, her foot tripping on something solid which lay beneath the mounds of twisted seaweed. Correcting herself, she disentangled her ankle from a knot of black weed. Nudging the thick kelp aside with her foot, she expected to find the carcass of a seal or porpoise, and certainly the wet, pale flesh which revealed itself as she parted the seaweed seemed to further attest to this. But the flesh seemed discoloured, and Flora stared open mouthed at the soft whiteness of it. In places there were patches of blue, purple, and yellowish bruising on the ghostly skin, blooming like crocuses pushing up through the last of the winter snow.

The flies swarmed.

Flora looked once more at what she had thought was long, black weed coiling around her foot and baulked in horror. Shakily, she bent down and moved the hank of hair to one side. Her hand brushed against something cold and clammy. Parting the kelp exposed a long, thin arm with pearly skin flung outwards, hand outstretched to greet the sky above, fingers delicately curled towards palm like a sleeping new-born.

Rising as quickly as her aching body allowed her, Flora stepped back and dropped her basket. Shells clattered and spilled over the shoreline. Abandoning the basket and its contents, she scrabbled back towards the path. Hobbling up the cliffs, she ran breathlessly back towards the settlement, her mind and stomach reeling.

CHAPTER FIVE

THOMAS

"SHE'S not one of ours. That much is certain."

Murray forced himself through the ring of men. He had heard the commotion when Flora MacKinnon had staggered into the village, breathless and shaken as she deliriously relayed her message of a body in the cove. Eagerly, he had followed the small band of men, who dashed over the cliffs to investigate.

He now found himself unable to take his eyes from the body, draped pathetically over the kelp, limbs spilling over the rocky shoreline. She was barely past womanhood. Seventeen, perhaps nineteen at most. Salty coils of jet-black hair lay matted around her face and fell in wet trails over her glistening, puckered skin. Her body was strangely blemish free, but there were faint bruises on her arms and wrists. She was as naked as a new-born. Murray felt his face burn with shame as he looked away.

"Well, somehow she's been spared the worst of the sea's wrath," continued Donald Gillies, tugging gently on his beard. "We should search the island to see if there are any others."

The oldest men in the group began muttering, heads bowed seriously, and brows furrowed, as if trying to supress their thrill at being active participants in a disaster that was finally not one of their own. The youngest, on the other hand, stood at the perimeter, shuffling their feet, and looking nervously at each other. Murray could feel his disdain for these men growing. They continued to talk quietly amongst themselves, while some of them parted from the group to search further along the cliffs and shoreline.

"Reverend?"

Jolting from his thoughts, Murray looked up to a circle of faces staring intently at him. It was the first time the men had even expressed awareness of his presence amongst them, let alone acknowledged it.

"This is surely your area of knowhow," Donald said, spitting into one of the rockpools. "Make use of yourself and stay with the body. Say your prayers over it so it won't come bothering us in the coming nights."

Murray was incredulous. "And where will you be, sirs? Surely you will need more than me to carry her back to the village."

One of the men laughed. "We'll not be taking that body anywhere, Father. Far better we leave it to wash back out with the tide. If she has come from the sea, then that's where she should stay; she'd only cause trouble here on land."

"This is pagan, superstitious nonsense," Murray declared. "This poor girl has the right to an honest Christian burial on consecrated ground. Have you no thought whatsoever for her soul?"

"Aye. That's what we're worried about," asserted Donald. "Mock all you want Reverend, but my conscience will be far clearer knowing she's off the island. It's inviting trouble, taking back a soul that the sea has already claimed."

They stood in quiet animosity as the tide began to creep around their feet. The impatient gulls were already circling above their heads, and in the ensuing silence the waves sighed softly against the shore.

"You stay here and chant your words over her," Donald said scornfully. "We'll go around to the other side of the cliffs and let you know if we find any others."

"I won't leave her lying here."

The men grumbled amongst themselves.

"Fine. Suit yourself," Donald sighed. "But no one here is going to help you carry her anywhere. If her spirit becomes restless, then you will take responsibility. We'll have no part in it."

"I should get some of the women from the village to help me carry her." Murray gestured towards the girl. "For decency's sake."

"Absolutely not. No one is touching her but you."

"Then at least give me something to cover her with, man! She can't be left like this; it isn't decent."

Glancing at the girl from the corner of his eyes, Donald reddened and quickly looked away. Fumbling at the pin which fastened at his shoulder, he untied his plaid and flung it towards Murray.

"Here."

Murray grasped at the coarse wool and gathered it up. Its folds smelled strongly of old sweat and peat smoke. Bending down, he draped it clumsily over the body's pale torso, trying desperately not to brush against her cold, damp skin.

The men began departing with barely a backwards glance, and Murray soon found himself alone with the nameless, lost young woman. Perching awkwardly on top of the seaweed, he clasped his hands together and lowered his head in recitation of the Lord's prayer. The words sounded hollow coming from his lips, their comforting familiarity only masking the intense sense of panic quickening inside him. His gaze flickered upwards towards the girl, whose naked form he would have to carry, whose weighty body would soon press against his own. He forced himself to think of the alternative. His conscience would not allow for her to lie entangled amongst the seaweed; to be picked at by tiny hermit crabs; to once more await the tide to pull her into its embrace, where she would soon sink softly into the depths. Murray's head swam and stomach churned as he braced himself for the inevitable task ahead. Reaching out, he leaned across the body and pulled the woman's arms to her sides, gently tucking the plaid around them as tightly as he could.

Pushing to the forefront of his mind, in resistance of any primary humanitarian urge, was the thought of how this young woman came to meet her fate. The obvious conclusion was a shipwreck, but without any wreckage this line of enquiry was inconclusive. There was also the matter of how she had become so unclothed, yet free from the obvious broken bones and abrasions that contact with the rocks would inflict: either she had done this to herself, or someone had done this to her. Murray looked around the body, overturning rocks and fishing his hands into the tidal pools.

Nothing.

Suspicions clawed at his skull: something must be missing from this scene. He turned and saw that the tide was now making its way back inland, the waves encroaching further onto the rocks with each swell. He would have to get her back to the settlement before high tide. If necessary, an examination of the body could be carried out discreetly; indoors and away from the elements.

When he reluctantly lifted her arms, he was surprised by how supple her joints remained; her skin was still soft and as tender as a bruise. Securing the rough, homespun wool around her, he fought back his discomfort and attempted to manoeuvre her upper body from the bed of kelp. Lifting her slowly, her face was soon pressed against his collarbone, her head tilted skywards. Her cold lips brushed close to his ear.

Then, amidst the frothy hiss of the sea, came a closer and more distinct sound. Murray at first mistook the whistling, grasping breath for a sudden gasp of sea air, but then he felt the tiny hairs on his neck stir. Startled, he pulled away, his heart pounding. He saw now, clearly, what his modesty had thus far blinded him to. He stared at the long, pulsating sinew stretching across the girl's neck. It was faint, but unmistakable.

Scrabbling to his feet, Murray scanned the edge of the cove and felt his stomach drop as he saw that the men had disappeared.

"Come back! Please! I demand it!" he screamed hoarsely, yelling desperately, despite an inner knowing that his cries would go unheard. Taking another look down at the figure tucked beneath the plaid at his feet, he stood breathlessly, looking at the slight but steady rise and fall of the skin which stretched tautly across her chest. Spinning wildly on the spot, he looked out to sea, knowing that soon the tide would swallow the rocks beneath his feet. Murray staggered forward. Flailing his arms, vainly attempting retain his grip on the slippery seaweed and uneven rocks, he skirted around the tidal pools and stumbled towards the far side of the inlet, where the path vanished into the sea. His heart pounded as he waited for the men to appear, but the creeping approach of the tide forced him back. He knew he could not leave her another moment.

Wading through the expanding rock pools, icy ripples lapping against his ankles, Murray returned to where the young woman lay. The tide was beginning to seep towards her head, and thin tendrils of her hair flowed into the approaching water. Murray could not tell how long he had. For all he knew she had already passed from one world to the next in the short time it had taken him to traverse from one side of the cove to the other. If she was alive, she was barely so.

Bending down, he scooped her into his arms with less trepidation than before, looking around frantically for the men to reappear on the cliffs above. Resolving to himself that help was not coming anytime soon, he braced himself against her weight and lifted her to his chest. She seemed lighter somehow. To his relief, he could still detect the faint pulse and the soft, whispering tickle of her breath against his throat.

Gradually, he made his way back towards the cliff path. His foot snagged underneath a rock and his ankle seared with pain. He persevered, limping forwards, clutching the fragile body against his chest as the tide snaked towards him. Stumbling onto the steep path, he struggled to get a foothold on the uneven dirt track, upon which loosened stones rolled and skittered beneath the wet, wooden soles of his shoes.

Under normal circumstances, this was a path to be navigated with a hand outstretched to help haul himself upwards. He tried cautiously to stretch one hand out to grasp at a clump of turf, but in doing so the girl's head lolled backwards and her upper body began to slip from his grasp.

The tide was now crawling forward; it had passed the rocks. The thick bed of kelp had now been swallowed up completely. Murray tried pressing on, but his unworkable shoes failed to get a grip on the loose earth. He scanned the tops of the cliffs and opened his mouth again to cry out, but his throat was dry, and no sound came forth. His chest tightened. There seemed to be only one dreadful option now available to him. Feeling the body sag against the brace of his arms, he began lowering her to the ground.

From high above him, a stone scudded towards him and bounced past his shoulder. Looking up, he exhaled with relief to see a shawled figure lowering herself slowly down the steep path.

"Mrs MacKinnon . . ." his voice cracked and came forth in a raw, painful pants. A few yards ahead of him the figure froze and lowered her shawl, staring dumbly at the girl hanging limply from his arms. Her mouth fell wordlessly open, and she stood in trancelike awe.

"Mrs MacKinnon, I need you to help me up. I can't carry her alone." He looked at her in stern supplication.

The old woman's arm jerked away from her side, and she met his eyes. Gently easing herself down the path, she held out her hand and hooked it around the crook of his arm. They slowly guided each other forward, the young woman cradled between them as they gradually ascended away from the encroaching swell below.

CHAPTER SIX

FLORA

FLORA led the Reverend towards her croft, her hand gripped tightly around his forearm. As they arrived back at the village, the girl's brittle body slumped against the Reverend's chest, curious faces peered up from the huddles of women who were gathered around baskets of gutted fish carcasses. Abandoning their labour, they rose steadily to their feet and clutched nervously at their shawls, weary of the peculiar bundle of skin and bones held closely within the stranger's arms.

"Flora?" Margaret Gillies approached her neighbour cautiously. The other women craned their necks. Eager to hear of the rumoured body found in the cove, their previous doubts of Flora's confused story dissipated. Flora gawked at her friend with wide, frightened eyes.

"Margaret, she's alive . . . She's alive," Flora spoke breathlessly.

"Who? Who's alive?" Margaret stammered, spinning around to observe once more the bundle in the Reverend's arms. She staggered backwards. "You don't mean to tell me . . . Flora, did you...?"

"The girl I found . . . In the cove. Margaret, she's still breathing."

At this point, the minister took a step forward. "It's true. She is alive, although barely. We need to get her somewhere warm, quickly."

Margaret looked quizzically at the clergyman and turned back to Flora.

"He's telling the truth, Margaret. You need only feel the rise and fall of her chest. Look! Here!" Flora lunged forward and grabbed her friend's hand. Parting the now damp woollen plaid away from the girl's neck, Flora placed Margaret's hand against the cold, clammy skin.

The look on Margaret's face was sceptical, but within seconds her perplexed frown was replaced by a look of sheer terror. She snatched her hand away suddenly, nursing it against her chest as if scalded by boiling water. Staggering backwards into the gathering crowd of her fellow women, Margaret struggled for some moments to speak.

"Flora . . . I know that this must be difficult for you more than anyone, but if you had any sense left, you'd take that thing right back to where you found it."

"She's little more than a child, Margaret! Perhaps there has been a terrible accident at sea. Donald and the others are out there looking for others as we speak."

"You know as well as we, Flora, that no ships would be anywhere near here in that weather." As Margaret made her assertion, several of the other women muttered their agreement.

Flora opened her mouth to reply but was assured to hear the Reverend's stern voice from behind her.

"It is not unreasonable at all to believe that a ship, having got into trouble last night, would have come here looking for a safe harbour," he lectured furiously. "What else could you possibly be suggesting?"

The women chattered angrily together. Flora looked pleadingly at her neighbours.

"I can't leave her out in the cold for the sea to take her . . ."

The widow, Ailith McQueen, emerged from the crowd, pinch faced and clutching her heavy, wooden walking stick. "You're a fool, Flora MacKinnon. Nothing mortal could survive being out in that swell for so long."

At this the women all recoiled one step further away from the Reverend and his burden.

"I'll suffer no more of this heathenish nonsense," the Reverend reasserted. "If this girl dies without any of you raising a hand to help her, then let it be on your conscience."

Forcing their way past the gathering onlookers, who quickly parted in fear of what they beheld, Flora guided the minister towards the threshold of her croft. As they neared the doorway, Morag came bounding towards them, weaving between their legs in ignorant glee.

At the door Ann and Mary, chased off the beach by the tide, sat jigging Mary's baby girl on their laps, Michael and Fergus having gone to repair the roofs of their crofts. As they saw Flora and her bedraggled companion approaching, they stopped and glanced at each other concernedly. Upon seeing the Reverend's wet, unearthly cargo, Ann screamed. She stood up suddenly and pressed herself against the blackhouse wall, a protective hand over her pregnant belly. Mary gathered her baby to her breast and the child, perturbed by this sudden change in its circumstances, began wailing.

"Flora, what is going on?" asked Mary tentatively, as she sat rigidly against the hard, stone wall of the croft, clutching her child tightly against her. Ann took a step forward, one hand still pressed against her bulging stomach.

"Don't let him bring that into the house, Flora." Ann glanced at the girl's sagging form, before quickly averting her eyes. "You know it doesn't belong here. I warned you that there's been enough death in here already; no sense inviting it back in. And for pity's sake, cover it up! We should not look upon it . . ."

"Please don't bring it inside, Flora!" begged Mary. "Get him to leave it on the beach for the tide to wash out."

Flora's heart thudded in her chest as she felt a sudden wave of resentment towards her sons' wives. She wanted to scream at them; to fly and spit oil like a fulmar warding intruding hands away from its precious young.

"She's alive!" Flora cried. "Why can't any of you see that she's alive and I need to help her? I found her and I can't leave her again!"

Ann and Mary looked furtively at each other.

"Flora," Mary said cautiously. "Please. I think it would be best if we went to fetch John. You're not well and no wonder after finding..." Mary trailed off and gulped back her words. "Anyway, this is John's house and he'll know what to do."

"You can keep *him* here," added Ann, her eyes fixed pointedly at the Reverend Murray, "just until we can get John and the lads back. Just so you can have someone to keep an eye on you."

"There is nothing wrong with me," said Flora, forcing back the urge to raise her voice again. "Go and get John if you wish, but nothing is stopping me from stepping foot into my house and bringing inside anyone I choose."

Ann stood and stared from Flora to the wet, emaciated bundle in the Reverend's arms. Without turning her head, she called out to her children, who had been running around behind the byre throwing clods of dirt at the sheep in the distance. Flora listened wearily as Janet and Malcolm's footsteps came thumping around the side of the blackhouse.

"No!" Ann screamed, turning in panic and gesturing towards the other side of the byre. "Don't come 'round this way! You stay exactly where you are and wait for me and your *antaidh* to take you home!" The running feet halted. Mary pulled herself and her baby up from the damp turf, making her way around the byre to chide the children away. Ann turned to follow but gave a last halting glance at Flora.

"We'll send the lads back, Flora." There was caution in her voice. "Just stay where you are. Don't *you* let her out of your sight." Ann threw one more pointed look at the Reverend and heaved herself along the outer wall of the byre, clutching her stomach as she manoeuvred towards Mary and the children, who were making their way towards their croft further along the bay.

Flora guided the Reverend over the threshold. As she entered, the smoky haze of the blackhouse wrapped itself around her and pulled them away from the cold air outside. Making her way through to her living space, Flora gestured hurriedly towards a low alcove in the back wall, where a pallet of straw and coarse wool lay half hidden in darkness. Reverend Murray gently lowered the girl's body onto the pallet, and Flora heard the soft rustle and crack of the bird down and seaweed which had been hastily stuffed into the thin mattress. She had not thought to use Donnchadh's bed again, but she found herself promptly dismissing away any thought of indecency as the girl's thick, salt encrusted mass of hair draped across the blankets. Flora reached out tentatively and brushed a hank of it away from the girl's face.

Her skin was still tinged blue in places. Her forehead felt cold and waxen: like a corpse. But to Flora's relief, the girl's chest still rose and fell in a slow but steady rhythm. Flora imagined the girl's mother, either dead or pining from across the sea, and emboldened, stroked the girl's cold cheek. Where had she come from? Flora quickly dismissed the most obvious conclusions she came to. Looking closely, no longer fearful, Flora scrutinised the girl's features: her square jaw and high cheekbones made her look deceptively local. Like an island girl. If she had lived, no doubt her own daughter would have looked something like this.

"Is she from Eilean Eòin?"

Flora had forgotten the Reverend's presence, but his question sharply punctured her thoughts. She knelt silently, contemplating before replying. "I have never seen her before."

"Then she must have been swept ashore. It just seems incredible, unbelievable almost that she could withstand the cold and the sea for a whole night . . ." The Reverend looked at her searchingly. Flora returned her gaze to the face of the unconscious girl.

"I would have thought," she began, "that as a man of the Church you would be able to explain this as an act of God."

The Reverend's face blanched and he looked to the rushes on the floor. Flora crossed the girl's arms against her chest and wrapped her carefully in two more woollen plaids, which lay by the side of the palette. The girl's black hair now lay fanned around her face like a halo. Flora wished she could see the colour of her eyes.

"Should we pray for her, Reverend?" she asked suddenly. The Reverend appeared dazed, but with a fleeting twitch of a nod, Flora followed his lead as he clasped his hands and bowed his head in silent prayer. Flora hoped in the ensuing silence to hear the girl's shallow breaths as she clung precariously to life's thin thread, but to her disappointment she could barely hear a sound. Even the tiny creatures which made their home in the rushes of the floor seemed to creep and whisper amongst the decaying matter with more vigour. Then, Flora heard the faint but recognisable voices of her family approaching the blackhouse. The door to the byre creaked open, and the Reverend rose to his feet. Flora remained seated, unable to tear her eyes away from the girl.

"I told you." Flora heard Ann's voice rising. "In Donnchadh's bed as well! But I tried, John. I swear I tried to stop her, but she just won't listen to reason."

Flora heard a large figure move across the room and kneel beside her. Two heavy hands fell on her shoulders. "Come on, Ma," Michael's voice commanded. "You need to come with us. Leave father and the priest to settle this, or you'll get yourself upset all over again."

"Michael," John's stern voice rose before Flora could even summon words. "Leave your mother be and take Ann back to the bairns. Then you and Fergus go and round up the men for a gathering." There was an uncomfortable pause. "Go. I'll take care of your mother." Hands were withdrawn from Flora's shoulders, and she heard footsteps retreating outside. Once the door was closed, the muffled but outraged tones of Ann's voice could be heard fading away into the distance.

"You should be on your way too, Reverend," John said.

There was a brief pause.

"I do not think it is your place to give orders."

"It is my house. I shall do as I see fit."

Flora tried to ignore the tension filling the air as she gazed tenderly at the strange, yet soothingly familiar young woman lying in her son's bed.

"So be it." The Reverend eventually broke the silence. "I will trust in your wife to attend to this woman, sir. But I will not tolerate it if any harm comes to her, you mark my words. If she awakes, you are to summon me: there are questions I have for her."

Flora saw from the corner of her eye the Reverend begin to leave, but his footsteps halted before reaching the door. "And you will let me know," Flora heard him whisper, "if the girl passes, although I would say it's a question of when rather than if. You will report it to me before word gets out to anyone else?"

"I can't promise you anything, Reverend. Now please leave us."

Flora listened and waited as the Reverend's indignant steps retreated and the byre door once again creaked shut.

"Are you angry?" she asked.

"No."

Flora felt her husband kneel beside her and place his hand over hers. "It's them who have lost their minds, not me," she said suddenly. "You can see as well as I that she's just a girl, barely more than a child. Look at her. Does she seem anything other than that to you?"

John seemed to hesitate, but clutching Flora's hand tightly he said, "Once people have calmed themselves, they will think more clearly about this and see that what you did was an act of kindness. Nothing more." John placed his arm around her. "I trust you, Flora. You always try to do what is right."

Flora flinched. Turning to face her husband she planted a kiss on his cheek and smiled shakily.

"I should go and stoke up this fire," John said, returning her smile. "She'll need as much warmth as we can give her. Only, do not get your hopes up, *mo chridhe*. I couldn't stand to see you upset yourself over this."

As Flora nodded reassuringly, John turned to tend to the hearth. Relieved, she turned her attention back to the girl and saw the pulse still throbbing in her neck. Flora knew that the Reverend was right and that her chances of holding on to life were incredibly slim, but still, she could not pull herself away. Having found the girl herself, she imagined it was natural for her to feel this way. To her alarm she found it was the same protective feeling she had experienced when each of her children were pulled from her womb and placed bloody, squalling, and vulnerable into her waiting arms: agony had transformed into a savage, aching want.

Flora took a bone comb from the pocket of her skirt and reached across to untangle the girl's hair from the debris left crusted in it from the shoreline. Flora pulled away a long strand of gutweed. Flinging it to the floor, she gently teased at the long, dark tresses. Humming to herself softly, she remembered using the same comb to untangle the thick, matted locks of a little girl's hair. The child had squirmed and whimpered, but soothed by her mother's kisses and caresses, her earthy brown eyes had closed, and she had soon fallen soundly asleep. Flora remembered the weight of her child in her arms, and the faint, little, beating pulse which had throbbed against the bare skin of her breast.

CHAPTER SEVEN

THOMAS

"I can promise you, Reverend, we searched every inlet and stretch of rocks this side of the island. There was nothing to be found."

"Surely you cannot be certain of finding anything until the tide goes back out. And shouldn't we be searching the other side of the island?"

A few of the men, who were sat against the village wall, laughed to themselves. A wider circle of haggard faces eyed Murray suspiciously as he perched awkwardly on a clump of mossy, tumbledown stones, his black clerical cloak draped beneath him. Murray felt their eyes on him. As they stared in silent mockery, it was as if they were reminding him that he was only invited into this circle by virtue of his sex. Every man on the island now had their faces turned to him; mistrust and in some cases, blatant animosity bore into his skin. He even drew a brief glimpse from John MacKinnon, but unlike many of the others, his expression was unreadable.

"There would be far more than just driftwood if any ships had run aground," Donald Gillies continued, rubbing his forehead. "A few planks of rotten wood are hardly unusual after a storm, and as for the other side of the island, nothing but sheer cliffs. But of course, Reverend, you're welcome to a rope and grappling hook if you fancy scaling them yourself, seeing as you're so determined to prove us wrong."

Again, some of the men laughed, but others remained visibly uneasy. Murray felt his frustration grow; the islanders seemed completely unmoved by the thought of the other helpless souls who could be cast adrift, left at the mercy of the sea.

"Well, if she isn't from a vessel, where else could she have come from?" Murray inquired, deciding it wise to change tack. There was a long pause, broken only by a few nervous coughs. Suspicion swirled through his thoughts. Perhaps he was finally getting through to them. Nevertheless, he balanced on an ever-slackening rope; on one hand he must root out the truth of the matter, but on the other hand riling the islanders would only serve to ostracise himself even further.

"No reason why she could not have fallen overboard from somewhere," Donald eventually said, stiffening.

"Or have been dropped," one islander muttered furtively. Murray thought back to the faint, violet bruises blossoming on pale skin. Being thrown against the rocks could easily have caused the girl to sustain far more serious injuries, but when Murray had held her, he could detect not a single broken bone or swelling.

"Perhaps," he said, "she was left there by someone. Perhaps she was never in the sea at all. Someone could have pulled a boat in at the shore and left her."

"Impossible," Donald responded quickly. "Not in that storm, anyway. No, Reverend, she came in with the tide." The men nodded in agreement, murmuring their assent.

"The women are frightened," Fergus MacKinnon spoke out tentatively, looking up into the intense scrutiny of his fellow islanders. "My Mary looked like she'd seen a ghost when she got back from father's house." Fergus looked shyly towards John. "Dismiss it as women's prattle if you want, but I trust the look on my own wife's face. I'm not comfortable with housing the girl amongst us."

Murray tried to repress a sneer. He had been waiting for someone to assert some primitive superstition. It seemed the rigid traditions of the island left the locals totally unable to view anything which upset their routines without a heightened sense of paranoia.

"Could she not be kept in one of the storehouses up on the hill?"

Michael added to his brother's concerns. "Surely if she's close to death, the cold will hardly matter."

"Not unless you want her tainting our food supplies," said a grizzled voice from the crowd. "Birds have been so scarce this year that I fear we'll be living off just potatoes come harvest time. The last thing we need is more bad luck"

"Finlay has a point," said Donald. "The furthest house from the village of course would be our new Reverend's." A sea of faces turned towards Murray. "Would a man of the cloth not be the best person to accommodate an unfortunate at death's door?"

Murray recoiled but forced a tone of indignation into his reply. "It would not be appropriate to house a young, presumably unmarried woman where there are no other women present."

"Why, Reverend, you can't possibly be saying that you, a man of God, would be tempted by a corpse? Things must be getting desperate on the mainland."

Murray's face glowed as some of the men began to snigger. "I have had quite enough of your accusations. I only meant she should have a woman present to administer to more intimate tasks. Whether alive or dead, the poor woman's dignity needs to be maintained."

"I am willing for her to stay with my wife for a time." John MacKinnon suddenly broke his silence, looking slowly around the circle as if daring to be contradicted. "I can't say I'm happy about it, but it is the best solution. Flora found the girl and given she is more than willing, I'd say it's fitting that she nurses her. I reckon either the girl will die soon or will barely hang on to life. That being the case, we should wait until the tacksman and his men visit in a few weeks and send her back to the inner isles with them."

This statement was met with muttered approval.

"That's settled then," said Donald. "Living or dead she'll be off our island soon enough and there'll be no more talk of her." Many of the men seemed relieved at the conclusion of the debate.

"As for the tacksman," Donald continued, "it is the case that tithes are looking sparse at present, so I propose another short trip to the stacks once the weather is settled. If we cannot pay Chief MacLeod our full due, he'll have to be satisfied with oil and feathers."

The men all voiced their agreement, and began to freely talk amongst themselves, seeming to signal an end to the gathering. As they gathered their plaids and eased themselves up from the grass, Murray manoeuvred his way towards Donald Gillies, who was conducting a hushed conversation with John MacKinnon. They both glanced towards Murray as he approached.

"I was hoping," he began, "I could commission some of the men to begin work on the chapel. The stonework can be preserved, but the timber from the roof will need replacing, and there is a risk that if left too long, there won't be much to salvage at all."

"You'll have to wait until the tacksman arrives to start bartering for your timber, Reverend," Donald replied distractedly. "I would not hope for much under the circumstances. Of course, you are welcome to pay your own tithe to get whatever resources you need."

"And salvaging the stonework? Could men be commissioned to do this?"

"You should have heard me earlier, Reverend: we have our own tithes to gather. The men will be up and down those cliffs continuously collecting birds and eggs for the next two weeks, perhaps longer. Your chapel will have to wait, I'm afraid." Standing up, Donald and John moved away, still conversing quietly between themselves. Seeing the futility of his endeavour, Murray marched back up the hill towards his croft, desperate to put as much distance between him and the settlement as he could.

As he passed the MacKinnons' blackhouse, he felt a fleeting desire to enter, and had to immediately repress this urge. After all, the stranger still lay in a state of oblivion, and Flora MacKinnon in her current state of mind, although biddable, was not a woman who could be coaxed into any fresh insights. No. He had no reason to enter the MacKinnon's croft, he told himself.

He thought back to what the men had said about searching the far side of the island; clearly no thorough attempt to get to the bottom of the girl's appearance had been carried out. He did not know for certain how large the island was, or how long it would take to navigate over and around it, but surely beyond the ridge at the top of the slope there would be a steady descent to the other side. Determined, Thomas Murray walked on.

※

Scree slid from beneath his feet and was carried by the wind back down to the bay. The climb had been arduous, but with each step away from the settlement, Murray felt a perverse longing to keep walking. Overhead, the sky had started to darken. Clouds which promised rain slowly started to roll forward. As he reached the peak, Murray could feel the ground become less sodden, and saw with some relief that his shoes had survived the ascent reasonably unscathed. Reassured he pressed onwards.

As he reached the peak, the dramatic landscape of the island spread out before him in waves and ripples. Light seeped from between the clouded sky and fell in pools across the bay below him. Further down the slope he had just ascended, a woman bent low as she corralled together a group of young, bleating ewes to shepherd towards the village for shearing; the breeze carried the ewes' cries up to the top of the hill, where they echoed amidst the quiet hiss of the ocean. Turning and descending the other side of the ridge, Murray saw the land rush downwards, before flattening out and vanishing between the sea and sky. It looked as if the island had simply been broken away; like a clod of earth abruptly severed by the heel of a boot. Murray steadied himself as he felt the wind pummel against him. Approaching the edge, the sensation grew stronger.

Bracing himself, he turned to one side and edged his way tentatively towards the sheer drop of the cliff edge. Coming as close to the edge as he would allow without the fear of the ground giving way beneath his feet, he looked down at the waves rhythmically beating against the cliff face; on seabirds swooping through the salt spray to their nests and piercing the sound of the sea with their harsh cries. To his right and left, the cliffs continued to fan out before him and plummet into the breathing waters. Straight ahead, the ocean spread out for miles. Murray peered down nervously, half hoping and half dreading to see limp bodies face down, being tossed about like rag dolls in the surf, perhaps some still draped futilely across the shattered hull of a ship. His face was greeted by the cold, salt spray and the stench of seabird droppings.

Nothing.

Nothing but sea and stinking white rivers of shit. Resigned, but hardly surprised, he decided to continue his trek around the northern edge of the island, which would take him past the same cove the girl was found in.

After a few hours of weaving along the island's jagged promontories and inlets, Murray was startled to arrive at the cove, the time scouring the shoreline having passed quickly but completely ineffectually. Combing the tidal pools for scraps of clothing, or any clue as to the girl's identity, was also proving to be a fruitless effort. Mindful of the tide, Murray listened as the sea sighed against the rocks, no doubt satisfied with its efforts to thwart his search.

He felt a tickling against his earlobe, as light yet irritating as the wing of a horsefly. He thought it nothing more than that, until he heard the voice. It was indiscernible, but female. It was seductive; it was impossible. Murray's head whipped around to confront his phantom, but naturally there was no one there. He shook his head firmly: it had been the sea, nothing more.

Overhead, a smudge of cloud covered the sun as it began to cast an orange light over the horizon, luring him away, dejected, from the empty stillness of the shore.

In his sleep, he was wading through the shallow breakers. Pushing through the foam, he pressed himself forward towards the rocky shoreline of the cove, feeling the icy cold seep through the cotton of his breeches.

A woman was standing on the shore. Facing the cliffs, she stood as still as a pillar of basalt. Suddenly, a gust of wind ripped the ribboned cap from her head and tossed it out to sea. A thick shock of copper whipped around her as the wind teased her hair from its pins; it flashed against the bleak palette of greys against which she stood. She was wearing the gown she wore for their wedding: a pale, yellow linen, and it rustled faintly in the breeze. He remembered how it once span and swelled when they danced a reel.

"Watch out for the tide, Thomas."

Caroline did not turn, and her voice seemed to float from nowhere.

He splashed towards her, but despite the waves sweeping towards the shore, each step seemed to bring him no further forward than the last, and the weight of the water pushed heavily against his thighs.

"Caroline!"

She did not turn. The waves gathered strength and suddenly he felt himself being sucked backwards, the cold water wrapping around his waist. He thrashed and flailed but was only pulled back further. Soon, the water reached his chest, his neck. Waves bobbed up and down and obscured his vision, slowly concealing Caroline from view. A voice lingered in the air once more, this time it seemed to change form from his wife's unmistakable trill to one of greater depth and coldness.

"The sea . . . She is coming."

The silty seabed gave way until he was out of his depth, and as he lost his footing and sank into the relentless swell, he felt cold hands caress his back, slithering onto his shoulders and pulling him down. What felt like long, wet hair wrapped sensuously around his throat and spread like oil in the water around him. As he was dragged under, he envisioned a woman's face, part encrusted in barnacles and sea welks, with colourless eyes which mirrored the gloom of the sea.

※

When Murray jolted awake, his eyes were greeted with nothing but the pitch darkness of the little box bed, which sealed him away from the fug of the blackhouse. He swung the wooden door to one side, desperate to be free of the sense of entrapment. Unable to settle, he sat upright, panting, but as he became more aware of himself, he noticed the damp sheets crumpled and wrapped stickily around his thighs. Mortified, he quickly kicked them away from his legs, and lay back down in the hope of less visceral dreams. Instead, he tossed about in a troubled half slumber, impatient for the light of day.

CHAPTER EIGHT

FLORA

KNOWLEDGE of the tacksman's imminent arrival had made the village thrum with the chatter and song of industrious women. At dawn their husbands, fathers and sons flocked to the cliffs in the hope of returning in the evening with baskets filled with eggs, oil rich fulmars, and tender fleshed puffins. During this time, the women sat clustered around the village wall, cleaning and scouring the wool of their scant flocks in buckets of water and bird oil. As they tugged and teased the matted clumps with combs, some of them sang, whilst others swapped gossip, their eyes occasionally straying from their work companions to watch their children, the youngest of whom sat contentedly on the grass pulling at clumps of wool, while their older sisters joined in their mothers' toil.

Regardless, Flora could not be drawn any further than her own doorstep. Perched with her back against her door, she scoured and combed, occasionally glancing across to the other women, knowing that they were furtively watching her; talking about her. She imagined it was with a combination of pity and scorn.

It had taken Flora three days to even reach the front doorstep after the girl had arrived. She could not be induced to leave her side for fear of her slipping away, alone, her soul trapped in the house with no one to let it out the byre door. Somehow though, the girl was still clinging to life. If, indeed, it could be called life. Over the past few days, she had occasionally stirred as Flora trickled water into her mouth, and gently forced small spoonfuls of porridge between her lips. The first time she had coughed Flora had nearly fallen backwards off her stool, so startled was she by those dry, rattling breaths. To begin with, Flora was determined to watch every heaving breath which wracked the girl's swollen ribs and had felt a growing anticipation whenever her eyelids fluttered. Still, she had not opened her eyes.

After those initial days, once it became clear that the girl would not die quickly, John had managed to coax Flora as far as the doorstep, but in another hour or so, she was resolved go back inside to check on the girl and offer her water. Flora put a hand down to massage Morag's ears as the sheepdog sat by her basket, snacking at the air as wisps of wool floated down past her face. Raising her hand to shield her eyes from the sun, Flora observed Margaret talking quietly to her sister and daughter, whilst discreetly eyeing her. Rising and setting down her work materials, Margaret paced towards Flora.

"Won't you come over and join us? You look lonely sat over here all by yourself."

"You know how things are, Margaret," Flora replied, roughly pulling at a knot of wool. "Someone has to keep watch over her, and seeing as John is away and nobody else has volunteered . . ."

"You never even asked us, Flora. Not once did you ask any of us if we'd be willing to help."

"And are you?" Flora looked up from her work. "You have certainly made no bones about how you feel. I've seen how you all skirt around my house, so full of nonsense you'd fear stepping foot in its shadow."

Margaret blinked. "Maybe that is the case." She stepped back and folded her arms. "But that doesn't change the fact that we all care for you. Given what happened with Donnchadh, it's obvious we'd be concerned, and it's understandable that you'd feel this way having just lost a child. Don't forget that many of us know how that pain feels."

Flora looked down and went back to her work, tugging at the stubborn woolly tangle.

"But you must admit, Flora," Margaret continued, "there's something not quite right about any of this. A slip of a girl like that somehow still breathing after all that time out in the wind and rain? It just doesn't seem natural, and we've had our fill of bad signs. So far, the harvests have been poor. You remember fifteen years ago. You remember how . . ."

"I remember it better than anyone." Flora continued to untangle the wool and swore softly when she tugged so hard a bone tooth snapped from the comb. She could feel Margaret's eyes bore into her.

"Well," Margaret said, "you can't say I didn't try."

Flora pursed her mouth and continued to tug at the wool. Flicking her eyes to one side, she watched as Margaret walked away, returning to her daughter's side and resuming her work with the other women.

Over the days since the incident at the cove, she had spoken to barely anyone other than her husband. On the few occasions that the Reverend had passed by her door, even he had seemed eager to avoid meeting her gaze or crossing too close to the house. On one occasion, she had watched him stall and falter for a moment, his feet poised to alter their direction, but after a few seconds he had jolted back onto his original path. The previous day she had observed him preaching by the ramshackle ruins of the chapel, and those who remained in the village continued to toil around him as he read from the Holy Book. His tone seemed distracted and lacked enthusiasm or conviction. A few elder women paused and sat on one of the walls to listen, but Flora suspected this was more to relieve aching joints than as a sign of sudden piety. She had hoped that this rejection would spur in him the desire to pass by, for he was still the only person who seemed as concerned about the young woman as she did. To her disappointment, he had marched back to his lodgings with his head fixed resolutely downwards, lost in contemplation as he drifted away from her.

Emerging from her thoughts, Flora looked down at the now

completely shredded hemp of wool that lay spread out on her lap, the comb now scraping feebly at the fabric of her skirts. A droplet of water fell from above and thumped onto her lap, spoiling her work even further.

Looking up, she saw the grey clouds overhead burst open and release heavy rivulets of rain. The women who remained by the village wall were already hastily gathering their work and clutching the material under their shawls, making their way towards the shelter of their crofts. Flora heard a plaintive whine at her feet as Morag pushed herself against the door. Sighing, Flora opened it and the hound bounded inside, and scurrying towards the leftover pile of hay in the corner of the byre, she curled up close to the wall, rubbing her nose against her paw. Now that the sheep and cattle were out grazing for the warm season, Flora could cross into the living space without having to lift her skirts out of any congealed straw and muck.

The girl still slept soundly. Nothing had changed since Flora had left the room. She felt a rush of relief, closely followed by a nagging sense of unease at how the girl had managed to remain dormant yet thrive off so little. A blush of colour was starting to return to those sunken cheeks, and her breathing grew steadier. Flora took a spoonful of porridge from the covered pot which sat cooling by the hearth and gently lifted it to her mouth; she wafted it under her nose and was disheartened when she refused to stir. Dropping the spoon back into the pot, Flora crossed the room and set down her load of wool. Resting on a stool, she listened as the patter of rain continued to bounce against the tiny sealskin window. She busied herself by lighting the hearth. Her thoughts turned to the now scant offering of dried fish and gannet meat resting in the storage hut: making a meal was becoming increasingly problematic despite the change of seasons. No doubt with the turn of weather John would return home soon. Supper would be expected.

As the flames crackled to life, the blackhouse filled with the comforting smell of peat smoke. Flickers of light danced against the wall. It was with reluctance that Flora got to her feet to once more to go outside into the rain and collect her limited ingredients from the storehouse.

Turning to head towards the door, Flora froze. She took a step backwards and the stool she had sat on clattered to the floor.

The girl was sitting bolt upright. She was facing the window on the opposite wall, and beneath thick, greasy curtains of hair, cold, grey eyes were fixed on the fat droplets of water rattling against the taut hide.

Flora edged closer, tentatively, as if approaching grazing cattle. As the light flickered from the hearth and cast Flora's shadow against the wall of the blackhouse, the young woman turned and raised her arm as if to peer through the gloom. Her movements were jerky, as if newly she were brought to life and adjusting to the sensation of movement.

"It's all right," Flora soothed, "It's all right."

As she crept closer, the girl shrank against the wall. It was then that Flora noticed the blankets fall away to reveal the tiny mark on the underside of the girl's arm as it was lifted to her face: a small, dark crescent which stood out against her pallid skin. Flora fell back. She had not noticed it before. When she had recovered the girl from the bay she had not seen her whole body, it either being enshrouded in kelp or else covered to preserve her dignity. But this tiny imperfection stood out to Flora. In the quick glance she had made she could not be certain if it was bruise, blemish, or stain, perhaps even a crust of dirt. Nevertheless, it was the size, shape and almost exact location which left Flora's head whirling.

She had seen a similar blemish before; many years ago, now. It had been on the body of her own little girl.

CHAPTER NINE

THOMAS

THE girl's grey eyes were frantic. Flickering from wall to wall and face to face, they eventually rested back on the shadow of water droplets falling steadily against the window. Propped up on the pallet bed, her hands trembled in her lap. Murray felt a muddle of pity and embarrassment when he saw Flora MacKinnon lean towards the girl with her hand reached out tenderly to part her hair. The hand was quickly flinched away from. Flora continued to shush and coddle the girl with unwanted attention, whilst the subject of her affections recoiled further into the wall niche, like a cornered animal.

Murray had been attempting to polish his shoes when he had heard the frenzied knocking at his door. He had opened the door to find John MacKinnon, wide eyed and dripping with rainwater, begging him to come and see to the awakened girl, for nobody else was willing to come. Whilst assuring the terrified husband that he was not a doctor and could be of little use, he could not help being drawn back towards the MacKinnon's croft. Upon entering the croft, he was immediately set upon by Flora MacKinnon. As she led him into the smoke of the blackhouse, he grew anxious over what he would find. Walking through to the living space he had looked on awkwardly at the object of their frenzied concern, and as he now gazed at the cringing creature huddled in the corner of the room, he felt an uncomfortable flicker of recognition. The young woman's stillness, punctuated by jerky, irregular movements and her fixed, empty expression were distressingly familiar. It would prove nothing to question her like this, he thought reluctantly, even if she was capable of speech.

"I think you should allow her some space, Mrs MacKinnon."

The woman, who had been humming softly, turned to face him. She opened her mouth to speak but was seemingly unable to find the appropriate words. She flushed and mutely stepped away.

"I don't know what to make of it all, Reverend," John MacKinnon said, as his wife settled down by the hearth and distractedly rubbed at the ears of a sleeping sheepdog. "I don't know what to do."

"You can't do anything, Mr MacKinnon. This girl's fate is in the hands of God. You can do nothing but carry on as you did before. Feed her, give her a roof over her head. Matthew: twenty-five, forty-five to forty-six."

The crofter stared blankly at him.

"For I was hungry and you gave Me food; I was thirsty and you gave Me drink; I was a stranger and you took Me in; I was naked and you clothed Me; I was sick and you visited Me."

"Is that what God tells you, Reverend?"

"In a sense, yes."

MacKinnon stole a sideways glance at the girl in the corner. She had turned her grey eyes from the window and fixed them on Murray. He felt a cold, invisible finger touch the nape of his neck as she quickly averted her eyes to stare once more at the window.

"Well, if you knew anything about us islanders, then you'd know that God's words are seldom new to us," MacKinnon lowered his voice to a whisper, "but something about her unnerves me."

Murray tried to flick away the implied insult, as well as his own growing unease. He wondered if his recital had struck a chord with the young woman, attracting her attention.

Once John MacKinnon had left the blackhouse, mumbling about going to find his sons, Flora got up and tried to return to the girl's side. Murray grabbed her arm. "Mrs MacKinnon, you must give her space."

Flora shrugged his arm away. "The way you men talk, it's as if she were a dangerous animal."

He winced. He had not heard her speak so roughly before and for once he felt a dangerous ferocity exuding from this gentle old woman's eyes.

"Quite the contrary. You know I do not believe in any of this superstitious nonsense about how she came to be on the island. What I see, is a frightened woman who has been subjected to a horrific ordeal. And as that is the case, she needs time to come back to her senses."

"A frightened child needs comfort and reassurance."

"She is not a child, Mrs MacKinnon. And no, she does not; right now, she is not in a fit state to be reasoned with. She needs time to understand where she is and that we mean her no harm."

"She's barely more than a child. You told me you have no children, Reverend. You don't know what she needs any more than the next man."

Murray struggled to contain himself. He had never been able to stand the insinuation that having children gave one a higher capacity for empathy. "Believe what you will, Mrs MacKinnon, but I have seen this sort of thing before. Whether you heed my advice or not is your decision."

"Where could you have possibly seen this sort of thing on the mainland?"

"My mother."

"Your mother?"

Murray shepherded Flora into the far corner of the room, away from the girl. "Back in '15, my father was killed at Sherrifmuir, fighting against the Pretender."

Flora remained silent, clearly unable to comprehend him.

"It was a battle."

Flora softened; her head cocked inquisitively. "I have never seen a battle before. We don't fight each other on Eilean Eòin. Not since the giants left, anyway."

Murray sighed.

"I am sorry. You must miss him terribly."

"Yes," he lied. "But after he was killed, my mother was never the same. My father was fifty-five by then, and he'd promised Mother it was to be his last campaign." He paused. "She just sat in her chair and stared out the window. Barely even looked at me. The physician told us it was just a temporary melancholic phase; it would pass. But months passed and still we could not get a word from her. Later, she started lashing out at us if we tried to help her; she cut my youngest sister's lip open with her wedding ring once, she hit her with such force. We couldn't go back to the physician then. I couldn't allow them to lock her up in some madhouse full of miscreants and fallen women."

Murray could not bring himself to look at Flora, but he felt her searching eyes sweep over him.

"It's been over ten years and she hasn't spoken since. My sisters in Inverness look after her. My younger sister still can't find a husband and I doubt now she ever will. Not with mother in the picture . . ." He trailed off, searching for words. "When I saw that woman just now, I could see the same confused look in her eyes. Now you must tell me," his voice became sterner, "do you know anything, anything at all, about how all this came to be?"

"What do you mean, Reverend?"

"Where this woman came from. How she came to end up stranded in that cove in such . . . an unseemly condition."

Flora Mackinnon blinked and stepped back. "I only sought to help her."

"And you had no knowledge of what happened to her?"

"How could I, Reverend? I found her this way."

"Yes, but . . . you did not observe anything, hear anything in the time you spent on the shoreline?"

"I'm telling you I only want to do what is right. That is all I know for certain, otherwise why would I care for her?"

The earnestness in the old woman's eyes disarmed him. He knew from her look that she spoke the truth. "You must do what you can, Mrs McKinnon." He glared down at her. "God will reward you for it. We must pray that she recovers enough of her senses to tell us her truth, so that no wrongdoing, if indeed she has been ill-used, may go unpunished."

Flora slumped to the floor. She seemed unable to gather her thoughts together. She looked up with terror in her eyes. "What if she does not improve, Reverend? She's young: surely she can overcome this."

"You must pray to God, Mrs MacKinnon. Only he can make that decision."

For a moment Murray thought he heard the old woman sob, but helping her to her feet, he saw her eyes were bone dry.

༄

Even as the mystery of the woman from the cove intrigued him, he also felt an oncoming dread of what truths he could possibly find in such a barren place. The island was closing in on him, and Murray felt the urge to escape. As the days passed and the tacksman's visit approached, he found himself contemplating an early departure from his current situation. But every time he was tempted, the thought of Caroline's look of disappointment grounded him.

This was the tragedy of island life; with only one ill fitted rowing boat and miles of treacherous ocean surrounding them, the inhabitants were entirely reliant on the bi-yearly visits from the outside world. Around him, the islanders hastened to their duties, spurred on by the thought of the tithes that would have to be paid and the bartering for additional supplies which could be made. The weeks of heavy rain and gale force winds had decimated their crops, and their sheep and cattle were sluggish from the lambing and calving season. Frequently, when livestock was born, islanders came to him to have their animals blessed. Murray had made it clear that such notions were Papist, and many a disgruntled old woman had slunk away from his doorstep, muttering angrily whilst clutching a newborn lamb still smeared in blood and trailing viscera. Murray's attempts at preaching were still largely ignored. Small groups of women sometimes sat with their archaic, whorl-less spindles and observed him at his outdoor lectern: a ramshackle pile of rubble outside the now ruined chapel. None of them appeared to be listening. To the local children he had become a daily novelty; they either stood and gawped at him, with grubby faces and sticky fingers twisting in their mouths or hid behind walls, giggling as they dared each other to flick shingle at him.

The chapel itself saw no chance of revival given the menfolk's preoccupation with the egg harvest. But for now, he knew he had to persevere. He could not turn back up at his home in Inverness after such a short period without losing even more dignity than he faced losing by staying. Each night he prayed that the tacksman would provide some comfort from the civilised world and bring him word from Caroline to lift his spirits and inspire him to a renewed sense of duty.

In the meantime, he had settled on the parable of the loaves and the fishes for his makeshift sermon. He had hoped that this would encourage productivity and be somewhat relatable to the islanders as they hurried to gather together whatever scant offerings they could to appease their distant laird. Standing atop the rubble of the chapel wall, he held his King James Bible aloft in one hand and began to haltingly recite the Book of Mark. The women and children scurried to and from various tasks, some stopping to stare briefly, while two elderly women knitted on the wall beneath him, occasionally glancing up from their work as his voice swelled.

". . . and Jesus, when he came out, saw many people, and was moved with compassion toward them, because they were as sheep not having a shepherd: and he began to teach them many things . . ."

A cow was giving birth, badly it seemed, in the paddock by the village wall. A cluster of women gathered around it as it bellowed pitifully, drowning out the sound of his words.

"... He saith unto them, how many loaves have ye? Go and see. And when they knew, they say ... Five, and two fishes ..."

The cow let out a dreadful moan, and the women clucked with concern. The two elders turned to watch before wandering across the paddock to either help or merely satisfy their growing sense of curiosity. The Reverend was no longer the main novelty of the day.

"And when he had taken the five loaves ... and the two fishes ... he looked up to heaven, and ... and blessed ... and brake the loaves, and gave them to his disciples to set before them; and the two fishes divided he ..."

A final muffled cry from the cow, and something dark and slick slipped out onto the grass. One of the women, her sleeves rolled up to her elbows and her forearms red with blood, clutched her hands to her mouth and screamed. Rather than tend to the calf or its mother, several took a step back. Their faces froze and all went silent. Murray's words halted. His sermon wasted, he slowly descended the wall and went to observe the source of the disruption.

Mercifully, the calf was born dead. Under the greasy placenta was a chaotic tangle of mismatched limbs emerging from a crooked torso. The face was split down the middle. Bulging, red rimmed eyes protruded from the centre of a malformed skull and its mouth and nose were pushed together in a human like grimace. The cow instinctively turned, and to Murray's revulsion, began licking clean its monstrous offspring.

CHAPTER TEN

FLORA

"AWAY! Away!"

Morag skulked from Flora's striking hand, retreating into the byre. Flora picked up the spoiled, half eaten bowl of porridge now lying upturned by the side of the girl's bed and drew it away before the dog returned for more. Scraping away the leftovers into a pot, Flora heard a faint whimper behind her. Thinking it was Morag returning for more of the girl's food, Flora turned around and prepared to scald the hound back into submission.

The girl was propped upright on the pallet bed, her head tilted back against the wall as tears welled up behind tightly shut eyes. Flora hastened to her side and held a tentative spoonful to the girl's mouth. The girl sobbed, turning her face to the wall. Pulling back, Flora hurled the spoon to the floor in frustration and dropped to her knees, rubbing her temples as she struggled to think of a way to feed her charge, who as her strength grew with each passing day also became more and more uncooperative.

In the days since she had awakened, Flora had tried desperately to glimpse the crescent mark on her underarm, but the girl was totally resistant to her touch. Flora could barely get close. On a few occasions, while the girl had slept, she had crept forwards through the light of the hearth to peer at that pale skin; it had still been there, and gentle probing had proven it to be more than just a smear of dirt. Nevertheless, Flora found herself doubting herself: was the mark a few inches removed from that same place she had observed in the past? It had been so long since Flora had held her daughter, and her memories of her had been twisted and rendered misshapen by time's cruel span. There was also a chance the mark could be a bruise and would vanish with the passing days.

"What do I have to do to get you to eat?" Flora murmured.

The girl picked at the drystone wall.

"Thinking of home? Your own mother must miss you."

There was no reaction.

Flora sighed. "How did you end up here, *m'eudail?*"

Flora saw the girl's head turn slightly and her hand tremble.

"You must be cold with nothing but that blanket on . . ." Flora hastened to the stone kist by her own bed. She pulled out an old, hooded earasaid and a rough woollen shift to go underneath the heavy, voluminous garment. The girl stared dumbly as Flora held them out to her.

"You can . . . you can dress yourself?" She gestured with the garments and, tentatively, the girl rubbed a section of thick plaid between her thumb and forefinger. Flora unrolled the shift and motioned to lift it over the girl's head.

The blow was sudden and fierce. Flora fell backwards, rubbing at her reddened cheek and grimacing from the dull ache in her hip flaring up as it hit the hard, earth floor. Slowly, she eased herself up onto her knees and shuffled over to the hearth as the girl snatched the clothes away and began examining them. Flora felt her face flush with humiliation as well as pain.

"Have it your way," she muttered, absent-mindedly stirring the pot of porridge, and trying to supress the burning sensation spreading across her upper thigh. She knew she could not blame the girl. The story the Reverend had told her of his mother's illness still lingered in the back of her mind, no matter how desperately she wished to suppress it, and had stirred every time she had woken to see the girl staring blankly into the dull, half-light of the morning. Even John was clearly unnerved; he now frequently left the croft before the sun rose. Flora desperately wanted the girl to recuperate, but also worried for the day when the girl recovered her wits enough to leave. The plan was still for her to leave when Chief MacLeod's men came to collect the tithes, but even now, sat nursing her bruised thigh, Flora could not imagine letting her go so soon.

She knew it was mad, but a desperate hope still clung to her that her motherly instincts could be founded in some truth. Perhaps if the sea claiming her son had been a reckoning, it had allowed for another to be brought back to her.

Hearing a muffled movement behind her, Flora cautiously turned to see the girl had managed to slip the shift over her head. To Flora's shock, she had almost eased herself to her feet for the first time since she had arrived. Unfurling the yards of wool, the girl stepped into the earasaid and draping it over her shoulders, started gathering the fabric at her waist. She appeared tentative and uncertain.

"Wait."

The girl tensed as she approached, but her body relaxed slightly as Flora gently took the plaid and pulled it together over her breast. Reaching into one of her deep pockets, Flora pulled out a pin decorated with a flattened coin and secured the material in place. As the girl examined the pin Flora brought a soft, leather belt from the kist and tied it around the girl's waist. Looking down at herself, the girl's lips twitched into what was assumed to be the briefest of smiles. Flora beamed.

"That's better," she laughed, wide eyed with joy, like a mother who had just seen her infant lift itself up into a half-hearted crawl. The girl peered nervously at her. Reaching out, she placed her fingers lightly on the starched frill which stood up beneath the shawl on Flora's forehead.

"Why, this?" Flora touched her brow. "Only married women wear this. You don't need to hide your lovely hair. Here." She dug further into her pocket. "My daughter used this comb. She had beautiful black tresses, just like yours."

The girl snatched the comb away, and to Flora's surprise immediately started tugging it through her hair, as if desperate to relieve herself from the greasy tangles which hung around her face. Clearly the girl still had some awareness of her appearance.

Flora turned and feigned interest in tending to the hearth, glancing over her shoulder occasionally to see the girl sitting on the edge of her mattress, deftly twisting sections of hair into a thick plait. A deep pleasure stirred within Flora. It was the kind of maternal satisfaction she had not felt in a long time, and it banished the pain from her bruised hip.

She heard Morag's feet clack against the floor as she crept back into the room, drawn by the warmth of the hearth and the smell of the fulmar meat simmering in the pot full of porridge; the dog sidled up to her and rubbed against her side, whining pitifully. Shooing Morag away with a spoon, Flora brought another oil rich bowl of porridge to the corner of the room, and pushing Morag's muzzle out the way, placed it in the girl's lap. The girl sniffed the contents suspiciously.

"It will get your strength up." Flora smiled encouragingly.

The girl ate a few half-hearted spoonfuls, but to Flora's dismay offered most of the bowl to Morag, breaking into a genuine smile as the contented hound licked the bowl clean.

"Or you could waste good food on the dog . . ." Flora tutted. Sitting by the hearth, she retrieved her spindle and set about the task of separating the large pile of cleaned fleece lying abandoned on the floor, slowly winding it into fibres. Normally Flora enjoyed the formulaic procedure of teasing and winding, as well as the rhythmic spin as wool became yarn. It allowed her to fully absorb herself in the routine of the task and push away any unwanted thoughts. But on this occasion, her mind kept straying back to the girl in the corner, and her shaky hands created yarn that risked becoming coarse and spoiled.

The girl was now watching her intently. Her hands tugged distractedly at the earasaid.

"Perhaps . . . you could help me with something," said Flora.

Later, when John returned from hunting at the cliffs, Flora saw his expression alter from disappointment at the scant bounty he was bringing home, to astonishment at the serene picture of his wife sat calmly spinning yarn, while a young, well dressed island girl knelt beside her, carefully pinching and softly pulling the wool which fed Flora's spindle.

***

At the foot of the hill which sloped upwards from the bay, there was a large, flat surface of exposed rock upon which the women gathered. Barefoot and sitting in a circle, their voices came together in song, their chants echoing around the village bay and carrying on the wind to the men at work on the cliffs.

They had come together to cleanse and thicken the wool, and the rock was the best place for it. Other than the damp, mouldering pews rotting in the cemetery, there was no abundance of wood on the island to serve as a big enough surface for the waulking, so the rock was swept bare and between them the women passed the large swathes of material clockwise around the circle, beating it in rhythm with their song.

None of the women could meet her eye. Unconcerned, Flora craned her neck to keep watch on her croft, anxious that the girl would soon grow bored of cleaning and preparing their bird haul. Like the spinning, the girl seemed to absorb herself in the formulaic sequences of each task and had needed little prompting in the process of clean decapitation, plucking, de-winging and packing the birds with salt. Feeling slightly reassured, Flora returned to the waulking. Across from her, Mary was dividing her attention between joining in with each chorus, beating the cloth with her feet, and nursing her daughter at her breast. Flora tensed and looked away. She felt a twinge of resentment as her own breast began to ache and throb beneath her heavy plaid.

The song began to quicken. The motion of hands and feet became more rapid as the cloth stiffened. Feet thudded and pounded against the dampened material. Soon, the women's song became a crescendo and then quietened, gradually coming to a halt as they stopped to examine the texture of the wool between their fingers.

"Flora?"

She jolted.

"Flora?" Margaret repeated. "What about you? Do you think it's done?"

"It's no good asking her," Ailith McQueen grumbled. "She's no more use than that tatty, old ewe over there. Might as well get yon wee lassie to do it." Ailith nodded towards the babe suckling contentedly under Mary's shawl. Flora bristled with anger but supressed the urge to bite.

"The weave seems good and strong to me," she said loudly. "Strong enough to barter for more grain at least."

Ailith snorted. Margaret shot her a reproachful look.

"There's no need for her to be silent, Margaret," said Flora, rising to her feet. "If she takes issue with my efforts, she had better tell me face to face."

"Sit down, Flora MacKinnon, before your legs seize up."

"Ailith, there's no need . . ."

"No, Margaret, I think Ailith had better speak up. Whatever she's got into her spiteful head about me you can trust will be disproven when my tithe is paid in full. I'd wager my contribution is bigger than her measly offering."

"Aye. No thanks to you," Ailith muttered.

Flora felt as if someone had punched her in the gut. Still, she was not prepared to back down. "And what is that supposed to mean?"

"Do I really have to be any clearer?"

"Oh, wind your neck in, Ailith McQueen," Margaret interrupted. "This has nothing to do with you."

"No, Margaret, I want to hear what she has to say about me."

The two women stared silently at each other. The others dared not break through the tension; some cast their eyes down and pretended to return to the task of testing the strength of the cloth.

"All right," said Ailith. "Firstly, it very much is all of our business, when a member of our community is not giving their full due, and believe me, that is what is happening here. Now I understand, Flora, that after Donnchadh's death we knew this first harvest would be hard for you, and I sympathised. I've been in the same situation as you many a time, and we always rally around to help our own." Ailith paused for breath, seemingly savouring the opportunity to make her opinion known.

"But this is about more than that," she continued her lecture. "Ever since you brought that stranger into the village, you've hardly raised your head to speak to us, let alone help us with our work; even today your mind clearly isn't here but elsewhere. Your poor John has been doing most of the labour, and from what I hear you've been using that sea bitch as some kind of servant around the house, doing chores for you as if you're above all the rest of us." Ailith spat in the grass. "Now I'm not denying there's some tender reason for you taking this stranger into your house. Sure, a soft heart like yours would easily be taken in by a young woman like that, but it should never be at the expense of your family and neighbours." Her voice rose. "Besides, rising back from the dead like that, what makes you so convinced she's even human?"

Flora had known this question would be asked at some point, and surpassing her own doubts came the urge to defend not herself, but the girl in her care. "You've been listening to too many tall tales. I've shared my food with her, slept under the same roof as her, and I have seen nothing more than a frightened child. You can come and see for yourselves that she's harmless."

"Harmless?" Ailith shrieked. "How can you say she's totally harmless? Don't think we haven't noticed that swelling under your eye. There's no way your John would ever have done that to you, although how that man has not raised a hand to you is astonishing."

"Ailith. Stop!" cried Margaret. "This isn't doing any good to anyone."

"No." Ailith rounded on Margaret. "I'm fed up with walking on tiptoe around her. She's not that much younger than I am: she can defend herself."

". . . Go on, then," Flora snapped, steeling herself. "Don't stop now. Clearly you have more venom to spit out."

"Ever since you invited this stranger back into our community, things have taken a turn for the worst," Ailith explained with relish. "Even you can't have failed to notice that the crops have rotted; the ones that weren't blown away by those storms have almost turned to mulch. The animals have been sickly; I've lost two ewes and I know I'm not the only one. My poor Rachel," Ailith gestured towards her youngest daughter. "Her cow died a few days ago, after giving birth to a monster, as no doubt you will have heard."

Rachel lowered her head. Ann, who had been silently looking down at her hands the entire time, looked fiercely up at Flora in stolid support of her aunt and grandmother.

"Almost all of us have had animals birthing stillborn young this spring," Ailith continued. "This is exactly what happened before the last great sickness, and you yourself know how bad that time was just as much as the rest of us."

Flora recoiled.

"I don't want to see another year like that in my lifetime," Ailith continued. "Something clearly isn't right, and I don't think it's any coincidence that this is happening now. It's as if life is being drained from the island."

There were a few murmurs of assent. Ann continued to glare, and her hand once more placed protectively over her rounded belly.

"Grandam is right," she murmured, finding her voice. "Something is draining life away from the crops and animals. Who's to say it isn't that thing you harbour in your house?"

"Aye," said Ailith. "Answer me that, Flora MacKinnon."

"She . . . she's just a child," Flora stammered. "There were signs of crop rot and animal deaths before she came to us."

"But it could have been laying curses upon us all this time." Ann had found her voice now and looked around her for support in her assertions. "If it is returned from the dead, perhaps it is only because of the life it is taking from us. I told you before, Flora, Donnchadh's death was a reckoning."

Flora opened her mouth to speak, but exhausted, could summon no retort. Standing tall, she could still feel the women's eyes boring into her, searching, probing her face for signs of weakness until she could stand it no longer. She spun on her heel and began walking away, ignoring the voices rising behind her.

Ahead, something ran towards her. Squinting against the glare of the afternoon sun, she saw Morag bounding up the hill, tail thrashing from side to side and letting out excited, guttural whimpers. As the hound approached Flora, she lay down flat with her ears pushed back in submission. Flora's heart tightened. Pushing past the dog, she lurched towards her croft in a blind panic.

As she feared, the door was open. There were discarded bird heads and wings carelessly thrown around the front of the blackhouse, but inside was a neat row of tightly packed fulmars and a basket full of feathers.

The girl had gone. Flora frantically circled the blackhouse several times to no success, and she cursed herself for not paying closer attention to the croft during the waulking. She scanned the settlement, but all had been deserted in the rush of the day's work.

Then, silhouetted against the sun, a figure appeared sitting astride the cemetery wall, looking out across the bay at the gentle rollers whispering against the shore. She had eased the earasaid from her shoulders, letting the sun cast a healthier glow on her dry, damaged skin. Flora stormed towards the girl.

"Don't you ever leave my sight again!"

The girl turned at the sound of the raised voice; the skin around her eyes was red. Flora baulked and her fury melted into concern.

"You can't just go wandering off," Flora reasoned. "I can't protect you if you leave."

The girl blinked and turned away, vigorously rubbing the plaid of her earasaid between her fingers while fixing her eyes once more on the sea. Flora motioned to touch the girl's arm and gently pull her away, but knowing her neighbours might still be watching thought better of it and let her arm fall back to her side. It was likely the girl would lash out and cause a scene.

"Flora!"

John had returned and was standing outside the blackhouse alongside a worried looking Margaret; from his hand dangled a brace of dead fulmars.

"Flora, get the dog in! It's out worrying the sheep. Leave the girl; she'll come back in her own time."

Flora reluctantly ascended the crest of the hill and gathered an overexcited Morag, dragging her back to the croft by the scruff of her neck, all the while trying to keep her eyes on the girl who still sat on the cemetery wall, eyes fixed on the bay.

The girl was out all afternoon, only not even returning once the sun had set and Flora was clearing away supper and preparing for bed. John refused to let her go and search, and after the confrontation with the other women, Flora feared the worst.

She lay awake, eyes straining in the darkness between the empty mattress on the floor and the entrance to the byre. She would not sleep with her growing unease. Flora bided her time, waiting until she was certain that John was completely still beside her before she eased herself from the heavy blankets and trod carefully across the living space. She pulled a shawl over her shift and listened. The night was still, but somewhere beyond the byre door there was a quiet commotion.

Flora strained her ears and heard it again. There was a soft sound of something thumping against the turf outside; a feeble rustling of tentative beats which made her heart catch in her throat. Flora slipped into the byre and reached for the door, ignoring Morag, who lay low to the ground, whining, the fur on the back of her neck forming a stiffened ridge.

As Flora greeted the cool night air, she peered into a silvery beam of light which fell from the full moon above, lighting a path forward towards the cemetery. As she stepped forwards, her hopes were answered as she beheld a hunched figure bent low, a few ells away from where she stood.

"Please come back inside, *m'eudail*," Flora spoke softly, anxiously reaching forwards. "You aren't safe. What is someone were to find you outside like this?"

The girl's head whipped around, and she stumbled backwards, dropping something which had been cradled in her hands. Flora gently knelt forwards.

"You should be sleeping," she said. "You need to get your strength back."

The girl seemed hesitant, and she eyed Flora mistrustingly. Nevertheless, after a pause, she rose from the damp turf, and Flora saw a cascade of feathers fall from her lap as she returned towards the warmth of the blackhouse.

Feeling the grass between her fingers, Flora's hands recoiled when they met with a familiar stickiness. Looking down, Flora saw the thing which the girl had dropped. It was a feathery mass coated in blood and oil, and as Flora examined it further, she saw unmistakably the broken, discarded wings and head of one of the fulmar chicks that had been collected earlier.

The wings lay neatly together, spread out one on either side of the head, as if in one last hopeless attempt at flight.

CHAPTER ELEVEN

THOMAS

MURRAY had never seen the island as busy.

Both men and women clustered together around the bay, hauling baskets and barrels filled with wool, feathers, bird oil and whatever other scant offerings could be gathered. Their expressions were anxious. There was very little of the usual chatter between women, and the men huddled in sullen groups, keeping a watchful eye on the flotilla of boats rowing towards the shore from the small ship anchored beyond the bay. For the islanders, this bi-annual visit from MacLeod's representatives was an opportunity to barter for goods. It had also become a kind of justification for their existence. In Murray's case, his anticipation derived from the promise of communication with the civilised world, and the prospect of word from the mainland. He had read Caroline's last letter to himself over and over. He was anxious for more.

Nearby, the MacKinnons were gathered around the produce they had collected for their tithe, the men waiting nervously while the women fussed over their children's appearances. Flora MacKinnon sat apart from the rest of her family. Next to her, the woman from the cove kneeled on the sand, neatly folding and re-folding the woollen plaid heaped in baskets by their side. A large space separated them from everyone else, as nobody seemed willing to set up their produce anywhere near them. A huddle of women kept nervously glancing back towards Flora MacKinnon and her charge, clutching their skirts towards their bodies as if anxious of trailing them in muck.

Even so, the strange, young woman appeared well dressed in comparison to the tired clothes many of the other women wore, having sacrificed their own best garments to appease the tacksman. Her hair had been braided underneath her hood. She looked like one of the Highland clanswomen who frequently drifted into town on market days in Inverness, reeking of smoked meat and damp; there was a savage dignity about her. She looked up from the basket and stared at him. Murray quickly looked down at his feet.

Over the past week he had been making regular visits to the MacKinnon croft, his previous trepidation about the place and its occupants having slightly abated. It had started during one of his attempts at preaching. Ever since the incident with the calf there had been even fewer women gathered in the pasture or at the cemetery wall, their attention now almost entirely on intensive wool production. On one such occasion he had been in the middle of a lacklustre rendition of book two, Chapter twelve of Corinthians. As usual, the islanders had continued to pass by him on their way to their daily tasks, and after a while he had been further disheartened by a group of women in the distance, who had drowned out his preaching with their shrill work chants.

Some time had passed before he had noticed the lone figure crouched by the wall; feathers stuck to her coarse woollen clothes, down rested in her hair and her hands were coated in the grease of seabirds. The girl had listened, seemingly transfixed, her eyes never leaving him. For the first time since arriving on the island, he found himself preaching to a willing audience, and holding the book further aloft, he had allowed his voice to rise and carry as if he were preaching to a crowd of hundreds. Still, she had listened. Regardless of whether she understood all his words, they clearly must have held some resonance as she sat serenely at his feet. His voice had swelled with a renewed sense of purpose. She had stayed and listened to his entire sermon, barely moving except to occasionally pull a feather from her hair and discard it, or to prop her face up with one elbow resting lazily on the remains of the chapel wall.

Afterwards, as he descended, she had lifted her arm, and for a terrified moment he imagined she would grab his foot or the edge of his coat. Instead, she held out a bird carcass. The headless body had been tightly wrapped in twine, the puckered flesh glistening with salt. It had occurred to him later that the gift may have been an offering of gratitude; perhaps she had remembered fragments of the day he had carried her over the rocks from the cove, and now she acknowledged him as her rescuer. He felt a certain discomfort when this memory stirred. Nevertheless, he overcame this with a forced sense of accomplishment that perhaps, finally, he had instilled in someone a desire for the gospels, even if that person was even more of an outcast than himself.

As he stood on the beach waiting for the boats to arrive, his eyes lingered on her. Flora had been the one to find the girl and she guarded her fiercely, regardless of the censure of her fellow islanders. But despite this, the stranger still seemed slightly afraid of her, and maintained a cold indifference in Flora's presence. Even as the tacksman and his men drew up to the bay, Flora MacKinnon faltered in her work and looked at the girl, hovering nearby as if debating whether to go to her.

Murray returned his attention to the boats and watched as its occupants leapt into the breakers and began hauling their crafts onto the beach. Donald Gillies was the first to greet the tacksman with a sweeping gesture towards the awaiting crofters and their produce. The man was not quite what Murray had expected. Absent from his person were the usual clan plaid and insignia, replaced with matching coat, britches and a pair of sturdy, but fine, leather boots. Under his hat was a reasonably well powdered wig. A far cry from what Murray had come to expect from the islands, this man could easily blend into a crowd on any of Edinburgh's commercial streets.

As the tacksman and his men began their inspections, peering into barrels and testing the texture of the crofters' wool between their fingers, Murray was disturbed by a sudden commotion behind him. A solitary pebble had been thrown in the direction of the unknown woman. Flora MacKinnon looked up and threw herself towards her charge, fussing over her with renewed vigour. The women around them spread out even further, but still cast curious glances in their direction.

"Sir?"

Turning back around, he saw the tacksman with his hand extended.

"The new curate, am I right?" The man's accent was clipped and refined: educated, Lowland, perhaps even verging on English.

Murray held out his hand in return, still felt distracted and on edge. "You are correct, sir."

"Rather you than me." The tacksman's smile was patronising, mocking. "Robert MacLeod. No close relation, but close enough to be tasked with carrying out this tedious assignment." He gestured lazily at the other men inspecting the islanders' produce, some now hauling baskets and barrels back towards the boats. "Still, one night on this barren hellscape is no doubt enviable to a poor bastard in your position," he laughed. "How have you been finding the locals? A charming people, aren't they?"

Murray took a moment to conjure an appropriate response. He looked back at the MacKinnons, relieved to see that whichever vicious person had cast the pebble had not renewed their assault. Nevertheless, he did not want to give this man the satisfaction of complaining. "We are all sinners."

MacLeod let out a shrill laugh.

"A churchman's answer if ever there was one!" he grinned, clapping Murray on the back. "No doubt you can tell me more tonight. The last curate was a terrible old bore. Half bloody senile; not that that is a bad thing on this place. It'll be nice to converse with another educated man."

"You will pardon me, Sir, but your accent does not read as Highland."

"Oh, Christ no, I left as soon as I could. Spent my formative years in the capital."

Murray flinched at the man's casual blaspheming. "Edinburgh?"

"Christ, no," he repeated, "London. Studied law for a few years at Cambridge, then spent my formative years in the City."

"In what capacity?" Murray tried to keep the jealousy from creeping into his voice.

"Oh, you know... This and that," the man said, flicking a sand fly from his cuff, seeming to grow tired of this line of conversation. "I can't say it benefited me much." He gestured at his person and swept his arm out as if to survey the area.

"On a serious note, I suppose I should tell you," MacLeod lowered his voice, but still puffed out his chest as he spoke, "the King is dead, long live the King."

It took several seconds for the news to register with Murray. Suddenly, he felt more cut off from the outside world than he ever had before. "King George is dead?"

"Well, the first one is anyway. We have a second German Geordie now." Again, the man seemed to grow bored and glanced distractedly over Murray's shoulder.

"Should you not announce it?" Murray motioned towards the islanders.

MacLeod snorted. "What difference would that news possibly make to them?"

Murray remembered Flora MacKinnon's confusion when he had talked about Sherrifmuir and conceded a nod of agreement.

"Happened in Hanover, or Flanders; somewhere far away from here anyway," Macleod continued. "Hopefully the next one will have a stronger pair of balls than the last."

"And has there been any word of the Pretender?" Murray hastily asked. "No stirrings from the continent?"

"Damned if I know," replied Macleod. "Doubt it though. From what I've seen, the Popish clans and sympathisers no longer have the stomach for it."

Murray's hopes at educated company were dwindling every minute he spent with this abrasive young man. All the same, he still longed for word from the mainland, his hunger for news from Caroline fuelled by the knowledge that halfway across the continent, a man he had never met had died.

"You will join me this evening?" he enquired. "I'm afraid I've little to offer other than my company, though."

"Of course," Macleod said. "I have some bottles of half decent wine back on board that I can smuggle past the locals. I have your letters as well, of course."

Murray's heart lurched.

"Until this evening then." The young man tilted his hat and walked away.

Still reeling from news of the king's death, Murray had almost forgotten the tumult behind him until he was shaken from his thoughts by a sharp, inhuman scream, more akin to the yowl of a beaten dog. Looking back, he saw the young woman clutching at the side of her face, scarlet streaming through her fingers. This time, a pebble had met its target.

He ran forward just as Flora MacKinnon was rushing to her charge's side, trying desperately to prize her hand away from her face, but the girl lashed out like a dog cornered in a fighting pit. She pulled against Flora in fear.

Murray span on his heel and rounded on the cluster of other women, who all remained silent, they themselves holding back as if afraid of their victim's ire.

"Who threw that?" he spat.

The women looked to their feet, some clutching their children against them and moving further down the beach towards the men. He could have sworn he saw Ailith McQueen's hand quickly vanish back into her pocket, the wrinkled face beneath her shawl seemingly twisted into a half concealed grin. Murray felt his temple throb with rage.

"If I find the person who threw that stone, I will see you hauled back to the inner isles with the tacksman and placed on charges of assault," he seethed. They did not look at him, but continued to drift away, his words failing to alarm them.

Murray heard a further cry and turned back towards Flora and the girl, but it was too late. Twisting free of Flora's grip, the young woman was pelting across the machair, her hood falling back and her hair streaming free as she fled.

He started to run in pursuit, but she was already vanishing from his sight. He turned again and looked to the remaining MacKinnon clan.

"What are you waiting for?" he cried. "Go after her!"

He was met by a sea of impassive faces, all except Flora MacKinnon who stumbled forwards on stiffened legs, her face bereft as she failed to keep up.

"You should never have brought her here." His words were savage, and he saw with a twinge of cruel satisfaction that this time they had hit their mark. Flora MacKinnon was out of breath, but she looked at him pleadingly; urgently.

He did not need any encouragement from the old woman, and was already running ahead, his feet almost tripping from under him as he propelled himself forwards too quickly for the rest of his body to catch up.

He circled the settlement, rounding on each blackhouse and storehouse before casting his eyes up towards his own lodgings on the hill. Making his way up the slope, he thought he saw a flash of plaid on the ridge. He pushed forward, his breath catching painfully in the back of his throat and his heartbeat pounding in his ears. As he neared the ridge, he came to the edge of an animal enclosure and hauled himself over the stone barricade, even in his haste still taking care to dodge the drying clots of dung cluttering the turf. He came to the opposite wall and saw the same splash of tartan against the grey-brown landscape, but to his dismay its wearer was long gone.

He picked up the course shawl, which was caught upon the drystone, tangled with mats of sheep wool. He yanked it and held it for a moment, feeling the remaining warmth of where fibres had met with flesh. There were a few flecks of reddish brown at its edge.

Remembering where he was, Murray looked up to see the entire island sloping downwards towards the sea. She was nowhere to be seen. It was as if she had vanished into the very air he breathed, leaving nothing but a tattered shawl.

He felt something whisper lightly against his ear. Remembering the sinister voice from his dreams, he swatted against his face and spun on the spot. The wicked suspicions of these savages were clearly taking their toll. Summoning himself back to stern reason with a shrug of his shoulders, he realised that he was still clinging to the shawl, its warmth dissipating against his sweat dampened skin.

❦

"If you want my opinion, she'll not have come far at all."

Robert MacLeod casually tapped the remnants of his clay pipe into the rushes covering the floor and stretched his feet out, resting them on the one remaining stool by the hearth, while Murray perched awkwardly on the edge of the box bed. He had spent all that remained of the morning and afternoon scouring the island to no success, raging with himself that he had allowed the woman to flee. Now he had to convey his concerns to the brash young man in front of him, still distracted by thoughts of where the young woman could have gone, but also needing to convey his story in a way which still sounded credible. The evening had been long, and with the lull in topics of conversation it was mercifully drawing towards its conclusion. Murray anxiously traced the seal of the topmost letter which sat on his lap.

"I thought perhaps one of the surrounding islands myself," Murray said. "Given that I couldn't find any wreckage she can't have been on any large craft."

The young man scoffed and drained the last remnants of wine from the bottle. "I meant even closer. Trust me, Reverend, she'll be a native."

"The locals have claimed they don't recognise her."

"They would say that, though," MacLeod smirked. "Think about it. There is absolutely no hard evidence from what I can see that would prove she has been washed up at all. Trust me Reverend," he continued, leaning forwards, "you would not believe the stories I've heard about these places. You know how it is: isolated communities; superstitions run rife; ritual sacrifice and all sorts of backwards nonsense. That is why you're here isn't it? To root out this sort of thing?"

Murray shrugged, as if he could shed his growing sense of inadequacy and watch it slither down amongst the rushes to lie, lifeless, alongside the discarded tobacco.

"I am a Highlander myself, sir," he eventually replied, "I don't think the people here seem a great deal worse than some of the rural communities back home. Just before I left, I heard of a witchcraft case up in Sutherland. Unbelievable. The supposed witch they tarred and burned was no more than a harmless old woman. Such barbaric beliefs have no place in this century."

"Yes, I had heard of that," said MacLeod, inspecting the bottom of the bottle for dregs. All evening the man had sat and drank, barely anything piquing his interest until talk of the girl. "Although I'd say we've all but stamped that out. Questionable from a legal standpoint too from what I heard; I've never heard of another case like it during my lifetime. Certainly, you wouldn't hear of any of this claptrap down in England, and if you ask me, Parliament will outlaw such superstitious nonsense completely within the next few years."

"So, you think there might be something similar going on here?" Murray was hesitant to feed the man's ego but felt compelled to discuss the matter further.

"Possibly." MacLeod leaned forwards. "I have to say, I would not mind meeting this *fille sauvage* of yours."

Murray baulked at the young man's brazenness.

"Tell me, is she pretty?"

"It's difficult to say," Murray said awkwardly, cringing away from the directness of the question.

"Could be quite the novelty on the mainland," MacLeod continued. The man was incorrigible. "Our very own Peter the wild boy. Wild girl in our case."

Murray stared blankly.

"Oh, you would not have heard, I suppose. He was the talk of London before the king snuffed it. Some poor, idiot boy they found wandering the woods somewhere in Germany, crawling around naked on all fours and growling like a wolf. The Princess of Wales, well, the Queen I suppose we should call her now, heard rumour of it and they sent him across the channel so he could be the latest plaything at court."

Disturbed, Murray considered what fate beheld the girl even if she left the island. Undoubtedly, she could not safely remain where she was, not given the growing tension amidst the community from the poor harvest; but the prospects of a vulnerable, lone woman of her age were not the brightest.

"I was hoping that a domestic position could be found for her. According to her current keeper she is very willing and able to work. In fact, she seems to enjoy manual labour. She may be illiterate, but I have observed signs that she understands some spoken word despite her current muteness. Unlike this wild boy, I believe she has skills which will re-emerge once she recovers from whatever trauma she's been through."

"Perhaps." The young man seemed unwilling to commit to an answer and, deprived of an opportunity to extoll on his knowledge and experiences any further, the room reverted to its gloomy, meagre form. MacLeod tapped the base of the wine bottle and ran a finger around the rim. "But it seems to me, Reverend, that given your precarious position here . . ."

Murray tried not to flinch.

". . . well, it seems to me that you'll have need of this young, wild girl if you are ever to build a successful case against any of this primitive, island nonsense. You say she may yet talk, well then, I would suggest making her talk."

Murray frowned. "Do you mean, sir . . . ?"

"Oh, I do not mean to infer anything sinister, of course," MacLeod laughed. "After all, as you say, we are men of more civilised society. I merely suggest spending some more time rooting around this issue. You seem to have gained some of her trust; well then, you are in a good position to uncover the truth of this matter. Chief MacLeod would no doubt be more than willing, I'm sure, to elevate a man of your stature and commitment to a better position within the Church, should your investigations help to bring about a solution to the growing inconvenience these islands give him." He looked pointedly over the rim of the bottle.

Murray understood. Nevertheless, he felt some trepidation. He tried to shake off his doubts, for Caroline would no doubt be proud to be the wife of a bishop; perhaps this is what would be the making of him after all. If it was evidence that was needed, it was evidence that he would acquire.

Standing up, MacLeod swayed slightly as he shook Murray by the hand. "Thank you for the hospitality, Reverend. I best be away before it gets dark; I can never stomach the thought of being stuck here after sundown."

After watching him stagger away, both men relieved, Murray turned his attention solely to the letters sitting on the edge of his bed: he could worry about the young woman later. As expected, the first was from the diocese, requesting a note of the progress which had been made since his arrival. Murray was tempted to put the letter to one side before responding. On the other letter, he recognised the feminine swirls of handwriting and was eager for its contents. His hand hovered over the unbroken seal. Responding to the first letter would no doubt be disheartening, but perhaps if Caroline lay by his side as a reward for the unenviable task of writing a response, it would be rendered more bearable.

Retrieving the bottle of ink from his father's chest, he found the contents clotted and unyielding. Warming it by the hearth, he rested a sheet of parchment on the unsteady table, inelegantly perched on a stool and set about writing his reply. He avoided specifics. Focusing on his remaining time rather than what had passed previously, he tried to write convincingly about his ambitions for the chapel repair. Hoping his prose would conceal his insecurities and lack of success, he signed off as an obedient servant and hastily checked it for errors. Satisfied, he folded and sealed it, putting it to one side and eagerly reaching for Caroline's letter.

He held the letter in his hands for a moment longer, imagining remnants of warmth from his wife's fingertips when she had delicately smoothed the creases of parchment. Having built up this moment for so long, he felt a tenseness in his stomach and a tight pain across his chest. His hands trembled as he opened the seal and observed the impeccable handwriting inside. Not a blot or smudge marked those elegant, looping scrolls. He read the letter slowly, a stump of a tallow candle burning low beside him.

My Husband,

By now you will have reached your destination, and I have no doubt you will be administering to the Lord's work as he intended for you. How I envy you, my husband. If I could, I would fulfil such duties myself, for I cannot think of a nobler purpose than spreading Christ's word to the disenfranchised. But I am merely a woman, and it saddens me that I am still unable to fully serve and fulfil my role as your wife.

My Husband, it pains me to tell you that shortly before you were summoned from me, I discovered that I was with child once again, and the babe quickened in me for a mere week longer before it bled from me. This is now the seventh child I have lost this way, if one does not count our beautiful boy, who God granted me one day with before he was taken. It is now clear that for whatever divine reasoning my body is unable to carry a living child. I did not tell you before you left because I was ashamed. I still am. You will have to forgive me for waiting until you were far away from me before disclosing this to you, and I understand if you are angry at me, but you must concede, Husband, that I am no longer able to be a valid wife to you, and our sacred vows are all that now bind us. I will not be with child again. I cannot suffer this even one more time.

As such, I relieve you of your husbandly duties. From now on we are Husband and Wife in name only. I know you have loved me, but it is with a deep regret that I can no longer feel the same intensity of affection which brought us together, and in truth you deserve better than me. I cannot tell you how sorry I am for you, but trust that should there be any scandal at my chosen solitude, I will ensure all censure falls upon me. I will tell them that my husband is away seeing to the Lord's work, and that I am content to be alone. Once again, I must confess myself guilty of envy, for I wish I could follow your path, for you are most fortunate to have been granted a purpose, whereas I must find a quieter way to be of service to God. Know that you will always be in my prayers, and despite the hurt I must cause you I hope that you will keep me in yours.

Your Wife,
Caroline Murray

Upon finishing, he read it again. Surely the words would imbue new meaning upon a second reading; the reality was too shameful to be true. His heart pounded. The room became a blur as he felt himself slipping into the smoky air. After what could have been seconds or minutes, he became aware that he was sat on the hard floor; his back resting awkwardly against a table leg, the letter still grasped tightly in his sweating palms. The world around him was silent and no longer real.

In a burst of frantic energy, he returned to his seat and reached for his quill, almost knocking over the bottle of ink with his elbow. He hurriedly scratched out his reply, barely paying heed to the mess of ink on his fingers and the smears of black along the parchment's edge. His writing was cramped, and letters spilled into one another. He read it back to himself.

The blur of words was desperate; unhinged. He read Caroline's letter a final time, and angrily slashed the quill across his own, tearing into the paper and blunting the tip against the hard, wooden table. Folding together his desecrated composition, he held it against the flame of the candle and watched dazed as it set alight. The paper curled and blackened, his words falling as cinders which burned the skin of his hands. He flung the remnants into the hearth. They crackled and hissed briefly, but soon collapsed on themselves and faded away into the ashes of the last, feeble flames.

He sat and stared into the dying embers.

He did not rise from his seat until the first chinks of early morning light seeped in through the window, casting shadows on the fragments which lay on the floor.

CHAPTER TWELVE

FLORA

As Flora lay awake, fear crawled over her. She rested on her side, staring into the dark recess where the girl's bedsheets were crumpled in empty disarray. Faint rays of light were beginning to seep into the fug of the blackhouse as dawn broke; the seabirds were shrieking and squawking from the cliffs as they began departing their nests for the sea. She had been coaxed to bed after hours of sitting and waiting, sifting through the embers of the fire, lifting her head only when the wind stirred at the door or the softest thud of a sheep's cloven foot trod across their threshold. Still the girl did not return.

"She will make her way back in her own time. She can't go far," her husband had reassured her. John's attempts to comfort her were hollowly accepted. They did nothing to ease the rising panic and fury she felt towards herself, as all of her protective instincts swept over her like the sea breaching a harbour wall.

John had already risen and sat eating the remnants of yesterday's supper. Flora wondered if he felt any concern for the girl, or if instead his feelings on the matter rested entirely on relief that she was no longer a burden to them. Even if she did not turn up at the bay in time for the tacksman's departure, Flora supposed it would be unlikely that John would accept her back into the household.

"Did you sleep?" John's voice was groggy, and even as he spoke, he did not turn to face her.

"A little," she lied. Slowly she eased herself up from the bed and masking the familiar pain in her joints, she began to slowly get dressed.

"Shouldn't you eat something?"

"I'm not hungry."

"You should eat before we meet with the others."

"Perhaps later."

"Eat something, Flora."

The hardness in his voice startled her. Her husband barely ever spoke harshly to her, especially since Donnchadh's death.

"I can't eat. Not until I've found her."

"She's not your responsibility!"

Flora withdrew from his raised voice. Morag skulked towards the byre, familiar with the angry tone of her master's voice usually being reserved for her.

"This has gone on for long enough," John continued. "There is talk, Flora. If anything, her running off is a sign you've pursued this too far. I'm tired of seeing you rely on strangers for comfort while ignoring the people who really care for you. How do you think me and the boys feel watching you isolate yourself like this? Fergus' first child is not even weaned yet and Michael's baby is due any time now: the way things are don't you think they have enough to worry about without you adding to their troubles?"

"They're men now. They don't need me to . . ."

"They need you to support their wives and children. What kind of woman spurns her own grandbairns?"

Flora took a step towards her husband. She understood now that urge to lash out, to push back against the incessant verbal attacks. Her rage subsided. She internalised her screams and spun on her heel, turning her attention to pinning her clothes in place. A hand rested on her shoulder.

"I'm sorry," he said, "but we can't go on like this. No stranger can bring Donnchadh back. We have to start moving on from what happened."

He pulled away from her when she laughed. Still, after all these years, her husband could never understand what ailed her.

"And what if she is dead, John? What if she has tumbled over a cliff? What if I could have saved her and failed?"

John was silent.

"You probably think that's for the best too, don't you?" Flora's voice trembled as the question escaped her. She could not fathom what compelled her to say it, other than raw defensiveness.

John turned to face her. A filmy layer of tears threatened to erupt across his face, but he quickly dashed them away and raised himself up to his full height. "Do you think you're the only one who feels guilty for what has happened?" John asked scornfully. "Every day I remember how our boy called out to me as the rope slackened. I remember the fear in his eyes when he saw I couldn't hold on to him. I am the one who must bear that burden every cursed day, not you. You couldn't possibly know how much I struggle to go to those cliffs every morning; watching young lads help their fathers; watching others being able to hold them steady and afterwards patting their sons on the back. I will regret failing our son for the rest of my life. But it always has to be about you, doesn't it?" His voice swelled.

Flora wanted to shout back but could not form the words to convey her true feelings.

"Instead, I have to be the one to tread carefully around you," John continued. "And as for the girl, you're right: it is better she's out of your hands. At first, I thought it might be good for you, but clearly, I was wrong. Like everything else, you become obsessed with things that are out of your control. Now neither of us have to take on an extra burden, and at our age, that's the way it should stay. Perhaps now you can spend more time with Ann, Mary and the grandchi . . ."

"How could you be so heartless?" she muttered across him.

"Me being heartless? Because I care more about you than some stranger you took in?"

"Because you have no idea how guilty I feel!" Flora screamed. "Or do you have a shorter memory than I thought, John?" She looked at him pointedly. "You remember our little girl, don't you? You remember how it was my fault she got lost and the sea took her? Babes were dying all over the island that year and I couldn't even protect her from myself."

John's face crumbled; every line and crease deepened and for all that he resisted, the tears in his eyes began falling in slow, steady streams through those cracks and valleys. His hands fell limply to his sides. With choking sobs, he clutched Flora to him.

"Is this why you've been so protective of her?" he said, as Flora stood stiffly in his arms. "I'm so sorry, Flora. I should have realised."

Flora hesitantly rubbed his back before he let her go.

"It's too late to save our girl," he said. "Our daughter is long gone, Flora, and you can't go on blaming yourself for something that happened so long ago. This girl is no replacement: you can't bring her back."

"I know," she mumbled her reply, desperate for an escape, regretting her outburst. "We don't need to talk about it, John. I'd rather just try to forget this argument ever happened."

"I understand." He kissed her head softly.

No, how could you ever understand, she thought bitterly.

※

The tacksman's departure left little reassurance. As it had always been, the wool, oil and feathers that were given would be rewarded when MacLeod's men next visited with renewed supplies of cereals, grains, and wood. This time, the islanders knew that their scant offerings would be repaid with minimal resources. In the meantime, they would have to be satisfied with the provisions which had been newly left to them as a result of their tithes from one harvest prior. As everyone hurried to plant and store what had been granted to them, dashing back and forth between the fields and the small, stone store houses which dotted the landscape of the bay, Flora took advantage of this time to covertly search for her lost charge.

The store houses were lumpen mounds rising out of the ground; the cold winds whistled through the drystone entrances to keep their food rations cold. Often the animals used them for shelter. It was not inconceivable that a human would do the same. So far, Flora had had no success, but as she passed by her neighbours, she saw how much more relaxed they seemed around her. Whereas a few days ago they had avoided even looking in her direction, now some of them ventured to greet her. Nobody questioned her about the girl's disappearance; perhaps they believed she had left the island with the tacksman. Or perhaps they did not feel the need to question it, the tacit understanding that she was no longer in the MacKinnons' croft comforting them enough not to assume worse of her. Margaret now regularly stopped as she crossed the field to converse with her.

"It's good to see you out, Flora. How are you keeping?"

"Well enough." Flora was evasive, eager to continue her search.

"I'm glad," Margaret had smiled encouragingly.

Later she had exchanged occasional gossip. Flora had tried to maintain a façade of normality by observing how Ann's stomach was swelling and how she would be due any day now. In exchange for news of birth, Margaret had reported how Ailith McQueen had been unwell, but that even at her grand age nothing seemed to have fazed her over the past few years; surely there was little chance that this time would be an exception. Flora had wished her well, but secretly thought of the widow's poisonous tongue being the true cause of her ailment.

Flora also felt disappointed not to be able to confide in the Reverend. She had informed him of the girl's disappearance and had been shaken when he appeared unconcerned. Since the tacksman's departure, he could be seen making hasty preparations for the repair of the old chapel, very seldom with assistance but nonetheless determined. Still an air of melancholy hung over him, which made him seem unapproachable, the thread of connection she once felt between them slackening day by day.

There was more pressing concern when the first potatoes of the season came up blackened and soft to the touch, their tender flesh turning to a mushy rot at the gentle prod of a finger. In the store houses the leftover oats omitted a musty smell, and flecks of green began to appear on some of the flaky mounds which remained. While the crofters' attitudes towards Flora had eased, the atmosphere on the island was tense and uneasy. Thankfully, they could no longer point the finger at her, but her own personal sorrow grew sharper as the girl's memory seemed to fade from the village. If people did think of her, they clearly chose to pretend her presence amongst them had never happened.

When her thoughts overwhelmed her too much for the pretence of routine, Flora slipped away to the solitude of the cove, part of her hoping that the girl would have returned to the place she was first found, sitting on a rock, gazing out to sea as the salt foam slowly gathered at her feet.

CHAPTER THIRTEEN

THOMAS

HE cleared out the wreckage, sweeping the debris from the foundations and tossing aside the sodden wood from what was once the pulpit. He imagined what he could rebuild if only he had the men and resources. A chapel could be raised up like a fortress, domineering the tiny, stone blackhouses which littered the barren landscape.

The chapel that had been built in the years prior to his arrival was even smaller than most crofts on the island: a hastily thrown together afterthought. And so, his ambition could be raised no higher than the musty wooden joints which propped up the remaining wall. A little wood had been gathered from the tacksman, but the men were reluctant to let him use it. The wood was reward for their previous offering to MacLeod and permitting it to be used on the chapel was lowest in their list of priorities. At the last village meeting it had been agreed that a limited amount could be used and some men could be spared to resurrect the drystone walls, but repairing their own storm damaged roofs took precedence. So, for now he satisfied himself with clearing the space for its rebirth, hoping someday it would grow into more than just an unwanted, half formed thing.

The islanders' defensiveness had cooled since Macleod's men's departure. As the prospect of a harsh winter of famine crept into their thoughts, they had let their guard down towards him, but only it seemed by mere inches. Standing on the beach on the morning the tacksman left, he had ensured that the crofters all saw their

Reverend hand over a small trinket in return for more timber, the sunlight catching on the flash of a silver ring. It was as he had intended.

He also remembered how as he had handed over his letter, the smug younger man had looked at him quizzically. "Only one?"

Murray had nodded solemnly, handing over the official looking document which would make its way back to the archdiocese. With a shrug of the shoulders, the man had pocketed it. As he watched the boats leave, Murray had felt no guilt, only trepidation at how he could repurpose himself. He still felt deep regret for the lost girl's disappearance. Without her, his preaching echoed hollowly. He thought of the roughness of her hand as she had handed him the stuffed bird; cold, calloused fingers brushing against his wrist. Her skin had been softer the day they had found her. He hastily snapped his thoughts away.

As he continued his task, the moistness from the grass began seeping through the cracks in the soles of his shoes, which were scuffed and worn from weeks of misuse. The island was shrouded with a fine, grey sea mist, hanging in cool droplets which clung weakly to the face and hair. The whole landscape was veiled in damp cloud. When the coastal fret moved in from the sea, the island seemed to be surrounded by impenetrable walls, the jagged cliffs disappearing into an endless grey. The sea and rocks still clung deceptively below, and one could easily be deceived that stepping beyond sight would simply lead into a vast nothing, rather than into a deadly plummet below. During these times, the men were reluctant to go fowling, which only made the islanders' moods dourer. Murray was sick from being surrounded by sky and sea; the fog it evoked only a sense of limbo in him. He was as tired of this spit of land as he was frustrated by its people.

Before he had left, the young MacLeod had mentioned that it would be more profitable to replace the entire native population with sheep, and as far as Murray could tell, many of the islanders already possessed the same kind of ignorant herd mentality as their livestock. He thought bitterly about how they selfishly clung together, and how in this herd no one dared step outside the group without swift condemnation. Although he prayed not to, he grew increasingly impatient with them. There were times when he hated them.

Furthermore, the arrogant young man, MacLeod, had only exacerbated his frustration with his situation, rather than relieved him by conjuring thoughts of civilisation. Murray did not understand how this man presumed himself superior. MacLeod too was trapped in a situation he deemed beneath him, and for all his talk of coffee house gossip in London, Murray had seen that on closer inspection, the man's clothes may once have been of quality but now were tired looking; his fashionable bag wig was also fraying and unkempt. The young man's shabbiness satisfied Murray that his coffee house days were long gone. Besides, he was quite gratified with having no one to talk to, for he was afraid his contempt would trickle through into any conversation given his current temperament.

He cursed softly as a splinter burrowed its way into the flesh of his hand. He flung down the rotten beam he was carrying and kicked it, watching as the soft, mulchy wood gave way to a reddish mush from which fat, grey lice scurried in alarm.

"Reverend?"

He spun around. Every unseen voice put him on edge these days.

It was only the widow MacKinnon. How was it the woman had such a habit of creeping up on one unannounced? She was like a fabled phantom; a sad banshee who heralded misery in her wake.

"I wondered if I could talk to you about something?"

Every thought within him was repelled by her question. "I am rather busy, Mrs MacKinnon . . ." He turned towards the pile of debris he was futilely piling up and felt a pang of embarrassment.

"You know I could ask my boys to help you with that?" Her look of concern disarmed him.

"Yes, well, I suppose that would be helpful, but . . ." His thoughts trailed off and he was left staring dumbly at her.

"I'm sorry to bother you, Reverend. I just feel I have nobody else who I can talk to about this."

The earnestness in her voice reeled him in further, and before she could say it, he already knew what this would be about.

"I'm sorry, but I have not seen the girl anywhere."

"But I thought, perhaps, you could help me find her?"

He felt conflicted. On the one hand he must be seen to be preoccupied with doing purposeful work, but on the other he needed the girl's safe return. He remembered what the tacksman had said about her, and her place in the island community. Who was to say whether she would be safest lost or found?

"I have a number of tasks to attend to, Mrs MacKinnon." He spoke bluntly, but with a lack of confidence. "If I happen to come across her, whatever her condition may be, I will of course let only yourself know." He cringed at his own stilted delivery. Adopting an officious air did not convince him that he was in charge of this situation.

But if Flora MacKinnon was disheartened by his curtness, she did not show it. Her face remained unreadable. As she gave her thanks and left him to his meaningless task, he felt a slight apprehension. Whilst this woman had willingly forged a tenuous bond to him, her unpredictability and almost hysterical possessiveness over the lost girl was starting to make him uneasy. There was, perhaps, no one he could trust on this island. A wave of anguish hit him as he thought of those on the mainland, his superiors in Edinburgh and his family in Inverness: there was nobody he could truly trust anywhere.

He struck out at the crumbling interior wall of the chapel with his fist, dislodging a loose piece of drystone. Cursing, he rubbed at his knuckles. The wall behind the crude stone alter had been the least damaged part of the construction, and as he clumsily pushed the loosened stone back into place, his fingertips brushed against something wet and mushy. Recoiling in disgust, he pulled his hand away expecting it to be coated in green moss and slime.

He examined his fingers; they were instead flecked with tiny white fibres, like those from the dampened pages of parchment.

He removed the stone and dug his hand into the recess behind. His hands touched sodden leather. Carefully withdrawing his arm, he held in his hand a small, bound pocketbook. The heavy rain which had helped destroy the chapel had trickled its way through the drystone to saturate the little tome, and Murray was afraid that opening it would only serve to emulsify the pages into a papery paste.

Intrigued, he carefully wrapped it in his handkerchief and placed it in his pocket, before heading up the steep path to his blackhouse, head bowed obliviously to the foaming sea which hissed against the shore.

※

Murray's bounty sat tantalisingly beside the crackling flames of the hearth, its pages drying slowly. For once it was swelteringly hot inside, but Murray was unperturbed by this, merely wiping the sweat from his forehead as he once more checked the book's suppleness. Finally satisfied, he cautiously removed the leather strap, only for it to immediately snap and break away. Eagerly, he leafed through the contents, careful not to damage the pages further, his fingertips barely grazing the corners as he lifted them.

To his dismay, he found the traces of ink had faded almost beyond recognition, the rain having done its work in erasing the words of his predecessor. Why the Reverend Buchan, whose pocketbook this must surely have been, would choose to deposit it behind the alter wall was beyond comprehension, unless it contained information either secretive or relevant to his successor. As Murray knew there was no threat of any of the islanders being able to decipher writing, let alone writing in a language they could not speak, he felt confident that the information within must be of some value. However, as he squinted to discern what had been written, he could only make out a few pages of what seemed to be numbers. No doubt a simple list of expenditure. Other pages contained traces of faded illustrations; Murray thought he could make out a sketch of the chapel and a plan of the village. With a growing scepticism, he turned over another page, desperate to find something more decipherable.

A firm knock at the door forced him away from his task. Frustrated, he shrugged on his clerical coat and opened the door to one of the many square-jawed, indistinguishable women of the island. Thinking she had come to clean or drop off supplies, he was ready to dismiss her, until he noticed the tears she was trying to hold back.

"Father, could you come quick please? It's my mother. We don't think she'll make it through to the end of the day."

Now accustomed to the false, popish title some of the islanders insisted on bestowing on him, he shrugged it off. Eventually he recognised the woman as the one whose cow had given birth that day in the pasture outside the chapel's burial grounds, her heavy-set brows and tawny skin marking her out as one of Ailith McQueen's daughters. He had wondered why Ailith had not been paying her weekly visits to the blackhouse of late, possessive as she was of her deceased husband's property, and untrusting of its current incumbent. Murray had assumed the old woman had grown tired and resentful of serving him, a development he had welcomed. He could now see from the bags under the daughter's eyes and her haggard posture that this was not the case after all.

"You do understand I will not say any last rites over her?" Murray asked the woman. "That is not what is done anymore, and it will do nothing to spare your mother's soul."

The woman looked confused. "We just hoped you would come and pray for her, Father. We've tried everything else. We fear she is cursed."

So, this was it? He was their last resort in a time of crisis. Or more accurately, God was their last resort, after every other heathenish quackery had been exhausted. "Lead the way," he sighed reluctantly, supressing his resentment.

As Murray entered the McQueen croft, his eyes stung from the smoke which filled the room. Peat was piled high on the hearth, spreading its warm, sooty scent throughout the blackhouse; it battled with the sourness coming from a wooden slop bucket at the foot of a bed, which was stacked haphazardly with heavy plaids and woollen blankets. The thick air made his eyes weep, and the heat was stifling. Approaching the bed, the bitter stench from the bucket became stronger. Murray glimpsed the contents of blood-tinged bile mixing with other bodily fluids and tried not to retch. Why had nobody had the decency to empty it before now? Underneath the pile of bedclothes, he could discern the old woman's face, which appeared hardened like a cracked walnut; oily strands of thin, grey hair stuck to the slick sheen of her forehead. Around the bed huddled several men and women, while a few feet away a sticky child played in the dirt, far too close to the raging hearth.

"Have you come to convert me?" a raspy voice croaked from the bed.

"Your family have asked me here, Ailith. Although I warn you, all I can do is pray for your soul, heedless of its destination. God is not some miracle cure. His will is unshakable, and his intentions cannot be undone."

"Hmmph." Ailith seemed unperturbed, almost amused. "God can take me as he finds me, even if that means entering his kingdom covered in my own piss and shit." She looked stonily at her children gathered at her side. "Make yourselves useful and find me some clean bedding."

"But ma," one of the women ventured, "we've used up the clean sheets . . ."

"Then go and get more from your Martin's house," the dying woman snapped, "and while you're at it, scoop up that brat of yours before he does himself an injury."

Some of the women clucked about their mother and, in some

cases, grandmother, concernedly before departing, while the men retreated to a corner, eyeing Murray suspiciously through the thick haze of smoke.

"Well then, Reverend. What prayers would you have us say?"

"There are no magic words you can say. You have to speak to Him in earnestness if that is what you want."

"Hmm." She looked contemplative, then grimaced. Whether it was from physical pain or some secret sentiment, Murray could not tell. "Perhaps then, you should do the talking," was the conclusion she came to.

Murray clasped his hands and began to utter the Lord's prayer, painfully aware throughout the entire procedure of the old woman's eyes boring into him, as if analysing every movement of his mouth for some sign of deception or insincerity. When he concluded, her eyes travelled from his face down to his naval.

"You don't carry a cross." Her voice was growing weaker as she exhausted her capacity for speech, and Murray had to strain to hear. Gradually grasping her meaning, he replied, "I do not carry one, no. But you have surely seen the one I have fixed to the wall back at the croft."

". . . You're even less like the last one then."

"Pardon?"

"Father Buchan always carried one at his waist." Her voice cracked and became barely a whisper. "And yours doesn't have the broken man hanging from it."

"The broken man?" Murray could not be sure he had heard correctly.

"Yes." Ailith glowered, frustrated. "Father Buchan would have us kiss it after he prayed over us. I wondered where yours was . . ."

Murray put a hand down on the floor to balance himself, heedless of the straw and filthy matter which would stick to it. The room swayed as the heat and pungent smells took full effect. Suddenly it all made sense: the islanders' stubbornness in not addressing him properly; their calls to his door for blessings of their livestock and last-minute rites; their resistance to abandoning idolatrous funeral practices and their resilience to his preaching. Composing himself, he decided that the best response for now was one of restraint. It would be an almost impossible task to explain the errors of past religious doctrines to a people barely acquainted with the concept of Christ.

"The Reverend Buchan was old fashioned," he said.

The old woman's eyes met his.

"He understood us far better than you," she murmured. "He never judged, he just guided. And his god was far more forgiving than yours..."

Murray rose to his feet, almost knocking over a piss-pot.

"You have my prayers, Ailith McQueen. May God grant you into his mercy."

The old woman opened her mouth to speak once more, but disgusted, he turned his back.

"You should be mindful of the tide, Reverend!"

Murray froze, his hand clutching the doorframe. Behind him, Ailith McQueen was reduced to a bout of coughing from the effort of her outburst, but soon summoned the strength to speak to him one final time.

"She caught me throwing stones, Reverend, for aye, it was me tried to stand against her, now look what has happened to me." She let out a harsh cackle. "You best watch out, young man. The sea is merciless, and she has no respect for your God. He cannot protect you; not now she is coming."

Murray tried to stifle the fear rising like bile in his throat as the words from his dreams echoed in his ears. Quickening his pace as he left the rancid miasma of the sick-house behind, his feet pounded the dirt and turf in contempt of the wretched place, the welcome wind whipping fiercely at his back, driving him further away.

He forced his mind away from fear and thought of the little book sitting back at his croft, its pages lying half open for him to decipher the possible dissension within. Outrage seeped through his every pore. He thought of how this explained why his predecessor had sought out an itinerant position and such remote congregants: not for any pure motive as he had.

He knew that there were small papist enclaves throughout the Highlands and islands, but practicing Catholic sermons was strictly illegal. With such knowledge, he hoped that Buchan had developed his views later, rather than infiltrated the Church and taken funding intended to promote true Christian knowledge in isolated communities. If only he had known before he had composed his last letter to the diocese...

His eyes continued to water, but he could not tell whether the tears came from smoke, wind, terror, or fury. He was tempted to take Buchan's pocketbook and finish what the rains had started; flinging it into the merciless sea or else leaving it to burn in the fire of the hearth. He was glad his croft was furthest from the village, and as he climbed towards it, he fixed his sight on the uppermost ridge without looking back.

As he climbed, a sudden movement caught his eye. Fluttering in the wind at the top of the hill was a flash of plaid which billowed around a lone figure whose hair, no longer braided, whipped bout her face.

The girl was crouched low, surveying the settlement below like an owl scrutinising the grasses below its branch for signs of movement. Murray opened his mouth to call out, but quickly thought better than to alert others of the girl's presence. Suddenly feeling the full force of Ailith McQueen's warning, he froze, but the girl seemed not to notice him, and in the gap between one heartbeat and the next, had disappeared over the ridge of the hill.

The moment had passed so quickly that Murray briefly doubted his senses. Whilst he was still relieved the girl was alive, he wondered how she had evaded the settlement for so long. Surely on a treeless island it would be an impossible feat? But then again, perhaps she had not needed to roam free. Perhaps she had sheltered with the animals in their tiny, stone enclosures during the day, venturing downwards later to find nourishment. Unlike the islanders, Murray took very little notice of the contents of his own storehouse and would not have noticed traces of food going missing; it was likely that as the furthest croft from the settlement, this was where she had sourced what little sustenance she could. Yes, this must have been the explanation. Talk of phantoms and vengeful sea witches was utter rot. It had to be.

Far from fearing her, he knew he would keep watch in the coming days; he knew that she would eventually come to him, whether he yearned for it or not. She would have no choice once starvation crept in.

He recalled his words to Flora MacKinnon from earlier that day and quickly decided that for now, he should rescind them. Knowing the current malcontent of the islanders, the girl would no doubt be endangered by their knowledge that she had possibly been taking their dwindling supplies, and he could not be held accountable for the actions of Flora should she force her female instincts over common sense. He retreated to his blackhouse. The day had had too many ponderous revelations and he was eager to sleep and forget all for the night.

In his dreams, Caroline returned. He had seen her this way before, in his waking hours. She was weeping, her face tormented as she struggled through the words of, "When I Survey the Wonderous Cross". He looked down at her from the pulpit. His memory blurred and as it shifted with the second stanza of the hymn, she lifted an accusing finger towards him before the water seeping through the tiles of the floor rose up and consumed them both.

CHAPTER FOURTEEN

FLORA

THE day of Ailith's burial was the hottest of the summer. As the matriarch's coffin was eased into the ground, the women's tears mingled with the sweat which beaded their faces, while children swatted at the air which grew thick with swarms of midges and horsefly. The ceremony was subdued. Although Ailith was the oldest amongst them, there was clear concern over the suddenness of her passing, and Flora was relieved to be spared from the usual keening and wailing. The Reverend seemed to share in her feelings. He hovered by the hollow of earth, chanting words which few understood but none saw fit to challenge, perhaps misled into seeing the islanders' unease as a display of growing tolerance. The same as it had fifteen years prior, this sickness had acted with swift brutality.

Ailith was soon swallowed up by peaty soil of the island. As Flora placed her stone onto the growing cairn, she thought of how some day, she too would become part of the dirt beneath her feet, her body consumed by the place which had been her only version of the world. She would much rather they gave her body to the sea.

The mourners began to disperse. The rest of the day would pass without work, as was appropriate for the days from a soul's passing through to burial. Flora's family flocked around Ann, whose bloated belly now meant she needed several arms to lean on as she shuffled back to the croft from her grandmother's burial. Flora assured John she would be home soon, but wished to sit some time with Donnchadh, her parents and siblings. Perching on the wall closest the sea, she allowed the sun to warm the leathery skin of her hands and face, ignoring the itch of damp wool rubbing against the rest of her body. She unpinned her earasaid and let her shawl fall softly onto her shoulders.

"Mrs MacKinnon?"

Hurriedly, she gathered the loose material back over her shoulders before turning to face the Reverend. He looked down at the grass as she fastened herself back together.

"Would you perhaps walk with me for a spell?" He extended his hand awkwardly, and quickly recovering from her sense of indignity she took hold of it gently, trusting that the walk would enable him to offer up some hope to her.

They made their slow procession along the cliff edge, the now calm sea stretching out before them. The Reverend's arm offered sturdy support, but there seemed to be no warmth or intimacy to the gesture, only reluctant necessity. His brow was furrowed beneath the shade of his hat. In one fleeting moment his face would express wide eyed desire to share in whatever thought or recollection occupied him, but with small, halting steps his mind seemed to repeatedly change.

"It is a hot day for walking," she offered. She had meant it to sound encouraging, but immediately worried it would seem accusatory. The Reverend halted and absent-mindedly examined his shoes. Flora grew impatient.

"Perhaps there is something you want to talk about?" she asked, summoning her courage. She hoped that news of the girl waited on the tip of his tongue. At the sound of her voice the Reverend's eyelids flicked upwards, and he stared at her, mouth half open in dumb surprise.

"Mrs MacKinnon . . ." He seemed to carefully construct and deconstruct his next words in his head, opening his mouth and then pausing, closing it again like a dying fish yanked from the water and held under the glare of the sun, dazzled and desperate. ". . . what do you know, or I should say, what can you tell me about the Reverend Buchan?"

Before he finally spoke, Flora had almost begun to speak her mind, summoning her own burning questions before the Reverend's words overlapped her own. She took a moment to process his question, staring in bewildered disappointment.

"He was . . . different to yourself, sir," she said hesitantly. He looked at her with stern concentration, as if he could scoop the words from her mouth and examine them, judging their quality like a crofter meticulously turns and probes at the crops he unearths from the dirt for signs of rot. Flora decided to choose her next words tactfully, hoping it would still lead to an exchange of information which satisfied them both.

"I mean, you are a lot more dignified, more level-headed than him, Reverend. A lot of the others liked him because he was more direct; he liked to talk to people about their private affairs and how God could help fix them."

He stared more intensely. A flash of annoyance indicated him heavy-handedly prising her words apart, eager to find the rot inside and discard them.

"I never liked or trusted him in the same way," she continued hurriedly; truthfully. "He was too prying for me and came across as insincere. The others liked talking to him and unburdening themselves, but that was never the way for me. I don't need God to forgive me anything, Reverend, I need God to let me forgive myself, and if this happens, I want it to be real, not because of the words offered to me by some priest . . ." Her voice wavered, finding it impossible to fully articulate what she needed to say. Looking up, she saw the Reverend's face soften.

"That's why I want to talk to you," she said, encouraged. "Since you came, I could tell you understood how it felt to be unseen by people. People only look at us on the surface and don't try to understand why we act differently, why I feel the way I feel. I shouldn't have to talk about my feelings or make a scene for people to consider that I might not be all right, that I might not want to just do what they do and pretend to be content with it . . ." Again, she could not find the words. Each time she came close to expressing herself the words ground to a halt in her mind, unable to wrap themselves around how she felt in a way which could be understood by anyone other than herself.

There was a long, pregnant pause. The Reverend shuffled his feet uncomfortably and once more directed his scrutiny out towards the sea, as if afraid to recognise the look in her eyes. She did not prompt him, instead choosing to wait quietly before he opened his mouth to speak.

"You mentioned the Reverend Buchan as being very... familiar with the other islanders," he said, returning his intense gaze towards her. "Did you ever see him behave in a way which you thought was... inappropriate towards some of the others? Was there any particular company he kept when he should have been alone?"

Flora was dumbfounded, and her frustration reached its peak. She could think of no retort. Before she could begin to respond, a female voice drifted towards them.

"Flora!"

She turned. It was Mary, panting as she stumbled in a clumsy, exhausted sprint along the cliff path. Drawing close to them, she stopped, placing her hands on her knees as she regained her composure.

"Mary?" Flora began to panic; for a moment she envisioned Michael and Fergus sprawled on the rocks beneath them. "Mary, what are you doing? Where's the baby?"

"She's back at the house ...," Mary said between breaths. "You have to come quickly, Flora ... It's Ann. Her time is upon her."

Flora extracted herself from the Reverend's arm. He seemed to teeter on the edge of saying something, but soon retreated, removing himself from the women's situation to scan the horizon.

Flora hurried back with Mary, eventually arriving at Michael's croft with her back and hip burning.

Michael hovered by the door. John and Fergus patted at him reassuringly as they remained outside, on the one occasion where the house became the sole realm of women. The children, Janet and Malcolm, played nonchalantly near the shoreline, skimming stones which scudded against the flat sheen of the sea. There was a low moan from inside and Michael's body bolted towards the door before he remembered himself and withdrew.

"It'll be all right, son," said Flora as she and Mary passed over the threshold. "Third one is easier than the first two. Your Ann will be fine." She squeezed his shoulder and was ushered inside.

Flora had to steady herself when she saw Ann. The belief in a straightforward labour evaporated into the thick air of the blackhouse.

All the women of the village had crammed themselves inside the house, filling every cranny while Mary rushed to sooth her sister-in-law, gently applying a damp compress to her forehead. Margaret Gillies seemed to assume charge over the situation, now being the elder of the village after Ailith's death. In the centre of this scene, sat Ann. Propped up by her fellow women on a wooden birthing stool, she snorted and sweated, her body straining and bucking sporadically like an animal immediately before slaughter. On the rushes below her open legs was a thick, black slick of blood. Her thighs were also coated in a sticky redness, which trickled down to the puddle on the floor in long, slow gullies. The room was pungent from Ann's oozing body.

The others held Ann's shoulders as she was caught in an agonising spasm. It was in this moment that Margaret slipped to Flora's side and whispered in her ear, "Flora, you have to go outside and send your boys away. Tell them it could be many hours, days even before this is fully over."

"Do you think she'll live?" Flora dared ask the question they were all thinking.

"I'm not sure. If the bleeding stops soon, then maybe. She's certainly strong enough. But the baby . . ." Margaret chewed her lip. "I've seen this once before, and if it doesn't come out soon, it will drown, if it hasn't done so already . . ." Her voice trailed off and the two women turned to look at Ann, who recovering from her seizure was looking to Mary, gripping her hand.

"Go and take the bairns over to your house," she said through gritted teeth, "someone will have to mind them." Mary kissed her friend's hand and hurried away.

Flora caught Mary by the wrist. "Tell the men not to linger outside," she instructed. "Tell them it'll be a long labour; no more than that."

Mary nodded, knowingly, suppressing the tears welling in her eyes before she departed.

"Get me water," Ann's voice slurred, her body now slumped against several of her neighbours. "And don't crowd me." Her voice was beginning to crack, and swiftly her abrasiveness turned into a pathetic wail. "I knew it was bad this should happen today! What chance could a child have being born on the day of a burial?"

"Oh, nonsense, Ann MacKinnon," clucked Margaret. "Ailith will be watching today. It makes sense to have new life replace an old one." Margaret cast a doubtful look at Flora, who prompted herself to action by helping to wash the blood away from Ann's legs. She gently sponged away the crusty veined pattern on Ann's inner thighs and wrung out the sopping cloth in a bucket filled with pinkish water. "The bleeding's stopped now, Ann," she said encouragingly.

"Aye. For now."

"Be hopeful, *m'eudail*," Flora admonished. "My last birth wasn't so different and you're a far stronger lass than I was. Now, have you felt any movement from the baby? Have you been pushing?"

"No. There's pain, but it's not like the last times. I can feel it hurting, but it isn't as sharp or sudden."

Flora looked at Margaret with concern. She took a deep breath before saying, "Right then. Well, if this babe won't budge itself, we better get him moving. Let's get you up and walking for a spell."

Ann finished sipping at the water administered to her by

Margaret's daughter, Elisabeth, before Flora and Margaret took her by the arms and gently hoisted her to her feet. They walked her back and forth from one side of the blackhouse to the other. Ann was uncomplaining, merely screwing her face up in determination whenever the pain struck.

They proceeded like this into the night. Whenever they could, they walked her, and when the spasms returned and the pain became too much, they held her steady on the birthing stool, watching as the blood which trickled forth from between her thighs became less and less. As the dawn light began to seep in, they made their decision.

"Ann," Flora whispered. Ann turned her head drowsily and stared though half closed eyes. "This baby isn't going to come of its own accord. Margaret is going to have to make a small cut and pull it out herself."

There were no protestations. Ann merely nodded her head, propping her legs up on Margaret and Flora's shoulders and bracing her body against the support of the surrounding women, who held her firmly as Margaret reached inside her. Ann dug her fingernails into the wooden legs of the stool, her face red and contorted.

With one final rush of blood, the baby came free. Flora caught it, quickly slicing through the cord with a gutting knife retrieved from her pocket, before scooping it up and hurrying it from sight while Margaret continued to empty Ann's body of the remnants of its pregnancy.

Flora examined the limp little body, its pudgy limbs dangling at its sides. She patted down the powdery skin; lips stained the colour of a bruise were delicately prised open with a finger, but there was no hint or whisper of a breath. When Flora withdrew her finger, it was flecked with blood. She wiped her hand across her skirt, nauseated.

"Is it man or maid?" Ann's voice floated through the miasma of the room, weak but demanding.

Flora turned, the child still drooping in her arms. "Maid."

Ann closed her eyes and tilted her head back, exhaling deeply, her face set in a frown. "Well, can I hold her?"

Flora brought the baby to her, and silently, without explanation, eased the child's lifeless form into Ann's waiting arms. Margaret shot a look of admonishment at Flora. Ann passed a hand over her baby's lips and gently pressed two fingers against its breast, the skin yielding to her touch like a clammy ball of dough.

"I'm so sorry, Ann," Margaret said, still frowning at Flora. "These things happen. You've got two fit, healthy children still, and you're strong and young enough to have many more. I know it won't be much comfort now but give it a few days and you will be thankful for that."

Ann's face crumpled and she began to wail, her body once more shaking. Flora had never seen Ann cry.

"She did this." Ann's words were spat in Flora's direction, her grief suddenly turning to anger, swiftly seeking out blame. "She brought that drowned witch into her home and everything's gone wrong since. It's hardly surprising since she cares more for dead children than living ones."

Flora fell back against the wall of the blackhouse. She drew herself into the shadows and tried to pull herself towards the door, her stomach lurching forward as if to be sick. The remaining women all looked to her, whether out of pity or consternation Flora could not tell. She only knew she had to get out.

"That was a wicked thing to say," Margaret said sternly. "I know you're upset, Ann, but there's no one to blame for any of this. You're hardly the first woman here to have lost a babe."

"Aye. You need to grow up, lass." Another one of her neighbours spoke up. "Now let's clean you up and then you can have a lie down. No use angering yourself."

The attention once more removed from her, Flora inched towards the door, still with her back to the wall. The women were trying to prise the baby away from Ann, who gave up her burden reluctantly and after some struggle, while her neighbours shushed and cossetted her, tutting and murmuring platitudes. Finally finding the door, Flora hastily undid the latch and stumbled into the damp morning air.

"It could have been worse," a woman's voice from inside soothed. "At least it was only a girl."

CHAPTER FIFTEEN

THOMAS

Murray's latest encounter with Flora MacKinnon had shaken him. He was now less torn about hiding the young woman's reappearance from her, and after the scant information she had offered to him regarding Buchan, perhaps he could use his knowledge of the girl to wheedle out more of the truth the next time they spoke.

After the women's departure, he had made a brief circuit of the island, eager to encounter the lost woman again. He hoped he could speak to her. Surely once he could do that he would fully accept that she was merely a woman of flesh and blood. There was a chance that in her absence, she had somehow recovered the capacity for speech and could herself answer many of the burning questions he had regarding the mystery of her presence. Part of him knew this was a delusion. Nevertheless, his desire to see her grew with an intensity he could not fully comprehend.

After a fruitless walk he had retired to the blackhouse, physically exhausted and unable to decipher his thoughts. Restless, he squinted by candlelight in another attempt to decipher Reverend Buchan's various scribblings. Frantically, he flipped through the pages.

Despite his former urge to destroy the book and his contents, he now realised how he could use this discovery in his favour. If he were to present evidence of popery to the diocese, which he planned to report as soon as the opportunity to convey letters was once more available to him, they would at the very least acknowledge his usefulness in uncovering dissenters. After consideration, he counted this as an opportunity, if not a victory. This revelation would send a clear message that he was effectively doing his duty. Driving out heathenism was one thing, but detecting popery could provide him with not just praise, but a promotion to an established parish, perhaps even a seat on the General Assembly in Edinburgh.

His fingers vigorously traced the jumble of letters and numbers across each page. He did not know where the Reverend Buchan had been sent subsequent to his departure from Eilean Eòin, only understanding that he had left after a sudden bout of illness. The man was significantly older than him, but without doubt still a danger. Buchan's promotion of popery in the isles could provide fuel for further insurrection should the Pretender once more cross the sea from Europe.

As he skimmed through the book, his enthusiasm weakened. On one page was what seemed to be a lengthy census of the population; the islanders reduced to a series of numbers across a page. Some were divided into households, whilst others were nameless. Shortly before Buchan's departure in March of that year, there were listed "three females", age and names left blank. Murray supposed they must have been birth records, as he had noticed previously that the islanders seemed reluctant to name their children prior to weaning. However, he could not recall seeing any more infants past suckling age other than the youngest of Flora MacKinnon's grandchildren, who nevertheless seemed significantly larger and sturdier than the average four-month-old child. Not that he knew much about infants.

There were some faint pencil drawings on the next few pages, almost too faded to decipher. They seemed to be images of the islanders. Clearly there would be little of use in these. Slamming the book down in frustration, Murray decided to retire early. In the last remaining heat of the day, he sat out on the step of the byre and practiced his Gaelic before attempting to read Knox. Having spent his time on purposeful distractions, he went to bed hoping that neither nightmares nor impure thoughts would return to torment him.

Creeping silently in the forgotten, drowsy gap between wakefulness and slumber, they eventually found him.

※

The next morning, there was a frenzied commotion at the bay. Coming to the end of a sparsely attended sermon, Murray watched as the group of men came scurrying over the edges of the northern cliffs, descending upon the bay like a string of ants carrying their struggling prey back towards the nest. They dragged a large net behind them; a net which bulged feebly. The women who sat by him abandoned their labours and ran, pulling their grubby children along with them in barely concealed glee. Doors flew open. The women burst into excited chatter.

"We've caught the witch!" a man called out hoarsely, as the women flocked around them. Children approached the net, prodding and kicking it before running away in mock terror as it thrashed violently.

Murray felt his heart catch in his throat. His mouth was dry and his stomach roiled. For a moment he could barely breath, and though he desperately wanted to run at the crowd, he found his limbs seized by a tension which froze him steady. His breath came forth in panicked, shaky bursts. After several more agonized seconds, his body bolted towards the shore, stumbling gracelessly as his legs regained their sense of autonomy.

As he reached the beach, the men were posturing proudly around their captive.

"Where did you find her?" some of the women asked breathlessly.

"Sitting on the rocks just north of the cove."

"Did she not change form and dive back into the sea?"

"Not this time."

Murray shoved the women aside, who tutted and glared at him

for disrupting their sport. Eventually he stood face to face with the leader: a squat, solidly built man of around Murray's age, who brandished a wooden club usually reserved for dispatching seabirds.

"I order you to stop what you are doing!" he panted, with as much dignity as he could muster. "Let her go."

"And let her cause more havoc to our crops and neighbours? Not likely," the man said contemptuously. "You should be glad, Father. We've caught a witch. Wouldn't you like to see her pay for her crimes against your god?"

There was a mutter of agreement amongst the crowd. Murray drew himself up to his full height. "There will be no talk of witches here. Now stand aside."

"You can look if you like, but you can't touch her, Father. Not until she's safely dispatched."

Urged on by dread, Murray lunged at the men and tried to push them aside. He bounced ineffectually against the broad width of their shoulders as they formed a barrier between him and their victim. He drove himself against them as they began to tussle him away. The surrounding women and children stood slack-jawed; no doubt greatly entertained.

It was at that moment that a strange, gurgling croak came from the net's captive. Murray stopped struggling and listened as the sound was repeated. Deposited to one side by the men, he cautiously craned his neck to peer between the coarsely woven squares which made up the alleged witch's prison.

He jumped back in surprise.

"It's a bird," he said, baffled, even though few were at this point listening to him.

He could have laughed. He felt a deep, calming wave of relief wash over him. He looked again at the net's occupant as it flapped its tiny, stunted wings. One could easily have mistaken it for a small person, so large was the creature. He had never seen a bird so large in the flesh. It had slick black feathers, topped by a small, white patch just above its bead-like eye; it stood tall on its ginormous webbed feet, craning its long neck in confusion as the islanders pressed in around it and it desperately looked for an escape. Its beak was sharp and razor like; no doubt it could be used to deadly effect should someone place their fingers too close. But by far the most unusual thing about it were its wings, which for such a large bird were shockingly tiny, occasionally flailing at its sides in a pathetic gesture of alarm.

"This is no witch, sirs," he said. "It is merely a garefowl. I have heard tales of such creatures existing to the far north."

"Trust us, Father," the leader once more turned to face him, "we've seen such things before. Whenever there's been some strife upon the island, one of these hags appears. You can hear her muttering; no doubt cursing us. If we release her, she'll transform into her true self and vanish beneath the waves."

"I've never heard such nonsense," he scoffed. "It is a dumb beast. It does no harm to you at all."

"Get him to clear off!" shouted one of the women. "He's always there to spoil things for the rest of us. Boring us with his preaching but scoffing whenever we want to do things our way."

The leader of the group of men circled his arm around Murray's shoulders and pulled him aside. "Listen, Father. This doesn't have to concern you. If you want to stay and see justice done, you are welcome, but if not, I strongly recommend you back off so we can rid ourselves of this witch and her curses once and for all."

"It is a bird," Murray repeated, emphasising every syllable and narrowing his eyes in open disdain.

The man crossed his arms. "It's a witch, Father, and if my suspicions are correct, you're probably partly to blame for her being here in the first place. We remember how you helped bring that woman back from the cove. It's no coincidence we found her in almost exactly the same place."

"You have some nerve," he raged. "This thing is no woman. You'd have to be either blind or completely stupid to believe it so."

"Have it whatever way you want, Father," the man replied stonily.

"Either way, like everyone else I grow tired of talking to you." He turned away and returned his attention to the creature, which now sat, snapping its razor-sharp bill pitifully at the growing crowd of onlookers.

Seeing the futility of the situation, Murray backed away. As he did a hoard of women surged forward. Descending on their quarry with sticks and heavy pieces of driftwood, they thronged around the net and began to mercilessly beat at the unfortunate beast. Children joined in, pummelling the writhing net with their fists. There were a few wretched croaks before blood began seeping into the surrounding sand, spreading into a rusty puddle of gore. Feathers flew everywhere. He lifted a hand to brush them away from his face before noticing to his disgust that amidst the carnage splatters of a stinking, red, oily fluid were beginning to mark his sleeve. Some of the smallest children nearest the front of the crowd were joyfully smearing themselves in viscera.

Sickened, Murray strode away.

Perversely, after the incident with the bird the islanders seemed sated. Convinced they had ridded themselves of the source of their troubles, their sudden outlet of bloodlust left them seemingly calmer and more respectful in the presence of their Reverend. A few days past where he was able to give his sermons without interruption, and a few of the men had even offered to start working on renovating the chapel. Perhaps, he thought, this small act of barbarism was worth it to bring about a greater good.

It was now the height of summer, and storm clouds gathered at night to disperse the heat of the day. In the evening, lightning shattered across the horizon like cracks spiderwebbing across on a broken windowpane. Fortunately, the storms remained distant, further convincing the islanders that the worst of their plight had been averted.

Murray sat up late, watching the ashen clouds roll across the sky. The soft rumbles of thunder soothed him. During the long days, stretched out by the summer's sun, he found ways to occupy his mind, but as the nights crept in, he dreaded being alone with his thoughts; dreaded the suffocating dreams where the sea came to claim him. He hardly ever saw Caroline in his dreams now, and when he did, she offered no warmth. At best she seemed indifferent, and at worst she turned to look at him with condemnation. He could not help but wonder what now occupied her, and whether she slept in the familiar, soft shell of their marriage bed, or whether she now kept the company of strangers; anonymous faces crowded his vision and mocked him for his hubris.

It was in these moments that he would toss the scratchy covers of his own bed aside and, throwing a coat over his nightshirt, stand out on the doorstep, breathing in the crisp, damp air as the storm crashed against the depths of the open ocean. He closed his eyes and put a foot forward into the wet turf, curling his toes into the earth, allowing the cooling sensation to numb his mind from turmoil.

As he stared into the night, still hung with remnants of daylight, a figure emerged slowly from the vaporous air. She stood about ten paces from him, her back turned and her bare arms outstretched to welcome the rain; her uncovered hair was hanging loose down her back in a sodden cascade. She reached up into the sky, tipping her head back and parting her lips, as if she could drink in the fresh, savage beauty of it.

Before he could control the urge, his mouth opened, but the sound that came forth was wordless and distorted by the storm. Still, she turned to face him.

His chest thudded in rhythm with the gently rumbling thunder. Feeling suddenly self-conscious, he gathered his coat around himself and stumbled back towards the byre door. The young woman stared. He stepped backwards over the threshold, and quelling his shaking breath and trembling hands, he softly pulled the door towards himself. He waited behind it a moment, listening intently. After minutes had passed, he began to ease the door shut, lifting the latch into place, before suddenly stopping himself. He stood still, the latch held loosely in his hand.

Reaching a decision, he let it fall, and leaving the door slightly ajar he retreated through the byre to his bed. Lying with the doors to the box bed still swung open, he listened again, uncertain and fearful of the decision he had made, his heart throbbing, his stomach churning. After an agonisingly long time, he heard the gentle pad of footsteps outside the door, followed by a slow creak.

The door groaned softly as it was closed. His breath quickened. For a moment he regretted his decision and was unnerved by the lengthy silence which followed.

He heard a movement close by him, but his growing alarm abated when he realised it came from the other side of the partition. There was a soft rustle of straw. Untensing, he fell back onto his bed and waited as the dry whisper of the straw being shifted against the partition wall faded into gentle, muffled breaths.

Murray clutched at his blanket and drew it up around himself. He lay awake for some time, feeling the space between his cocooned body and the wall behind his bed constrict and press against his side. He could not tell if he slept.

The next morning, he slowly eased himself up, and with tentative footsteps, peered around the corner of the byre. The front door was placed firmly, but carefully shut. No trace of her remained.

CHAPTER SIXTEEN

FLORA

"Can she really think me such a callous creature?"

Flora stood at the doorway of Michael and Ann's croft, a basket of puffin eggs cradled beneath her arm. She stared pleadingly at her youngest daughter-in-law.

"She doesn't want to speak to you, Flora." Mary's face was sympathetic, but she rubbed nervously at her wrist and her eyes looked to a spot over Flora's shoulder.

"I told Michael I'd be willing to help until she builds her strength back up," Flora continued. "I can even take the children if she'll let me. She cannot possibly expect you to mind them all day with a baby of your own. She can't really think I would do anything to harm my own grandchildren . . ."

Mary glanced quickly over her shoulder into the house and shrugged uncomfortably. "There have been others who've come round to help. Rachel . . ."

"Rachel McQueen?!"

Mary shrugged again and fixed her eyes on the ground.

"She buried her mother only a week ago." Flora was incensed. "Why would Ann want help from her aunt when the bairns' own grandmother lives but minutes away?"

"She thinks you're a bad influence."

Flora bit her lip. The basket of eggs sagged in the crook of her arm.

With an awkward smile and a look of pity which Flora flinched from, Mary took the basket into her hands.

"I'm sorry, Flora," Mary said, lowering her voice. "She's still a little emotional after the birth. Give her a bit of time and she'll come round."

"Mary, you have to understand that I could never hurt a child. I may have spent too much energy on other things, but not at the expense of my family. There was never any malice in anything I've done."

"I know." Mary placed a hesitant hand on Flora's shoulder, but quickly snatched it away, as if scared to be seen. "I don't think Ann believes you caused this; she's just looking for someone to blame. It'll pass."

"How does she fare?"

Mary sucked her breath in through her teeth. "Physically, she's getting better every day. Her cut has healed over properly, and she can walk a little now."

"I'm glad."

There was an uncomfortable pause. Flora hoped for Mary's resolve to soften.

"I'll tell her the eggs were from you, Flora."

As the silence was broken, Flora saw to her disappointment that the expectation had been for her to leave. Mary was once more clutching self-consciously at her wrist.

"Thank you, Mary. Tell her I'm glad she is feeling better."

Mary nodded, but did not raise her eyes to meet Flora's. Inching backwards, she gently closed the door once more. To Flora's unease, Mary held one hand behind her back, and Flora could have sworn she saw a thumb held between two fingers in a clear gesture to ward away black magic.

Flora tried to convince herself otherwise and slowly trudged back along the side of the bay towards her own croft. As she skirted the village wall, she saw the men were finishing their meeting. Her husband and sons were giving Donald Gillies their full attention as he closed the discussion, but Flora felt eyes follow her as she crept past them; she was mindful to respect boundaries and not be seen lingering to listen to men's talk. She already knew without looking that it was the Reverend who stared. He would be at his usual place, hovering at the edge of the circle, awkwardly perched on the stone wall, neither fully included or fully apart.

As she passed them and the men begin to disperse, she sensed the familiar, tentative tread of his ill-equipped shoes.

"Good morning, Reverend."

Turning to greet him, she caught him off guard. For a moment he seemed to fumble his words. "Mrs MacKinnon." He approached her and removed his hat. "I had been hoping to speak with you about a private matter."

Flora's chest throbbed.

"Of course, Reverend. You may talk to me anytime. Now, if you wish." Flora tried to check the eagerness in her voice.

"I had thought, perhaps, that we could conduct our conversation back at my lodgings." He glanced over his shoulder anxiously. "Somewhere we won't be disturbed."

"Of course." Flora's voice caught slightly. Her experience of private conversations prepared her for an array of tragic news. "Lead the way."

Clumsily taking her arm, the Reverend led her up the hill towards Ailith McQueen's old croft. She barely registered the discomfort in her hips as she climbed the sloping incline; barely registered the slipperiness of the grass under her feet. Her mind flew to the darkest places. She saw the girl's broken body shattered on the rocks below the cliffs, surrounded by frothy, white breakers, her skull cracked just like Donnchadh's, her life flowing in red rivulets back to the sea.

Arriving in the warmth of the blackhouse, Flora perched on a stool opposite the Reverend, her body taut with worry.

"I asked you here," the Reverend began, clearing his throat, "to make a proposition which I think might offer some security to us both."

Flora shifted forward, her fears turning to confusion.

"With Ailith McQueen's passing, I have need of a housekeeper." Flora frowned and tilted her head, eager for explanation.

"What that means, is a respectable woman to help with the upkeep of the house. Cook, clean, and the like. As you can see, without my wife I am rather at a loss for such things." He held his hand out and made a sweeping gesture. Flora's eyes followed and could immediately understand his concerns. The hearth was poorly lit; the bricks of peat stacked haphazardly around the edges. The room was in general disarray. Around the window was a scattering of dead moths. The rushes had clearly not been swept and were emitting a musty scent which overpowered the fire; a stale smell also came from the basket on the table which contained old potatoes clearly harvested prior to the Reverend's arrival. Flora tried to temper her revulsion at the waste of good food, especially given their current circumstances. The only other food which had been brought from the storehouse was an unappetising plate of dried fish.

"I see the problem," she said tentatively, uncertain as to why this request needed to be given in private.

"I understand you might have reservations, Mrs MacKinnon, but rest assured I spoke to your husband earlier at the meeting about this. At first, he was unhappy with the idea of you being treated like a servant, but I assured him I would of course pay you generously in coin. Anything I give you can be used to buy supplies when the tacksman returns before the winter months. You would have access to enough money to see you and your entire family through 'til spring."

At first Flora was angry. She was furious with herself to have thought the Reverend trusted her enough to make this appeal without the consent of her husband, and that his motivations were anything other than practical.

"Well, for coin I don't see how I could possibly refuse," she replied, tempering her frustration and disappointment.

"I'm relieved." The Reverend offered a strained smile, which appeared unnatural on his sombre face. He paused. Flora observed the now familiar look he gave when he felt conflicted and was ruminating over what he could and should say. "There is of course, a rather particular reason why I asked you specifically to help me in this matter," he continued.

Flora held her breath.

"Whilst I of course respect you as a hard-working woman, Mrs MacKinnon, my main reason for asking you, and you only, to keep the house, is strictly between us." He drummed his fingers on the table and with his other hand scratched at the back of his neck. He seemed utterly terrified of what he needed to say. "Lately," his voice wavered, "I have observed a certain young woman we are both acquainted with, both up on the hill and outside my lodging." He hesitated before continuing. "Over the past few nights, I have kept my door open to allow her to sleep in the byre, purely out of concern for her safety and to provide her with decent shelter you understand." His voice regained its self-assured tone. "So, you see, I cannot allow anyone else in the house but you. You are the only person here who I trust with this knowledge, as I have been increasingly concerned of what others may do to her if she were to be found. I have seen . . ."

He trailed off. Flora had sat listening breathlessly to his revelation, and the feeling of unease in the pit of her stomach transformed into overwhelming elation. She felt dizzy; disorientated. In a sudden motion she bolted from her chair and kneeling at the Reverend's feet, grasped his hands and lay her head on his lap, almost laughing with the purest joy she had felt in years. Sensing the Reverend's unease and discomfort, she sprang from his lap, and correcting the chair she had tipped over, sat back down. To her growing jubilation she found she could not stop herself from smiling.

"Oh, Reverend," she gushed, once the room had stopped spinning, "I cannot tell you how relieved I am to hear that. I have been so worried about her . . . Of course, I will come here and help take care of the place. I'll make the byre ever so comfortable for the poor child. I can barely wait to see her..."

"I really do have to warn you," he interrupted, "we must be extra vigilant so that nobody else learns of this. Only you and I can know. You must understand that this is strictly for her safety, and as soon as the tacksman returns she must go with him. She cannot keep hidden forever, and we must hope that we can avoid her being discovered over the next few months. You must not let your emotions get the better of you, Mrs MacKinnon. We cannot afford to alarm her, or risk being caught."

Tempering herself, Flora reflected on how the girl's skittishness had torn her from safety the last time she had been under her protection.

"I understand, Reverend," she said, meeting his eyes in what she hoped would be an adequate gesture of her sincerity. "I won't tell a soul, and rest assured if I see her here, I will not do anything to risk her safety."

"Good. Then it's settled." There was an edge to his voice, and Flora recognised that he was not fully assured. She hoped she would prove him wrong.

For what remained of the morning, she swept and replaced the rushes on the floor while he sat quietly contemplating his books. She ventured out to the storehouse to replace the peat on the hearth and ensured that it would provide substantial fuel for the fire before she readied herself for departure, promising that she would return in the evening to prepare a decent supper. Rising from his seat, he thanked her, and to Flora's surprise took one of her hands gently into his own.

"Before you go, I just wanted to say that I am sorry for the loss of your grandchild."

Flora was touched.

"Thank you, Reverend. It happens. Better for Ann that the baby departed early and did not linger for a few days. Those are always worse..."

The Reverend's hands slipped suddenly from hers, as if stung. Flora raised her eyes to meet his and saw to her horror that they seemed to be suppressing tears.

"I'm sorry. I had not meant to . . ." her words faded, and she allowed him a brief moment to compose himself; to once more assume the solemn, dignified expression and posture she had become so accustomed to.

"Do not concern yourself over me," he said, taking a breath. "It is only that around a year or so ago I lost a child of my own under quite similar circumstances."

"I'm so sorry."

"No one has anything to be sorry for. God willed it." He looked faraway, wrapped in memories too difficult to fully express. "My wife had been with child many times before, but had never managed to carry one to full term. This one was different. She almost made it through to her lying in when the pains came on her too early. The child was born alive, but small and feeble. A boy."

Flora placed her hand on his arm in a gesture of sympathy, but he barely seemed to register her presence anymore.

"He lingered a day and a half. He was to be called William, same as my father. I'd never seen Caroline so happy, until she wasn't, and then I'd never seen her so heartbroken." He frowned, his brow furrowing over his next words. "The worst part is, I don't remember feeling anything at all. No sorrow. Not over the child, anyway. I only remember how she changed from that day . . ."

Flora placed her hand on his shoulder, willing him to meet her gaze. He flinched from her touch but met her eyes.

"I understand," Flora said, drawing her hand back.

She felt the threads between them tighten. She had no choice; not to keep the trust of this man could undo the knots in the net she weaved beneath herself, plunging them all back into the depths.

CHAPTER SEVENTEEN

THOMAS

MURRAY hoped he could trust Flora MacKinnon. As the woman cheerfully busied herself preparing a puffin for supper, she hummed a lively melody, her mood buoyed completely by the secret he had shared with her. Now it was their secret, and the notion greatly unnerved him. After much contemplation, Murray realised he had had no choice; it was both unfeasible and improper that he should be the girl's sole guardian, and without someone from the community to assist him, he highly doubted the young woman's presence could have remained hidden for much longer. Still, Ailith McQueen's warnings rang in his ear, and despite his reassertions of rationality, he was nervous allowing this strange creature into his abode. But he needed her here. She could give him the evidence he needed to elevate his position beyond anything that his detractors would ever have thought possible. It would take time, he knew, a little gentle prying here and there. With patience, he would extract the truth from her one way or another.

As the acrid scent of the bird pervaded the air, Murray found himself surprisingly eager for this barely adequate supper. He had grown used to the strong taste and fatty texture of seabird meat, and though he still wished for a leg of mutton, this meal would no doubt provide far more sustenance than the scraps of salty, dried fish he had been relying on for almost a month. Flora was preparing a meal for three. He had cautioned her that the girl had not yet appeared before darkness began descending, and for Flora to hope that they would somehow be reunited was incredibly optimistic.

Still, the woman seemed to be lingering for as long as possible over the meal. The notion that all three of them could sit down for a shared supper, sat in polite discourse like relatives gathering after Sunday service was, to Murray's mind, quite frankly absurd. In fact, he shuddered at the thought.

He hoped that the old woman would leave soon and kept gently reminding her of her own obligations by verbally admonishing himself for keeping her away from her husband. Flora seemed unperturbed. There was an air of excited tension about her, as if she were a cat sat expectantly by a crack in the wainscot, patiently waiting for a mouse to appear. It was profoundly disturbing.

Murray planned that as soon as the woman had departed, he would place a plate of food in the byre, next to the deftly arranged woollen sheets Flora had draped over a mound of fresh straw retrieved from the storehouse. As he contemplated this, there was a light tug at his sleeve.

"It's almost ready. Would you prefer me to serve it now, or should we wait a little longer?"

Flora hovered eagerly at his shoulder, her eyes wide and expectant. Murray had always found it difficult to be fully present around excess female emotion, and under the circumstances it seemed unwise to allow the woman to linger and build up her anticipation until it boiled over. Moreover, he was uncomfortable with how he himself had let his guard down around her earlier in the morning. It still unnerved him to know how vulnerable she made him.

"I would much prefer to eat now, Mrs MacKinnon," he replied, shifting in his seat. "I do think you should get back to your husband soon. I expect he will worry if you do not return before dusk."

"Oh, he will be fine; he has his supper. I am far happier waiting to see if I can help in any way when . . ."

"I fear you would be wasting your time," he snapped.

Flora took a step backwards and he immediately regretted the brusqueness of his tone. He needed this ally. "I only meant that I cannot guarantee she will be here. I cannot keep her locked in, so to speak, so we must allow her to come and go as she pleases. Having you here is simply a precautionary measure, you understand?"

"I understand," Flora mumbled her reply, her eyes downcast like a chastised child.

Murray softened his tone. "If we are to keep this between us, we will need to be discreet. If you should linger too long there is bound to be yet more talk. We have a few more months at the very least before we can take further action, so we must avoid suspicion as much as we possibly can."

No doubt reassured to be part of this wretched conspiracy, Flora's body untensed and she offered him a wan smile. She returned to her labours, scooping greasy stew from the pot hanging over the fire and slopping it onto plates.

They ate in silence. He felt uneasy the entire time, and it did not help when Flora's eyes twitched towards the byre door, her eagerness enhancing his trepidation so that each mouthful of food became increasingly difficult to swallow. After their uncomfortable meal Flora left briefly to scour the plates in the water barrel outside. In this merciful interim he pored over his books in the hope that this would settle him.

When Flora returned, her mood seemed to have lifted.

"I will leave you to your labours now, Reverend, and I'll return in the morning." She spoke in an almost cheerful tone. However it had manifested, he was grateful for her imminent departure. Flora hurried to gather her basket and shawl, before bustling out into the evening air, leaving him alone to contemplate what came next. On the table opposite him a plate of stew lay congealing, the top layer forming a skin.

Murray tried to shake himself from his apprehension. It was ridiculous that this young woman should unease him so, and now that he had alerted another to her presence, there was no hint of indiscretion about such an arrangement. When and if the girl appeared, he would simply offer her food, and attempt to make her aware of their plans. He reminded himself that this was an act of mercy as well as necessity.

As darkness began to seep into the blackhouse, he forced himself into his usual night-time routine. Studying Knox for the umpteenth time, he found the words blurred across the page as his mind wandered elsewhere. Casting the book aside, he went to his father's chest and retrieved a fresh sheet of parchment, as well as quill and ink. If he could not focus on the words of others, perhaps he could channel his frustrations into drafting a letter to the diocese, relating his predecessor's transgressions. His quill hovered over the parchment for some time.

In a brief opening of inspiration, he placed his quill into the inkpot and began to write.

The creak of the door left a pooling blot where his first words should have been. Smearing his elbow in ink, he crumpled up the page and retreated to perch on his bed, out of sight of the entrance. The clawing in the pit of his stomach returned. He assured himself that he was being absurd, and that this churning feeling was simply due to the unpleasant diet he was forced to keep. Summoning his dignity, he took up the plate of stew and turned towards the byre.

His body jolted when he saw that she was watching him. She stood, peering around the wooden partition, her eyes fixed on him and her expression unfathomable. Ignoring the thrumming in his chest, he straightened and corrected himself. Seeing her up close, he observed how her lank hair hung in clumps over her shoulders; how her clothes and exposed forearms were caked with dried mud. Unnerved by the silence hovering between them, he gestured clumsily towards the plate of now gelatinous stew on the table.

"Would you care for something to eat?" His voice shook, and he felt suddenly foolish for speaking to someone of such primitive appearance in such a formal manner. Another part of him was embarrassed at being judged by those probing, grey eyes.

The young woman took a step closer. Eying the food on the table, she turned to him like a child asking for permission. He tentatively stepped aside, nodding his assent, and she lunged towards the table.

Pulling out a chair, she set upon the food, scooping it eagerly into her mouth with disgusting abandon. Murray sat opposite her. He watched, repulsed yet fascinated, as she sucked the grease from her fingers and slurped at the juices which trickled down her chin.

Murray tried not to wrinkle his nose as the smell of her became more apparent; after weeks of having nothing but the rain to wash herself with her skin omitted a sour aroma which caught at the back of the throat. She was close enough for him to reach out and touch her, and he could easily dissect every small detail of her wasted appearance. He could observe the dark half-moons of dirt under her fingernails; the pink line around her shoulders where her skin had been burned by the sun; the way the light of the lantern highlighted the delicate, little hairs which stood up on her neck. Murray looked away, ashamed.

Glancing up from her food, the girl reached across the table. At first, he flinched away, but chastised himself when he saw the outstretched spoon in her hand.

Her lips curved upwards.

He shook his head at her offering, and she quickly resumed her hasty consumption of the meal. When she had devoured all that remained, she sat back and calmly took in her surroundings, her eyes eventually falling upon him.

He cleared his throat. "I don't think you're a simpleton, you know," he began.

Her eyes widened.

"You may not speak, but I have no doubt you understand me perfectly well."

Easing herself forward, she placed her elbows on the table, her head resting on her hands in rapt attention, as if keen to illustrate his point to him.

"You and I . . ." he chose his next words very carefully, "given time I hope we may become friends. Perhaps you will learn to trust me? I am on your side, so you may tell me anything and I shall not use it against you." He observed the young woman shift in her seat, so he swiftly decided to change tack. "You no doubt understand that you cannot stay on this island. We must keep you safe until there is an opportunity for you to leave." He tried to keep his words as simple and concise as possible, but the young woman did not seem confused. She seemed to pause and think a moment, before, to his relief, she gave a slight nod.

"You will be in danger if you stay here." Pausing, he thought back to the incident on the beach with the strange seabird. He forced the image from his mind. "There is only me and one other who know that you are here, and that is the way it must stay. There will be an opportunity in a few months for you to leave; until then you must be as . . ." Murray searched for the right words, ". . . discreet as possible. Do you understand?"

She nodded her head, this time in a clear, affirmative gesture.

"I do not expect you to stay locked away until the end of summer, but if you do go outside, you must stay away from the bay and the village. Cover your head and avoid people whenever you can . . . Although, to be fair, you seem to have done a rather good job of that so far . . ."

She looked upwards at him through her dense eyelashes and smiled wryly. He felt his body tighten. He clenched his fists against his knees, quickly shaking off the feeling before proceeding.

"You are of course, still welcome to eat and sleep here. Flora MacKinnon, the woman you stayed with last time, is the only other who knows you are here. She cooked your food this evening and she will be the only other person to come and go. You can trust her; I have no doubt whatsoever that she won't breathe a word of this arrangement to anyone else."

Her face had fallen into a frown, and her fingers scratched nervously at the tabletop.

"You do not need to fear Flora. She has your best interests at heart, I assure you."

She ceased her scratching and again stared openly at him. The skin on his forearms prickled and his cheeks glowed.

"A bed has been made up for you, should you want to . . ." His voice trailed off as he watched the young woman's attention drift elsewhere.

She was looking to a spot above their heads, and as he followed her gaze his eyes fell on the simple, wooden cross he had affixed to the wall. When he looked back to her, he saw how her mouth parted in seeming adulation.

"Do you wish . . . would you like to pray with me?"

Studying him, she copied his motions as he knelt and clasped his hands. He tried to focus all his attention on his prayers but grew painfully aware of the sinful pride he took when she repeated each of his gestures of devotion. Although she omitted no sound, her lips moved in time with his. He felt a strange stirring of blasphemy in the air, for if this woman truly was of such evil intent and origins, he should not be allowing her to do this. Allowing her to mirror his actions was absurd, conflicting and yet strangely tempting. He had a horrifying realisation that his part of his unease was from a desire to reach out and touch her; touch her in all her bedraggled beauty to feel if she were made of warm flesh or see if she would pool coldly against his fingertips and shift her liquid form to swallow him whole.

Culminating his worship with a fervent amen, Murray rose, and the girl shuffled backwards. She smiled up at him, the fire casting a flickering dance of light and shadows across her face. Stepping back, he eased himself away from her.

"I plan to retire soon." He said it in the hope she would retreat to the byre, allowing him to be away from her eager, searching eyes.

Her smile widened and she rose. With small steps backwards, she moved silently across the room and eased herself into his bed. She held his gaze, and tucking her feet beneath her, she began deftly unpinning her mud stiffened earasaid.

For a moment he froze with horror, then lurching forward he

grabbed at her wrist and lowered it to her side. They both hung in a strange tableau.

He became aware of the searing of her flesh where their skin touched. Was it terror or craving he felt? He quickly pulled away from her and clasped his hand to his side.

"This is my bed." He tried to sound firm, but his voice wavered. "Flora MacKinnon has prepared a space for you in the byre. Do you understand?"

She looked at him intently, frowning slightly. Slowly, she eased herself to her feet. Surely she was not so ignorant as to not be embarrassed by her conduct, but he could not decide if this would make her actions better or worse.

She offered him a parting look before she slunk away. Raising a finger, she pointed towards the now empty plate of food, then laid a hand across her abdomen and smiled wanly in an expression of simple appreciation. He nodded towards her; his words stuck in his throat.

Later, when he tried to retire, he noticed the dampness of his sheets, and the briny smell which clung to them.

※

Sleep that night was impossible, so Murray lay unplagued by dreams. Nevertheless, his thoughts drifted back to his parish in Inverness and recollections of past sermons resurfaced from his conscience.

He saw a young woman, propped up on a stool by the alter, sobbing hysterically whilst her mother attempted to comfort her. The mother shot a hateful look towards the man standing at the frontmost pew, whom Murray was railing against from the pulpit. The youth kept his face to the floor. Every eye in the church fixed on him in condemnation, while Murray directed a tirade against the sin of fornication. The young man's parents sat behind their son, their faces also downcast from shame and mortification. Murray remembered the whole process feeling surprisingly easy at the time.

For ten Sundays, he had delivered the public rebuke, and received a hail of praise for his steadfast and powerful delivery of each sermon. He had been proud; sinfully so. He was courting Caroline at the time, and the exhilaration brought about by her admiration had made him bolder in his pursuit.

Afterwards, there was rarely a cause to deliver a rebuke again. It seemed the whole congregation became more steadfast in their commitment to God, not daring to face the wrath of their new Reverend.

But now he found himself in a community who deemed themselves beyond rebuke, and he himself felt borne along with them, thrashing in vain against the merciless current.

CHAPTER EIGHTEEN

FLORA

FLORA could not relieve the tension which was building up inside her. Afraid that in her nervous excitement she would give herself away, she occupied herself with solitary tasks, excusing herself from the backbreaking work of cutting peat with the others to pluck sea whelks from the harbour wall. The ruse seemed to have worked. After the paltry harvest of the past few weeks, nobody questioned the urge to gather what remained of the little food left to be salvaged.

The previous evening had been difficult. As much as she tried to suppress her feelings, her desire to see the girl had only been briefly abated once she left the Reverend's house to wash his plates. That was when she had seen her. The girl had hovered briefly by the stone outhouse, frozen still and watching Flora intently. In a flurry of excitement, Flora had made the regrettable mistake of going back inside to collect her basket and shawl before departing, only to find that as she left the house again, the girl had vanished from sight. She had scoured the hillside to no avail, returning home heavy hearted. As she contemplated the brief encounter, she desperately hoped that she had not scared to poor girl away again, and decided she must check in with the Reverend as soon as possible to assure herself that this was not the case.

Slowly straightening her aching back, Flora waded back towards the sandy bay. The whelks in her skirt pockets clacked gratifyingly against her thigh. Janet and Malcolm were playing by the shoreline, making unsuccessful attempts to skim stones across the breakers while Morag snapped at their heels, desperate for attention. Flora called out a greeting.

The children froze. Malcolm stood, almost comically, with one chubby fist in mid-air enclosed around a pebble, his mouth agape. Suddenly the stone fell from his fist, causing Morag to yelp as it narrowly missed her head. Turning away, Malcolm sprinted across the sands, his tiny feet pumping the air as he ran. Janet stood and stared, but made no attempt to approach her grandmother.

Flora's felt a fluttering in her chest. Attempting to smile, she approached the girl with a small offering of whelks in the palm of her hand.

"How would you like a wee treat, *m'eudail?*" she asked warmly. "I remember how much you used to love these when you were your brother's age. Why don't we find something to pick at them and cook them at grandpa's house?"

Janet chewed her lip and glanced nervously over her shoulder.

"Ma says we shouldn't talk to you . . ." she mumbled.

The fluttering in Flora's chest became a heavy, plummeting feeling. She had hoped that Ann would have softened during her slow recovery, and she had certainly hoped that Michael would have spoken firmly to his wife in defence of his mother.

Janet must have sensed her grandmother's sentiments, for in the stretching silence between them she turned on her heel and ran in pursuit of her younger brother. The only being that remained was Morag, who wagged her tail eagerly and pushed her nose up against Flora's skirts in supplication. Flora pushed the creature away and set off resolutely towards the Reverend's house. As she walked past village wall, the grey clouds which were smeared across the blue summer sky erupted into a heavy downpour which saturated the ground. Flora welcomed it.

To her relief, the Reverend was still at home, not having yet departed to attend the morning meeting or supervise the men rebuilding the chapel walls. As he opened the door to her, she noticed that the byre had indeed been slept in the previous night.

The Reverend ushered her through to the living space. He seemed exhausted. Tender, darkened skin had formed under his eyes. His shoulders, usually pulled tautly behind him by the restrictive, mainland cut of his clothes, sagged, his arms falling limply to his sides.

"Do you wish me to come back later, Reverend?" Flora eyed him with concern as she began to sweep the old rushes from the floor. He sat himself by the table, his head balanced precariously by one hand, the other of which traced the strange scratches and squiggles which lined the pieces of parchment in front of him. He looked up blearily.

"No, Mrs MacKinnon, you can stay," he rattled, his voice clearing. "I must go and see to the chapel. Before I go though, I need to raise a rather delicate issue with you. A favour if you will."

Flora waited eagerly for clarification. More than ever, she desired a more active role in their shared endeavour, as to her dismay it seemed that her own family were drifting further from her, relegating her to a mere spectator in their grief and toil.

"When you return this evening," the Reverend explained slowly, "I would like you to set out fresh clothes and set out some warm water for bathing."

"Of course, Reverend."

"Not for myself, you understand."

"Oh." Flora tempered herself. "I see . . ."

"When our visitor was eating last night, I noticed that she was in a rather unpleasant condition. This is not a dignified position for a young lady to be in, so I had hoped you could attend her just for this evening; make some excuses for your slightly prolonged stay . . ."

"You can trust in me, Reverend."

The Reverend paused and quickly scanned her face before proceeding. Flora caught the searching look, even if he had intended otherwise.

"I will of course, remove myself for a walk while you attend to her. It would not be seemly for me to stay." He cleared his throat and awaited her reply.

"I will be here."

"Good." He began to shrug on his constrictive jacket. "I shall see you tonight. Perhaps a little later than usual?"

She smiled and nodded her head assuredly as he donned his hat. Leaving the blackhouse, the Reverend clumsily allowed the door the swing shut behind him, leaving Flora alone to her tasks. She cleared the musty smelling rushes and filth from the blackhouse floor and set out to retrieve fresh ones. As she left, the damp air hit her and clung to her face, the heavy shower having settled into a fine, gossamer web of mist.

She would tell John that she would be attending the Reverend later this evening, on account of him being delayed from overseeing the chapel. She doubted he would even notice. Since Ann's misfortune he had drifted even further away from her and seemed caught within his own thoughts whenever they were home together. Most of the time he would watch her concernedly, and in bed he would do no more than let his arm fall over her, seeking her out and hugging her to him as if afraid she was no longer there. Flora was thankful for the temporary reprieve from scrutiny. She had no doubt that John would shake free of this sullen spell in time, as he had so often done in the past.

She breathed in the coolness of the morning. Her spirits buoyed with anticipation as she walked into the haze.

※

"I am going to the Reverend's now, John!" Flora called over her shoulder, pinning the heavy wool of her shawls into place. Under her arm she carried a bundle of clothes, carefully concealed beneath the folds of her earasaid, while in her other hand dangled a large bucket.

John did not even glance up at her and continued to pick at his meagre meal.

"Did you hear me earlier, Flora?" Still, he did not look up.

Flora held back, masking her frustration. She was in no place to handle one of her husband's interrogations tonight.

"About the poor bird harvest?" she asked. "It's probably just the bad weather, John. You know how things get during these kinds of summers; it's hardly surprising there aren't as many chicks this season with these winds blowing the way they have been. Things will improve."

"We're going back out to the stacks."

Flora's breath caught. ". . . the stacks?"

"Aye. I told you earlier." John's eyes finally met hers. "It was decided at the meeting this morning."

"When?"

"As soon as possible."

Flora floundered around for the right words. "Well," she began, "I'm sure things can only improve then. Soon we'll have plenty of meat and it will barely even matter that the crops have been so poor this year."

"Is that all you have to say about it?"

"What more do you want me to say?"

John turned back to his food, dismissing Flora with a wave of the hand. "You best be heading off to that priest of yours. Make sure he pays you money up front this time."

Flora paused on the threshold, but thinking better than to encourage further discussion, she left. Tracing her steps back towards the Reverend's croft, she felt a growing disquiet. She shook it off, determined that John's melancholy would not distract her from the task at hand, certain that any worries about food supplies would be short lived and unfounded. They had been through far worse times after all.

Arriving at the Reverend's door, she took a deep breath before knocking, and she wondered whether the girl had already arrived. The Reverend greeted her at the door, nursing a plate of leftover stew from yesterday.

"She is here," he said. "I have set out food for her."

Flora entered, her breath quivering: she worried that her sudden presence would cause the girl to flee again.

"I have told her you are coming," the Reverend said, watching as she stood hesitantly by the entrance of the byre.

The room smelled fresher as Flora entered and observed with pride her work from earlier that morning. The air mingling with the peat smoke was crisp and clean, allowing her body, if not her thoughts, to relax as she entered the living space.

A small cry caught in her throat as she noticed the girl mutely watching her from the table, her eyes searching Flora over questioningly. The girl's habit of total stillness seemed to make her manifest from nowhere. There was a long, expectant pause before the Reverend cleared his throat and announced his intention to leave, seemingly unaware of the tension which gathered thickly in the space between the two women.

"I will be back before dark."

Flora observed how eager he was to leave. To her surprise, she also noticed the girl casting him an accusatory look, her brow creased and her fingernails worrying at the tabletop. The Reverend avoided the girl's gaze and Flora felt her anxiety deepen. Although she trusted the Reverend, it was without doubt that he was a man of integrity, she had a fleeting thought which greatly disturbed her. She watched the girl's eyes follow him out of the blackhouse, her hands tautly gripping the chair she sat in as if she were having to pull herself back from running after him. Flora tried to dismiss the feeling. It was only natural that the girl would seek out greater protection than that which an enfeebled, old woman could provide. As the door slammed shut, the girl returned to her plate of half-eaten food, pushing the remnants around with her spoon like a sullen child.

"Well." Flora forced a smile. "We have some nice, clean clothes for you here. I suppose I should heat some water so we can scrub some of that dirt from you."

The girl did not respond. Flora, unperturbed, set about collecting rainwater from the barrel outside, before returning to warm it by the hearth. As she did so, she continued her one-sided chatter, partly to calm herself and partly in the hope that it would ease the girl's caginess.

Testing the water with a finger, Flora motioned to the girl that it was ready for her. The girl shuffled forward in her chair and looked down at the water mistrustingly.

"It's all right." Flora splashed the water playfully, then plunged her arm into it, knocking at the base of the bucket to demonstrate its shallow depth. "It's only to wash with. You're in no danger from the water here."

Clutching at her wrist, the girl looked up. Flora smiled encouragingly. Slowly, the girl eased herself forward and with small, halting steps approached the hearth; with a hesitant hand, she reached out and held her palm over the surface of the water, moving it gently back and forth before gently submerging it.

"See?" Flora said reassuringly. "It's lovely and warm, isn't it?"

Having suitably calmed herself, the girl began to unpin her muck stiffened earasaid. Dry, claylike shards scattered across the floor. Perhaps replacing the rushes should have waited an extra day, Flora thought with a sigh. The girl paused as she held her clothing up around her shoulders and frowned at Flora. There was a thinly disguised warning in her eyes.

Understanding the girl's message, Flora turned to face the opposite way, fixing her eyes on the wooden cross which hung from the wall. She heard the heavy sound of cloth falling to the floor and the tentative rippling of water. Flora could hear the girl gently splash water onto herself, trickles of which began to seep onto the floor beneath her feet.

Flora wanted to steal a look. She needed to see if the mark on the girl's arm was still there

Trying to appear distracted, Flora made an appearance of clearing the table. Sinking her head low, she moved past the girl, plates stacked in her hands to be taken outside to wash. Lingering by the byre, she stole a fleeting glance over her shoulder.

The girl's skin was still as pale as she remembered but had acquired a greater softness and roundness; gone were the harsh angles and jutting bones which she had seen before. The mark was still in place: a small, maroon crescent blossoming on her underarm.

Flora crossed the room and picked up the swathe of dirty wool which had fallen from the girl's body. She took it outside and beat at it by the narrow stream which ran down from the hill, scrubbing the rough weave until it yielded grey swirls into the frothing water. Roughly shaking the material dry, Flora paused as a handful of stones and black bird feathers fell from the heavy folds of material to the grass at her feet. She examined this strange pile of tokens, trying to shake off the chill which greeted her when she remembered the little hands which had grasped at rounded pebbles, seashells, and feathers in infantile glee, stuffing these childish treasures into her mother's basket when she thought she was not looking.

❧

As Flora re-entered the blackhouse, the girl had finished washing and dressed herself in her new clothes. She was wringing her long, tatted hair out over the bucket. Flora watched as the droplets trickled down and fell into the grey, swirling water. The girl appeared more relaxed than when she had left her. She looked up at Flora, and loosely gathering a soft fold of wool between her fingers, she smiled broadly. Flora inclined her head slightly in acknowledgement of this expression of appreciation and hoped the girl could not see that her hands were shaking.

As she began stacking the clean dishes on the table, she peered slyly over her shoulder once again. The girl's hair was thick and black as ash, just as hers had once been. There was surely no evil in the child, but surely Flora's nagging hope of her being more than a stranger to her could not be true. Flora felt an unusual pressure building up behind her eyes and, alarmed, rubbed away the tears before they even had a chance to fall.

Behind her, Flora heard the girl let out a low grunt. Turning, she saw her trying to prise the knots from a hank of hair with her fingers, her mouth a thin line and her eyes watering from the effort.

"Here." Flora approached cautiously, her hand retrieving the bone comb from her skirt pocket. The girl did not hesitate to take it.

"You should let me," Flora said, feeling emboldened. "If you hold your hair, it will be easier and less painful."

The girl's eyes slowly searched Flora's face. Seemingly satisfied, she sheepishly handed back the comb.

Flora slowly teased out the tangles from the roots, working her way down the long, dense strands, the girl only occasionally wincing. Flora felt the damp weight of the girl's hair with immense pleasure, her fingers gently caressing coarse tendrils, close enough that she could take in the heady scent of it; it smelled of rain on lichen. She remembered the same process from fifteen years ago. She thought back to the times her daughter had been perched on her lap and afterwards had nuzzled into her mother's bosom, any hurt from snagged hair forgotten. Flora took a strand from near the girl's face, her hand slightly brushing against the softness of her ear. The girl flinched and pulled away. Unlike her child, this young woman cringed away from her touch.

"I'm sorry."

The girl nodded, but shyly held out her hand to retrieve the comb. Flora obliged and sat down opposite her.

"Keep it."

The girl looked surprised and motioned towards herself.

"It's yours," Flora nodded. "I have my own at home."

The girl's body and face relaxed as she moved herself closer to the fire and Flora; a brief flicker of a smile manifested briefly then disappeared like a ghost. Seizing the opportunity, Flora thought of all the questions she wanted to ask.

"Do you remember your name? I would like to call you by something."

The girl shook her head, not looking up as she carefully fondled the bone comb in her hands, gently rubbing its smooth surface.

"Well . . . I wondered if you would mind me calling you something. Perhaps I could call you Agnes? It was my daughter's name, you see, and you have such beautiful hair, just like her."

The girl looked up and cocked her head. She mouthed the name to herself and seemed to contemplate deeply, experimenting with the way her tongue and lips wrapped around the word. Returning her gaze to Flora, she gave an assenting nod.

Flora beamed.

Agnes returned her gaze to the comb in her lap, and Flora grew braver.

"Why did you run away from me?" she queried quietly. "You should have known I would not harm you."

The girl looked up, her grey eyes bulging. After a long silence she shrugged her shoulders weakly, returning her gaze to the fire.

"You know it was me who rescued you?"

Agnes frowned. With a quizzical look, she gestured towards the cross hanging from the wall. Flora took a while to decipher her meaning.

"The Reverend came later," she said. "I was the one who found you. Don't you remember?"

Agnes did not respond, but her frown deepened as she returned to examining the glowing embers of the hearth. The fire hissed.

"What happened to you, *m'eudail*? How did you come to be here?" Flora asked the question gently. She wanted to take the girl in her arms and hold her, and she longed for the answer which would allow her to do so once more. Whatever had happened, however impossible it seemed, she needed to hear it. Whatever miraculous act of mercy had preserved this girl, she had to know, even if it seemed unbelievable to others. Any answer would suffice if it could somehow bring her child back.

The girl stared at her and tears began forming in her eyes. Flora reached for her, but she pulled away again, weeping and shaking, rocking herself, her arms wrapped tightly around her body.

"Do you remember, *mo cridhe*? Do you remember anything?"

Agnes' eyes glistened in the dimming light, her fingers rubbing at the fibres of her fresh clothes.

Flora waited, barely breathing.

The girl shook her head, her eyes still staring resolutely into the fire.

Flora opened her mouth to speak, but before she could find the words, she was interrupted by the door creaking open, and the sound of the Reverend's tentative footsteps approaching through the byre. The girl quickly rubbed the tears from her face and Flora stood up, preparing reluctantly to leave.

"I will leave Agnes in your capable hands, Reverend."

"Agnes?"

"Yes. That is her name."

The Reverend eyed her suspiciously but did not question her further.

Before she left, she ensured the byre was comfortably arranged with fresh bedding and blankets. As she departed the girl was beginning to bed down for the night. Slowly closing the door behind her, she caught a last glimpse of the girl's curled up form; her hair fell softly over her cheek, and beneath those thick curtains, Flora caught the unmistakable glimmer of fresh tears.

※

When Flora returned, John was already in bed. He sat up, waiting for her, his expression sombre. Flora began to undress, preparing herself for an admonishment for her poor timekeeping, or for once more forgetting to collect the money which had been promised to her for her services. To her relief he remained silent, waiting for her to ease herself into the tight bed space they shared. Tucking herself under the covers, she lay her head down, hoping that if she appeared tired, she would avoid any potential confrontation.

"Fergus visited earlier."

Flora sat bolt upright.

". . . is it the baby?" She turned to John, wide eyed.

John did not return her gaze, but instead settled himself down, facing the wall.

"The baby's fine. It's Mary: she has the sickness."

CHAPTER NINETEEN

THOMAS

"If we go too soon, we'll have nothing left to ration come the winter..."

"And if we don't go now, we'll all be starving before winter even gets here."

"It has already been decided." Donald Gillies' voice cut decisively through the male clamour. "We depart in two days' time. At first light. That gives us enough time to patch up the boats and strengthen the ropes."

As usual, Murray hung back from the circle. He had made a substantial effort to be present for each of these morning parliaments, but rarely was his presence given much consideration. His requests for more work to be done on the chapel had failed miserably, and now the ramshackle building existed in a disused, roofless limbo, the weather once more seeping into the bones of the building and threatening to reduce it once more to a mouldering pile of rubble. He knew that resurrecting the building's cause was futile. Food supplies were dangerously low, and since Ailith McQueen's death there had been a steady increase of illness blighting the islanders, although so far only striking down women and infants. Now there was a desperate tone to this normally stoic meeting of men. Members drifted away from the group to care for their sick loved ones, while those that remained started to bicker amongst each other, no-one fully committing to the other's plan of action until either Donald or John MacKinnon held court.

"If the weather turns again, then we wait until it clears," Donald continued, responding to another panicked protestation from one of the younger men. "But otherwise, we go, and that's my final word on the matter." He turned to his companion. "John?"

The elder MacKinnon had said very little. Murray had avoided meeting the man's eyes, which throughout the meeting had maintained a steely contact with his own. He felt as if he were a specimen being pinned against the anatomist's table, layers of flesh slowly being peeled away.

"As you all know, my boy Fergus' wife is sick, which is why he would not attend the meeting today."

There were a few conciliatory looks exchanged before MacKinnon continued.

"You all know my opinion on the matter: we have to act. The food from the land is not sustaining them, so the sooner we can get to the stacks, the better."

Some men looked solemnly into their laps, but most mumbled their reluctant assent.

"I am however," MacKinnon began, patiently waiting for silence, "I am however interested to hear what our esteemed Reverend has to say about the matter, he of course being the only man amongst us with neither a woman nor child of his own to look after."

Murray dug his nails into his palms, and there was a barely suppressed snigger from some of the younger men as they turned to observe him. John MacKinnon's eyes continued to bore into him. With a creeping dread, he wondered how much the man could know. He felt a growing heat spreading up the sides of his face to the tips of his ears, but sat upright, attempting to weaponise his superior stature.

"I think that given the circumstances, what you propose is the best course of action for the present."

There was a smattering of surprised voices, and he tried not to appear smug as he saw their expectations of him wither. No doubt they had prepared themselves for another lecture on the rashness of their actions.

"And what will you do while we're out there, risking our hides?" MacKinnon's stare was fierce and relentless. "Stay here with the women?"

The younger men hooted with unrepressed laughter. Even Donald Gillies, with his stern face and weathered brow, had to look down at the ground and could not prevent his broad shoulders from shaking.

"Actually, sir, I see no reason for not coming with you."

As quickly as the cacophony of humiliation had started, it fell into a deep silence. All eyes were now upon him. Murray tried to keep the horrified realisation of what he had just said from showing on his face.

What could possibly have compelled him to make such proposition? Yes, he was tired of being mocked and ridiculed, but surely not enough to disregard his life in such flippant fashion. He could try to convince himself it was to finally gain the men's respect, but he knew that at this point any reverence from these cruel, hardened people meant extraordinarily little to him. He prided himself that his reasoning was to build himself back up in his own esteem. Of course, it had nothing at all to do with escaping the visitor concealed within his lodgings. It could be nothing to do with the confused feelings of fear and longing he felt for this strange woman. Those feelings were not rational, and therefore were not worthy of acknowledgement.

He looked squarely at John MacKinnon and was relieved to see the look of condemnation had changed to one of bafflement.

"I don't see why you would be surprised, sirs," Murray addressed them all. "I am young enough and fit enough. I'm also the son of a soldier, and as such I won't balk at danger if it's necessary." Internally, he congratulated himself for maintaining his composure amidst his body's roiling protestations.

"Well," Donald Gillies began, "I dare say we are all are surprised, Reverend, but I hope you know what you're getting into. Out there, we will not tolerate anyone slowing us down or putting us in danger." He adopted a serious tone. "Understand this, if you go out there with us, we won't be risking our lives to throw a rope over the side and rescue you if you slip, or if you're swept away from the boats."

The small group of younger men eyed him eagerly, sneering as they barely suppressed their amusement at the premise of him injuring himself, or worse. For a moment, he felt strangely fearless: the reality of what he had set himself up for did not seem real, and all that remained within him was a strange kind of determination. It was not quite bravery, that would be absurd, but an inconsequential regard for his personal safety; a looming chasm which he stared down into, daringly raising an ankle without committing to the next step forward.

"I understand what I am doing, Mr Gillies. Rest assured I will offer what I can."

Donald Gillies sucked the air in through his teeth. "It is decided, then. Two days' time, weather depending."

The men began to drift apart, some to tend to their families and others to prepare their boats. Before John MacKinnon could leave, Murray grabbed him by the shoulder.

"Have I done something to offend you, Mr MacKinnon?" he asked bluntly.

MacKinnon's brow creased.

"I'm no fool. Whatever scheme you have planned, you can keep my wife out of it," MacKinnon replied, prodding a finger into Murray's chest. "And you can pay us the money she's still owed."

"Rest assured, sir, if I were the type to scheme, there would be nothing shameful about any of it." He tried to keep his voice steady, but inside he felt even more rattled than when he had proposed to haul himself up a five-hundred-foot-high sea stack. "As for your wife's pay, you can rest assured she will receive what she is owed in full the next time I see her."

"She'll not be going to your house today," John MacKinnon responded quickly. "As you heard, our Mary is sick, so Flora will not be attending to anyone else. You can pay the money directly to me."

Fishing around in the bottom of his coat pockets, Murray managed to summon enough coinage to satisfy the old man for the time being, who stood clumsily pawing at the little metal discs in a pathetic charade, pretending he could count them.

"My prayers are with your daughter-in-law, Mr MacKinnon. I trust your wife will visit me again once she is well?"

The man's eyes darted upwards, distrusting and scrutinising. "We shall see. I can hardly protest if you continue to pay her, but I have my eye on you, Reverend."

Murray watched the man leave with increasing anxiety, but perhaps, even if he did suspect the truth, MacKinnon could still be trusted. There was no doubt that the man loved his wife, and would keep their secret if the alternative meant stirring up his neighbours' animosities against Flora.

As he passed the MacKinnon's croft, he saw no smoke rising from the roof vent. Clearly, they were all gathered to attend to the daughter-in-law at the son's house, so any attempt to locate Flora and warn her would be useless.

Then, just as Murray was about to turn away, a blackhouse door crept open and Flora swept out, as if summoned by his thoughts alone, her arms loaded with heavy blankets. She stopped suddenly as she spotted him and peered furtively around. She trotted over to him with quick, light steps.

"I can't come to you tonight, Reverend," she whispered. "I will try to come by tomorrow."

"I have just spoken to your husband, Mrs MacKinnon. I know of your current situation."

"It's awful." She looked down at the damp wool clenched between her fists, which was pungent with the sour tang of sweat and vomit. "Mary is in a bad way. I don't think she'll make it through the night." She looked up at him desperately. "I can't bear to think of my son being left without her; he's such a gentle boy. Could you perhaps come and see him, Reverend? Offer a few prayers for Mary?"

"I do not think I would be well received at present," he replied. "I do have to tell you something important, though."

Flora's body went rigid.

"In two days, I will be accompanying the other men to the stacks." He looked away as alarm spread across her face. "That means for the few days I am gone, you will need to see to our visitor's needs on your own. I know this is a precarious position to put you in, but I fear we have no choice."

"But why?"

"She will need someone to continue feeding her and making sure she has adequate shelter."

"I mean why are you going to the stacks?"

He struggled for an answer.

"I am fit enough," he replied quickly, trying to keep his uncertainty from showing. "It would be wrong for the other men to go and for me to stay."

Flora searched his face. She seemed to struggle for a moment, glancing around her to check no one was watching. To his great discomfort, she grasped at his shoulders.

"Come back in one piece, Reverend. I need you to keep her safe."

She offered a weary, unconvincing smile, no doubt intended to be reassuring, before darting away from him, hurrying along the side of the village wall with her head down.

Unable to fix his mind to any task, Murray headed along the cliffs, his mind lurching from one concern to another. He walked for hours.

He had almost completed an entire circuit of the island before he stopped to rest. Perched on the clifftops, he observed far off on the horizon three blackened pillars of rock, glinting wetly in the afternoon sun, their jagged sides plunging treacherously into the churning waters below. Below him, the seabirds seemed to mock him with their cackling chorus, and his stomach churned in motion with the treacherous waters which surrounded him.

Tentatively, he shuffled forward to the cliff edge and forced himself to his knees. He looked down. Fighting the dizzying notion which overcame him as he gazed down upon the swirling, foaming waves, he stretched out a shaking hand. Cold, salt droplets spattered his palm. A familiar thrumming fell against his ear, more urgent than ever before.

"*She is here.*"

Suddenly, a clod of earth gave way. He watched as the rocks tumbled and fell into the swell, disappearing in a heartbeat into the great, grey beast which roared beneath him. Murray scrabbled to his feet.

He backed away slowly, before turning on his heel and heading back towards the settlement. But before he could take five paces, he keeled over and retched dryly into the grass. He pressed his head against the cool, moist earth for a moment before rising, fixing his gaze away from the cliffs at the gently rolling heather which stretched across the centre of the island; it was dappled with green, lichen coated rocks which held none of the hardened threat of those which rose from the sea.

A speck of plaid flashed across his vision.

She was sitting on a cushion of mossy stone, her arms stretched out leisurely behind her. She had been watching him.

※

Later, he watched her from the warmth of the fire. The meal he offered her that evening was meagre without the supervision of Flora MacKinnon, but nevertheless she had eaten ravenously, as if anxious it would be taken from her before thoroughly consumed. He also provided her with ale, bartered for from the tacksman after his visit.

Murray felt immensely uncomfortable without another female presence in the room. After picking apart and demolishing her supper, the young woman sat with him by the hearth, calmly listening as he read aloud from the Book of Psalms. Her eyes glittered. A foamy bead from the ale he had offered her clung to the corner of her lips.

He focused his attention on the page in front of him, although in theory he could recite most of the words from memory. They were all for her benefit, for he could not focus on their meaning while she stared at him, so instead they provided a faint, droning accompaniment to his thoughts.

Despite his reservations, she did not pry into his feelings, nor did she demand a divine reasoning for her own. This girl expressed no shame or awkwardness about her appearance, or in being alone with him. He realised that any attempts to distance himself from her at this point would be nothing less than a betrayal.

Upon concluding his reading, he looked up and saw her gesture to take the book from him. As he offered it, she snatched it away and pored over the words, her fingers tracing the edges of the pages with narrow-eyed scrutiny. A thought struck him.

"Can you read?"

Still transfixed, the girl shook her head slightly. He supposed the notion had been a rather far-fetched one. Nevertheless he needed her to recount her truth to him, and if this was the only way, slow and laborious as it would undoubtedly be, then so be it.

"Would you like me to show you?"

She looked at him questioningly. Seeing the seriousness in his face, her mouth twitched into an eager smile, and she nodded vigorously. Shuffling her stool closer to him, she drew herself to his side.

He inched away as her arm brushed up against his own.

"I won't be able to show you overnight," he warned, "but we can make a start."

Crossing the room, he opened his father's chest and retrieved parchment, ink and quill. Sitting back down, the young woman watched carefully as he methodically unfolded the paper, uncorked the lid of the ink bottle, and dipped the quill into the viscous black fluid. As he hovered over the page, she reached out and ran a finger along the feather quill, watching as thick drops of ink spattered against the yellowing parchment.

He grimaced but persevered with his endeavour.

"We shall start off with something simple." He hesitated as he came to a swift realisation. "Do you know your real name?"

The girl sighed and rolled her eyes. Placing her hands out, she spread them apart in a quick motion which seemed to express both frustration and bemusement.

"And the name Mrs MacKinnon gave you . . . Agnes? How do you feel about being called that?"

She shrugged her shoulders.

"I suppose it would make sense to call you something," he conceded. Agnes seemed as good a name as any. "Do you really remember so little of yourself?"

Petulantly, the girl pursed her lips.

Suddenly, she placed her hand over his own, moulding it around the quill. She looked at him expectantly. Resisting the urge to snatch his burning hand away, he gently prized her fingers loose.

"Let me show you first."

She watched avidly as he drew an alphabet at the top of the page, before writing in bold letters underneath.

Thomas.

"These are all the symbols which can make up words," he explained rapidly, indicating the jumble of letters at the top of the parchment, "and this is my name."

Her eyelids flickered upwards, and she smiled.

He had not shared his Christian name with anybody else since leaving Inverness, not even Flora MacKinnon, but now he had done so without even thinking. The name felt foreign, even to him. Suddenly, what he was doing felt like sacrilege.

He cast aside this uncertainty, and over the next hour went over the phonetic sounds of each letter. When pronouncing his name, he got her to trace a line between each syllable and their alphabetical counterparts. She identified them all correctly, even down to the silent *h*. He was surprised at what a quick learner she was and wondered if there was some trace of knowledge which had lain dormant in her mind. Perhaps with further instruction, memories would begin to resurface.

While he contemplated this, Agnes sat and silently formed his name with her tongue and lips. She turned to him and repeated the action, this time pointing to the name on the page and then placing her finger on his shoulder. She looked thrilled at her discovery.

"I think that will do for now," Murray said, clearing his throat and gathering his writing tools.

Insisting on sharing the burden, Agnes picked up the bottle of ink and placed it back inside the chest. Before returning to the hearth, she stopped for a moment and traced her finger around the carved coat of arms on the lid. She turned to him questioningly, gesturing at the emblem and then at the parchment in his hand, as if he had failed to include a valuable component to her learning.

"No, that's not a letter." Murray shook his head and to his astonishment found his mouth curving upwards into a smile. "That's a coat of arms, in this case the coat of arms of His Majesty's army: my father was a soldier. The trunk belonged to him."

The girl sat back down and hunched over, resting her chin on her hands in a now familiar habit. She gestured for him to sit on the stool next to her.

He did so, but still reserved a few inches between her seat and his. She looked at him expectantly, and he was surprised that he did not mind discussing his family with her. After all, he thought, who was she to judge?

"My father was killed in battle twelve years ago. He was already an old man by then, but it still came as a shock to my mother." He waited for the look of sympathy, or for the reassuring hand on his shoulder, but to his relief neither gesture came. "I have two sisters. Elizabeth is married and when I left her, she was heavily pregnant; for all I know I have a nephew or niece by now."

There was still no reaction. Agnes sat quietly listening, her expression neutral, but attentive. Perhaps she simply did not understand.

"My youngest sister Frances still lives with my mother," he continued. "She looks after her. Since my father died my mother has been . . . not quite right."

He looked at Agnes and saw that what constituted right and not right, meant little in her company.

"I don't think I ever quite lived up to my father's high standards," he continued, pacifying himself with a thin smile, which was closer to a grimace. "I couldn't be the son he wanted me to be, so instead I became a minister, like a second son rather than an only son, while he, an old man, still went off to war every couple of years."

The girl observed him with rapt attention. She could not possibly appreciate the nuances of such family dynamics, but she seemed to hungrily digest each piece of personal history he could offer her, as if she were trying to fill the void of her own past with the memories of another.

"I don't miss him."

It was the first time he had acknowledged it, let alone said it out loud.

"He was not a bad father," he paused, "but I'm glad he isn't here anymore."

Exodus: *Honour thy father and thy mother so that you may have a long life in the land that the Lord your God is giving you.* But what kind of land was this for God to have given?

Agnes rested her hand against his arm. His skin no longer seared from her touch. Looking at her he saw glimmers of understanding, which sparkled on the surface of a much deeper, more unfathomable depth. He had not told her about Caroline. To his alarm he realised that he had not even thought about Caroline until this moment.

He pulled away from her.

Clearing the evening away, he closed his father's chest and indicated that their time together had drawn to a close for the night.

There was a poorly veiled look of disappointment in her eyes as she made her way across the room to the byre.

"Before you retire . . ." he began.

She froze at the partition wall, her face suddenly lifting.

"I will be away for a few days, so Mrs MacKinnon will try to attend to you in the meantime."

Agnes' face fell once more. He did not clarify where he was going and for what purpose. He did not think it necessary and had still not fully accepted it as a reality. Perhaps he could surprise her by returning with food to fill an entire larder; present himself as a man who could brave the elements and return as victor and provider.

"I will leave the door unlatched for you. You can still come and go as you please," he instructed. "Only . . ." He paused for a moment. "Please do take greater care to avoid detection. I want to see you when I get back."

The girl looked up at him, and he felt a sinking feeling in his stomach. Why had he said something so foolish? Besides, was it even true? Had he not wanted to leave her?

"How else will we continue your reading lessons?" he said, in a poor attempt to mask his indiscretion. She did not seem to notice, and with a parting look slowly disappeared behind the partition.

Murray breathed a sigh of relief. Straightening his own bedding, he noticed that he had left Buchan's notebook under his pillow. In his distraction over the past week, he had almost forgotten about his predecessor's treasonous activities. He picked it up and moved to put it back in the chest. Crossing the room, he flicked through the pages absentmindedly, shaking his head at the tedious itineraries and lists, skimming past crude sketches of people and barren landscapes. Why had the man felt the need to hide such an innocuous tome? Sighing, he bent down to place it back in the darkness, but fumbled and watched as it fell, its pages splayed across the floor. Retrieving it, he paused before closing its pages.

Surely, it could not be? With a jolt of disbelief, he almost dropped the book again.

He froze and examined the face which stared back up at him from the page.

The sketch was no work of art and was lacking in detail, but the similarity could not be dismissed; the way the figure's dark sheath of hair fell in lank tendrils around her face, the way her shawl fell around her jutting collar bone.

Hungry, charcoal eyes stared back at him from the page. It was the same expression that had fixed on him mere moments before.

Horrified, he flung the book away and retreated to his bed.

In his dreams, the eyes still followed him.

CHAPTER TWENTY

FLORA

FLORA was grateful to escape the noxious air of the sickroom, even just for a moment. She took a clean lungful of air, savouring the freshness, before teetering away from Fergus and Mary's croft, the slop bucket clutched precariously in her hands. The bucket was full almost to the brim and the contents sloshed threateningly. Flora grimaced. She tried not to dwell on the sickening substances swirling within the vessel.

As Flora approached the bay, she lowered her burden and reluctantly peered at what was inside. Each pail grew worse. At this point nothing that was evacuated from Mary's body resembled even the most revolting of human excretions. Instead, Flora looked down upon a white, foamy liquid which looked as if it had been skimmed from the rolling surf of the advancing waves. Even the smell of it matched the brininess of the sea. If Flora had not seen the pitiful way in which Mary had repeatedly filled her slop bucket, she would not have believed that this was where the vile fluid originated from. With relief, she tipped the bucket over the side of the harbour wall. Flora watched as it merged into the currents, twisting and reaching out in varicose streams until it completely vanished amidst the froth of the breakers.

Flora levered herself up. As she turned back towards the croft, she became aware of the women lining the edges of the beach, heads lowered, furtively studying Flora from beneath their heavy, cloaked earasaids. There was an increasingly nervous energy surrounding the women of the village, especially where the MacKinnon family were concerned. Flora tried to ignore their scrutiny and solemnly pushed her way back through their clandestine stares. Before she could return, she was accosted by Margaret Gillies.

"I'm so sorry, Flora. First your Donnchadh, then Ann's babe and now Mary. There's something not right about all of this, surely now you must see that?"

"I really must get back, Margaret. My boy needs me."

Margaret quickened her pace to match Flora's own.

"I thought we were friends. You do know you can talk to me?"

Flora halted. She turned and cast a pleading look at her old neighbour: the woman who had been her childhood playmate when her siblings either outgrew or predeceased her.

"Please, Margaret. I really cannot talk about this now."

With a lingering look, Margaret turned on her heel and stomped away, her skirts catching on the wind and swirling about her.

When Flora arrived back at the croft, Fergus was already outside. It had become increasingly difficult to have Fergus hovering by Mary's side as greater indignities were thrust upon her poor, wracked body, making her barely resemble the respectable wife he had known. Flora admired her boy's devotion. She wrapped her arms around his heaving shoulders and pulled him to her as she had when he was a child. His body stiffened as he tried to compose himself, as befitted a man.

"I can't stand seeing her like that, Ma," he said, his voice reduced to a hoarse whisper.

"I know, son, but perhaps you shouldn't. You know Mary would not want you to see her in such a state either."

He nodded, stifling a sob.

"I'm still going out with the other men tomorrow. Mary would expect it."

"Are you sure?"

"Yes. I don't want my child to starve."

Flora considered that by the time the men came back, it would probably be too late for Mary. She would be lucky to even survive another day and perhaps this would be a mercy. Flora contemplated warning her son of this, but held back, hoping that sparing him being present for the worst was the most humane course of action. Her mind then strayed to Mary's baby.

"You know, Fergus," she began, "I will care for the babe when Mary..."

Flora trailed off as she saw the look of agony form on her son's face. She placed a firm hand on his arm.

"It isn't nice to think about, but at this stage I think you have to accept what is going to happen. Can you do that for me, son?"

Fergus nodded, the muscles in his face taught as he held himself together.

"Your Da and I will take the child in. You know she'll be doted on with us, and you can visit her whenever you like."

"I appreciate that, Ma," Fergus sniffled. "But Michael and I have already spoken of this matter, and Ann has agreed to take her."

"Ann?" Flora was incredulous. "But she already has two bairns of her own to look after, and she's still recovering from her last labour."

"Ann insisted she take her. Besides, according to her she still has milk to spare." Fergus flushed crimson.

Flora thought of protesting, but fearful of stirring further conflict she let the matter drop.

"Have you named her yet? It seems like a good idea to do so before..."

"I'm calling her Mary," Fergus interrupted. "It's the only thing she has left to give."

The conversation ended abruptly as Fergus re-entered his home. Flora followed, steeling herself not for the stench, moaning and painful contortions, but for the recriminations which would no doubt follow her from this charnel house. She felt her position as matriarch slipping. No longer an anchor for the family to hold fast to, she was becoming burdensome; an old woman whose mental and physical state made her surplus, her metal rusted and the rope which moored her straining to be cut loose.

The following morning the boat was heaved to the shore and the remaining women, those who were not ill or tending to the sick, flocked to the shore to watch their men depart. Leaving Ann to relentlessly tend to Mary, Flora lingered nervously on the edge of the bay. John and the boys were loading the nets into the boat, and although John affected to be in high spirits for their boys' sake, Flora knew better. The sea was mercifully calm. Still, the craft lurched forwards in the surf, restrained only by the men who held it steady as the others prepared baskets, coils of rope and sea-stained grappling hooks, the sea eager to thrust them forward towards the distant peaks of jagged rock.

The Reverend helped load the boat. He looked ridiculous in his wooden soled shoes and fine coat as he clumsily navigated the shallows, heaving heavy cargo from the beach. Flora observed the older men's dismissive glances and the barely restrained snickering from the more youthful amongst them. Even some of the young women seemed to bob their heads together, their lips sucked in from restraining their mirth. Casting a condemnatory look, Flora pushed her way forward and waved for the Reverend's attention, paying no heed to the whispers and questioning looks which fell on her.

Noticing her, the Reverend seemed relieved. Throughout the proceedings, he had appeared dazed, but Flora could still see the nerves that were masked beneath the trancelike way he went about each task. As he approached, he affected a steely expression, but a muscle in his cheek twitched.

"I can trust that you will keep everything in order, Mrs MacKinnon, while I am gone." He gave her a knowing look.

Flora nodded.

"I will spend as much time keeping your house in order as I can, Reverend."

"Good." He seemed reluctant to depart. He rubbed his palms

together anxiously and peered over her shoulder, rather than directly meet her eyes.

Remembering why she had wished to talk to him, Flora picked up a sealskin bag by her feet and carefully pulled out a pair of boots. They were made from the neck and skin of a gannet; the leather was supple, but the oiliness helped make it weather resistant.

"I thought these would be of use to you," Flora said, holding them out to him. "You would not want to ruin your current ones."

The Reverend took them and held them between two fingers, his expression doubtful.

"They stretch very well," she replied, before quickly looking around and lowering her voice. "They belonged to my youngest son, only do not tell anyone that."

Finally meeting her eyes, the Reverend gave Flora a look which she chose to interpret as gratitude. After nervously glancing over her shoulder once more, he joined the other men. An oar was thrust into his hands and scrambling up into the boat, the Reverend set off. Flora exchanged a wave with her husband and sons, who had not wanted a protracted departure, instead preferring to say swift farewells and set about their business as soon as was possible. She watched the boat retreat into the distance.

The women seemed reassured: the sea was calm, and the skies were clear of clouds. Flora did not allow herself to fear, for all the signs pointed to a safe crossing and perfect weather for catching those young fledgling birds still reluctant to leave their nests. Soon the women dispersed and went back to work, but Flora chose to edge away from them. She needed a moment to herself to be away from the inquiring voices and covert stares that were swelling up around her. Now that the Reverend had gone, she had temporarily lost her ally. Her husband and sons had also taken all remaining affection with them.

Nevertheless, Flora's mind thrummed with anticipation. She felt buoyed by the opportunity to dwell on her thoughts regarding their mysterious visitor. Needing to get away from her neighbours, she carefully trod back towards the cliff path which would take her to the cove, and to the spot where she had found her girl lying at the edge the sea, tethered by the slimy umbilical cord of surrounding seaweed.

As she rounded the side of the chapel, away from the other women's scrutiny, Flora observed a lone figure sitting on the tumbledown wall gazing out at the boats which bobbed ever further from the shore. Flora's heart beat violently. Hobbling towards the figure, her suspicions were confirmed as she saw the breeze whip a strand of black hair from beneath the girl's hood. Flora thundered towards her. Agnes turned at the last minute, just as Flora grasped her arm in a vicelike grip.

"We told you to stay away from the settlement!" Flora's previous caution around the girl dissipated as her maternal concern took control of her. "If someone other than me came around that corner and spotted you . . ." Flora dared not finish her sentence.

Agnes struggled and yanked her arm free, her eyes glistening with tears which she angrily dashed away. She pointed out to sea before looking back at Flora challengingly.

Flora's initial fury softened.

"The men will be back in a few days at most," she said. "The sea is peaceful. There is nothing to fear."

Agnes seemed unconvinced and moodily began picking at the fibres of her clothes, a gesture Flora was now greatly familiar with and knew signalled frustration. Fearing a curious neighbour could stray along the path looking for her, Flora pulled Agnes up, and taking her arm in the crook of her elbow, urged her along the cliff path.

"We need to take you away from here," Flora warned. She thought of how easily the girl engrossed herself in simple tasks. "You can help me look for shellfish in the rockpools."

Agnes reluctantly followed her along the path, still occasionally glancing back at the boats drifting towards the horizon. This compliance was at least progress from before, where the girl had resolutely refused to allow Flora to even touch her. Now she seemed too preoccupied to even notice.

As they approached the cove, Flora led Agnes carefully down the steep path which wound its way down the cliff face. The girl clung to her arm and for a moment it seemed to Flora that she was the one being guided, her companion appearing like a daughter cautiously steadying her aging mother down a treacherous stretch of ground. Flora was comforted by this thought.

As they reached the bottom of the path, the girl suddenly froze. "What is it?"

Agnes started trembling uncontrollable, her mouth opening and closing in a terrified mockery of speech. Omitting a pitiful mewing sound, she tugged on Flora's arm, attempting to propel her back the way they came.

Flora felt suddenly foolish. Of all the places, why would she have brought her here? Perhaps the girl's memories were starting to slowly resurface. Flora grew fearful. What could she possibly remember?

"The tide is out," Flora said, but her voice trembled. "It can't reach you here."

Agnes shook her head. Regaining some movement in her legs, she took tentative steps backwards, clearly desperate to escape the place where she was found.

Flora felt cruel; it was futile continuing across the rocks. Turning her away, Flora ushered the girl back up the path. Agnes shivered and quaked in her arms, and her breath came forth in short, laborious gasps which rasped against Flora's ear. It was only when they reached the top of the path that her body relaxed.

Letting out a sob, Agnes abruptly clung to Flora, pulling at the fabric of her shawl and burying her face against her neck. Surprised, Flora wrapped her arms around the girl. She shushed and cooed at her, rubbing her back, and feeling the warmth of her radiate against her breast. Despite her terror of what could have resurfaced in the girl's memories, Flora savoured the brackish scent which clung to her skin and cradling her in her arms, was overwhelmed with love.

"Hush now, *mo cridhe*."

Agnes fell limp, her breathing settling into a steadier pace. Extracting herself from Flora's arms, she shakily lowered herself to the ground and stayed there until the tremors left her body. Flora allowed her to sit, before gradually easing her back onto her feet.

"We can't take you back through the village," Flora said. "Do you know the way over the ridge to get to the Reverend's lodgings?"

Agnes' eyes were glazed. She nodded.

"Go up the hill and come directly to the house once the sun is setting. Stay away from the other crofts."

Agnes exhaled heavily. Flora could not tell whether it was from frustration or an attempt to regain self-control. Without a parting word, the girl suddenly vaulted away, her clothes flying behind her as she bounded up towards the uppermost plateau of the island, where she would have nought but sheep and a few cattle for company. Flora watched her go with relief. Whilst she had relished the opportunity to hold her in her arms, she felt a nagging sense of dread at what the girl's memories could have provoked. She walked very slowly back to the village, not wanting to return to the company of others just yet. For her son's sake only, she would go to Mary.

Trudging back through the village, Flora ignored the other women who were scattered about the settlement in small huddles, some tramping their dirty cloth in large wooden tubs, whilst others patched up a large piece of sailcloth. Thankfully, they largely ignored her. As she approached Fergus' house, she felt a growing apprehension at what she would find. When she had left her, Mary had fallen into a deep sleep, her eyes sunken into her skull and her skin cold, clammy and tinged blue, as if she were already a corpse. After the agonising way that Mary's body had spasmed over the past few days, this slumber had seemed merciful. Flora knew better. This long, restful state, although seemingly painless, was in her experience a prelude to death. Flora braced herself.

As she approached the front door of the blackhouse, there was an unnerving quiet. Pausing to listen, she began to hear Ann's anguished sobs. Mary's suffering was over.

※

They buried her the same day. Worried that whatever harmful entity had overtaken Mary's body would spread to others, the women hastily wrapped her in a sailcloth shroud, binding it together with salt stiffened rope. With hesitant hands, they carried her body outside to the cemetery. Mary was offered none of the usual ceremony. Normally the body would rest for days with the family, with nobody permitted to return to work until after the burial. This time none of the women could afford to miss a day of work while their men were away at the stacks, let alone allow the infected body to remain and fester inside the confines of her former home. There was a solemn silence at the graveside. None of the customary wailing or keening. Instead, they were surrounded by the patter of a sudden and unexpected shower of rain, which began to fall in fat droplets onto the surrounding burial cairns.

Flora winced as she bent down to help the women scoop and scrape the earth from Mary's makeshift grave. They used whatever tools were available, as well as their hands. Grit dug into the delicate skin beneath Flora's fingernails, one of the only soft places that remained of her body. Beside them lay not only Mary's lifeless form, but also the smaller shrouded figure of one of Ailith McQueen's many great grandchildren, who had passed the previous night. The child's mother clung to him, sobbing silently and reluctant to let go.

Flora remembered fifteen years before, when the graveyard had been swamped with bodies. They had been piled high and had begun to stink in the sun, before being dumped into the large pits dug for their disposal. Flora was grateful that she had not lost one of her children that way, as so many others had that year.

Ann stood nearby, supported by the arms of her fellow women, still recovering and unsteady on her feet. She looked defeated. Flora could see that the death of her closest friend would harden Ann even further and when she caught her eye she was forced to look away, chastised and shamed, as if she had somehow allowed this tragedy to befall them. Flora kept her eyes to the earth. Soon the corpses were gently laid down in their grave, and the women hastened to scoop the dirt back into the pit to cover them. The cairn they erected was small, and many chose to wait until the men returned before placing their stone.

"I would like to call a meeting."

Flora turned at the sound of Ann's tearful voice punctuating the quiet.

"We can't allow things to get worse than they are. Something must be done."

Nervous chattering began, and Margaret Gillies stepped towards Ann, putting a comforting arm around her.

"Ann is right. We will gather at my house immediately."

A throng of anguished voices shouted out their concerns in unison.

"But it is forbidden!"

"Only the men can call a meeting!"

"These are desperate circumstances," Margaret called out, drawing herself to her full height. "It is not the first time we have spoken like this when the men were away. We must seize the opportunity."

Flora felt herself being swept forward amidst the tide of women, each eager to have her voice heard. They entered the Gillies' croft, the largest on the island, and spread themselves around the living space until every corner and bed niche was filled. What remained of the female population of the island crowded around the hearth or propped themselves up by the outer walls, while others spilled into the byre. Some clasped their infants to their chests, whilst their older children roamed free and played in the field outside, grateful to be afforded an afternoon free from work. Flora stood near

Margaret, uncertain of how much input she would be permitted to have. It was Ann who first addressed the gathering.

"How can you all stand by and do nothing while our mothers, sisters and babes are dying?" Her voice was breaking, and tears spilled freely down her cheeks. "If the harvest is poor, then we need to find other ways to survive, to keep our children alive. How can we . . ." Ann's voice trailed off. Her face was red, and she was breathing heavily, her fists clenched at her sides. Margaret rubbed Ann's back and took over.

"I understand why our sister Ann is frustrated. We cannot allow pestilence and poor luck to devastate our community as it did before. Are there any suggestions for what actions we should take to stop this?"

"We should pray!" Rachel McQueen spoke up. "Remember how Father Buchan taught us that God would take mercy if we repented our sins?"

"Pshaw," scoffed one of the McCrimmon girls. "What good did that ever do us?"

Rachel bit her lip. "We could try. Father Buchan said it only worked if you repented in earnest."

"And what sins could any of us possibly have to account for?"

"Aye! We've done nothing so bad as to deserve this. We're victims of God's wrath if anything."

The bickering continued unabated for some time before Margaret was able to summon some calm. Flora looked to Ann, who was now kneeling on the floor, sheltered by a small huddle of sympathetic bodies. When Ann looked up, her face was gleaming with sweat and tears; her hair was in disarray. The stare she gave her was one of pure venom. Flora baulked. She wanted desperately to say something before Ann could find the strength to open her mouth, but she was beaten to it.

"I know of someone who may have something to answer for," Ann seethed.

All eyes turned to Flora. She withered under their gaze, but tried to appear bold, for how could they possibly know what truly shamed her? As for saving the girl, she held no regret for that whatsoever.

"I know the grief that Ann feels, so I forgive her for her harshness to me," Flora began, "but nothing I have done started this. If you think that girl I found in the cove was some kind of evil being, then why would it be the case that the worst of what has happened began only after she vanished?" Flora spoke this part clearly and forcefully. "The illness only started after the tacksman's visit. Yes, the crops rotted earlier, but that's not something we haven't faced before during a bad summer." She tried to temper her tone. "I am sorry for your losses, Ann, but there is no connection here at all. You're only saying this because you want someone to blame."

Horrified, Flora watched as Ann lunged forward, shrieking, her arms outstretched and her fingernails raking thin air. A group of women pulled her back and restrained her.

"You've brought her amongst us! You know what you've done!"

Flora's heart quickened. She could not give away what she knew. Instead, she despaired to see her eldest son's wife bearing such ignorance and animosity towards her and began to fear that this growing rift could not be repaired. Two of the women led Ann outside, who for her part omitted heart wrenching sobs which wracked her entire body as she limped away. Most of the other women turned their faces downwards, seemingly embarrassed by this sudden outburst. Some still edged away from Flora. She looked indignantly at them.

"And you say I've gone mad with grief!" Flora remarked. "I'm not the one who slaughtered a bird, thinking it was a witch, wasting what was probably good meat in the process!"

To her credit, Margaret approached her neighbour and placed a loyal hand on her shoulder.

"We achieve nothing by turning on each other," Margaret said sternly. "We all know that Ann has had a difficult time over the past month, and we must be supportive of her, but not at the expense of any others in this room."

There was a smattering of whispers, and Margaret allowed for the commotion to die.

"We all agree that God has offered us nothing," Margaret continued, "which leaves us with the question of what can help us?"

Another hush descended as the women contemplated.

"My mother spoke of the fairy pool up on the hill," Rachel McQueen said quietly. "They used to leave offerings there for the *fae* in exchange for good fortune."

The last thing Flora needed was for people to begin trudging up to the centre of the island, where Agnes was most likely to be found roaming.

"We have nothing of worth to offer," she said. "The little food that we do have is hardly fit for the *fae*, if indeed any of them remain after all this time."

Flora was relieved to see many nods of agreement.

"This is true," said Margaret. "Besides, it is the sea that has been the source of many of our woes, starting with the storm. Perhaps it is her we should try to appease."

"A sacrifice?"

"My mother also spoke of taking a lamb from each family and giving it to the sea," Rachel spoke up again. "It's only since these priests started coming here that we were stopped from doing it. Perhaps it could help us now?"

"Can we afford to give up our livestock?" asked Margaret. "Some of us have had no luck with lambing this year."

"Some of us have only one sheep left!"

Many clamoured to agree with this statement.

"What else do we have to give?"

Margaret frowned, contemplating.

"We must not spare that we cannot afford to lose until we are certain it will help," she declared. "Until we have a clearer idea of what evil we face, we shall make what little offerings we can to the sea."

The women seemed to reach an agreement, with some pledging

to pour their ewe's milk from the harbour wall, whilst others unpinned brooches and pins in readiness to forsake them over the nearest cliff. Flora was relieved she had given away her daughter's comb. She made a show of unpinning her shawl and with the others, walked out along the cliff path.

As they approached, the women lined up like warriors, holding out their fists and flinging their precious items into the roaring maw of the oncoming tide. Trinkets of bronze and silver sparkled briefly in the air before falling rapidly, being consumed by the grey and white mass of waves beating against the cliff face. Whilst some mourned marriage gifts and heirlooms passed down from their mothers' mothers, Flora felt nothing.

The sombre procession soon dispersed, but some of the women lingered and sang a lament, as if willing the sea to hear them and pity them. A painful memory rooted Flora to the spot. She remembered how in the absence of a body, her fellow women had stood with her at the edge of the same cliff and intoned a song of mourning for her daughter. Time shifted and she was once again the raven-haired beauty of fifteen years past. The women's mournful harmony echoed against the rocks and stretched out over the cold mirror of the ocean.

She was grateful to leave. Flora did not go back to her own croft, but determinedly headed towards the Reverend's lodgings, where she found the company she sought. Agnes was already huddled by the hearth, having started a fire herself. Thankfully, she did not offer any inquiring look or make any demands. Flora busied herself for the remainder of the day in preparing a meal of dried fish, limpets and seaweed, having at this point exhausted the storehouse of any remaining bird meat. Agnes still accepted the dish graciously and devoured her food.

Later, after Agnes had slunk down into her mound of hay and wool, Flora crept into the byre and stood watching. She slept soundly. Without a hood, her dark hair was draped over her shoulders; one of her arms was splayed above her head and her fingers curled inwards towards her palm. Flora quietly knelt. Ignoring her aching hip, she lay herself down at the edge of the straw bed and soon found herself falling into a peaceful slumber.

It was only later that night, when the wind whipped up and with a howling fury pounded against the blackhouse door, that Flora awakened. In the distance she heard the faint, ominous rumble of thunder.

CHAPTER TWENTY-ONE

THOMAS

As the sun began to set, the men launched the boat. They had rested briefly in a small drystone bothy, clumsily constructed to cling to the side of the largest sea stack, trying to fit as much sleep into the day before they could begin their night's expedition to the rocky pillar furthest away from the land. This sheer pinnacle housed the largest of the gannet colonies, and it was there that they hoped to harvest their quarry. At night, the birds would return to their roosts and, in their slumber, become easy prey to the swift hands which would pin their wings and snap their necks.

Murray felt dizzyingly nauseous. The bobbing motion of the boat and the uncomfortable hours spent trying to ease himself into a semblance of comfort on the cold, stone floor of the bothy, had made his head and muscles ache. Thankfully, the other men had not noticed, or else feigned ignorance. Perhaps they simply did not care. Murray squinted through the salt spray and fading light at his companions. Unlike their journey from the village bay, the men had now fallen silent, no longer singing their shanties in rhythm with the movement of oars. Instead, they seemed totally fixated on the impending hunt. The world around them had followed suit; the deafening cries of thousands of seabirds had fallen to a low chatter as the birds began to bed down for the night.

Murray was relieved at this. His coat now bore the rancid evidence of their arrival at the stacks, where birds had swarmed in unfathomable numbers above them, turning the surface of the sea into a viscous slick of white and green as putrid missiles had fallen from the air. Even though the bird's daytime assault had ceased, the air still reeked from the calcified stains which thickly coated the surrounding rocks. Murray hoped that the remaining elements would be kind, as already a steady wind was increasing the motion of the swell which slapped against the sides of the boat.

They had positioned him at the very back. In front of him sat a father and his son, who looked young enough to have only recently exchanged skirts for breeches. As he sat close to his father, the boy's neck craned to observe his surroundings with an expression of both wonder and barely concealed fear. The child's feigned stoicism brought Murray's own anxiety bubbling up from within his chest. He could feel the cold chill on his shoulder transform into the stern, ghostly hand of his father as the soft swoosh of the oars echoed his heartbeat. Above him, the darkening silhouette of the stack loomed ever closer as darkness crept forward over the overcast sky. The men lit an oil lantern, and they lowered their voices to barely audible whispers.

The stack loomed closer. Murray looked upwards and balked as he finally saw the scale of the gargantuan pillar, which rose sharply from the sea until high above them it sheered away into a sharp, serrated edge. He thought of dagger blades and hounds' teeth; their pointed shape a warning against anyone who dared to trifle with them.

As they approached the lee side of this broken column, the sea surged forwards, carrying the boat in its wake. The sky was now cloaked in darkness. The rocks appeared black against the glint of the sea as it shot forth white tongues of foam to thrash against the stack's base. As the men were carried forwards, the eldest of MacKinnon's sons stood precariously on the bow of the boat. Taking two thick, heavy coils of rope under his arm, he waited until the breakers swelled up towards the rock, before leaping nimbly onto a small ledge.

Murray watched in awe as this bulky young man gripped onto the tiniest cracks and crevices, shimmying upwards in a seemingly effortless ascent to a rusted spike, which had been driven precariously into a crack in the cliff face. Michael MacKinnon deftly secured the ropes tightly to the metal post, knotting one around his waist and climbing back down to tie the end of the other to the ring on the front of the boat. MacKinnon passed around the rope which held him, and there was a nervous energy as the men in turn all began to tether themselves to each other. The rope was passed to the back of the boat, and the last to encircle it around themself was the small boy. Nothing was passed to Murray. His stomach clenched. Did they expect him to climb without rope? If so, he would refuse. As godless and dangerous as these men were, he would not allow himself to be deprived of anything they possessed; plunging to his death was only the second thing that crossed his mind after this conviction.

"Why am I to be deprived, sirs?"

As soon as he spoke, a dozen indignant faces turned to shush him. John MacKinnon looked at him with steely intent and pressed a finger to his lips.

"You'll wake the watchman," he whispered.

"The watchman?"

"The King of the birds keeps watch over his flock at night. Make the slightest noise to give the game away, and he'll start up a warning call. That'll be all our chances gone." John pointed upwards towards the far side of the rockface.

King of the birds? Such absurdity was difficult to take with any degree of seriousness. However, as Murray looked up, he saw that there was indeed a large gannet keeping sentinel from a rocky promontory, its silhouette faintly coming into focus as his eyes adjusted to the twilight. He licked his lips and lowered his voice.

"But why have I not got any rope to tie myself with?"

John shot him a look of contempt. "You'll be staying here with the boat, Reverend. We need someone to stay here, and when we kill a *guga* we will throw it down and you will catch it or fish it out of the sea."

Murray supposed he should feel slighted for being given a task which seemed more suited to the small boy in front of him, but instead felt a reluctant relief. Although the sea swelled around him in a sickening motion, lurching to and fro, it was still immensely preferably to ascending above it, risking either a plunge into the icy water or a bloody end on the rocks which peeked threateningly from below the surface.

The child had started trembling. His father was speaking to him quietly as he knotted the end of the rope around him. The other men bent forward and gave him pats of encouragement. With rising disgust, it dawned on Murray that as the boy was the last to be tied, he would be first to ascend and kill the bird keeping lookout. This seemed a perilous tactic to rest the entire success of the mission on. Before he could express his outrage, John MacKinnon again turned to whisper in his ear.

"It needs to be someone small and light footed to catch the bird off guard. It's the first task all of us do as young lads coming out here for the first time. Like all of us, Eòghann has been trained up by his father on the cliffs at home, so you can take that look of judgement from your face, Reverend."

He supposed the custom made some sense, but still felt affronted by this harsh initiation into the hunt. No wonder the boy trembled, knowing the responsibility which weighed upon his young shoulders. Murray's thoughts strayed once again to his own youth. If he had been born on the island, would his father have expected him to put himself in such peril for the sake of tradition? Undoubtedly so. His father's disappointed face clouded his memory; a reprimand from the past. Even now he cringed away from that pointed look of shame.

As the boy fumbled with the knot at his waist, Murray expected a tut or look of consternation from the father, but instead he looked on enviously as the man simply took the boy's hands in his own and they secured the rope together. No words were spoken between them, but their eyes exchanged a meaning only they fully understood. With one last squeeze on the shoulder for encouragement, the boy was lifted ashore. The boat rocked groggily. Even if he did not fully appreciate the stakes of this expedition, Murray felt his fear building as the child gripped the rocks at the base of the stack to begin slowly inching up the towering monolith.

The shadow of the bird did not stir. The only sounds which punctuated the gaping void in which they waited were the muted roar and hiss of the waves. They waited breathlessly.

A gasp caught in Murray's throat as the boy's fingers slipped from the rockface, only for his hand to then swing outwards and grasp at a barely noticeable ledge, which created a precarious pathway to where the watchman sat. The child made the manoeuvre look effortless. Getting down on his hands and knees, the boy crawled slowly towards his quarry, his eyes trained on the bird. He paused with one hand poised in mid-air like a stalking cat, navigating where to place himself in a way which did not draw the attention of the bird. Murray felt the cluster of men on the boat tense. The boy's hand descended and felt around for a decent hold.

The loosened stones fell with a crack against the cliff face.

The boy froze. In those agonising few seconds, Murray saw the watchman's silhouette ruffle itself and raise its wings. Instinctively, the boy raced forwards, alerting the bird. The gannet issued a loud staccato of throaty gurgles and flapped its wings ferociously before taking flight. The men, who had been watching avidly, uttered a collective, despairing groan as suddenly, from all around them, thousands of bird cries echoed in return and began swooping from their nests. The boy covered his head with his arms as gannets dived towards him and bloodied his scalp with their dagger-like beaks. Murray felt the rush of air from their wings brush against his face as they crowded into the sky around them. The boy's father tugged frantically at the rope and the boy began to shuffle backwards, cautiously descending through a hail of feathers and bird shit.

At this point, Murray assumed the men would resign themselves to failure. Instead, they rallied themselves. Grappling at the rock, they ascended in the desperate hope to recover any chicks still sitting vulnerably on their nests. They worked fast. In minutes they had shuffled around ledges and over jagged promontories to places beyond Murray's sight, melding seamlessly into the darkening sky. In spite of himself, he admired the men's determination and their gritty defiance of misfortune.

He braced himself. Any moment he expected the dispatched chicks to come tumbling from the sky. He waited for the splashes or thuds of their broken bodies landing in and around the boat.

Minutes passed. None came.

In those endless minutes, he became increasingly aware of the rhythm of the boat as it rose and fell in the swelling waters. He felt a weightlessness in his chest and the taste of bile rose in his throat. The waves were getting higher. He could not hear a sound from the men, and other then the thrumming heartbeat of the sea as it met the rocks, the air around the stack had fallen eerily quiet. Straining to hear above the water, he realised that the birds had departed. No longer did they fill the skies with their guttural alarm cries; no longer did they swoop down to ward their attackers away. The air rushing past his face was no longer from the wings of a thousand seabirds, but from a gathering wind which whistled along the edge of the boat; the salt spray which flecked his face was now mingled with a mist of rain. In the distance, the sky rumbled.

He felt a surge of terror. The rope which tethered the patched-up, ramshackle boat to the stack was swaying violently in the gathering wind. A sudden gust caught him off guard and buffeted the boat to one side, making it lean perilously in the water. He crouched low and clung to the wooden planks. Squinting in the wind and peering up at the stack, he grew increasingly alarmed as the men showed no signs of descending. Surely the thunder would have hastened their return.

A crack of lightning lit up the horizon, but the men were nowhere to be seen. In that split second as the skies were illuminated, he saw that the iron spike which tethered the men to the rock had slipped down into a widening crevice, loosened by the ferocious wind. Never mind the broken-necked carcasses of the birds, when would the shattered bodies of the men start to fall? He thought of praying, but to his contempt he instead found himself letting out a terrified whimper as once more the boat tilted in the stirred-up surf, threatening to tip over into the icy, foaming water.

He realised then that God did not care for the likes of him. A storm was God's creation, and here he was, a servant of the Lord, caught up perilously in its merciless grasp. What had been the purpose of his calling? To whom had he been trying to prove himself? His thoughts drifted back to his father, the archdiocese, and for the first time in many nights he thought of Caroline. All of them had deserted him. He could almost hear them chanting his failures, his ineptitudes, and his negligence. But he would not be a man cowed by the thought of dying. If he were to face his maker, he would at least offer Him a noble death.

Bracing himself against the boat's bow, Murray cautiously levered himself up. Spreading out his arms to grip the sides, he tried to find his balance. He stood, breathing deeply, preparing himself. Screwing his eyes shut, he leaped at the rocky ledge in front of him.

He landed on his chest, winding himself, but was thankful not to feel the freezing embrace of the waves. The cold water still soaked through his clothes, forcing him to drag himself forwards, his palms burning and his fingernails scraping painfully against the rough, craggy surface of the stone shelf.

The wind made it close to impossible to look up, but Murray had no choice. His eyes stung as he peered upwards towards the metal shaft, which was now closer to being uprooted from the crevice it had been haphazardly embedded into. It was not high up the cliff. Still, it was not low enough that a fall from that height would not fracture bones. Perhaps he could wait. Surely by now the men were on their way back down. But as he held his face towards the raging sky, he saw how the rope still stretched tautly up into the darkness, and how the hook which held it there would soon shake itself free. He had no choice. Without the others, he would be trapped amidst the elements, barely able to navigate or row the boat back himself in the unyielding swell which stretched out in every direction.

Steeling himself, he grappled at the rock face. Hauling himself up onto the first of a series of narrow ledges, he pressed his face to the cold wet rock as a gust of air thrust his body forwards. The spike was no more than a man's length away. He reached out and stretched his arm as far as he could. He was met with thin air.

The surface of the cliff was slippery, and without a firm handhold he would plummet back down to the ground in an instant. Stretching further, he managed to hang on to a thin ridge with the tips of his fingers. Finding his footing, he heaved himself towards the rope. He hugged the side of the crevice which secured the men's lifeline, his sodden clothes clinging to him uncomfortably as he positioned himself as close to their dislodged anchor as he dared. Turning to the gaping abyss above him, hair whipped across his face in a salty tangle. Slowly, his eyes began to adjust to the gloom and fret. Above him he saw the faint figure of a man emerging from the darkness, his body swaying unsteadily from the rope which tethered him to those above.

Murray cried out. His voice was lost amid the roaring waves and the screeching winds. Straining his body as far as he could, Murray grabbed onto the rope; the blistered and cut flesh of his palms throbbed sharply as they encountered the coarse, salt encrusted fibres. With as much urgency as he could muster, he tugged the cord.

He waited. From above there was a muffled cry, and as Murray held on, he felt the line loosen as the man descended.

"What are you doing?" The words were barely audible above the crashing elements, but the voice was unmistakably that of John MacKinnon. The elder man came closer. In his terror, Murray found himself unable to respond, his mouth opening and closing but no sound coming forth. Hoping MacKinnon would be able to see him, he pointed upwards at the metal spike.

Another strong flurry threw him against the cliff. Murray clung on, but above him he heard the sickening metal clang as the iron rod came loose and scraped against the rock face. If it plummeted further, it would drag those above with it. Steeling himself to look back up, Murray saw the whites of John's eyes widen with a dawning horror.

The seasoned fowler descended rapidly, pulling the rope so his companions would swiftly follow. Levelling with Murray, he instinctively took hold of the Reverend's coat sleeve and urged him to descend alongside him. Murray scrambled downwards, his feet skidding and his elbows scraping along the surface of the cliff. He barely felt the pain. In a tenth of the time it had taken him to ascend, he placed his feet back onto the ground.

John had beaten him and was already securing the boat. Soon, all the men had returned, and were eagerly cutting themselves free, barely recognising how close they had all come to a shattered demise on the surrounding rocks. A fractured fork of lightning cleft the sky, closely followed by a roll of thunder. The storm was coming closer.

Leaping back into the boat, they departed hastily. Murray barely registered what was happening, the perilous lunge forwards across the divide between land and vessel having passed in seconds, the drive for self-preservation forcing him to do things he would never contemplate under saner circumstances. As he observed his companions, he saw on their faces not fear, but bitter disappointment.

"Nothing." It was Donald Gillies who spoke first. "Not a damn thing."

It soon became clear: the nests had been empty. The bird colony had been left as bereft of young as their pursuers.

※

They left the stacks behind them as soon as the first slithers of light sifted through the gaps in the bothy's wall. None of the men had slept. Unable to flee further, they had retreated to their semi-inhabitable refuge, blistered, windswept and defeated. The storm had reached a crescendo soon after they retreated, and Murray had spent the night shivering under the heavy, sodden wool of his coat, half expecting the drystone to come tumbling down around him, providing him with a burial cairn which in time would no doubt be dragged away by the sea.

The men did not speak as they hastily set sail the following morning. They seemed merely thankful that the weather had calmed enough to permit them a clear passage back home. This time there was no singing to ease the strenuous motion of their rowing, and no eagerness to hurry back to the women who waited nervously on the shore. The little boy whose first hunting expedition had bestowed upon him the expectation of failure, frequently looked up at his father, seeking reassurance. His father never returned his gaze. The men dared not even look at each other.

The only exchange Murray had been offered was a reappraising stare from John MacKinnon. Whilst Murray knew the men owed him for their safety, he could see that no gratitude would be forthcoming. Instead, the men seemed almost ashamed to be around him; no doubt humiliated by the prospect of being indebted to one they had so callously mocked and belittled. John's gaze still conveyed the same undercurrent of distrust, only this time there was also uncertainty. Murray did not care for the appraisal of savages, but he sought approval in himself. He tried to convince himself he had been brave, but he knew he had not; he had merely done what was necessary to survive. His father would have thought him no more noble than the ragged men who surrounded him.

Their arrival back onshore was unceremonious. The women had been waiting since long before dawn had broken, no doubt kept awake by the raging storm. When they saw the men's empty baskets, their relief swiftly turned to despondency, and they went about unloading the boats with a slow, reluctant resignation. Murray pushed passed them. He could not bear to see Flora MacKinnon's searching face among that crowd, or contemplate the absence of his own wife and family at his side.

He did not look back as he strode towards the hovel he was forced to call home. As he arrived at the door, he felt a fleeting moment of trepidation before swinging it open and entering the smoky gloom. The croft was empty; the fire burnt out. He felt a flicker of disappointment. The attention of a dumb, mute girl, witch or no witch, was all he had left. Tearing off his sodden coat and boots, he flung himself onto the bed.

He slept through most of the day. On the few occasions that he woke, he turned away from what remained of the daylight and faced the back of his box bed. His eyes traced the whorls of wood which swirled and dipped before his vision. Suddenly, he was back out at sea. He screwed his eyes shut, returning to a semi slumber where time seemed to stagnate and blur the boundaries between dream and reality.

It was almost completely dark when he heard her come in. Spectral-like, she navigated her way through the murkiness of the blackhouse to light the oil lantern with a small flint and steel fire striker he had left by the hearth. He sat up and waited.

When she turned, she saw him, but rather than startle herself she stood still. Her breath was heavy, and beneath those curtains of wet, black hair, her face was inscrutable. He pulled himself to his feet. He did not know what to say to her, but every base impulse was now sharpened; his previous burdens and commitments seemed to slough off him like a cliff edge sheering itself into the sea. He tried to speak, but before he could she hesitantly wound her arms around him.

Where once he would have pulled away in terror, now he did not. She held him close, her body pressed against his own, radiating a flooding warmth. Now there was no distance left between them. The air around them was bitter from the lack of hearth fire throughout the day, but now he barely even registered the chill. He could have pulled back. He could have stopped himself, even as he buried his face within the intoxicating scent of her damp, peaty hair and felt his body tighten, convulsing in response to every fleeting touch. Still, her hands found their way around his body, branding his skin. He stood apart from her. She trembled slightly, but he could not tell if it was from the cold. He could have stopped himself. Then, reaching out, she clasped her hand around his wrist, and in his mind, he had been ensnared.

The simple gesture conveyed all he needed. If this was bewitchment, he allowed himself to succumb to the inevitable. In the space of a breath, he stepped out beyond the precipice and into the abyss.

CHAPTER TWENTY-TWO

FLORA

FLORA'S fingers were stiff from plucking. The cold of the Autumn was beginning to sharpen the air, seizing her bones as she and the other women sat by the harbour wall, away from the saturated grass. Together they removed the precious oil and feathers from what remained of the fulmar harvest, their hopes of a healthy winter supply of gannet dashed by the men's failed hunt. Earlier that morning the men had left the village for the surrounding cliffs, desperate to gather any seabirds that remained. John had barely spoken to Flora. All the men seemed ashamed to even acknowledge their wives, mothers, and daughters.

Across from Flora, Ann tightly clutched baby Mary to her breast, guarding her fiercely. The child gurgled contentedly; she appeared unfazed by the absence of her mother, and waved a chubby fist at the soft, white feathers floating in the air, giggling when a plume landed on her cheek. Flora tried to keep her resentment from showing. Several times she caught her daughter-in-law staring at her with narrowed eyes, but whenever Flora attempted to return the younger woman's attentions, Ann would hastily look away, lavishing more attention on her infant charge.

"I still say it's our fault."

The women looked up as Rachel McQueen broke their silence. Having drawn their attention, Rachel shyly lowered her head.

"Harvests failing is no new problem," Flora snapped, her patience fraying. "If you'd lived as long as I, you'd know that."

Rachel bit her lip, subdued. Flora snatched up a bird carcass and firmly pressed its bill against the side of a bowl, watching with a frown as the stinking, amber secretion trickled downwards.

"But still," another young woman added, taking up Rachel's cause, "I say a bigger sacrifice was needed. Who's to say the sea wasn't offended by what little we gave?"

Margaret Gillies looked up despondently. Like Flora, she had been unwilling to speculate, but now gave a reluctant nod. Flora did not know what to believe. She of all people knew sickness and famine were a hazard of island life, but she also suspected the sea could, in one way or another, return the value of what was offered to it.

"But what kind of sacrifice would be needed?" Rachel asked.

"We don't have much we can offer." Margaret chewed her lip. "Perhaps one of our flock could be spared, given how little wool they are providing us."

A few women nodded eagerly, but Flora frowned at her friend.

"We can't afford to be hasty. Our flocks can be used to barter with the tacksman for more supplies come winter. Surely we can't give up one resource for another when we don't know for certain it will even work?"

Margaret appeared hesitant, her eyes shifting between her friend and the cluster of younger women, who eyed her eagerly.

"I understand your concerns Flora, and I share them. But . . ."

Margaret's speech was interrupted, and everyone's attention was drawn to Ann, who had risen abruptly and was now stomping away from them, the baby reaching over her shoulder to snatch at the feathers which flew up into the air behind her. A few of the women arched their eyebrows at each other and returned to their work, whilst others examined Flora with a sideways glance. Flora looked to Margaret, who offered a weak smile and shook her head.

"I cannot have this." Flora stood up. "If anyone has anything to say about me or my son's wife, say it. I do not care. But if she can storm off then I don't see why I should stay and keep you from your gossip." Flora walked away, not waiting for a rebuttal from Margaret.

Not looking back to see if the women were watching her or talking amongst themselves, she steered herself in the opposite direction of Ann, away from the settlement and towards the chapel. As she passed by the cemetery wall, she noticed the Reverend was standing nearby, overlooking the half-built walls and making markings in a small book. Flora had not visited or spoken to him since his return from the gannet hunt, but she had heard the whispered snippets of rumour. Apparently, he had helped to return all the men safely from the stack during the storm, and as such her neighbours had adopted a less chilly attitude towards him. Some of the women had, without incentive, even encouraged their husbands to offer their brute strength in rebuilding the chapel. Flora had nevertheless kept her distance, but the dull ache she felt only throbbed harder the longer she waited.

Flora thought of the strange scars and markings that she had seen suddenly blooming on Agnes' skin. The more she thought about it, the more anxious she became to see the marks again, to see she was not deluding herself. She would relish the opportunity, just for a few hours, to dress and talk to the girl, to keep her company while soaking oats or gutting fish. She could not wait any longer. Her mind made up, she strode towards the Reverend's side.

He saw her approaching and lowered his book. He no longer seemed uncomfortable when she was around him, and instead examined her sternly. Flora did not balk under his gaze.

"Mrs MacKinnon," he greeted her coolly.

"Good day, Reverend. I wondered if I might talk to you?"

His hand jerked slightly and a muscle in his cheek twitched. Flora had become familiar with these slight movements enough to know that despite his steely exterior, there were things he hid from her.

"What is it you would like to ask?" The tone of his voice suggested he already knew.

"I was wondering how our charge was keeping?" Flora lowered

her voice. "I have not seen her in days and would like to continue my services for as long as we must keep her on the island."

The Reverend appeared uncomfortable. He could not meet her gaze.

"I have not seen her much myself," he replied, looking once more to the chapel. "She has been eating and sleeping well, from what I can perceive. There really is nothing else I can tell you about the matter."

"Perhaps I could come by this evening? You must be desperate for a decent meal."

The Reverend seemed to take a moment to gather his thoughts. Again, she observed that subtle facial tic.

"You could come over in the evening for a brief spell. I feel that you have got the household in enough order that I shall not need your services in the morning anymore." He spoke hesitantly. "I dare say, for the young lady's sake, you could visit early in the evening to see to her needs."

"It is no trouble to for me to cook and clean for you during the day. John is happy as long as I'm paid," Flora exclaimed, feeling slighted. "I can do any task you put to me. And I . . ."

"It's not that I don't appreciate your efforts," the Reverend cut through her words. "I just feel it would be safer, you understand, if you were to come less frequently. I fear your husband suspects something and it would be more discreet if you could come at an agreed time in the evening. I cannot afford to take too many risks."

"I understand." Flora tried to keep the disappointment from her voice. She could live with only having one opportunity per day to spend time with Agnes and was determined that these visits would happen. Nobody would keep her away.

The Reverend paused over his next words, finally settling on a curt farewell and a dispassionate promise to see her that evening.

"Wait!"

He halted.

"There is something else I have been meaning to ask you,

Reverend. I . . ." Flora could not think of how to say it. Thoughts which had been plaguing her for weeks now seemed impossible to translate into words without sounding foolish. "It's more of a spiritual question, you see."

The Reverend cocked his head and narrowed his eyes. "And what spiritual question might that be?"

Flora braced herself. Better to just say it.

"I wondered, Reverend, if there was some way that the dead could return to the living. Would God allow that?"

The Reverend stared at her in thinly veiled disdain.

"I mean, if a person was taken before their time, could it be possible for them to visit their loved ones again?"

The Reverend inhaled sharply. He rubbed at his temple and sighed.

"There is no possible way that the dead can return, Mrs MacKinnon. They are no longer a part of this earth. You can perhaps hope to see them in what awaits us after this life, but beyond that they are lost to us. Any speculation otherwise would be sacrilege."

"No. I understand. I am sorry to have asked, Reverend."

Flora saw the scrutiny and derision in his expression, and it dawned on her that these stirrings of hope she had been experiencing were best kept to herself. She could live with secrets; after all, silence had been her constant companion for many years. Perhaps she was going mad. Perhaps hope was forcing her to deny the reality of the regrets which plagued her, but as she left the Reverend's incriminating gaze, she looked out pleadingly across the frothing waves which rolled beneath her, crashing and plummeting into one another in a nauseating dance.

"Please," she whispered desperately. "Please let me keep her this time."

"John?"

John's face peered up from the warmth of the hearth, its glow emphasising all the cracks and crevices of his face. Flora entered tentatively and placed her basket on the floor next to a sleeping Morag. She turned away and appeared to look busy in an attempt to conceal the flush of excitement which ruddied her cheeks. Although their encounter had been brief, Agnes had looked healthier than ever: less melancholic. Flora approached her husband. He sat contemplating the embers, his bowl of pottage sitting half eaten on his lap, just as it had been when she had left him.

"He paid me this time, John." Flora extended her hand to show him the coins. "I told him I would go back tomorrow."

John squinted at the coins in her hand but made no move to take them. "Tell him there's no need," he muttered, returning his gaze to the flames.

"But why? I thought that's what you had been waiting for?"

"We don't even know how much they're worth, Flora." John poked at the hearth. "Do you really think what he gives us would be enough to barter with the tacksman? You know how it is with those mainlanders; they'll con us and then they'll laugh at us."

Flora sat down at his side. "You can't know that."

"I do," John responded firmly, but his next words were barely audible, as if they had been intended for himself alone. "Besides, I don't like to admit it, but I owe the man more than money."

Flora remembered the rumours about the Reverend's role in the failed hunting expedition. "Is that why you've been avoiding him?" she enquired. "I heard how he saved you and our boys back on the sea stacks. Perhaps now you'll see he's a decent man deep down. I can see why he can come across as a little gloomy and abrupt in his manner, but people are complicated, John. You know that."

John looked at her steadily. "You would tell me, wouldn't you?"

"Tell you what?" Flora's face blanched. She wondered how much her husband could know. She reached out and took his hands in hers.

"You would tell me if there were more to this than you keeping his house clean and preparing his suppers."

"Of course! What else could there possibly be to it?"

"You aren't hiding anything from me, Flora?"

"No! Why would I be?"

"Then why do you barely even look at me these days?"

Flora pulled her hands away abruptly. "We've been over this. It seems you aren't happy with any answer I give you."

"Ever since Donnchadh died you've been this way."

"What do you expect?"

"It's more than that, Flora."

"Then what?"

"I'm your husband. You share your secrets with me, not him."

"I'm not sharing secrets with anyone."

"Then why are you like this?"

"I have said all I need to say." Flora rose and began preparing the niche in the wall which served as their bed, shaking the blankets free of debris.

"You always do this. You're more like a stranger these days. We sleep in the same bed but you lie apart from me."

Flora's shoulders stiffened. She tried not to respond.

"I just don't understand it!" John's voice rose as she heard him becoming more frustrated. "If there's no secret then what's the fascination? You're too respectable to be his servant, but you're too old to be his whore."

In the space of a breath, Flora whipped around and held her hand up to strike. John rose so quickly his stool clattered to the floor. He was wide eyed. Morag had woken from her slumber next to the fire and skulked slowly backwards into the byre with her hackles raised.

Flora's hand continued to hover mid-air between them before it slowly fell back to her side. She stumbled backwards, feeling a solid mass of dread clog her throat. John's eyes filled with anger and hurt as he took a decisive step towards her. Flora put her arms out to shield herself, but when John saw this he halted, and his eyes softened.

"You can't think..." John stifled a sob. "You can't think I would do that to you? I promised on our wedding night that I would never do that to you."

Flora turned once more to the bed, her body heaving. She could not look at him. She could not bear to stare into those eyes which pleaded with her for understanding and intimacy when she had none left to give, even to herself. She felt his strong arms seize her by the waist and hold her, his head burrowing into her shoulder as he kissed her fiercely on the neck.

"I'm so sorry, *mo cridhe*," he gasped. "I'm so sorry."

She stood and tolerated his caresses, his wet face pressed against her as he forced back yet more tears. "I'm so sorry," he breathed softly against her ear. "Please. Please, come to bed with me." He nuzzled his face into her neck and whispered the words, "I love you", over and over, as if the mantra would bring her back to him. Her heart twisted with pity. She laid a palm against his cheek and stroked it, returning his words with touch.

She let him lie her down and she let him undress her. When she needed to, she turned to watch the dying embers in the fire. All night he held her close. All night she lay and worried about whether her girl was safe and warm.

CHAPTER TWENTY-THREE

THOMAS

AFTER his return from the sea stacks, many of the village women began to regard him in a different light. Although they never expressed their gratitude openly, the anonymous baskets of dried puffin and fish left by his door on certain mornings were evidence enough of a shifting attitude towards him.

Disappointed by their menfolk, it almost seemed as if the women had taken control of the settlement. Each morning, Murray was alarmed to see a string of young men waiting reluctantly by the walls of the chapel to offer their services. Beyond the walls, their mothers and wives hovered watchfully, trying and failing to seem preoccupied with their work while carefully monitoring the situation. Their influence grew even more apparent when, during the morning gatherings, the men finally parted enough to allow him to sit in their circle, rather than have him perch awkwardly just beyond the perimeter.

Murray was unnerved. Whilst once he would have welcomed these developments, his attention was now preoccupied elsewhere; particularly, with concocting excuses to extract himself from his responsibilities as missionary curate. He was contracted to stay until the following summer, but he now accepted that he did not want to remain much longer, and when the tacksman returned for the final harvest in a matter of weeks he fully intended not to linger. Schemes formed in his mind, but none developed fully. Nevertheless, he knew the young tacksman was pliable; no doubt he would be willing to take back additional passengers. But where would he go? He could not return to Inverness. He would need to find a parish further away, as although the thought did not appeal to him.

Adding greater fuel to his desire to leave, was the overbearing presence of Flora MacKinnon. The woman had been true to her word and visited every evening, despite his repeated attempts to keep her at bay. If anything, Flora seemed increasingly reluctant to leave in the evenings, especially when Agnes was present, and would look for every excuse to be alone and tend to her. He worried over how much she could know, but as she administered to her fabricated duties each evening, it became clear from the naïve smile which warmed her face that she suspected nothing of either him or her doted upon charge. It became clear to him that Flora had no intention of parting with the girl. When they did leave Murray knew the old woman would be overwrought with despair, but this could not concern him. It would be better for Flora MacKinnon to dedicate more time to her own family, as God intended for women like her.

As Flora administered to the girl's hygiene, Murray walked a brief circuit around the chapel and village bay. When he returned, Agnes was scrubbed and cleansed within an inch of her life, sitting in a clean wool shift with a discernible look of resentment in her eyes. The old woman was tugging a comb through her hair and as he approached her charge glared at him imploringly.

"I think that will do for tonight, Mrs MacKinnon."

Flora was startled, not even having realised he was there she stared at him slack jawed and cow eyed before realisation dawned. Her face suddenly became veiled by her usual habit of melancholy.

"Are you sure there is not more I can do for you, Reverend?"

"You have been most attentive. Thank you." He removed two copper farthings from his coat and placed them in her hand. She examined them, befuddled, before placing them in her pocket. She gave a slight nod and a murmured thank you before heading towards the door. Before she left, she motioned to the bed she had made up in the byre.

"I brought more blankets for you, Aggie," she addressed the girl. "It's getting so much colder, and you must keep yourself warm."

Agnes, who had been eagerly awaiting Flora's departure, turned away rather than offer a response. After seeing the old woman out, Murray returned to find the girl still facing the opposite wall, her shoulders shaking. Concerned, Murray turned her towards him. Her mouth was twisted into an inhuman grimace, like a snarling dog, and to his utter revulsion he saw that she was in fact laughing, although she uttered no sound. Murray backed away from her and pretended to tend to the hearth. While he found Flora MacKinnon increasingly insufferable, mockery and scorn were incredibly unattractive traits for one to possess.

He felt a hand slip over his shoulder and another snake around his chest. He felt his base urges stir as the weight of her head fell against his shoulder and rested, warmly, in the curve of his neck.

"No," he snapped. He pushed her away abruptly and she glowered at him, wounded and angry. "You cannot behave like that around guests. You were incredibly foul mannered. It isn't decent."

Agnes shook her head uncomprehendingly. Again, she attempted to reach out to him and take him by the hand, but he hastily extracted it.

"No," he repeated. "You cannot expect such things every night. For a man and a woman like us, it is proper that we should know each other fully."

She threw herself onto a stool and arched her eyebrows. Still, he had had no success in subduing her wild whims, and even less success at extracting any information of value from her to help in any case against the islanders. Perhaps it was nobler to cultivate this young woman's intellect, rather than force evidence from the semi scrawled words of what would be perceived as a vulnerable, half-witted girl.

"Perhaps we should go back to your letters. Then we can understand each other better."

Her sideways stare was reluctant, but he was determined to

rise above it. He would prove she could be tamed. While he still contemplated the sketch he had found in Reverend Buchan's notebook, he was reluctant to share with her anything other than the Gospel, which she was slowly and shakily translating into her own cluttered scratchings; she could be a demanding but diligent student when she was in the right frame of mind. Nevertheless, part of him feared exposing her true nature. He wanted to know the truth about her, but now he was fearful of sullying his perceptions of her. Perhaps the sketch was mere coincidence? The women of the outer isles had a similar bone structure; an almost indistinguishable look etched into their faces by the savage wilderness they had made their home. And so, the Reverend Buchan's book remained untouched at the bottom of his father's chest. His fascination and fury over his predecessor's transgressions fell into the debris which cluttered the back of his mind, alongside another, now unspoken name.

Fetching parchment and ink, Murray carefully observed Agnes as she attempted to trace the words he dictated from the Gospel of Mark. After some time had slipped by, she was starting to flag. Looking at him steadily, she shook her head and put her hand over his own, indicating for him to stop.

"You must learn these things," he sighed, closing his bible. "You will not remain here much longer, and you can be more than just a fishwife. Do you want to spend forever scratching your existence from the limpets on the rocks, or do you want a chance for a better life? If you write for me, I can make it so."

Agnes furrowed her brow. Grasping the quill in an awkward fist hold, she dragged it once more across the parchment. Murray squinted to decipher the word:

where

He sat back, unwilling to meet her scrutinizing gaze.

"I do not know. First we must go to the inner isles; I will need your help in something. Then . . . Somewhere better."

when

"As soon as the tacksman returns. We are trapped until then."

She scribbled furiously and jabbed at her words; her wide eyes pleaded with him.

you   me

He studied her words carefully, their meaning slowly dawning on him. To his growing discomfort he saw that she was beginning to weep. The soundless racking of her body unnerved him. Murray placed a tentative hand on her shoulder and in a gesture of rare affection, parted a straggling strand of hair from her face. Her body quivered under the tenderness of his touch.

"Do you . . ." He hesitated. "Do you wish to stay with me?"

Her silent sobs halted, and she clasped his hand. Drawing it to her face, she held it there against her cheek, her trembling subsiding. His mind was in turmoil, but suddenly the questions which had been plaguing him for the past weeks found a resolute yet daring answer. There was no going back to Inverness. Perhaps this was the opportunity he wanted: the opportunity to start his life afresh, far from the contempt and judgement of those from the past.

"We will go together. You and me. I will prove them all wrong: I will be free of them! We will find somewhere far away from here where you and I can live respectfully . . ."

She seemed bewildered. The thoughts which he had agonised over now appeared fully formed and irrepressible.

"You will not be my servant. We will be as husband and wife. Do you understand me?"

She nodded vigorously and clung to him.

"It does not matter who you are. The past does not matter," he murmured, but more to himself than to her.

He felt the rise and fall of her chest as her heart pulsed against his own, just as it had on the day he had found her. It had been so long since he had been held like that. Finally, here was a person who needed him, who relied upon him and would put complete trust in a life shared together.

He felt her fingers venture across his collarbone, reaching to unbuckle the starched stock which encircled his throat, drifting further still. He put his bible to one side.

※

He choked on the heavy, stagnant air. A brackish stench travelled through his nostrils and caught at the back of his throat. Mist swirled around him and filled the air with moisture, through which only blurred shadows were discernible. He stretched out his arm tentatively, before thrashing it from side to side like a blind man trying to navigate through a dense, web shrouded thicket.

His hand fell on something damp and coated in a thick slime. As he pulled away, he noticed the green crescents beneath his fingernails and caught the musty scent of rotten wood. His lip curled in disgust, but again he reached out. As he felt his way along the sodden barrier, the wood turned to a pulp under his palms, and his fingers brushed against long strands of weed. There was something rough and jagged against his hand. He felt around further: barnacles and limpets had buried themselves into the decaying wood. He brushed against the hard, conical shell of a whelk, and listened as it dropped and clattered against a hard floor. Something crunched beneath his feet.

He slipped on the sticky carpet of sea moss sprouting beneath him. His hands stung as they supported his fall. The floor slowly came into focus, and beneath the layers of green and purple there was a hard, smooth surface of black and white tiles.

There was movement. Much movement. Dozens of strange, grotesque organisms with many bristling tendrils unfurling from their tiny bodies swarmed over the floor. One collided blindly with his hand and stretched out a hairy leg, probing his skin for a path forward. He cried out in disgust and flung the vile creature away. As his eyes were drawn upwards, he saw the silhouette of another wooden structure. It was unmistakable.

He looked up at the pulpit of his parish church in Inverness. It was now collapsing in on itself, as if under immense pressure from an invisible weight. Squinting in the green tinged half-light, he saw the shadows of pews stretching out before him. Not a soul was there. He thought he heard hymns, but the voices seemed distant and indistinct, muffled as if underwater. Was that Caroline's voice he heard? Or was it his mother's? He could hardly discern the difference.

He moved forward slowly, pushing his body through the thick air, down the aisle and towards the door. He placed his hand against it, but it did not give. Someone or something seemed to push back from the other side, and the wood buckled and pushed itself out towards him. It too was coated in algae.

"Thomas."

There was a voice beyond the door, but it was so quiet he questioned its validity. He pushed again, this time with his shoulder. The door did not budge. As he applied his full body weight to the task, his eyes caught a trickle of water seeping in through the wooden slats, pooling around his feet. Cautiously, he began to retreat. There was a low groan from beyond the door as the wood creaked in protest at the pressure being applied to it from outside.

He looked to the windows. Outside there was nothing; only a vast, blue-green emptiness. He caught the voices again.

> *"When I survey the wond'rous Cross*
> *On which the Prince of Glory dy'd,*
> *My richest Gain I count but Loss,*
> *And pour Contempt on all my Pride."*

He called out. No one came. The door buckled further; its moans deepened and became a cry of agony. It would not hold. The little light that remained in the church was dimming, and darkness was looming forward.

> *"Forbid it, Lord, that I should boast,*
> *Save in the Death of Christ my God:*
> *All the vain Things that charm me most,*
> *I sacrifice them to his Blood."*

They did not come for him. But the sea was already there.

Its icy fingers slithered down his throat and wrapped around his lungs. With a ferocious roar it was unleashed, and it caught him.

The nightmare halted abruptly, and Murray awoke to the comforting crackle of the peat fire. There was a hand resting upon his chest and a cold ankle looped around his lower leg. Remembering where he was, he pulled the blankets towards himself and turned away to face the warmth of the hearth.

CHAPTER TWENTY-FOUR

FLORA

"Is this your doing?"

Flora had been taking Morag onto the hill to herd their flock when she was accosted by Ann. The young woman gripped her by the arm. The past months had not been kind to Ann's once solid girth, and Flora felt a twinge of pity when looking into her wasted face, rendered demented by the hairs flying free from under her threadbare shawl. Michael stood behind his wife, ready to lead her away. But Ann was not to be cowed.

"What is it you accuse me of this time, Ann?" Flora tried to keep her voice level and glanced over her shoulder distractedly to check Morag had not fled. Panic seized her insides.

"You can tell her." Ann whipped around to glower at Michael. "It's your blessed mother after all."

Michael shrugged his broad shoulders. "I've already told you, Ann. Ma has nothing to do with this. It was mine and Fergus' decision, no one else's."

"Nothing to do with what?"

"Don't keep hiding behind your son, Flora. I know you will have been the one to get him working on that building for that stupid priest of yours." Ann's face was red, but her expression remained deadly serious. Flora could have laughed.

"Is that all you are angry about?" Flora scrutinised her daughter-in-law's face. "Michael, take her inside, before she catches a chill."

"You just don't care, do you?" Ann shrieked. "You just don't care that your own grand bairns are going without food. You'd rather your sons bowed down to that black clad buffoon than go out and provide for their families!"

"I have nothing to do with their decision!" Flora snapped. "Ann, I feel sorry for you, I really do, but you need to get it into your head that no one is conspiring against you. Sometimes terrible things happen. Strong women like us need to press on and find a way forward."

Ann breathed heavily; she seemed unable to form words. It was Michael who moved forward to put a comforting arm around his wife, all the while looking at Flora with unspoken apology.

"I can be spared for a little while, *mo cridhe*." Michael spoke in a soothing tone, rubbing his wife's back as if she were a babe with colic. "I told you the Reverend saved us on our last hunting trip. I have no doubt he will fully reimburse us for our time. Will it not be a good thing to have money in time for the tacksman's visit?"

Ann yanked herself away and took a step towards Flora. "I know what you did, Flora MacKinnon." A knowing and vicious smile crept across her anguished face.

Flora tried to retain her composure, determined not to look away.

"I have no idea what you are talking about."

"You." Ann spat out the word. "You put a curse on me and Mary. You summoned that witch. All because you're jealous. Yes, that's right, jealous!" Ann let out a cackle of laughter.

Michael looked torn between protecting his mother and soothing his wife; he dithered between them with dumb eyes. Flora could have slapped him. She opened her lips to defend herself, but Ann cut her off before she had a chance to speak.

"It's because Mary and I have daughters, and you don't. So now you've taken one of mine and you took Mary out of pure spite so you could get your hands on her child."

"Michael, take your wife away," Flora said through gritted teeth. "She does not know what she is saying."

"Oh, I do! I know fine well what I am saying. I'm not the one who's gone mad."

"Ann, please . . ." Michael may have been physically strong, but he seemed totally lost in the current situation.

"Don't patronise me, Michael," Ann hissed. "She is a vindictive woman, your mother."

"Please leave, Ann, before we both say something we regret," Flora warned. "You are not well."

"No, you are not well! We all know, Flora. No one admits it to spare your feelings, but we all know it was your fault your own daughter drowned all those years ago."

Flora staggered backwards. Ann could have hit her, kicked her, beaten her with stones: nothing could hurt as much as those words. She felt Michael rush forward to support her from falling.

"That's right." Ann's face was triumphant. "What kind of well mother would neglect her own child enough to let her wander off into the oncoming tide? You are the one to blame for your own misfortunes, Flora. Even Donnchadh was spoiled rotten and not given time enough with his father to learn how to properly tackle those sea stacks. You are a terrible mother, Flora MacKinnon, but I will make damned sure you do not drag us all down with you."

With a parting look of contempt, Ann spun on her heel and stormed off. Flora had felt sympathy for her, but now she wished she were young and fit enough to race after her; she would pull out that poisoned tongue and twist her knuckles into those spiteful eyes.

Michael righted his mother, then gazed wistfully after his wife. "I'm so sorry, Ma. She'll apologise, I know she will. She just isn't in her right mind still."

"You are her husband, Michael." Flora shot her son a steely glare. "You ought to keep better control of her. Now leave me alone."

Michael looked wounded but obeyed his mother's request and followed his wife.

Flora marched forwards up the hill after Morag without looking back. She would not allow Ann to scare her. Ann could never understand the sacrifices she had made for her family. Scrambling upwards, she set her mind to the task ahead. Soon the livestock would need to be brought back down to the bay to winter in the byres, and soon the tacksman would return to collect MacLeod's last levy of the year. That was where her real worry lay, for that was when she and Agnes would be parted again. If only she could find a way to stop it. If only there was a way to keep her by her side.

It was not long before another child died. This time it was one of Donald and Margaret's grandchildren, barely a month past its first name day. There was a hastened period of mourning, then the customary gathering at the cemetery, but by then they had all become numb to the procession of death, and only the mother wept.

It was only a week later, when the women gathered to waulk the last of the year's wool, that the mood started to change.

Flora had hardly spoken to Margaret for over a month, and now as they sat side by side among the circle of younger women, dully trudging their feet against the tweed in time with their chosen dirge, Flora could see how reluctant her neighbour was to even meet her eye. Ann, thankfully, was not present. Ann never seemed to be present anywhere in those days and dedicated almost all her time to nursing Mary's child. Instead, her daughter Janet had joined them, old enough now to beat her tiny feet in rhythm, but young enough for it all to still seem a novelty. Flora smiled at her granddaughter and felt a pain in her chest when she did not smile back.

Soon the song came to a stop, but none of them seemed to have the energy to begin anew. Margaret's bereaved daughter, Elisabeth, subjected them to a fresh bout of sobbing.

"I cannot stand this anymore." One of the youngest in their circle, a brawny, recently married McCrimmon girl, Cora, stood up. "We can't go on like this. Something needs to be done."

"And what could that possibly be?" Flora asked bluntly, tired of the same outbursts from the younger women in the group. They were not used to suffering. They thought they were entitled to a life without it.

"Well first off, we should speak to the men. Force them to listen."

There was a grumble of assent.

"I agree," offered Rachel McQueen, tragedy making her bolder. "We should have made a larger sacrifice last time. Clearly that is what is needed. But when have the men ever listened to us? They're down there at their meeting right now, and since when have they ever invited our opinion?"

"Then we force them to."

"That is not how things are done," Flora muttered.

"We don't care about how things are done anymore. We need drastic measures," Elisabeth gushed, angrily dashing the tears from her face.

"Offering up what we cannot afford to lose will only cause more hardship." Flora tried to cut through their growing hysteria. "I'm sorry to be so brutal about it, but bad winters come, and bad winters go. It's a terrible reality but it's one we just have to accept and push through, no matter the cost."

"I would expect that kind of coldness from you, Flora MacKinnon." Elisabeth regarded her icily. "Mother, won't you say something?" She looked to Margaret. "We must go and demand action from the men. We should go right now."

"Aye," added Cora. "Tradition be damned."

Margaret sighed heavily and pinched her brow. Flora put a hand on her friend's arm.

"Margaret," she whispered. "You know we have been here before. It will pass. Things always pass."

Margaret slowly looked up. She seemed to have won the battle within herself, but her face was etched with regret.

"Very well," she said. "Tradition be damned."

There was a raucous cry from the younger women; they hastily began to fold away the cloth and rallied together down the slope, making their way towards the settlement.

"Margaret?" Flora looked at her former friend.

Margaret blinked away tears. "I'm sorry, Flora. But we can't just stand by any longer." She heaved herself up and followed her fellow women, leaving Flora behind.

Seeing no other option, Flora rose to pursue them, eventually coming within sight of the men at their morning meeting. Upon catching sight of the mass of women, they stopped their talk and stared, dumbfounded at what marched towards them. As they came closer, Flora caught sight of the Reverend, standing out in his clerical garb, his mouth agape. Some of the older men in the group, John and Donald included, glared at them with barely concealed outrage. Emboldened, some of the women stepped forward and broke through their circle.

"Back to your work, wives!" Some of the men began to shout out, but they were soon overwhelmed by a chorus of angry women's voices.

"Not until you do something about this sickness!"

"Aye. We don't want any more of our bairns dying! You men don't know what it's like: you've been spared the worst of it."

Trying to push back against the rumbling tide, Flora watched as Donald Gillies cut through the women's collective outrage.

"What means this, Margaret?" He looked to his wife. "This is men's business being discussed. You know it is forbidden for women to attend a gathering."

"We know, Donald, but as you can see, we have all had enough." Margaret spoke as if preaching a sermon. "You men failed to bring us succour from that disaster of a hunt, and now you seem to have given up entirely on trying to spare us more grief. You men are so unimaginative, so we must find other means to get ourselves out of this mess. We demand action."

"The best way to do that is by dedicating yourselves to your work." It was Donald who first rebuked his wife. Flora struggled to hear a discernible word as the women, spurred on by this reprimand, clamoured to have their say.

"And what have you men done to help recently? All you do is sit and talk!"

"We demand a sacrifice be made! Like in the old days."

"Yes. A sacrifice! What is one sheep worth when your children are dying?"

There was a silence amongst the men. They seemed in deep contemplation, searching for a way to appease their wives and daughters. Flora was the only one who noticed the Reverend leap to his feet.

"I cannot allow this! Sacrifices are pagan superstition. We should seek to appease God only. You must take to prayer, for He alone will decide your fate."

"We're done with your God!"

A chorus of women rained their retorts down on the Reverend, until Margaret once more took control.

"We have pleaded with God before," she said. "Reverend Buchan gave us reason to believe, but nothing good ever came of it. We have our own ways on this island, it is about time we went back to them!"

The women erupted with shouts of approval.

"So, Donald," Margaret continued, "and all the rest of you. What is it to be? Will you hear us? Will you do right by your families?"

Donald and John stared at each other. Many of the other men seemed already to have reached a decision and were nodding their heads in unison. Flora caught John's eye, and watched as he turned away, frowning.

"You may take one old ewe from each household. No more." Donald's voice was solemn. "You may do the deed in two night's time, at dawn; before the rest of the flock are brought in from pasture."

The women cheered. Some rushed to their husbands and embraced them, while the men still seemed weary of their presence in this strictly male space.

"I cannot condone this." The Reverend was still standing. "You are all lost if you agree to this affront to Our Lord."

"We have listened to your input, Reverend," said Donald. "I respect you have your own reservations, as do I. But this is not your decision to make now."

Flora watched as the Reverend turned red and marched away, his heavy cloak catching in the wind. As he passed Flora, he did not turn to acknowledge her, but instead issued an order, so quiet she was at first uncertain if it was not the wind passing by her ear.

"You are to come with me at once."

"I . . ."

"Now."

Flora glanced around nervously. No one was paying them enough heed to notice her separation from the group. It was only John's eyes she could feel boring into her as she followed the Reverend up the slope towards his croft. Perhaps it would arouse his suspicions further, but Flora knew she could appease John later. As she struggled up the hill after the Reverend, who strode forward in wide, determined steps, she wondered what the urgency could be. He had not called on her of his own free will for weeks.

As they entered his dwelling, he slammed the door firmly and ushered her into the living space. As she took a seat by the hearth, he looked at her sternly.

"There are now two pressing matters I must address with you."

"Oh?" She cocked her head, trying to affect an appearance of calmness which she did not feel. Whereas before the Reverend seemed awkward during their interactions, now his presence filled the room and loomed over her with stern authority. It unsettled her.

"Firstly, we should address the disgraceful display I just bore witness to." He glowered at her. "I would hope that none of that was your doing. I had after all, assumed you to be one of the more God-fearing people on this wretched rock."

"I had nothing to do with it, Reverend," Flora replied firmly. "If anything, I spoke out against the idea of a sacrifice! You can trust me, I swear it."

"I believe you." His expression did not show it. "But the fact remains, I cannot persist here much longer. Not under these circumstances. I have tried and laboured to bring this island round to God, but just as I think I have made some progress, I am thwarted once again by the stubborn heathenness of your people." He paused. "Which brings us, quite conveniently, to my next matter." His voice rose and he paced the floor. It seemed to Flora that he was not even addressing his rantings at her anymore. "The tacksman will return in less than a month and I intend to leave with him, which means, Mrs MacKinnon, our time here together will be at an end."

Flora shifted her body weight. "But I thought you were to remain until next summer?"

"Out of the question." He stopped pacing and turned to face her. "Especially not after today. I will go and report my findings to your laird, MacLeod. I cannot tolerate it here any longer, and neither can she."

"She?"

"You know of whom I speak."

"Is she unwell?"

"Quite to the contrary, but the longer she stays here the greater risk she is under. You saw the bloodlust in those harridans' eyes earlier. I will not allow her to stay and be at risk."

Flora knew this was coming, but still she felt unprepared for the blow.

"But then perhaps the sacrifice will be for the best, Reverend? Perhaps afterwards things will die down, and she will be safe. I will keep her safe. If they harm her, they will have to harm me."

"It is impossible, Mrs MacKinnon! Do you understand me? Impossible!" He threw his hands out in a gesture of exasperation. Flora had never heard him raise his voice to such a fury before. She turned away from him and set her eyes to the floor.

"It matters not how attached you are to her," he continued.

"You are one woman; you cannot protect her forever. She will leave with the tacksman, and I will accompany her. That will be the best outcome for all of us. I can at the very least assure her safety better this way."

"But . . ."

"No, Flora."

She looked up as the sound of her given name escaped his lips for the first time. He wielded his next words like daggers.

"You belong here. We do not."

Flora fought back the burning sensation building up behind her eyes. She would give no one the satisfaction of seeing her cry. She lowered her eyes and steadied her voice so as not to betray her distress.

"You don't know that."

"What did you just say?"

"I said, you don't know that. You certainly don't know where *she* belongs." Flora looked up at him through clouded eyes, her fists clenched in her lap. The Reverend took a step back. She gained strength as she observed him wither against the back wall.

"I pitied you when you first arrived here," she continued, glaring at him, "because I know how it feels to be misunderstood. Because you do not seem to belong anywhere either. You say you have a wife, then why does she not follow you here?"

A shadow seemed to pass over his face. He placed his hands flatly against his stomach like a shield. "I would choose your next words very carefully, Flora MacKinnon."

There was a thinly veiled warning in his eyes. She could have dared herself to go further, to pick at his weaknesses the way a fingernail burrows into a recently formed scab. But then she thought of Aggie. She did not want to lose those opportunities to be with her; not when they would soon be so cruelly cut short. She fought against the rage building within her and, calling upon years of practice, set her voice to compliance.

"I understand you, Reverend. You of course, know what is best for us." She levered herself to her feet in as dignified a way as possible. "Will there be anything else?"

The Reverend's shoulders dropped, and his face softened. Once more she caught a glimpse of the anxious young stranger out of his depth. The moment was fleeting. He stood tall in his fitted black, like a flustered raven.

"A small matter." His eyes shifted towards the byre. "I will need you to attend to our mutual friend this evening. She has . . . I wish for her to stay here with me from now on. Allowing her to continue coming and going as she pleases is too risky, do you understand?"

"Yes, of course." Flora did not envy the man having to restrain her girl by keeping her indoors. It would be a necessary evil, Flora tried to convince herself, but overriding this urge to protect, came an aching dread at what was to come. Flora knew how it felt to have a child prized away from her and could not bear the pain of it again. She could not let it happen. She would find a way.

CHAPTER TWENTY-FIVE

THOMAS

MURRAY felt some relief that his days on the island were numbered. By now he had already secured his belongings and gathered what he deemed suitable coinage for their safe passage; not that much would be necessary. Murray speculated that from Robert MacLeod's easy corruptibility, the promise of a cask of wine would be enough. He hoped the foolish youth's love of extravagance would not urge him to demand more, and he also hoped that the man's base curiosities would not put Agnes in harm's way. No doubt there would be some insinuations made. But what did it matter anymore?

He grew restless. His only occupation now was in overseeing the reconstruction of the chapel building. There was some satisfaction in watching each stone put in place, knowing that it brought him gradually closer to departure, although he very much doubted the men had the resources they needed to complete their task. But that did not matter either. By the time the islanders allowed the structure to fall into ruin again he would be gone, and therefore could not be blamed. He had already prepared his letter to the Presbytery in Edinburgh. It was appropriately brief and pragmatic. Judging by the prior appointment of Buchan, the Church clearly viewed Eilean Eòin as a lost cause, and at least he had the satisfaction of stating he had rooted out popery. As far as he was concerned, the Kirk owed him release from his current post, and surely it would not be too difficult to find him another?

Murray contemplated this as he directed Flora MacKinnon's sons over the careful resurrection of the chapel's walls. It was bitterly cold, and the light was starting to fade. Thank God he would not have to see through the winter in this place.

"... I said we're almost ready, Reverend."

His head snapped up and he blinked at Michael MacKinnon. "What?"

"We're almost finished the chapel walls. We can make a start on the roof tomorrow, with your permission of course." The young man's face seemed earnest enough, but his brother Fergus avoided Murray's eyes as he collected his tools and made his way home. Murray took a moment to gather his thoughts back to the present.

"Oh, yes, I see. That would be appropriate. Yes," he stammered his reply and gave a wave of the hand.

"Are you well, Reverend?" Michael frowned.

"Yes. Fine. Thankyou." He stared at the young man, willing him to leave. "That will be all for today. You should return home before it gets dark."

"Well, actually, Reverend, there was something else." Michael looked down at his feet. "I never got the chance to thank you properly for what happened back at the stacks. I suppose this building is my thanks, but I know you mainlanders like words better than deeds sometimes, so . . ." Michael shrugged, alternating his gaze between the ground and Murray's face.

"I appreciate your gratitude, but there really is no need, Mr MacKinnon. Now if you will excuse me . . ."

"But I think there is, Reverend. Especially now you've been giving work to my mother. My parents need the extra tithe to pay the tacksman, and my mother needs to keep her mind occupied." He seemed to struggle with his next words and gazed into the distance. "I worry about her. Everyone seems to have turned against her but you."

There was an uncomfortable silence before Michael continued.

"She was always quite fragile minded, even if she does not show it. When I was a child and my sister died, she shut herself away for weeks afterwards. Fergus and I really worried after Donnchadh's death. He was always her favourite, and to be honest with you Reverend, he was a spoiled boy. Ma did not keep a tight rein on him, even when he . . ." Michael seemed to rethink his next words. "Even when his behaviour was not right."

Murray grew impatient. How could this possibly concern him?

"Is there something else you want to tell me, Michael?" He stared at the young man, who quickly looked back down at the turf. Murray felt some satisfaction in knowing he could now subdue the burly simpleton with no more than a look. Michael shuffled his feet.

"Nothing, Reverend. Just Donnchadh and some of the other young lads, they . . . Well, you know how young lads can sometimes be." He attempted a hearty laugh. He stopped when he met Murray's frown. "Anyway, all in the past now."

Murray sighed. "You should get back to your wife, Michael."

Michael's face darkened in the dimming twilight. "Ann does not talk to me much these days, Reverend. She's taken against my mother something terrible, and now she seems to distrust me too." He looked drained. "I wondered, perhaps, if you could speak with her. Talk to her about forgiveness, and all that?"

"I very much doubt your wife favours me over yourself." Murray kept his voice level. "You are her husband. Only you can discipline her."

"There is truth in that, Reverend, I cannot deny you that," Michael laughed half-heartedly, seeming to have mistaken the admonishment for a joke between men. "Are you married, Reverend? I suppose not, if you have come here alone."

Murray's face coloured.

A sly smile crept across Michael's face. "I bet you've been very lonely these past months, am I right?" The man's grin widened. "You are still young after all, not like the old man you replaced, and though he may never have had much to do with them, even he knew the value of a healthy population of women!"

Murray recoiled as Michael slapped a heavy hand on his back, as if he would share in his crude attempts at conversation. He pulled himself away roughly and Michael's face fell.

"As I said, sir, you should return to your wife." Murray took another step back and glowered. "Whatever perversions or vices you insinuate, I suggest keeping them to yourself, or taking them up with God."

"Well, Reverend." Michael arched his eyebrows. "Far be it for me to question what the Lord wants. I may not know what perversions or vices are, but at least I can share in a joke."

He was relieved when Michael turned to go, but just as he got to the cemetery wall, the young man shouted back, "You'll never fit in here with the rest of us, you do know that don't you?" When no answer came, Michael shook his head and continued onwards to his croft.

※

Murray flung his hat onto the table and sunk down onto the wooden stool. He slouched forward, staying that way for some time, rubbing his forehead, before he noticed his breath forming icy clouds in front of his face. He turned. The hearth was barely smouldering, and Agnes was nowhere to be seen. He sat up. How long could she have been gone for the fire to have fully extinguished itself? Looking to the window he saw that darkness had almost fully settled and, panicking, he rose to go to the front door.

Before he could even take a step, the door creaked open, and in she strode. She smiled at him, brazen, as if nothing were amiss. Bending down to the hearth, she took his tinder box and began to strike flint against steel. Murray swooped down and grabbed her by the wrist. She did not pull away, but looked up at him through her tangle of hair and reached out with her free hand to touch his face. He batted it away.

"How could you do this again? How could you be so careless?"

She blinked.

"I told you not to leave during the day. Not under any circumstances. Do you understand me?"

Snatching her arm from him, she furrowed her brow and continued to chip away at the flint. Murray watched the sparks catch and begin snaking into flame, but he could not let this transgression go. He wanted to shake her, to hold her to face him until she could fully understand how much anxiety she had caused.

"You wilfully disobeyed me." His voice caught in his throat. "Do you understand the lengths I have gone to, the risks I have taken just to keep you safe?"

She did not look at him but continued to watch the fire forming. He felt his ire rising to the point he could contain himself no longer.

"Why am I constantly being thwarted by women?" He was alarmed to hear his voice rise to an unrecognizable pitch. "Why can't you simply do as you are bid?"

Agnes slammed her palm down on the cold, hard floor and her furious eyes locked with his own. Murray recoiled.

She stood up and looked down on him, before turning to head once more for the door.

"Wait! Please!" He could not believe how pathetic he sounded. "I am sorry," he gasped. A lump formed in his throat. "I just cannot bear the thought of losing you. You are all I have left . . ." He trailed off as his own words hit him. It was true; he had just not fully accepted it until now.

Agnes paused at the entranceway and once more turned her gaze towards him. Her expression was sullen, but there was a hint of vulnerability and tenderness in the way she lowered her eyes. It was only then that he realised that he was still on the floor, crouched down in the filthy rushes as if in prayer, while she held herself above him. Embarrassed, he unfolded his legs and rose to his feet, until he once more dominated the space with his height.

"When we leave here," he steadied his voice, "when we are married . . ."

Agnes' head lifted.

"When we are married, you can go outdoors as you please." He watched her lips twitch into her twisted, inscrutable half smile. "You can even have your own little garden. Perhaps you will pick flowers..." Murray's voice trailed off as unwelcome memories rose up like the tide colliding with a cliff, chipping away slowly at the foundations of the land.

Agnes must not have noticed his anguish, for rather than hold back any longer, she now clung to him, her head resting against his chest. He wished he could separate himself from her just for this moment, but within him came the unbidden desire to be held, to be touched. More than that: to be needed. There was a silence that hung between them, and he felt her breath quicken as she leant against his shoulder. He held her at arm's length and stared at her, scrutinising her expression. She looked away.

"What is it?" His hand fell against her face and directed it back to him. "There's something else that's troubling you. I can tell."

She pulled away and turned her stool towards the hearth, her body tensing. He wished more than ever she could talk to him. Leaning closer to her, he caught her once again in his arms and felt her thin body press against him. Their eyes met. Shakily, she took his hand in hers and laid it flat against her stomach. His eyes widened.

"...are you...?"

She nodded, her expression unfathomable. Murray rose from his seat and held his head in his hands. Of course, this would happen; he should have thought about that, but he had been in denial the entire time.

Murray paced the floor. He reluctantly thought of Caroline, whose broken body had never been able to support a living child, except for the one time when she had borne their son, only to lose him within hours. If that was a holy union, how was it that God had not blessed it with children? And now this: this union not founded on marriage vows, but on happenstance, had been consecrated with new life. He stopped pacing and looked at the young woman. Her flushed face appeared innocent in the golden glow of the fire, like the faces of stained-glass women gazing up at the crucified Christ. If his former marriage were in error, could it not be that God was now righting his mistake? They were, after all, as good as married. He bent down and held Agnes' hands. Soon they would be wedded in a proper ceremony, far away from the horrors of Eilean Eòin.

"All will be well," he spoke tenderly to her. "The tacksman will be here soon, and both of us will be off this island for good. Your child will want for nothing, and we will be happy. I promise you that."

CHAPTER TWENTY-SIX

FLORA

IT was the morning of the sacrifice, and Flora had barely slept. The sky outside was still black, and for the first time in years she rose before her husband, who was turned to face the wall, still sleeping, or at least pretending to. Flora sat on the edge of the bed. She began her morning ritual by vigorously rubbing her knees, which had become red and swollen overnight. When the warmth returned, she rose to her feet and began pinning herself into her clothing. She clicked her tongue and Morag, who was curled up close to the hearth, pricked up her ears.

The dog followed her to the door. As Flora pushed against it, the wood moaned and refused to budge. She leaned in with her shoulder and applied the full weight of her weakening body, then stumbled as the ice sealing the door cracked and fell in frosty shards around her. Morag shook herself, while her mistress stepped out into the cold. The ground had formed a hard crust overnight, and the air was tinged with a blue grey light as the dawn slowly struggled to assert itself over the freezing mist, which formed over the low-lying ground. Perhaps the cold would delay the other women. Perhaps they would not come at all.

Then Flora heard the voices cutting through the mist, starting as a whisper that echoed hauntingly against the barren landscape. Shadows began to form. Flora watched as her neighbours, all bundled in wool, drifted in and out of her vision like ghosts, all heading in the same direction. She followed anxiously, struggling to keep up. Near the cliffs to the side of the bay stood a small storehouse and sheep pen; the chosen ewes had been herded there the previous day, and now it was time for the deed to be done.

As Flora climbed along the cliff path with her fellow women, she saw that the younger amongst them were limping under the weight of the large stones that they carried; thick ropes were tightly wrapped around these rocks. Flora understood. It was important that they gave their sacrifice whole. Spilling blood with a slit to the throat would be robbing the sea of its prize. It would be like gifting broken crockery, or half eaten bread.

Soon the blurry silhouette of the domed storehouse loomed into view; a slight hump on the horizon before the land sheered away into thin air. The women formed a semi-circle around the perimeter and some of them eased their burdens to the ground with a soft exhale. Flora looked at the bound rocks and a memory surfaced. When she was a child, her father's sheepdog had fallen on the rocks and broken its spine. Her mother had told her not to take heed, but she could not help noticing her father cradling the poor beast in his arms, carrying it out towards the shore: it was the first and only time she had seen her father's eyes brim with tears. They had secured the animal with rope and tied a rock around its neck before dropping it in the water. Her father assured her it was a quick and merciful death: with luck the dog's neck would break before it even hit the water, and if not, the sea was a gentle killer. More importantly, it was the way it had always been done.

Flora noticed that Morag had fallen behind, and was skulking a few yards away, her ears pushed back, whining. She turned and fondled the animal's ears.

"Hey," she soothed. "What's the matter, hey? What's the matter?"

Morag barked and slowly began backing away.

"What's the matter you dumb dog?"

Morag's lips curled back, and her eyes were wide as they stared fixedly ahead. She let out a low, tremulous growl. "Stupid beast," Flora muttered, returning to where her neighbours stood.

The women bided their time until yellow beams of light began to seep through the dense cloud. Flora looked to her right and saw Margaret squinting up at the hazy sunrise, before moving with assertive strides towards the sheep pen. Flora followed with the others, her skirt swishing silently through the dew coated grass, the wool clinging damply to her legs. As they approached the gate, Flora noticed that Morag had turned on her heel and fled. The animal always was skittish, and even she felt unnerved by the silence and the solemnity of her fellow women, who did not chatter or cluster together as was their custom during shared labours.

As the haze started to clear, their silence ended. There was a sudden uproar amongst those beside the pen, and Flora could see that not only was the gate open, it had also been torn from its post and hung crookedly to the side. She rushed forward with the others, who then scattered and threw themselves into a desperate search. The sun had now broken through the cloud and Flora could see clearly enough that their efforts were in vain: the ewes had gone.

It was then that she heard the frantic barking from beyond the storehouse. Lifting her skirts, she ran stiffly around the enclosure to the edge of the cliffs, where Morag was running in circles, tail between her legs. When she saw Flora, she flattened herself upon the ground and whimpered. Flora edged closer, cautious of slipping on the wet grass. She peered downwards.

The foamy water that slopped against rocks below was stained with red. The broken bodies of the ewes lay limply between sea and land, their lifeless limbs splaying outwards as they were pulled to and fro in the shallow breakers. Flora pulled herself back from the precipice and retched. She knew what would come next, as soon the others surrounded her, drawn towards the cliffs by Morag's yelps. There was a collective gasp as the women saw what lay below, and a smattering of anguished cries.

"Come away!" It was Margaret who barked the order, ushering her own flock away from the sheer drop. The women hung back, and it was then that the whispering started. Flora's shoulders shook.

Panting, she hung back from the others, her eyes closed firmly so she could not see their suspicious, recriminating glances.

"How could it have happened?"

". . . the wind was still last night."

"Perhaps something spooked them? They could have broken the gate themselves . . ."

"I think it's fairly obvious what has happened."

Flora cringed against the wall of the storehouse as Ann's voice rose from the crowd.

"We all know the only one among us who objected to a sacrifice in the first place. And why might that be I wonder?"

Flora could feel Ann's eyes upon her.

"Ann, what could you possibly be suggesting?" Margaret's tone was harsh, but Flora could see from her neighbour's awkward stance that even she was unnerved.

"It's her!" Ann screeched; her finger pointed at Flora. "She's to blame for all of this! Her and that sea witch!"

"Calm down, Ann." Margaret held the younger woman by the shoulder, but Ann yanked her arm away.

"I've been telling you all this for moons now." Ann shot another poisonous look at Flora. "Perhaps now you will listen."

Flora wanted to speak, to defend herself, but she felt worn down. The others were now chattering in hushed tones amongst themselves, stealing glances at her as they allowed Ann's words to leach into their minds.

"Think, Ann." Margaret again tried to assert her dominance over the group. "Why would Flora do a thing like this? That's one of her sheep dead on those rocks."

"Why would she care for that when she has dark magic to sustain her?" Ann hissed. "Look at her there. She can't even bare to look you in the eye. Look at her!"

Flora did not need to see that the women had all turned to face her. Her eyes were fixed down upon the grass. She felt a familiar hand rest upon her arm.

"Go on, Flora," Margaret whispered. "Tell them. Tell them they're talking nonsense . . . Flora?"

Flora could not summon a reply, and Margaret's hand retreated slowly.

"See. She knows what she's done."

The mass of women seemed to collectively draw in their breath, and in the brief stay of condemnation Flora pushed herself forward. Barging her way through the throng, she stormed back down the cliff path, her eyes stinging. She dashed at them with her wrist and kept marching, Morag following faithfully behind her.

"That's right, run away!" Ann's voice rang out from behind her. "But there's a reckoning coming for you, Flora MacKinnon, you mark my words!"

Flora pressed forward, determined to put them all as far behind her as she possibly could. She stumbled back towards the village, wishing for nothing more than the warmth of her own hearth, keeping her head cast down, refusing to look back. As she reached her own croft she hesitated. Nervously, she glanced behind her. The village was deserted. It was only the Reverend, standing sentinel by the walls of the chapel, who observed her with his scrutinising eyes.

CHAPTER TWENTY-SEVEN

THOMAS

WHY not go

Murray lifted his head and met her gaze. Her hand was poised over the parchment, and in the dimming firelight her expression was eager. He frowned.

"I've told you," he explained. "The tacksman will return within the month." He waited patiently while she furiously scribbled her reply.

Go now. Take boat.

"The nearest island is well over a day away," he replied. "Do you know which direction to row?"

She looked down and bit the inside of her cheek.

"We would have to do it at night." He put a tentative hand on her lap. "At the very least we would get lost, and you can't risk losing the child."

Her leg twitched away from his palm and she wrapped her arms around her body, binding herself against his touch. He slowly retracted his hand but would not remove his gaze.

"Don't you fear the sea?" he asked.

She refused to look away from the crackling hearth. Murray leaned into the warmth, forcing her to turn to him.

"I know you still won't talk about what happened to you . . ."

She hugged herself tighter.

"But is there nothing you can remember yet? Anything?" he appealed. "Help me understand. If you can help me, we can end this; we can bring justice to those who have harmed you."

She closed her eyes.

Murray jabbed at the parchment on her lap. "Show me. Try to remember something about where you came from. I've told you everything about me; I need to know whatever I can about you."

She pressed her hands against the side of her face and opened her lips, baring her teeth in a silent scream.

He reached out and brushed his fingertips against her cheek, until she opened her eyes. "Please." He gently held the back of her neck. "Just tell me what little you know."

She took a breath, but her hand shook as she once more took the quill and wrote her response.

Like here

He pulled back from her. Could this confirm that she was indeed a girl from the islands? He thought of the tacksman's assertion that she was, and the imperfect sketch in Reverend Buchan's notebook. "Like Eilean Eòin?"

She shook her head and swept her arm around the room, indicating the hearth and the box bed.

"A house like this?"

She nodded.

"Where?"

She rolled her eyes and once more applied ink to the parchment.

Do not remember

"How about your family?"

Another shake of the head.

"Anything at all?"

She seemed to think. Murray was on the verge of giving up his quest for truth when she began drawing an image. The lines were shaky and imprecise, but there was no mistaking the splaying pattern of veins and arteries spreading from a central root.

"Trees?"

She scowled and examined her drawing carefully before her lips twitched into the slightest of smiles. She silently repeated the word to herself.

Not an island girl after all then, or at least not from any of the outer isles. "Then how did you come to be here?"

Her quill hovered over the page.

Do not remember

He sighed. He allowed her a few more minutes of staring into the flames before he continued to probe her for information.

"But what do you remember?"

He watched her anxiously, waiting for her to throw the parchment to the ground or storm through to the byre. Instead, she was totally still, her eyes fixed and her body frozen. The fire flickered. Murray waited and watched as she wrote three more words.

Cold Dark Wet

He stared at her inquiringly, but she had already turned away. As if awakening from a vision only she could see, she rose to her feet and curled up on the bed. She did not move for the rest of the night.

※

He needed to know more. The desire was eating away at him, and he could no longer commit to his imagined life away from the island until he had once and for all assembled the truth. It became clear he would get nothing more from Agnes. The next morning she rose as normal and busied herself with stacking peat, smiling at him and excitedly embracing him as if nothing had happened the night before.

He reluctantly realised that the only other person he could discuss the matter with was Flora MacKinnon. The woman had made fleeting visits to fuss over Agnes over the past few days, but otherwise she seemed to have become a hermit, rarely if ever leaving her croft to participate in work. Murray had heard something of the failed sacrifice. He was grateful such an abomination had not gone ahead, but he could not imagine the old woman bold enough to have unleashed the ewes herself. No doubt the enclosure was shoddily constructed, just like everything else on this island.

He seized his opportunity to talk to Flora the following day. He cornered her outside by the water barrel, eager to usher her around the back of the blackhouse, out of the eyeshot of the village. She looked thinner than before, and her winter earasaid hung from her in heavy folds. Her eyes flitted nervously back and forth.

"Mrs MacKinnon. I have to speak to you."

She did not reply.

"I need to know everything you know about Agnes. Tell me about how you found her."

Flora's fingers clawed at the sleeve of her earasaid. "There's nothing more to tell, Reverend. I found her exactly as she was when you first saw her."

"Mrs MacKinnon, I am quite tired now at how little anyone on this island seems to know." His voice rose as he failed to contain his frustration, and she flinched. "I spoke with Agnes last night and she tried to tell me what she remembered, but every time I pry further, she shuts down. Now what kind of trauma could have caused her to do that?"

"I don't know," Flora mumbled, looking to the ground.

"To hell with your evasiveness! I think you do know something," he hissed. "The way you coddle her, it's as if you feel guilty about something."

Flora looked at him with fury. "I am kind to her. What mother could fail to be moved by her plight?"

"That's as may be." He tried changing tactic and decided to gamble with a half-truth. "But I have evidence that Agnes was on this island long before you found her in that cove."

Murray knew he had broken through the woman's tough exterior, as she suddenly fell back, crumpling against the drystone. He waited for her to speak.

"I think she's my daughter."

"What?" He could have sworn he heard wrong.

She slowly lifted her face, and beneath her hood her expression was defiant. "I said, she's my daughter."

He was silent for a moment.

"But you told me your daughter was dead."

"Yes . . . I mean no," Flora stuttered. She looked confused. "I mean, I believed her drowned. But now I think she has come back to me."

Murray peered into Flora's face. He was repulsed: clearly the old woman had lost her mind, her sanity eroded by years of loss and hardship, and he had helped fuel it.

"Flora MacKinnon." He lowered his voice, trying to keep his tone gentle, to show that he still felt a trace of compassion for this woman. "This girl cannot be your daughter. It is impossible. Do you understand? Simply impossible."

"I thought your God allowed for miracles."

"No. Not ones like this." Before she could argue with him further, he continued, determined to appease her. It was after all now clear that the woman could no longer be of any use to him. "I understand you have suffered. But suffering must be accepted; sometimes terrible things happen to us, and they are simply not meant to be fixed."

Flora unfurled herself and took a step towards him. For a moment he thought he would have to restrain her.

"I am fully accepting of suffering, Reverend." Her voice shook. "I would never have felt complete love if I had not received the suffering caused by losing it. You would know that too."

His hand involuntarily reached up and fell against his heart, and with that final barbed remark she swept past him. He watched her retreating down the hill, his hand still pressed against his chest. He stood in the frigid air, the cold suddenly jolting him out of his reverie as he tried to shake off the creeping feeling of dread which accompanied Flora's departure. So, what if this madwoman could not help him? He would search for the truth himself, and if he did not find it, then what did it really matter that the girl's past remained far from his present? He would build a new future on the path that was revealed to him.

He began his search for remnants of truth in the place he had found her: the rock-strewn seclusion of the cove. The tide was far out as he traversed the slippery edges of the tidal pools, skirting around slick patches of slime yet still sliding into water enough to get his ankles wet. He looked towards the tideline. Two crows cawed as they pecked savagely at a dead gull.

What was he doing here? What could he possibly find when the tide so relentlessly rearranged this stretch of land to suit its whims? He half-heartedly examined the rocks for marks, stains or scratches, but the notion was absurd considering the layers of living matter encrusted and coated on every surface. He turned back towards the cliffs and started back. Surely this endeavour was a waste of his time.

It was then he noticed the low opening in the cliff face. Natural curiosity drew him towards it, and he scrambled over the mountain of rocks littering the path to the entrance, before ducking down and peering inside. Murray wished he had brought his father's tinder box, but he could immediately see that beyond the entrance the stooped passageway widened into a cave. He could hear the slow, steady drip of water as it fell from a height. He quickly looked around and, as suspected, there was no one in sight.

Bending low, he crawled through the cave mouth. Mercifully, it soon widened and grew tall enough for him to crookedly stand, his hunched shoulders scraping against the damp rock. A small chink of light fell against the smooth pebbles which lined the floor, before vanishing into blackness. He took a moment to close his eyes, enjoying the solitude which removed him from the savagery outside. He ran his hands over the walls, staining his palms.

His fingers brushed against something wet hanging from the wall. He drew back in disgust but squinted to examine what was there. Reaching out, he grabbed on to the rough fibres of a rope grown green with algae. Following the rope upwards, he came to a knot, and beneath that was a cold, hard ring of rusted metal struck into the rock face. He had seen this before. His mind raced back to the fowling expedition, and the crude metal anchor which had held the men together.

The end of the rope was frayed. His hand traced the wall behind it. Scratches. Gouges. As if someone had struck at it with something heavy. And then, caught between the metal and the coarseness of the rope, a long strand of knotted black hair.

He fled, pulling himself through the cave mouth, launching himself into the sunlight, away from the cold, the dark and the wet. Steadying himself against the cliff, he heaved until his stomach was emptied.

CHAPTER TWENTY-EIGHT

FLORA

FLORA'S eyes focused on nothing but remained open. She had refused to get out of bed, and instead remained coiled towards the wall, facing away from the warmth of the hearth well into the late hours of morning and past midday. She was dimly aware of John trying to rally her, but it was no use. Now he had left, and all the better for him if he stayed away from her. Flora pulled the heavy blankets up over her shoulders, bunching them under her chin and shivering. It was getting cold. Perhaps the fire had already died.

Her body was numb, but her mind drifted back and forth between oblivion and memories of her heated exchange with the Reverend that had taken place the day before. The young man she had pitied at the side of her son's grave, the man she had felt she could relate to in all his strangeness and otherworldliness, was lost to her. Perhaps she had misjudged him, or perhaps he too had known there was something not right about her, something insidious that plagued her and could not ever go away. And now he was taking Agnes from her. In mere days, the tacksman would return and the girl would be smuggled away under cover of darkness without so much as a parting glance.

Flora pulled the blankets up around her ears to dull the faint sounds of activity coming from outside. The other women were busy scraping together what they could in time for the final harvest, and the men were away collecting fulmars for oil. Nobody had visited her since the day of the sacrifice. Nevertheless, she still heard their muffled voices whenever they dared stray past her front door;

even without hearing their words, her neighbours' tones dripped with accusation. Flora did not know what would become of her once the harvest was over and the winter set in. She did not know how her fellow islanders would deal with her. Right now, though, she could not bring herself to care. All she wanted was sleep.

The sound of the door creaking open disturbed her rest. She wished John would just leave her be. It did not feel as if he had left her for that long, and she had presumed he would still be at the cliffs, fowling. But then again, time seemed not to register to Flora in her self-imposed seclusion, for she could barely tell if she was sleeping or awake, and perhaps the hours had already slipped away from her into evening. Reluctantly, she rolled her body over.

It was not John who stood by the hearth, but Margaret. Her neighbour bent down to tend to the fire, adding an extra sod of peat and stoking it enough for it to begin flaring back into life. Slowly, Margaret looked up and came towards the bed. Flora tried to turn away.

"Don't you dare turn away from me, Flora." Margaret's voice caught in her throat. "I'm your oldest friend. I have always sided with you."

Flora focused her eyes on Margaret. Her neighbour was indeed close to tears.

"Oh, Flora," she sobbed. "What are you doing to yourself?"

Flora said nothing. She could not think of words which held any meaning; there was no point in saying anything. She stiffly levered herself up onto one elbow, the thin bones of her arms snapping into place.

"I cannot protect you, Flora," Margaret continued, trying to set her voice firm. "Not when you are like this. You were always the strong one out of both of us. The Flora I know would never stoop so low."

Flora looked away. Words began to slowly form in her head, but she could not summon the energy to say them.

"Do you remember," Margaret's mouth twitched into a smile, "when we were girls, and we would go to the kissing rock?"

Flora turned to face her friend.

"The boys teased us that the first to jump from the edge of the cliff onto the rock would be the first to find a husband," Margaret laughed shakily. "I was always too scared, but you told me you would do it just to show them up, and I never believed you, but you did. My heart caught in my throat when I saw you hop across, but you made it look easy." Margaret fixed Flora with a stare. "I never said it, but I was jealous of you. All the boys loved you. Donald thought you were jumping for him that day, but I knew you were just returning his taunts and leaving him for me. You were always the prettiest, the bravest, and in the end, you got the best man."

Flora stared back at Margaret and opened her parched lips to speak. Her voice was cracked and wheezy. "I know John sent you," she said. "But I don't need your help, Margaret. Not this time."

"Yes, you do!" Margaret cried. "John is scared for you, Flora, and none of this is fair on him. Just look at yourself! You're wasting away to skin and bone." Margaret shook her head despairingly. "And trust me Flora, the others have not stopped their talk. Once the harvest is over, I doubt they will hold back much longer, not now you're turning the whole island against you."

"And what would you have me do?" Flora's words rattled in her throat. "They are only foolish young girls. Ann has turned them all against reason, not me."

"Ann is mad with grief," Margaret replied. "No one would take her seriously if it weren't for how you respond to her attempts to provoke you. You've cut yourself off!."

She could do nothing but stare blankly at Margaret, who continued her onslaught unabated.

"Where is that fight I always admired in you? The Flora I knew would have laughed at all these accusations and put the others in their place, while still finding enough compassion to soothe Ann's sorrow."

Flora was about to speak, but thinking better of it she bit her lip.

"Flora, please listen to me," Margaret sighed, "the best thing you can do is get out of this bed and carry on as normal. If the other women see you behaving in a normal way, they may stop paying attention to Ann and see that you're still one of us."

"And if they don't?"

Margaret paused. Her voice trembled. "Then I will not be able to stop them."

"Not be able to stop them, or won't stop them?"

Margaret stood up abruptly. Her mouth was a thin line and her eyes were crinkled in an effort to stave off the tears. "Get out of bed, Flora," she said. "I don't know what you've become, but God help you if you don't." Margaret spun on her heel, throwing her hood over her head. Flora watched as her oldest friend marched away from her, closing the door firmly on her way out.

She sat up. Perhaps Margaret had a small point about getting out of bed. Even if she could not stomach work and the thought of being in the company of the other women, she could still go outside and find Agnes. The Reverend may have contempt for her, but she would not allow him to shield the girl from her completely. There were things she had to tell her.

※

Flora bided her time, waiting patiently behind the shelter of the Reverend's storehouse for Agnes to appear. She was fairly certain that the Reverend was not at home, but she could not take any chances. Where she hid was beyond the sight of the village bay, and she had made sure that no prying eyes had been watching her as she hurried up the hill, away from the malicious gossip which no doubt was now circulating against her. Flora huddled in her earasaid, ignoring the stirrings of winter seizing up her hip.

It could have been an hour that passed, perhaps more, before Agnes emerged from behind the far wall of the blackhouse, hooded and quick footed as she walked towards the storehouse, a basket in her hand to gather what little remained of food supplies. Flora knew the Reverend could not be home. There was no chance he would risk Agnes leaving the house alone, even for an instant. Seizing her chance, Flora stepped from behind the wall and stood at the storehouse entrance.

Agnes dropped her basket and made to run, but seeing Flora's face she seemed to relax a little. Flora gestured for her to follow her into the storehouse. The girl took a quick look around her, and tentatively crouched down to enter through the tunnelled entrance. Inside the storehouse was dark and the air was dry. The floor dipped down to form a hollow in the earth which kept the space secure from the elements outside. Flora squatted down amongst the barrels and baskets of dried and salted meat, resting her back against the stacks of peat sods.

"I need to talk to you," she began. Agnes looked nervous, and Flora did not know what to say or where to begin. She took time to form her words, aware of Agnes' growing sense of discomfort from the way she rocked on her heels. "The Reverend spoke to me about how he believed you to have been on this island before the day I found you. As you are leaving soon, I . . ." Flora's words trailed off. Agnes frowned at her.

". . . I just needed to say that I love you, and I am sorry."

The girl's expression softened to what seemed to be one of pity, and she reached out to hold Flora's hand. Flora gripped it tight and pulled it to her lips, kissing it. She felt Agnes' hand strain against her touch, so she dropped it, not wanting to frighten her.

"I do not want you to go, *mo cridhe*," Flora breathed, staring into the girl's eyes. Agnes frowned again and shook her head firmly.

"I will make up for what happened to you. I promise." Her voice broke. She held the tears back. A question formed on her lips before she could reconsider her right to ask it; before she could register her dread at what the answer could be. "Are you her?" Flora's mouth was dry as the words escaped her. "Are you, my Agnes?"

The lines furrowing the girl's brow deepened into a look of pure bafflement, and in an instant Flora's hopes crumbled. She had imagined a moment when her daughter would fall back into her arms, the two clutching at each other and sobbing in the shared relief of reunion. But now her dreams began to shatter. Deep down she had known all along that her belief in her daughter's return was too good for her, but she had repressed this knowledge, determinedly persevering with what little faith she could muster until she rejected the very foundation of her being.

"I remember now." Fragments of Flora's memories took her to a place she had denied even existed. She knew now that this girl was not her own, but she was another's; another mother's from across the sea who no doubt mourned the loss of a child. Another mother whose child she had failed to protect. "I am so sorry . . ."

Flora tried to reach out to her again, but the girl pulled away, visibly unnerved. She backed away slowly, retreating through the hollow entrance and retrieving her basket.

"Please," Flora begged. "Don't go."

Flora followed her back towards the blackhouse, but Agnes turned and stretched out her hand as if pushing back an invisible force. Flora froze. The girl looked at her with both fear and compassion, a compassion which she had in no way earned. Flora watched as Agnes turned away and retreated inside.

Reaching up, she felt her skin scorched by the tears streaming down her cheeks. She had not cried in a long time. She did not deserve tears; she deserved her suffering, there was never any point in crying about it, but now she could not stop herself.

A rending, inhuman wail pierced the air around her, and she was alarmed to hear the unfamiliar sound coming from herself. Picking up her skirts, she pulled herself from the grass and ran as fast as her aging body allowed, barely knowing in which direction she was going, but knowing she needed to put the settlement as far away from her as she could.

CHAPTER TWENTY-NINE

THOMAS

MURRAY shrugged his coat on to combat the chill; even indoors with a fire fully lit, the first stirrings of winter were rapidly seeping in. He paced the living space, arms wrapped around himself as he contemplated his next course of action. The events of the previous day still pierced his every waking thought: the madwoman's ravings of a long dead daughter, the cave with signs of untold horrors clinging to the wall. He wondered what it could all mean, but every answer he pieced together was more appalling than the last.

He looked across the room at the curled form nestled inside the panels of the box bed, and the feeling of dread returned. It was now well past midday, and despite rising early, Agnes had returned to bed, her mood inexplicably turned to melancholy once more. He could not bring himself to wake her. He hoped she slept, for he feared the moment she woke and he would be forced to interact with her. Last night he could barely even look at her without conjuring in his mind the worst possible scenarios of how she had come to intrude on his life, but he knew he could share none of this with her. He could not risk revisiting such intense traumas on her: not now she carried his child inside her. As he looked at her, she barely stirred, her face resting in the soft crook of an arm. Her eyes appeared closed.

Murray knew he could not prolong the inevitable; he had to have answers, and if she could not provide them, he would seek them out however he could, even if a large part of him feared what those answers could be. Flora MacKinnon was a lost cause, but he had remembered another source of information which could help him piece the truth together.

His eyes strayed to his father's wooden chest. Treading cautiously across the room, he gently eased open the latch. The old hinges let out a strangled moan. He froze and looked up to the bed. She continued to sleep soundly. All the better for the baby, he thought. Inching the lid open, he quietly felt around the contents of the trunk, until his hand rested on cold leather. He slowly extracted what he needed.

Still kneeling on the floor, he frantically thumbed through the pages of Buchan's notebook. Surely there was something he had missed. His hands stiffened on the page where the sketch of a raven-haired girl gazed back up at him from the parchment. There were dozens of similar sketches scattered throughout the book; she and her drawn companions could be anybody, he remonstrated with himself. His eyes flickered through the rudimentary census lists. He looked to the very last record and again saw the words, "three females", followed by a blank space which trailed off into nothingness at the end of March: barely two months prior to his arrival.

He tore onwards, frustrated by the ambiguity of the clues which had been left to him. He wanted to tear the damned thing apart, and as his hands fell upon the final page, he took a fistful of paper and ripped it from its binding, scrunching the loose sheets up and throwing them to the floor. Closing his eyes and biting his lip, he brought the wounded tome to his face and pressed his forehead against the open cover, trying to stop himself from crying out. He bit down on his lip until it hurt, and as he took the volume away from his face, a tiny bead of blood stained the inner lining. He scratched at the mark roughly with his thumbnail, scraping the thick parchment insert as if picking at a scab.

Just as he was about to hurl the book away, his thumbnail came to an abrupt, involuntary halt. He retraced his path across the inner back cover and again he felt it: an unmistakable ridge. He followed the edge upwards and around into a perfect square encased beneath the lining: it was as if a piece of paper had been folded and sealed inside.

Murray rose quickly to retrieve the small gutting knife which lay on the table across the room. Returning to his space on the floor, he stabbed into the back cover of Buchan's book, slicing deftly along the edges of the lining. He trembled as he peeled back the sheath of oiled parchment and saw what lay hidden inside was, indeed, a carefully folded paper. Murray unfolded it cautiously. It was a letter: undated, unsigned, and unsealed.

Dear Sir,

You will forgive me for not addressing you with appropriate reverence, but I am unwilling to divulge names should my note stray into false hands. You may trust the gentleman who accompanies this letter; he is another true man of God.

I was much interested in your description of the island upon which you find yourself, and much moved by the plight of its inhabitants. You are doing the Lord's work in finding healthy and faithful souls through which to assist in the growth of this populace, as it is clear this community, which has suffered so poorly, cut off from the sins of the outside world, is one which may easily be persuaded to following the cause. I regret to report that the situation in Ireland does not fare much better than Scotland or England at present, and we are subject to many reprisals from those who have sold their souls to keep their hold over the land, and threaten us with barbarity and violence. Nonetheless, the ordinary people here side with us, and so it was not too difficult to find three local girls of childbearing age, who with the closure of our Holy convents, have nowhere else that will claim them. They will no doubt prove worthy wives and mothers of Christ's soldiers.

This cargo will be brought to you in the early hours of morning, although I cannot promise on which day, and you must be ready at all times to welcome them. You will recognise my man, and he will in turn convey my blessings directly to you.

Have hope. Our hour is almost upon us.

Written by the hand of your most Humble Servant and Brother across the water.

Murray's vision returned to the space he occupied on the rush strewn, dirt floor. This confirmed his suspicions about his predecessor, but he could never have imagined a connection with the woman who now slept in his bed. For whom else could she be but one of those chosen girls? His head spun as he rose to his feet. He stormed out of the blackhouse, barely taking heed of the noise of the door as he slammed it shut behind him.

Outside the sun shone as a white haze, low in the sky as it shied away in the ever-shortening days. An icy breeze seared the back of his neck as he strode towards the settlement, his feet carrying him to the crofts nearest the sea. Flora MacKinnon was his last resort.

※

"Mrs MacKinnon!" Murray pounded his fist against the door again, his knuckles scraping against the rough wood until he felt a splinter burrow its way into his skin. Unperturbed he continued to hammer at the door. "Mrs MacKinnon, I'm not leaving until you open up and talk to me!"

He pressed his ear against the wood, hoping to hear the latch slide open. He was drawing a crowd of onlookers. All around the settlement, village women looked up from foul smelling mounds of fulmar feathers, some of which fell like downy snow onto their hair and faces, rendering them almost inhuman and even more repellent to him. They abandoned their work as they stared at him with barely concealed relish, their bestial faces no doubt carved into expressions of malice. He could hear their intrigued whisperings behind his back.

Enraged, he turned to confront them, but instead came face to face with John MacKinnon. The old man's expression was stern but etched with worry.

"It seems you and I are searching for the same person, Reverend."

Murray shrank away from him. There was still blood and oil encrusted on his hands from slaughtering birds.

"I have to speak to her at once," he said, refusing to be intimidated.

"She's not at home. I returned about an hour ago and could not find her anywhere. I had assumed she was with you."

Murray frowned, trying to think of a way to combat the knowing look which had formed on MacKinnon's face. As he sought a retaliation, the old man had the gall to place his bloody hand onto Murray's shoulder and guide him into the blackhouse.

"Come," he said gruffly, closing the door behind him. "You've drawn enough attention to us as it is. Now get inside."

Murray shrugged off the man's hand and refused a seat by the hearth, instead choosing to stand imposingly by the wall, his arms crossed as he looked down on the short, stocky islander. "I need to speak to your wife, sir."

"I understand that," MacKinnon scoffed. "I can hardly help you when she is not here."

"Then, where is she?"

MacKinnon's face fell. He began stoking the fire. "Flora sometimes wanders when she needs to clear her head," he said, his tone uncertain. "She'll no doubt be back in a few hours. Before it gets dark."

Murray almost felt pity for John, but he disregarded the sentiment entirely by reminding himself of the real reason he was there. Who knew how much this man was hiding from him?

"It is urgent that I see her as soon as possible."

John met his eyes. "It's about the girl, isn't it?"

Murray felt the room spin. He stared at John, open mouthed, unable to form a coherent thought as terror rose in his throat like bile.

"There's no need to look so shocked, Reverend," John continued, shaking his head. "I've known for a while now that Flora had another reason for visiting you so often. I tried to keep an eye on her the last few times, but this morning she would not even get up from the bed . . ." John's voice trailed off, and concern seemed to overtake the condemnatory look he had spared for Murray.

"Who else knows?" He broke the impending silence, fearful of what the answers could be, and ready to bolt out the door in an urge to protect his unborn child.

"No one as far as I'm aware," John replied. "Do you really think I would tell anyone else and risk my wife any further harm?"

Murray supposed not. Even though he could never trust the man, it was obvious to even the most casual onlooker that John would do anything to defend his wife's reputation. The intensity of the man's feelings was as undeniable as it was pitiable.

Murray re-established his dignity by stepping away from the wall and straightening. "In that case, Mr MacKinnon, you can tell me what happened to her."

"To Flora?"

"No. To the girl."

John looked to the fire again. "I honestly cannot tell you."

"I think you can."

John paused. "I do not know for certain."

"Liar."

John returned his gaze to him, and there was fury in his eyes. Murray stepped back.

"You have my word, Reverend. I know little and my wife knows nothing at all, which is how I would like to keep it." John locked his eyes onto his, unblinking.

"Mr MacKinnon," he softened his tone, "I know that Reverend Buchan brought young women from Ireland to Eilean Eoin. Is she one of them?"

John paused, seeming to be in deep contemplation, as if being struck by an idea which had barely yet occurred to him. "Perhaps," he said eventually. "I don't know. I wish I did. But it seemed impossible given what happened..."

"And what did happen?"

MacKinnon gave him a sidelong glare, but quickly looked away, his expression one of shame.

"I will get to the truth, Mr MacKinnon. For the sake of your wife, I would think very carefully before you hide anything from me."

At the mention of his wife, MacKinnon's eyes widened with panic, and his tone became desperate. "It's not a case of hiding anything, Reverend. All I know for certain is that shortly before Father Buchan fell ill and left, some amongst us petitioned him for help."

"The girls from Ireland?"

"Yes." John slumped onto a stool and sat with his head in his hands. "You will have noticed yourself that there are not enough children on the island, or women of childbearing age." John rubbed at his brow. "We never recovered from the sickness fifteen years ago. Put us all together and we are barely more than four families remaining; not enough to sustain our way of life for our grandchildren. We needed help in rebuilding our people, and Father Buchan was all too happy to provide us with hope for the future; with young, healthy bodies who could help us remain here forever. Nobody else was ever willing to help us. Your lairds and bishops would happily see us shipped out and replaced by mere animals, we are of so little value to them."

"Reverend Buchan was using you." Murray's voice was cold. "You were just a means for him to further his own cause."

"I don't think that," John said pointedly. "There was goodness in that man. He may not have been one of us, but he knew what we needed."

Murray shifted uncomfortably, feeling the barbed contempt in MacKinnon's words prick at his ego. He reared up angrily. "I do not have time for this," he hissed. "I need you to tell me what happened to those girls once they got to Eilean Eoin."

The old man paused. "I can tell you that the women did not accept them." John continued to stare venomously. "They would not let them into their houses; said they were replacing their own daughters. I had little to do with them once they were here, and they were housed in one of the larger storehouses for a time, until a few days later when Father Buchan had to be removed from the island."

"And then what happened?"

John rose and turned to peer through the oily skin of the window. "That, I cannot say for certain. I do not want to know for certain."

"You must tell me!" Murray could see from the man's evasiveness that he was edging closer to a truth he did not want to acknowledge.

John turned again to face him. "So what?" he spat. "So you can stand in judgement of us? So you can justify your own faults by condemning everyone else and claiming you are above it all?"

Murray did not flinch. "Just tell me what you know," he said, casting aside the insinuations about his character.

"You must believe me on this." John's eyes did not waver from his. "Flora knows nothing about any of it. I kept all suspicions from her. She barely even knew of the girls' presence in the first place. She lives in her own world."

"I am not here to judge your wife. I only want to protect the girl."

John took a deep breath, making it look as if it were the last gulp of air he would ever take. "After Father Buchan left," he began, "many of the women still wanted nothing to do with them, so we decided to just send them home when another ship came." He paused and looked to the floor, forcing Murray to lean forward to hear what he was saying. "But others must have driven them away from the village. The weather was bad; they could easily have died from being out amongst the worst of it. And some of the younger men, they . . ."

Murray's heart was thumping against his chest. ". . . Go on, Mr MacKinnon."

"They . . ." John's voice cracked. "You have to understand that I only know this through rumour from my sons, who I will have you know were not there and played no part in this . . ."

"How about your youngest son? He was alive then."

"Donnchadh may . . ." Tears welled in the old man's eyes. ". . . Donnchadh may have been there. I only heard rumours." John looked to him with desperation. "That is another reason why Flora can never know any of this. I will not have her suffer any more."

"Mr MacKinnon," Murray steadied his voice, "are you telling me that those boys took those young women? That they . . . That they performed unspeakable acts upon them?"

"I do not know," John repeated, his voice breaking into a sob. "I do not know. But you know how some men can be when they are young and foolish. They get carried away . . ."

"They get carried away?" Murray was appalled.

John put his head in his hands. "Do not make me condemn my son, Reverend. If he had any part in it, it is my fault. A father should set an example for his son."

"That's as may be." He tried to keep his voice level, but outrage stirred within him. "But you and anyone on this heathenish rock could have spoken up to protect those women, but you did not."

"We did not even know where the girls were! We thought they must be dead. If I could have stopped it, I would. But none of the women wanted anything to do with them."

"Even your wife? She is a kindly woman; surely she would have done something to protect them?"

"I told you, Reverend, Flora had no part in this!" The man's hands clenched into fists. "Now if you have what you were looking for, I need you to leave. I won't have you here when Flora returns."

Murray backed towards the door, cautious of riling the man further.

"I just need to know one more thing, Mr MacKinnon, so that I know for certain," he said. "Was the young woman found in the cove one of those girls?"

"I barely glanced at them," John replied. "If she is, then I do not understand how she came to survive for so long . . ."

"And the other girls?" Murray hesitated, already knowing the answer. "Reverend Buchan referred to three women. What got to them first: being cast out into the cold, or your boys?"

John looked up at Murray with bloodshot eyes. "I only know what I have told you."

Murray felt a wave of nausea. Sickened to his core, he stumbled back out into the cold air, leaving the old man to wallow in his grief. When he looked up, he saw that the settlement was still filled with staring faces, all turned in rabid inquisitiveness towards him. They disgusted him. Even if these women were not guilty, some of their sons and brothers undoubtedly were, and yet they turned a blind eye to all but themselves, huddled together like a colony of gulls, fiercely pecking at any intruders who sought refuge near their nests.

"God will judge you." He spoke the words out loud. Loud enough for them all to hear and loud enough to vent his disdain. Furious, he pushed his way through them, swiping feathers away from his face, heading beyond the chapel and up towards the cliff path. He knew exactly where Flora MacKinnon would be skulking, and he had no intention of sparing her his wrath.

But then he heard a voice; separate, yet somehow in unison with the crowd of women behind him. A voice which existed both in isolation and as part of a congregation.

"And God will judge you too."

CHAPTER THIRTY

FLORA

CORMORANTS brought bad tidings. Cormorants brought omens of death. On a jagged throne of basalt, the lone bird stretched out its black, skeletal wings, saltwater dripping from the tips of ragged feathers, returning in droplets to the sea. Veins of white foam swirled into the cold, grey waters, ebbing and flowing towards the cove.

The sea raced forward to meet the land, and Flora eagerly embraced it. Falling to her knees on the edge of the rocky shoreline, sheltered from the watchful eyes of the settlement, she let herself cry. Water and froth lapped towards her in placid ripples. She let the damp soak through her clothes; barnacled rock scraped against flesh, while the salt stung her skin. There was not a soul to share in her torment. That is how she wanted it, for that was no less than what she deserved.

Flora let her shawl fall away from her face and allowed the breeze to free tendrils of her hair. She wondered how the girl, not her Agnes but another, had felt in those agonising hours that she was stranded on the shore. Had she been mercifully unconscious to what was happening to her, her mind dazed, or had she been fleetingly aware of her situation? Did she cry out for her own mother to save her? It would have been so for her own Agnes, when her little girl's face disappeared beneath the waves, when her eyes grew misty, and her mouth filled with water. She would have cried out for her mother. Cried out for a mother who had abandoned her.

Flora's knees buckled beneath her, and she choked on a heaving sob. She should have sacrificed any attempt at fulfilment all those years ago. She was sure now that Donnchadh was punishment for the choices she had made.

A stone fell behind her and skittered to a halt against her leg. Raising her head, she sensed a presence approach her. She turned, her eyes filling briefly with hope.

"It's you." Flora's face fell on the Reverend, his stern figure a towering pillar of black. His cheeks were drained of any remaining colour and his eyes were furious.

Flora recoiled but did not rise from the ground. She pushed back her matted hair with a trembling hand, self-conscious of how she must look to this man. She suddenly saw herself as she was: a dishevelled, rapidly aging woman, her face no doubt streaked an angry red where the tears had flowed. Gone were the days when men would be enraptured by her beauty. She looked down at the bony hands resting on her lap. Had they seen her now, they would no doubt have mistaken her for a banshee, her howls of despair promising misfortune to those who saw her. She hated being seen like this.

"What do you want from me?" Flora could not meet his eyes at first, but when she did, she immediately looked away again. She shrank from him, crouching down further into herself. On seeing the wrathful look on his face, she reached out behind her and felt around for a rock, feeling compelled to defend herself if it came to it. Her life may be worthless, but she would not see it lost at a man's hands. The Reverend's eyes never left her, and when his voice came, it was cold and hard.

"I spoke to your husband." As the words escaped him, Flora's head jerked up. "He told me everything."

"Everything?" Flora rose unsteadily to her feet, her fear giving way to confusion. "What could John possibly know?" Her face blanched. "You did not tell him about the girl, did you?"

"He already knew," the Reverend replied, his voice sharp as a knife edge. "You need not fret about that particular deception. He has kept it to himself, all to protect you."

Flora winced, repelled by the way in which he spat out that final word.

"He also told me about the girls from Ireland," he continued. "The ones brought here all those months ago. You must have known."

"I knew of them. But I barely ever saw them." Flora had dreaded this moment. The moment where the truth would be exposed to her for what it was, and all her desperate imaginings would be quashed. "But they went missing. I thought they were dead . . ."

"Two of them are," the Reverend snapped. "All because of how you and the rest of your kind raise your damned offspring."

"I . . . I don't understand."

"Do not," he paused, and his voice became a deadly whisper, "tell lies to me. You know. Whether you have even accepted it is immaterial; deep down I think you know."

Flora clasped her hands over her ears and turned back to the sea.

"Don't turn your back on me, Flora MacKinnon." The Reverend lurched forward and grabbed her by the arm, turning her to face him. He spoke through gritted teeth. "I know what those boys did. Donnchadh and the others. They took them, and they had their sinful way with them, and when they tired of them, they left them to rot. Left them to be carried away by the sea like old sheep carcasses!"

He tightened his grip around her arm. Flora felt speckles of saliva against her cheek. She tried to pull herself away, but she was no match for the strength of an adult man. She opened her mouth to scream, but her throat was dry.

"I didn't know . . ." she sobbed. "I swear to you I didn't know."

He flung her away from him and she fell against the rocks, winded, her palms stinging as they scraped against wet pebbles. She lay still for a while, shielding her head with her arms, waiting for the blows to rain down. None came.

She peered from under her raised elbow and saw that the Reverend had kneeled down beside her. His lips pressed into a thin line and his eyes once more bored into hers.

"Tell me," he said. "Tell me all you know, or so help me I will make sure that no one on this island goes unpunished. I will report what I know, and you will be arrested and tried for concealing murderers in your midst. Do you understand me, Mrs MacKinnon? Or would you prefer it that I see you and your kin hang? Believe me, I would take great satisfaction from that."

Flora trembled. On Eilean Eòin they had no such punishment as hanging, but she had heard of what they did to people on the mainland. She imagined the rope chafing against her neck as it slowly throttled the breath from her throat, her legs dangling helplessly beneath her. She would be taken from her home and paraded before strangers, having to withstand their jeers and taunts as they came to gawp at the savages from across the sea. No. She would not let herself die in such an undignified fashion. Steadying herself, she breathed deeply.

"I did not know," she repeated, lowering her arms, and meeting his eyes. "All I knew was that they disappeared, but I barely ever saw them; I had nothing to do with them. Some of the others wanted them gone, but I never spoke a word for or against them."

"And your son?"

"I . . ." Her voice trailed into a sob. "I suspected. But I never thought it was as bad as that. I thought him and the other boys were just joking with each other; I did not think they would actually harm anyone!"

"Well, they did. And the worst part is that no one stopped them. No one questioned it."

"And if it's true, I am sorry for it!" she cried. "I wish I could excuse my son, but I can't. I am a bad mother. I've known that for a long time . . ."

The Reverend said nothing, but continued to kneel before her, his face mere inches away from hers.

"Do you . . ." she began. "Do you think she's one of them? One of the missing girls?"

"Of course, I do," he said. "The fact that she survived is miraculous, but how could she be anyone else?"

Flora turned slightly and looked to the sea, which lapped ever closer towards them.

"I wanted her to be someone else," she muttered.

"We have discussed this; the dead do not return. Your daughter is dead."

"Yes but . . ." Her voice trailed away, making him lean forward to hear her next words. "You don't understand. I wanted it to be her, because . . ."

"Because what?"

"I thought maybe God had forgiven me and brought her back in exchange for Donnchadh."

"And why would God do that?"

Flora looked up. "You say God is merciful."

"God does not toy with the boundaries between life and death. What is gone cannot return."

"But she was not meant to leave me so soon. It was my fault."

The Reverend paused and edged away from her. She did not look at him; she did not want him to see the guilt which wracked her every breathing moment now exposed upon her face. "I killed her."

"What?"

"My daughter." Her voice was steady now. "I killed her."

The Reverend leapt to his feet and stepped back. She could see him from the corner of her vision holding an arm across his chest, as if guarding himself from her. She did not know why she had said it, but she immediately felt the weight of over fifteen years of torment, deceptions and emotional self-abuse shift slightly, easing from her careworn shoulders.

"You murdered your own child?" The Reverend's lips curled into a grimace of disgust.

"No!" Her cry was frantic. "It was not like that. You have to understand, I never meant for it. I could never, I would never . . . I just . . . couldn't keep her alive."

The Reverend narrowed his eyes, still cautiously edging away from her. Flora wrung her hands in a pleading gesture, willing him to understand, willing him not to condemn her. Her next words rushed forward in an unstoppable torrent, the truth she had held inside her for so long finally escaping from her lips.

"My daughter was weak, Reverend. Always sick. If not in the body then in the mind, at least." Her voice caught on the memory and choked. Still, she could not stop herself. "I knew there was something not right; even at three years old she could barely walk or talk . . . And when the famine came, when the sickness came, I could not protect all four of my children. Donnchadh was not even weaned, and it would have taken him first, I know it. I could not let my children suffer in such a way, but I could not keep all of them alive. I was starving for them, and Donnchadh . . . my milk was drying up . . ." Flora clutched instinctively at her breast. "He would not stop crying."

"So you . . . so you chose your son's life over your daughter's?"

Flora felt a solid lump form in her throat. His words stung her, and she wished that she could fully deny them. "No," she began. "I mean, it was an accident. At least at first . . ." Flora's knees buckled beneath her and her whole body began to shake. She wished she could curl up on the shoreline and wait on the cold, wet rock for the sea to come and swallow her up. "I can still hear her crying out to me," she said shakily. She clutched her head in her hands, desperate to ward off the memories. Like a keening woman at a burial, she began to scratch at the roots of her hair.

The Reverend drew back further, his expression one of pure horror. She saw the grotesque reflection of herself in his eyes and baulked. What could be more monstrous than a mother who knowingly delivered her child to death?

"Please," she whispered. "Don't go."

"I won't hear any more."

"Please don't leave me here. Pray with me, Reverend. Tell me God will forgive me for my sins . . ."

"I cannot absolve you, Flora MacKinnon." He was already turning to walk away. "You must live with your sins. I will not help you."

She dove forwards to clutch at his feet, but he had already drawn away. No matter how much she cried out, she could see he would not be swayed to turn back to her. She watched as he scrambled back up the cliff path, his silhouette fading into the dimming light of the oncoming evening. She was alone. After years of denial, she allowed herself to sink beneath the surface of her memories.

※

The day had been a bright one. No mist or portents of misfortune hung on the horizon, only a crisp, Autumn breeze which brought with it clouds the colour of goose down. Flora's shoulders had ached from the weight of Donnchadh, who rested, swaddled and cocooned against her back. She could remember the feel of him struggling under the constraints of his woollen prison. The material had dug against her jutting collarbones. Her stomach roiled with hunger pains. Whenever she had bent down to collect a meagre meal of cockles and seaweed, she swayed on her feet, her vision suddenly fading and returning with each throb of her temple. Donnchadh would not stop crying, and the air wrung with his piercing screams. She knew he was hungry. But she could not feed him. Not yet.

Tottering along the shoreline of the cove, her little girl led the way. Barely able to keep herself upright, she would stumble, grazing her knees on the edges of rockpools. But she did not complain. Agnes had giggled as she plunged her arm into the icy pools and ripped up balls of slimy weed. Flora had eased herself up and watched as her child planted herself against the rocks nearest the water, dangling her feet in the surf. She had watched as the little girl felt around her and picked up stones, hands gently caressing them and marvelling at their smoothness. She placed several favoured ones in the folds of her plaid. Agnes seemed totally oblivious to her mother's desperate search for sustenance, and Flora had felt a sudden pang of resentment. Her baby son's cries grew louder and summoned her attention away from her daughter.

Shrugging the sling from her tired back, Flora lay Donnchadh against a rock and checked him over. Un-swaddling him, she examined the swollen belly; the ribs poking through his chest like a baby bird's; the tiny, stick thin arms beating feebly at the air.

"Hush, *mo cridhe*." She picked him up and bounced him against her chest. "Shh, shh."

Donnchadh's mouth roamed searchingly amongst the inner folds of her shawl. Flora had tried to let him latch against her breast, but when nothing came forth, he squealed and once again began bawling.

"Oh, hush. Please hush..."

Flora's eyes had filled with tears of frustration, and she tried to offer him a finger to suck, but he batted it away. Flora lay him back on the ground and clasped her hands over her ears, wishing she could do something to make it stop.

"Please, stop. Oh please, just be patient." Her voice had been clogged by tears.

Flora had not known how long she had sat like that, listening helplessly to her baby's cries, but before long she noticed the rivers of sea water snaking around the rock she knelt on. The tide was coming in. Sweeping Donnchadh into her arms, she had once more secured him to her back, trying to ignore his flailing protestations. She turned to look around.

Agnes was gone.

Flora scanned all along the shoreline, but her daughter had been nowhere to be seen. For a moment had she panicked, but soon that panic was subsumed by an even worse feeling. If she searched for the child, the tide would cut her off and trap her and Donnchadh in the cove. Donnchadh's screams had continued above the rushing swell of the water, and Flora's breasts throbbed. Any more days without food for herself, anymore days without milk, and her son would die. There had been no doubt about it. She could not continue to feed them all.

Without stopping to think for any longer, without stopping for any weakness or doubt to emerge and stifle her instincts, she ran from the shoreline and scrabbled up the cliff, not daring to look back. She had tried to keep her mind blank, for there would be time for regrets later; now she had to act. It would be easy to explain away: Agnes got lost. It was not a lie. She did not know where the girl had gone. She had just wandered off, as little girls were often bound to do. No questions would be asked. Flora wished she could move faster, but her weak, malnourished legs now tired easily and the backs of her wasted calves ached. She pushed herself onwards. The child had gone missing. She had wandered off. It was as simple as that.

Soon she reached the cliff top, but before she could set one foot in front of the other, a single, shrill sound pierced the air, momentarily masking Donnchadh's cries. She halted. The sound had echoed all around her.

"Mammy!"

In that moment, her resolve had crumbled. Spinning around, she had slid back down the slope, mindless of the scree giving way beneath her feet. Panting, she did not stop for breath, but had run over what remained of the rocks, leaping over tidal pools, and clawing herself back upright when she fell against the shore. Her hands were a reddened, bloody mess as barnacles and limpets shredded the papery skin of her palms and dug beneath her nails. Finally, she reached the edge of the sea.

The saltwater sloshed up to her knees and stung her legs as she waded further out into the breakers. She scanned everywhere. Her daughter was nowhere to be seen.

"Agnes!" she howled, without even registering the thought to cry out. She screamed the name again, as loud as her tear choked voice would allow her.

No one cried back. Flora had strained to hear: nothing but the triumphant roar of the sea and the frantic wails of her infant son had answered her plea.

She fell back and sank down into the foaming breakers, allowing the cold to wash over her lap.

"Agnes . . ." She sobbed to herself, quietly, staring numbly out at the vast grey abyss.

The light was dimming. She had not known how long she had been there, but it was only when the other women had found her, alerted by the sound of Donnchadh's cries, that she had allowed herself to be dragged away.

CHAPTER THIRTY-ONE

THOMAS

By the time Murray reached the sanctuary of the croft, his hands and face were numb. The frosty air had bitten into his skin, but he was senseless to the cold. His mind reeled over the hideous knowledge which had been imparted to him, and he felt more than ever the urge to escape the barbarous place which blighted his hopes of a meaningful life. Just two more days until salvation arrived. He prayed the weather would settle for the tacksman's return, for the thought of no imminent rescue was too horrendous to contemplate for long. If he could not leave soon, it would be difficult to convince himself that he should not attempt some daring escape, even while restricted by access to one inadequate rowing boat and an inability to navigate the treacherous ocean currents. Any flight of this nature put himself in peril and his unborn child at risk. At the door, he leant his forehead against the cold of the frozen wood and tried to overcome a wave of nausea.

They were animals. All of them. Unable to tame their base instincts, they were beyond God, and he could not spend another moment near their company lest they should rip him apart. Pressing against the door, he felt it give way in a flurry of tiny white shards as he stumbled into the blackhouse. He resolved to not leave the safety of the house again until he was sure the tacksman had arrived. He closed the door heavily behind him, securing the latch firmly and frantically looking around for some form of barricade. As he approached the living space, he watched his breath form a mist before him. Agnes had clearly neglected the hearth again. Perhaps she was still sleeping. He approached the partition cautiously, and it was then that he noticed the destruction and chaos which lay beyond.

Not only was the hearth extinguished, but the remnants of last night's embers were also strewn amongst the rushes to form an ashen snow. The stools had been upturned. One of them lay with a broken leg, as if it had been flung against a wall. Broken pots and bowls had been swept from the table and shattered. Murray looked to the far wall, where the cross had once hung; now it lay amidst the debris, deep gouges scratched into the varnished wood. In a blind panic, he swept into the room, scanning the ruin. The bedsheets were flung from the box bed.

Murray felt a swollen mass of dread in his throat. Amidst the fear building rapidly within him, he seethed with wrathful thoughts. If they had taken her, he would knot the noose himself. He staggered back across the room, desperate to find her.

It was only when he stumbled that he noticed the pitiful figure huddled half under the bed, curled around his father's old chest. Hair covered her face, and he moved it gently aside. She stared into nothingness, not moving, and for a terrible moment he thought she was dead.

". . . Agnes?" He put the back of his hand against her cold cheek, and only then did she stir.

"What happened? Who did this?"

She turned her head, and her eyes met his. He pulled away from her, for her face transformed from impassive to a vision of fierce, pointed contempt. Tears had streaked her cheeks and turned her face into a red, swollen mask.

It was then that he remembered the chest, which he had abandoned in his hurry to leave and find answers. It was still open. As he looked upon it now, he saw its innards had been torn into, its paper heart ripped into a blizzard of parchment. On one of these fragments, he discerned the fractured pieces of words:

My Lovi ng Hus band,

He raised his head slowly, daring himself to meet her intense gaze.

"You do not understand."

She pushed herself up to rest on one elbow and glared at him. Gone was the illusion of innocent naivety which he had read in her face. Instead, he saw her: he saw all the desires, hopes, fears and contradictions that made up the human soul. There was no savagery in her expression, only hurt. For the first time he saw himself reflected in her eyes, and he had to force himself not to look away.

"I promise you, that binding is now over. There is nothing for me to go back to."

She did not respond, nor did she take her eyes from him.

"Don't you see?" he pleaded, clawing at the ground and picking up the ruined crucifix, which he thrust before her. "God has given us both a new beginning. He has seen how we have suffered and given us a new life through which to find our true purpose."

He reached out to grab her hand, but she snatched it away and pushed herself up against the wall.

"There is no sin in it," he rambled. "There cannot possibly be sin in taking the path God presents us with." He paused and scrambled for a coherent thought. "You and I . . ."

She blinked.

"You and I . . ." he began again. "We are the same."

Slowly, she rose to her knees and knelt forwards. He felt a sudden lightness in his chest, and his lips parted. For a moment he thought she would kiss him. It was only when he felt the gobbet of spit spray across his cheek that his delusions were broken. His hand went to his face. Wiping away the saliva with his sleeve, he fought for words, but could not find them. She continued to stare, her face still.

It was then that she rose to her feet and looked down upon him as he knelt amongst the scraps of torn letters. Her lips curled at the edges. With a rasping, whistling gasp, rusted words came forth from her long silent throat.

"I know myself."

He strained to hear her. To him, the sound was otherworldly, so much so that he questioned whether he had even heard her speak at all. But her expression was one of conviction, and as he knelt before her, he began to fear her for the first time. He rose unsteadily, and tentatively held his hand towards her.

"Please," his voice shook, "you can't go. You're all I have."

She took a step backwards, evading his touch.

"If you leave now," he continued, "they'll hurt you. Without me you are not safe."

He made a mad dash towards the gap between living space and byre, holding his arms out as if to entrap her. Seeing this, she ducked down and tried to pass under his outstretched arm, but quickly he grabbed her and held her to him. She struggled, her legs bucking and her hands thrashing dangerously close to his face. As he evaded her sharp nails, her knee jerked up and crunched hard against his abdomen. He dropped her and fell to the ground, winded and breathless.

Through a dark haze he saw her standing over him. She seemed to hesitate, but before he could recover, she darted beyond his sight. He tried to call out to her, but when he did bile rose in his throat and all he could let out was a choking cough. He heard the door slam. Trying to rise, he wrapped an arm around his torso and groaned. His muscles spasmed and his head swam, causing him to fall backwards onto the hard floor.

Staring at the rafters, he thought he saw another figure momentarily kneel over him, bending forwards and tilting its coppery head in a scrutinising way. Her face was blurred, like a smudged oil portrait. She looked like a surgeon standing above their newest dissection; a lifeless body unearthed from hallowed ground with folds of flesh peeled back and pinned against the floor.

". . . Caroline?" he gasped.

"This is what God wanted you to do, Thomas."

The words, which had once given him hope and purpose, now

rang mockingly in his head. He closed his eyes, not daring to open them again until his head had stopped spinning and the searing pain in his stomach had faded to a dull ache. Persevering through the intense discomfort, he pushed himself into a sitting position, and from there forced himself to stand. He swayed on his feet. Determined, he struggled forwards, staggering through the byre.

He collapsed against the blackhouse door, driving it open and falling into the frostbitten air. All around him was a dense haze of ghostly, white mist, encircling him and dragging cold fingers against his face. It was the kind of impenetrable mist that one could grab fistfuls of, letting it filter through fingers like curdled milk. Spinning on the spot, he tried to get his bearings, squinting through the fog. After several circuits of the blackhouse, he ran a few yards down the slope, hearing the frozen turf crunch beneath his feat, hands outstretched like a blind man.

She was gone.

CHAPTER THIRTY-TWO

FLORA

IN the end, it was the fog that drove Flora back home. Returning to the present, she forced herself up the cliff face and shambled reluctantly towards the settlement, her bones grinding together in the biting cold. She did not want to return, but evening was setting in and instinct led her by the hand towards the warmth of her own hearth. John would no doubt be frantic with worry. Flora did not know how she could face him; how she could persevere with the pretence of a love that she had long ago broken. It was her fault. Her heart was still locked in place, and even after the relief of admitting her burden, it did not bring her the sustenance that she craved.

She did not think the Reverend would reveal her sin to the others, not when he held such disdain for her fellow islanders, but there was still a part of her that almost wished for it. As she skirted the cliff path, the ruins of the chapel slowly loomed into view. Its ragged stonework still slumped inwards, defeated, peering through the top of the white mist which twisted through the burial cairns surrounding it.

Flora veered off the path, impulsively driven towards her son's grave. As she drew close, the mist parted to reveal the proud structure, constructed as a final act of love, still standing in a neat pyramid which drew up to her waist. The stones were sealed together by frost. Flora eased herself down and clutched at the uppermost stone, once more giving in to tears. She sat and allowed herself to weep, listening as her sobs rang quietly around the small cemetery. She was surprised at how she sounded, and was perturbed by the low, whining cries which echoed back to her. It was as if she were listening to a ghost of herself.

It was only after some time, that she realised that her own tears had stopped. Still, she heard the faint, disjointed sounds of a soul in distress. She rose to her feet and carried herself towards the abandoned remains of the chapel.

It was there she found her, curled into herself like a woodlouse, cowering on the stone floor which was once an altar. Flora placed a protective arm around her, alarmed at how close she had come to the walls of the village.

"Agnes?"

The name sounded strange now, knowing that it did not truly belong to this outcast, but Flora still held her as if she were her own. Despite what had happened, she realised that her feelings had not changed, and if anything, her love for the abandoned girl had grown stronger than ever.

"You should not be here," she whispered, smoothing her hand across the girl's tangled hair.

Agnes looked up at her; her eyes were wide, as if she had only just noticed Flora's presence.

"What happened?"

The girl flung her shaking body into her arms, and Flora cherished the moment. No longer flinching from her embrace, Agnes let Flora hold her.

"Hush, *mo cridhe*." She kissed the top of the girl's brow and rocked her, gently, as if soothing a babe. "Hush, now."

Agnes' shoulders eventually stopped shaking, and she once more looked up at Flora through teary eyes.

"What has happened?" Flora repeated softly.

Agnes looked at her pointedly, then turned her gaze up the hill, towards the Reverend's croft. It was then she noticed the faint bruises blossoming on the girl's arms. Flora's heart froze.

"Did he . . . Did he hurt you?"

The girl looked frustrated, and opened her mouth as if wanting to speak, but could only omit a throaty, garbled croak. Flora thought she saw her shake her head, faintly.

"Help me understand. Did he do this to you?"

Agnes bit her lip and closed her eyes. She again tried to open her moth to speak, but nothing came out. Flora grabbed her by the wrist to stop her from dashing her fists against her forehead. Grasping her arms firmly, Flora waited until the girl had somewhat calmed herself, before gently lowering them. As she tried to draw back, Agnes pulled against her, taking her firmly by the hand.

The girl looked meaningfully at her, so Flora let her arm go limp, and let her hand be guided. Agnes drew it towards herself, and let it rest flatly against her stomach. Flora frowned, confused, until the girl fixed her with tearful eyes, continuing to hold Flora's hand against her abdomen. Flora felt the slight swell of the girl's belly, once hollow from hunger. She kept her hand there a moment longer, her mouth opening in realisation as she felt the tender, ripening flesh beneath her palm.

Flora drew back, speechless, and horrified. The girl could surely not be more than a few months pregnant, at most; that was what Flora told herself. She felt a slight relief, banishing from her mind the thought that the child could be anyone's other than the Reverend's. She dwelled upon this notion, simmering with a rising anger at the man she had unburdened her innermost self to. She had allowed him to examine her soul, thinking she could somehow relate to the torment within his own. But now she saw him as a shallow hypocrite, his words of God's judgement as meaningless as the protection he had promised to provide.

"I wish I had never left you," she said bitterly, her voice choked with tearful fury. "I wish I had never trusted him."

The girl seemed embarrassed, and was unable to meet Flora's eyes, instead looking sidelong towards the wall, chewing on her lower lip.

"How could I let this happen?" Flora rubbed at her brow. She wished she could scream but grew afraid of attracting the attention of the village women, who would no doubt be milling towards home for the night.

"I have to hide you. I have to get you away from here." Flora looked up towards the girl, her tears subsiding and giving way to conviction, her maternal urge to protect suddenly overriding any feelings of self-condemnation or pity.

It was then that the sound of a loosened stone skittered through the early evening mist, and both women heard the distinct sound of a footstep. Flora froze. She grabbed Agnes and hugged her to her chest, as if she could conceal her from whoever was standing behind them. She turned slowly, expecting to see the Reverend's slender, black silhouette looming over them both.

It was Ann. Half concealed behind the chapel's doorway, she stared at them both open mouthed, her basket lying at her side, the contents scattered. Baby Mary was strapped to her back, and the child gurgled to herself in blissful ignorance, her growing legs dangling at Ann's waist. Flora could not tell how long her daughter-in-law had stood there, but it was clear that there was now nothing she could do now to hide her charge.

"Ann . . ." Flora pleaded, looking to her desperately. "Please."

For a moment she thought there was hesitation in Ann's eyes. Flora rose, shielding Agnes with her entire body.

Ann peered behind her at the cowering girl, and her lips curled back.

"You will pay for this, Flora MacKinnon. You and that sea witch."

Ann began slowly backing away, her lips still frozen with the vehemence with which she had spat out her threat. Flora made to run at her, but Ann bolted, discarding her fallen belongings and disappearing into the mist.

It was too late to stop and think. They needed to go now. Flora pulled the girl up and breathlessly dragged her through the cemetery. Agnes pulled against her; her expression had transformed from sorrow to terror. Flora grabbed her by the shoulders and stared steadily into her eyes.

"We have to get you off this island."

The girl stiffened, but Flora continued to pull her towards the bay.

"We have to get you away. Right now."

CHAPTER THIRTY-THREE

THOMAS

THE blood formed a frozen clot in his chest, through which he could feel his heart pulsing. He heard the sound again: a distant, incomprehensible scream. Ignoring how his feet slid against the slippery turf which sloped away beneath his feet, Murray raced down the hill towards the settlement, pushing himself forward with his hands when he fell against the needles of frozen grass. Arriving at the islanders' crofts, his breath quickened from both exertion and fear. The white mists began to clear as he approached the village paddock, and he saw a crowd of flustered women swarming around a lone figure. The figure's cries pierced his eardrums, full of a mad, wordless vitriol.

His worst fears were temporarily assuaged, as his vision fell upon Ann MacKinnon, her hair and clothes in disarray as the other women flocked to calm her. He could barely discern a word amongst her hysterical ramblings. A young child dangled from a sling on her back, struggling to grip to its mother's sides as it slid down the woman's hip. Ann MacKinnon hardly seemed to notice.

"It's her! I saw her!"

The terror came coursing back through his body like the tide.

Other women began to add their voices to the commotion. "Calm yourself, Ann. Who are you talking about?"

"Her!" Ann shrieked, and her child started crying. "The witch. The one who came from the sea. The one who turned into a bird. The one we thought we had killed! I saw her. I saw her summoning up curses with Flora. I told you all that it was them all along!"

A hush descended, and many of the women turned to exchange weary looks with one another. Murray tried to push his way through the crowd, but the women were clearly distracted and did not even acknowledge his presence.

"Are you sure, Ann?" Margaret Gillies stepped forward and gathered Ann's wailing child to her. "It's hazy. Perhaps you saw something in the mist and got confused." The gathered women looked doubtfully at each other, but Margaret persevered. "I still don't believe that Flora would do anything to harm us."

"I know what I saw!" Specks of saliva flew from Ann's mouth, conjuring up images in Murray's mind of a rabid dog.

"It was her!" Ann repeated. "And Flora was with her."

Murray heard the women's whispers spread throughout their gathering, and his anxiety grew. Still, they ignored him. Unable to make himself heard over the crying child and the distraught young woman, he felt invisible, like a ghost at its own funeral.

"Ann . . ." Only Margaret Gillies' voice remained level and cut through the frenzied chatter. "You have to be sure about this."

"She's sure, Margaret! What more does she have to say?"

A chorus of women joined the fray.

"Aye! She's been telling us for months that something wasn't natural about our sufferings, and we could all see that something's not been right with Flora."

The women all nodded their assent. Even Margaret looked contemplative as she lowered her head, seemingly unable to dispute their point.

"They were at the chapel," Ann continued. "I heard them talking; summoning something evil no doubt, and when I followed the sound, there they were, huddled together, cursing us. It's no wonder I found them on a burial ground!"

"And to think, on top of the bodies of our own kin!"

A few of the women let out a collective moan of exaggerated despair, before once more turning to the head of their pack.

"We must find them, Ann. You must lead the way!"

Margaret Gillies tried to appeal for calm, but it was to no avail, the women were ravenous in their persecution, and began making their way across the paddock towards the cemetery. Murray followed, although his limbs were almost rigid from dread.

"Stop!" His voice was hoarse, and completely ineffectual. He tried to grab a woman's arm and push her aside, but she only shook him off; her lips curled in disdain as she noticed him.

"Keep away, priest!" she spat. "You have no authority over us!"

Murray fell back from the woman, but still he tried desperately to barge his way amongst them. Soon they approached the cemetery and, clambering over to the half-constructed walls of the chapel, they scoured around the burial cairns. When it became apparent that the two women had fled, they once more came together.

"This is hallowed ground!" Murray stood atop a tumbledown wall and tried to shout above them. "You should all go home! Go home to your men!"

The women turned their backs to him, just as they had when he had first confronted them after his arrival on the island.

"We should search the shore!" Ann cried, and the other women cawed their agreement.

"Please," Margaret Gillies coaxed. "Don't hurt Flora. We must search for the girl, but we cannot hurt one of our own."

"That didn't stop her from hurting us!" Ann turned on Margaret with furious eyes. "If Flora gets in our way, then whatever happens to her is through her own fault."

Margaret's face blanched. Clearly the younger women were now beyond her control, and if their respected matriarch no longer held sway over them, it was obvious to Murray that his attempts to stop them were hopeless. As he stood on their fringes, Margaret suddenly turned to him and put a clawing hand on the sleeve of his coat.

"Reverend," she said breathlessly, "you have to go to John. Find John and keep him away from here. He needs to be kept away. Do you understand?"

Murray stared at her, uncomprehending, but gave a slight nod.

Seemingly satisfied, Margaret gave him one last pointed look before retreating to pursue the mob of her fellow women.

Murray wasted no time. He ran, not in the direction of John MacKinnons croft, but towards the cliff path which rounded the headland and led to the rocky cove where he had confronted Flora only hours before. He could not have cared less for the MacKinnons in that moment; he had no other intention than to find Agnes. As he panted his way up the narrow track, he heard flustered, high pitched cries from below.

"The boat! It's gone!"

"They must have taken it!"

Spurred on by panic, Murray tried to push through his exertion and move faster along the cliff path. Even, if they had taken the boat, they would have to navigate the shore of the island before they could push into the calmer seas which stretched towards the inner isles. Murray's mind worked frantically. What could Flora Mackinnon possibly be thinking? Miles of ocean surrounded them. Without supplies and the skill to navigate the treacherous waters they would easily die. He had to find them. He had to protect his child. He had to save the future he had found for himself.

Below him, the mists were clearing. The women had evidently had the same idea, as they too were heading towards the cove, but taking advantage of what remained of the low tide, they were swarming over the rocky shoreline beneath the cliffs towards the headland. He quickened his steps. He had to outpace them and reach the cove before they could manage to scrape around the jutting rockface. Looking beyond the receding mist, he saw it: a little, wooden boat hugging the shore, pulling into the isolated cove at the other side of the sheer premonitory which separated them. He still had time. Ignoring the cries of the rabble below, he pressed on.

As he circumnavigated the cliffs, his feet slid away from the narrow path. Skidding along the icy ground to the very edge of the precipice, a sod of dirt gave way beneath his feet. Feeling himself keel over into mid-air, he let out a sudden shout and grabbed at the frosty turf. His fingers grappled at the edge of the land, and he tried to haul himself up. Feeling his fingernails curl against the hard dirt, he heaved himself upwards. There was purchase beneath his feet, but he could hear the clods of hardened earth beginning to tumble away beneath him and bounce against the cliff face.

Taking a breath and gritting his teeth, he pulled his upper body against the crumbling earth above him. The ground was giving way beneath his hands, and his fingers were stiffening from the cold. He could not die like this. Not now. With one final pull, he kicked against the crumbling dirt falling away beneath him and launched his body against the ground above. As he levered himself up by his frostbitten hands, the remnants of the cliff edge fell with a crack onto the shore below. He wriggled wildly on his elbows and stomach, sliding away from the abyss. Flashes of white pierced his vision, accompanied by the shadowy, ethereal figure of a woman in a crisp, yellow dress. He screwed his eyes shut before the phantom could speak.

He lay for a moment, the pain from the blow to his abdomen resurfacing. Turning his cheek against the cold ground, he looked to where the sea met the headland. The two women in the boat had vanished from his sight.

CHAPTER THIRTY-FOUR

FLORA

Flora watched the girl shivering and knew that it was not from the cold. As she drew the boat into the cove, she quickly scouted the shoreline, but was relieved to see that nobody had yet caught up with them. Looking back to Agnes, she saw the girl wrap her arms around herself and blink rapidly, eyes darting around at the grey waters sloshing against the side of the boat, as Flora swept the heavy wooden paddles through the shallows and into the inlet. It had been a struggle to convince Agnes into the boat, but with perseverance and steady encouragement she had had been forced to confront her anxieties. She had no choice. As they neared the headland, they had both heard the women's cries, and Flora rowed faster, ignoring the pain and weight of the massive oars, designed for several grown men rather than an aged woman.

She felt the boat scrape against the rocks entering the cove. Stepping into the surf, she held it steady, then began to pull away. Panicking, the girl scrambled to the front of the boat, thrusting her hand out to grip on to Flora's.

"No," Flora said, trying to hold back the tears which pressed hotly against the back of her eyes. "I can't go with you. You have to go alone."

Agnes gripped her hand tightly against the damp wood of the boat's bow. Her mouth worked in a silent plea. Flora reached out and pressed her hands to the sides of the girl's panicked face.

"I belong here. I cannot leave. But you . . ." Flora stroked the wet tendrils of hair away from Agnes' face.

Agnes' jaw trembled and she moved her eyes up towards the towering cliffs, as if checking for something.

"You can't go back now. Do you understand me?" Flora held the girl's face firmly, guiding her gaze back to her. "Not for anything. Not even for him."

The young woman's eyes grew filmy, and she broke down, collapsing into the older woman's arms. Flora leaned across the boat's bow and held the girl's head against her shoulder. She shushed her softly, before hastily pulling away.

"Go. Now." Flora's words were firm. "Row around to the back of the island and then keep going. Row and don't stop. Even when it gets dark, keep rowing. Don't stop. Go straight and by the end of daylight tomorrow you should have reached the nearest isles. Do not stop rowing until you find land, do you understand me? Don't stop."

Agnes hesitated, but Flora pressed her fingers into her outstretched wrist.

"Go. Don't stop."

The girl looked terrified, but she nodded shakily. Flora did not tell her of the fierce currents, or of the biting winds which could sweep her off course and into harm's way. She did not warn her that miles of ocean separated her from refuge, and that without a direct course hunger, thirst and cold would soon take their toll. She could not let herself consider these things for long. If she stayed, they would find her. If she stayed, they would not let her live. This was her best chance. Flora did not need to clarify any of this, for looking into Agnes' eyes, she could see that the girl too knew what could face her.

Flora tried to push the boat away, forcing an oar into Agnes' hands.

"Please," she whispered. "Go."

Agnes seemed to contemplate for a moment, but before Flora could push her away again, the girl plunged a hand into the fabric folds of her earasaid and pulled something out. She held it in the palm of her hand, and then uncoiled her fingers. Flora looked down on the familiar, bone hair comb, the surface smoothed with age and some of the teeth now snapped away.

Flora reached out, and placing her hands beneath the outstretched offering, she closed the girl's fingers back over her gift.

"Keep it." Flora's voice shook. "It's yours."

She let the girl hold her hand a moment longer.

"They'll be coming for you." Flora sniffed back her tears and tore herself away. "You have to go. Now."

The girl clumsily took the oars and began to push away from the rocks. Then, as if reconsidering, she stopped and looked back at Flora.

"Go!" Flora shouted, falling to her knees against the shore. "Go now!"

The girl's cheeks were streaked with tears, but she heeded Flora's words and paddled into the surf, turning the boat around awkwardly and bobbing along the side of the cove, pushing out towards the furthest headland. Flora watched her struggle to move the hefty paddles against the relentless pull of the tide, and the boat spun around a few times before it righted itself. Flora chewed at her lip, fearful that she would not be able to navigate around the side of the island in time.

"Don't look back," she murmured, but she did not know if her words were for the girl or for herself.

Tearing herself away, she quickly made for the path up the cliff face, knowing that she needed a vantage point to make sure the girl made it safely from sight. She was braced to encounter Ann and her neighbours. No longer fearful of them, she hoped she could sidetrack them if they were heading rapidly towards the cove. And so, she hurtled forward, her breath steaming the air before vanishing into the frigid evening mist, as below her the sea boldly roared its threats for all to hear. Occasionally she looked back from her ascent to see the boat still bobbing in the shallows, the girl still hugging the rocks, as if too afraid to cast herself out further. Reaching the clifftops, Flora edged along to the jutting promontory which separated the cove from the village bay, hoping to get a vantage over the water, while also bracing herself for a confrontation.

It was then that she heard the wild voices echoing from below. Casting her gaze downwards, her eyes navigated the sheer drop. Trailing rapidly along the rocks which clung to the cliff side, were her fellow women. They picked their way over tidal pools, looking like tiny insects traversing rutted ground, and they were almost rounding the headland.

Flora's heart leapt. From her great height, the women looked to be mere moments away from spotting the boat, and with the girl still skirting the shoreline, it would not take much time or guile for them to fall upon her. She staggered back towards the cliff path, but did not have to go far to see that the boat was almost exactly where she had left it. The girl was trying to strike out past the northerly cliffs, but the breakers kept sweeping her back, over, and over, holding her against the land in a tormenting game which she had yet to conquer.

"Don't fight it," Flora uttered through gritted teeth. "Keep your strokes short. Loosen your grip and it will carry you." Still the girl was swept backwards as she thrashed the paddles in a desperate, exasperated motion, and Flora could see she was close to giving up the battle. There was no time.

Flora wavered on the spot, before again dashing to the cliff edge to observe the gathering below. They were still relentlessly pressing forward. She tried calling out, but they seemed not to hear her above the constant rumble of the sea. She began to run back to the cliff path, but then chastised herself, for there was no way she would make it down to the cove before the mob rounded the promontory and spotted the girl making another failed attempt to cast off. Flora knew the girl could do it, but for that she needed time. Flora looked down from the dizzying height, trying to steady herself, and saw that one of the women at the head of the crowd was already clambering over the large rocks which bridged the gap between one side of the headland and the other; she was reaching out to pull others up after her. Flora could already tell from the colour of the plaid that it was Ann.

Scanning the turf around her, she looked frantically for a distraction, but the ground was frozen and yielded nothing. Short of kicking away the eroding cliff edge herself, there was nothing she could offer as an obstacle to stop the women from reaching their destination, and she was still cautious of causing them harm. She hobbled back a few paces towards the cove. Still the girl had not struck out. She whipped her head back towards the other women. They were almost in sight of the boat.

Flora's breath quickened. She could think of no other way of halting them.

She shuffled towards the sheer edge of the cliff, her feet disturbing some of the earth and sending small clumps of dry dirt plummeting below. She steadied herself. The wind whistled past her ears, blowing her shawl away from her face; the air on the clifftop was cold as it greeted her face, but it felt beautiful. Even the sea, in all its merciless savagery, was beautiful, as the deep, green scent of it surged towards her. Seconds stretched out.

She looked down. There were no jutting ledges to disturb the sheer path downwards, only empty air. She waited just a fraction of a moment longer, until the women were at the most outward part of the headland, but not quite close enough to see what lay beyond, or to lie directly beneath her.

Flora kept her eyes open.

She let herself fall forward into thin air; her arms outstretched to catch the sea's breath. For a fleeting moment, she was a young girl again, leaping fearlessly into the void, the wind whipping through her star flecked hair.

CHAPTER THIRTY-FIVE

THOMAS

He saw her fall, but could not believe the vision was real until he heard the screams of the women below. Rousing himself into a delirious frenzy of motion, he pulled his body back to the cliff path and staggered down towards the cove, fear plaguing his every step. He barely remembered the minutes that carried him down onto the rocky shore, as everything that fell within his sight was blurred by vivid thoughts of what he would find waiting for him on the rocks. He scrambled over the southern edge of the cove, moving mindlessly towards the mass of women, who swarmed forward to encircle something, their heads bowed. Some were whispering, one of them was crying, while another screeched hysterically. Only Ann MacKinnon stood silently, her face tilted down in open mouthed terror. Murray pushed through their ranks, and this time the women fell away before him.

Flora MacKinnon's shattered body was sprawled before him, her face mercifully concealed amidst a slick splash of gore. He stared at the scene in trance-like awe, until coming to his senses his eyes swept over the circle of women, looking to the shoreline beyond them. He could not see her. Perhaps she was safely cocooned somewhere, perhaps even waiting for him.

"We can't leave her like this!"

It was Margaret Gillies' voice which first fractured his thoughts, followed by a chorus of women.

"She jumped! I saw her do it."

"Perhaps she was trying to fly."

"If it was her who summoned the sea witch, perhaps now both their spirits will be banished."

"Maybe the witch was Flora all along. Are you sure you saw her with a girl, Ann?"

Ann MacKinnon remained silent.

"However it happened, we can't bury her now."

"But this is our kinswoman!" Margaret cried, kneeling to lay a hand against the thing that was Flora MacKinnon. Upon touching the wrecked body, she swiftly drew her hand away, wiping the red on her skirts. "Oh, Flora," she gasped, her body rigid from the horror of it all. "What have you done to yourself?"

Murray observed how Ann MacKinnon shuffled back from the ring of women, and thought he heard her quietly murmur something to herself.

"She did not have to do that."

The other women failed to notice, for their attention was now solely on the body. They were all perilously close to the tideline, which would soon consume the stretch of rocks.

"What are we to do with her, then?"

Murray looked: all the women were now staring at him. He knew what he should say, but he could not find the calm needed to structure and articulate his thoughts. His mouth was dry, and he could not think straight, so he pushed back through them and headed towards the cove.

He waded ankle deep in the oncoming tide, looking out towards the placid, indigo sky which beckoned in the night. The moon had risen, and the sun was casting what remained of its dim warmth over the sea, which was now dappled with white light. As he walked, he saw a smooth path amidst the water's rolling reflection; a winding scar upon the surf where a boat had recently traversed the shallows. Suppressing the cold sensation which swept down his spine, he looked back, but the women were still occupied. Trudging forwards, he came to a halt by the entrance to the hidden cave. Perhaps there was still a chance. He felt along the algae-stained stone, bent down, and peered into the gloom. Water dripped steadily from the rocks above, but there was not a soul to be found hiding in that haunted space, and he soon realised what a fool he was to even imagine it. He continued onwards, but soon the tide came to push him back from the northerly edge of the cove. She was gone.

When he returned, the women were no longer squabbling, but standing in quiet, concerned contemplation, none of them willing to take responsibility or offer any consolation for the tragedy which lay broken at their feet. Instead, it fell upon Murray to speak.

"How can you just stand there?" There was a tremor in his voice. "Clean her up. Somebody will have to take her before the sea does."

The women turned to him, startled and uncertain. Each of them looked to the body and took a step back, some holding their skirts away from the blood. Even Margaret Gillies, Flora's staunchest supporter, was cowed by the dreadful display which lay at their feet. Ann MacKinnon still hung back, and to Murray's revulsion he saw that she still had the young child tucked away amongst her skirts. The infant looked dazed and baffled.

"I'm not touching her," one of the women said, looking appalled at the mere thought.

Some of the others muttered their assent, but none could meet his eyes, not even Margaret.

"The men will be coming soon," she murmured. "They will be looking for us. We should get back before the tide comes in."

"And what about the body?" Murray asked.

Margaret paused. Looking down at the remains of her neighbour, she seemed torn between emotions.

"There is so much blood," she breathed, her face pale. "Perhaps it would be best, if . . ."

"Come on, Ma." A younger woman stepped forward and took Margaret by the shoulder. "What good does it do any of us to linger. If there has been witchcraft at work here, the body could be cursed."

"There are no curses," Murray snapped, his temper fraying as he willed the women away, back to their men. "But I will concede there is an issue with burial . . ."

The women looked to him questioningly.

"I saw her fall," he continued, trying to keep his tone cold and level. "And to me I say it was deliberate. And that being the case, she cannot be buried on hallowed ground."

"Are you saying she jumped, Reverend?"

"Yes. She died in sin."

"Oh, Flora . . ." Margaret wrung her hands.

"I told you she jumped. She was trying to fly!"

"Shush. We have not the time for this. We need to get back before the tide comes."

The women once again grew fractious, and some began to drift from the group.

"I'm going back to my man. I won't stay here with that thing."

"Aye. There's an evil here that I don't want to infect me too. I don't want to end up like Fl . . . like her."

"But how about the girl? Shouldn't we find her? Ann?"

Ann looked dumbly at the speakers, as if she had only just heard them. Her lips worked, but she seemed incapable of answering.

"If there was a witch," another woman spoke up, "I say it was Flora who first found her, so it makes sense that she would disappear alongside her. The evil dies with those who conjured it."

As the women were talking, Murray was looking to the clifftops. Specks of orange light had appeared up above, and he knew that the men were now on their way. He pushed back through the women, wanting no more in that moment than to escape before the men descended. He needed to be far away, where he would not be able to hear the anguish of John MacKinnon or his sons as they discovered the gruesome sight that lay beneath them.

The water was already seeping beneath their feet, and many of the women were now retreating rapidly up the cliff path. Even Margaret Gillies, with one last anguished look behind her, was being ferried away by her daughter. Only one woman remained. She stood opposite him, her eyes fixed on the body, her child whimpering anxiously at her side as it tugged its guardian away from the encroaching tide.

Murray made to escape, but Ann fixed him with pleading eyes which shone beneath the ragged curtains of her loosened hair.

"Say some words over her."

"What?"

She had spoken so quietly that for a moment he questioned whether she had said anything at all.

"Before we go, say one of your prayers over her."

Murray was about to dismiss her, but he saw that there was earnestness in her eyes. He bowed his head and watched her carefully as she did the same. He muttered a few words: fragments of psalm twenty-three. They held as little meaning for him as they no doubt did for the miserable wreck of a woman standing opposite him. When he concluded, she raised her head, only just seeming to notice the now squalling infant clinging to her legs. She nodded shakily, and with one last trembling look at her mother-in-law, she swept the child into her arms and retreated after the other women.

Murray waited a moment for the woman to leave, the water now creeping up past his ankles. With repulsion he observed the swirl of crimson amidst the grey. Flora's arm had been flung out at an unnatural angle, but now it was swept up and seemed to reach out to grasp the cold hand of the sea.

Alarmed, he rapidly made for the clifftops. He could hear the women's cries as they confronted the men and could hear the shouts of confused panic coming from those who approached. Murray took himself off the path and made to loop around the northernmost edge of the island, to vainly search the dark crests of coastline. As he walked, he occasionally looked back to see the dim lights swarming in a long trail down the cliff path, but the tide was cutting them off. Even if they hoped to recover Flora MacKinnon's mangled body, it was clear that the sea had already claimed its prize.

"Only one passenger?"

Murray snapped from his thoughts and met the man's enquiring gaze. It was a stern, middle-aged and world-weary face; tanned and leathery like the face of a sailor.

"Yes."

The man arched an eyebrow and made a small note in his ledger. He snapped it shut and scanned the lacklustre activity taking place in the bay from his perch at a fold-out trestle table. The man seemed to be a walking contradiction: his accent reeked of the Islands, but like his gaudier predecessor, his conservatively grey stockings, breeches, and jacket lacked any indication of Clan affiliations.

"What happened to the gentleman who came last time?" Murray probed. "A Robert MacLeod, I believe."

The tacksman sniffed. "Men like that never stay long," he said scornfully. "They take what they can profit then disappear until the next time they run out of coin. Scavengers." He spat into the sand.

The man then swiftly returned his attention to the islanders' paltry provisions, as unlike the previous tacksman he seemed totally disinterested in idle chat. Murray followed his glare. Chief MacLeod's men were hastily rolling barrels of bird oil and feathers towards the waiting boats, many of them returning to collect more, then appearing baffled when nothing else was offered. A rough queue of islanders had previously formed before the trestle table, waiting to collect what little they were owed while the tacksman had acknowledged their tithe with a customary flick of his quill against the pages of his ledger.

Now they stood, huddled in the cold. Women shivered alongside their thin, hollow-eyed children as they waited for their men to gather the meagre supply of wood and salted meat they had been provided with in return for their previous offerings. Murray could feel no pity. He noticed Michael and Fergus MacKinnon amidst the crowd. They seemed to be slumped inwards on themselves, defeated by loss, and they reserved their glowers for him alone. John MacKinnon was absent. Murray was thankful that soon he would no longer have to see any of them ever again, especially after what had been taken from him.

He had scoured the entire island in the few days between Flora MacKinnon's reckless act and the return of MacLeod's men, shunning the company of anyone but himself. Nevertheless, it was a desperate act, for after several circuits of the coastline it became abundantly clear that the girl had gone. He hoped she and his child were safe; not drowned, starved, or dashed upon the rocks, but the chances of finding them amongst the other islands were slim to none. Slowly, he was forced to acknowledge his fears that a second chance had been taken from him.

"Will that chest be coming with you, Reverend?"

He returned his attention to the tacksman, who motioned towards the heavy, carved wooden monstrosity that sat squatly upon the pebbly shore. For a moment he deliberated emptying the ugly thing of its contents and leaving its hollowed out, wooden carcass for the islanders to scavenge.

"Reverend?"

His thoughts returned to the present. "Yes," he said clearly. "Yes, it is coming with me."

"Very well." The tacksman motioned towards two idle men, who took up the chest and heaved it into one of the waiting boats, before folding up his table and depositing that alongside it. "After you."

The tacksman swept a hand towards the boat, and Murray waded out into the surf, leaving the uncertain ground of Eilean Eoin behind him. He hauled himself into the boat. Even the thought of seasickness did not hold any deterrent over him now. As they rowed away, Murray watched as the islanders scurried forward and collected their wares, retreating gradually into the mist.

The boat approached the northern headland and drew towards calmer waters, where a sloop was waiting to return them to the inner isles. As they rounded that jagged promontory, Murray turned his face away. He knew that John MacKinnon would be sitting by the clifftop, a position which his family and neighbours had tried and failed to shift him from during daylight hours. Murray avoided looking at the land until they had drifted far away from the cove. He did not want to cast his eyes on that terrible place again.

As they drew away from the island and its cluster of sea stacks, the swell calmed and carried them gently towards the sloop. Murray peered over the bow waves at a murky, grey vastness which stretched out beyond the horizon. His fingers gripped tightly at the boat's sides.

"Excuse me!" he cried, raising his voice to be heard over the gentle swoosh of the water beneath them. The tacksman turned and looked him up and down disdainfully.

"If you have forgotten anything, you're out of luck. I won't be turning this boat back for anyone."

"It's not that. I just wondered . . ." Murray took a moment to formulate his words. "I just wondered if on your way here, you had come across a rowing boat, not dissimilar to this one. There would have been a young woman rowing it."

The tacksman frowned.

"A young woman, you say?" He looked contemplative, and in the brief silence between his words, Murray felt his hopes lift ever so slightly. "Odd for a woman to be unaccompanied," the tacksman continued. "But, no, Reverend I have seen no such thing."

His heart sank and he turned to stare into the dark waters, wondering how deep they plummeted.

"Was she a local girl?" the tacksman queried.

Murray looked up. "Just someone I fear is lost."

The tacksman's frown deepened, but he shrugged his shoulders and turned away, thankfully asking no more of him.

Murray watched as the island retreated into the fog, the last blackened pillars drifting from his view.

My Lord MacLeod,

As requested, herein lies a true and honest account of my time in the position of Missionary Curate on Eilean Eoin. I have reported back my findings to the Diocese of Inverness-shire, and once again humbly apologise for the early termination of the aforementioned post. I write to you currently from Fort William, having recently returned from a tour of the Isles, where I had reason to pursue some enquiries of a personal nature, which I shall not tire you with. I will instead be succinct and endeavour not to encroach much further upon your patience.

Your Lordship may recall that I was tenant on the island from the month of April. It was from that time that I had some moderate success in the rebuilding of a chapel on the Isle, in which any subsequent curates may find a suitable space to administer to Worship. I must, however, regrettably report that the people of the island are stubbornly resistant to proper religious observance, and despite my many efforts in preaching and administering the Gospels, they showed little sign of change in this matter. They still persist in folkish superstitions regarding magic and Pagan lore, with these heathenish beliefs being used to explain their misfortunes, rather than the untenability of their current way of life. I have observed unchristian funeral rites being administered, and was unfortunate enough to witness the slaughter of a Garefowl, which the islanders insisted was a witch. I have even borne witness to sacrifices being offered, which, mercifully, I was able to prevent from going further. It is a wonder they did not in fact cause harm to myself, although I doubt it was for want of trying.

As was previously reported to the Presbytery, my predecessor, the Reverend Buchan, exploited their gullible natures by preaching Popery. It is only through my ingenuity that this scandal was uncovered, and as such Buchan has been excommunicated from the Church. It is indeed my earnest hope that he is soon flushed from his hiding place and faces the full force of the Law *for his deviance and deceit. It is therefore of little wonder that the people of Eilean Eoin are inclined towards a malicious nature, and they are somewhat to be pitied in their ignorance. They lean towards Papism precisely because it falsely promises them a salvation that has thus far alluded them. These are a people of desperate want, and I have witnessed both disease and famine taking a toll on their population. This incessant cycle of struggle has made them cruel, and though one might wish them towards Enlightenment, they doggedly dig their heels into the past, where one fears they will forever remain.*

It is therefore my advice to you My Lord, and I humbly bow to your intent, that you desist in the facilitation of the island's survival, but instead think of what would advantage both yourself and those poor, unenlightened souls that remain. Surely the land could be better utilised through grazing, and the people fare better from integration with those from the Inner Isles and the Mainland, who could employ them in more profitable industry. By hook or by crook, they should be guided into the modern age.

Your Lordship's Obedient and Most Humble Servant,
Thomas Murray
Fort William, November 22nd, 1727

EPILOGUE

THE SEA

FLORA'S bones moved with the tide. They followed in the wake of the ocean currents that wrapped themselves around the island, gushing forth from the vast expanse to the west and winding down from the creeks and estuaries which breached the land to the east.

On the ragged clifftops which overlooked this relentless torrent, a man sat in silent vigil by a small, stone cairn. John MacKinnon had constructed this unrefined memorial with his own loving hands; with rough, calloused skin which longed for the touch of a memory. The winter winds beat at him, yet still he returned to this spot, day after day, hoping to find communion with those who had already left the land behind them. His living family surrounded him as the sun set, swaddling him in their own love and coaxing him away. But the day came when he no longer needed the company of the dead, and as his own strength waned and he too departed, others would maintain those monuments of stone.

Beyond the horizon, a ship skimmed over the waves, heading towards another new world, but one still constrained by the confines of the Earth. Onwards it sailed, and the man who could not find the purpose he had previously sought, looked forwards, towards a land of ancient forests which men now plundered for sanctuary. Thomas Murray had heard that the colonies of America were rich with opportunity: a place where lost people were driven to wander. He would find some shade amongst those towering trees, but no shelter from the darkened hollows within himself.

As those currents which carried the ship forward swirled and pushed back towards the east, they weaved around the islands and met with the mainland. Tracing them back to their roots, a river surged and pulsed down from the mountains, cold and clear. Eventually, it wound down past a drystone bothy, a place that some would call a hovel, half hidden amongst the scree and stunted trees, where a young mother sat beside the frothing waters and sang softly in muted tones, tenderly teasing a bone comb through her daughter's downy hair. The water lapped gently at her feet, seemingly at peace.

Unmoved, the remaining torrent rushed on.

That foamy deluge poured down into the sea. It pushed out into the deep, green depths and moved ceaselessly, sweeping back and forth, clearing away the remnants of the foreshore, until only ripples remained.

This book has been typeset by
SALT PUBLISHING LIMITED
using Neacademia, a font designed by Sergei Egorov for the
Rosetta Type Foundry in Czechia. It has been manufactured
using Holmen Book Cream 65gsm paper, and printed and
bound by Clays Limited in Bungay, Suffolk, Great Britain.

CROMER
GREAT BRITAIN
MMXXV